"The best fantasy novels invent alternate worlds in order to illuminate our own. *Wings of Ebony* is one of them—a bold, inventive, big-hearted and deeply perceptive vision of a Black girl's journey to reclaim her magic from forces determined to destroy her. The parallels to our current reality are unmistakable and the book brings us all a much-needed ray of hope."
—Nicola Yoon, #1 *New York Times* bestselling author of *Everything, Everything* and *The Sun Is Also a Star*

"*Wings of Ebony* is an intense, page-turner of a book about magic, sisterhood, community, and family. Debut author J. Elle offers us a richly wrought world, weaving together past and present with a rare blend of deft insight and keen humor that leaves the reader wanting more."
—Sabaa Tahir, #1 *New York Times* bestselling author of *An Ember in the Ashes*

"There is little on earth more powerful than seeing a reflection of the self, not only as it is, but also as it COULD be. *Wings of Ebony* is a rooftop-shout of affirmation that black girls from ALL walks of life are magic."
—Nic Stone, #1 *New York Times* bestselling author of *Dear Martin*

"A remarkable, breathtaking, earthshaking, poetic thrill ride bristling with magic, life, and so much love. Rue and her incredible adventures will change the world."
—Daniel José Older, *New York Times* bestselling author of *Shadowshaper*

"A powerful, thoughtful, and masterful exploration of #BlackGirlMagic that enthralls you from the first page and refuses to let you go."
—Alechia Dow, author of *The Sound of Stars*

"A heart-racing thrilling fantasy that sucks you in from the very first page. J. Elle has such a voracious voice and she's about to change the game!"
—Tiffany D. Jackson, author of *Grown* and *Monday's Not Coming*

"J. Elle has crafted an unapologetic heroine determined to save her block from agents of stolen magic in this immersive hidden world. A thrilling and irresistible new saga about loyalty and lineage."
—Kim Johnson, author of *This Is My America*

"Debut author Elle's characters shine with determination and heart. The tough realities of living in an underserved community fortify Rue against great odds but also influence her reluctance to accept kindness and support. Rue grapples with her sense of community, family, and duty; despite the size of her foes and fears, she never stops fighting for justice. Heart-stopping action and intrigue from cover to cover." —*Kirkus Reviews*

"This is the debut fantasy we need right now!" —*Ms.* magazine

"To offer much more story would be to undermine the care with which Elle tells the story of a girl discovering the breadth of her power and the richness of her cultural heritage. But allegory abounds, touching on systemic racism, the destruction of communities, colonization, and the ways—good and bad—our lives and actions are interconnected." —*The Houston Chronicle*

"A riveting first installment in a duology that reminds us of the power of Afro-futurism and the Black fantastic ... With Rue at their side, a new generation of readers will feel empowered to love the Houston of their minds and bring to life the worlds they imagine." —*Texas Observer*

★ "An ode to family, true belonging, and magic. Highly recommended for all collections." —*School Library Journal*, starred review

"Full of grief, love, and vengeance, this poignant debut encourages readers to embrace the whole of their identities to overcome pain." —*Publishers Weekly*

WINGS OF EBONY

J. ELLE

A DENENE MILLNER BOOK

SIMON & SCHUSTER BFYR

NEW YORK · LONDON · TORONTO · SYDNEY · NEW DELHI

SIMON & SCHUSTER BFYR

An imprint of Simon & Schuster Children's Publishing Division

1230 Avenue of the Americas, New York, New York 10020

SIMON & SCHUSTER BOOKS FOR YOUNG READERS

and related marks are trademarks of Simon & Schuster, Inc.

For information about special discounts for bulk purchases, please contact Simon & Schuster Special Sales at 1-866-506-1949 or business@simonandschuster.com.

The Simon & Schuster Speakers Bureau can bring authors to your live event. For more information or to book an event, contact the Simon & Schuster Speakers Bureau at 1-866-248-3049 or visit our website at www.simonspeakers.com.

Also available in a SIMON & SCHUSTER BFYR hardcover edition

Interior design by Hilary Zarycky

The text for this book was set in Adobe Jensen Pro.

Manufactured in the United States of America

First SIMON & SCHUSTER BFYR paperback edition March 2022

2 4 6 8 10 9 7 5 3 1

The Library of Congress has catalogued the hardcover edition as follows:

Names: Elle, J., author.

Title: Wings of ebony / J. Elle.

Description: First edition. | New York : Simon & Schuster Books for Young Readers, [2021] | Series: Wings of ebony ; #1 | Audience: Ages 14+. | Audience: Grades 10-12. | Summary: Half-god, half-human Rue is snatched from her Houston home to Ghizon, a secret land of gods, by her estranged father, then must face an evil determined to steal everything from her.

Identifiers: LCCN 2020009140 (print) | LCCN 2020009141 (eBook) | ISBN 9781534470675 (hardcover) | ISBN 9781534470682 (pbk) | ISBN 9781534470699 (eBook)

Subjects: CYAC: Magic—Fiction. | Fathers and daughters—Fiction. | Gods—Fiction. | Sisters—Fiction. | Good and evil—Fiction.

Classification: LCC PZ7.1.E438 Win 2021 (print) | LCC PZ7.1.E438 (eBook) | DDC [Fic]—dc23

LC record available at https://lccn.loc.gov/2020009140

LC eBook record available at https://lccn.loc.gov/2020009141

For O.C. and Amelia,
who held on to me tightly,
determined to help me be all that I could be.

And for you, reader,
there is an ember in you that's hungry to burn.
That is your magic.
Let it.

CHAPTER 1

BULLETS DON'T HAVE NAMES.

But if they did, chances are one would have mine. Or someone brown-skinned like me.

Metal slats chill my legs and I shimmy sideways, craning for a better view from the bus stop, careful to keep the onyx stones fused to my wrists covered.

Up all night, I watched the sun rise like a traitor to the chill set in my bones. A yawn scratches at my throat, but my lungs refuse to breathe. Any moment Tasha will step out, her tie-dye drawstring knapsack on her back and her purple fuzzy phone clutched in her fingers. She always oversleeps. But she won't be late. Not today. She—like me—probably couldn't sleep, knowing we had to face today. Had to relive what this day means.

One year ago today, Moms died, shot dead on her stoop. No explanation. No investigation. Just blood, pain, and lots of tears. So many tears.

Since then, it's been Tasha, and me. Separated, living in different places.

But not today. Today my little sister won't be alone.

My eyes sting. I blink the tears away as a bass-filled trunk rattles by, blasting some rapper whose name I can't remember. I'm home. It's good to be back . . . even if I can't stay. I sigh, but my shoulders cinch instead of sink.

Construction crews spill out of work trucks across the street, bringing the block to life. Chiming bells snatch my attention. Kiki's wig shop? They opened early as hell today. Two doors down, dudes in glistening chains, hoodies, and baggy jeans chop it up, slapping hands and giving one-arm hugs. My niggas. The whole damn block is family. Neighbors are aunties. I got more cousins than makes any sort of mathematical sense. You can't work that shit out logically with a family tree chart. The block is fam. Just the way it is. The way it has to be.

But even families keep secrets. I tug at my sleeves.

I lean back, slipping my hood on, face cloaked in shadow. I'm not trying to get tripped up with questions about where I've been. Some shit's just too wild to even *try* to explain. And where I've been this past year—the place I'm forced to now call home—is wild AF.

A jumble of voices pulls me around, twisting in my seat. I keep my head down, hoodie up, until their footsteps are faint patters. I exhale, my knee still bouncing.

Six a.m.

My sis takes the bus to school because it's too far to walk, and everybody at the house is off to work well before the streetlamps stop buzzing. Any moment now, she'll be out the door and find the gift I left on her step. A gift I wish I could hand to her if the risk wasn't so great.

As far as folks know, I disappeared a year ago. They probably think I'm locked up in juvie somewhere. It's not true. I've been in juvie twice. Two times too many. Being snatched from home before Moms was in the ground makes my insides ache more than how it felt sleeping on a cold cell floor.

And the bastard who took me left Tasha.

Such bullshit. "She isn't full blood," he'd said. We got the same mom, different dads. I tried to tell him the whole block is fam—that I can't be pulled from home and just forget where I'm from. It don't work like that. But he wouldn't get that because he's not from 'round here. Home won't ever be "behind me."

He wasn't hearing it. "Once you leave this place you can't ever come back . . . ever," he'd said without explaining. And for 364 days I didn't.

But Tasha won't be alone today. Today, she has me. Even if it means breaking their dumb-ass rules to leave her this gift.

She will know I remember.

I tuck my curls inside my hoodie and swipe the screen on my wristwatch. It warms, glowing a dull blue. It's barely breakfast time and this Houston heat is straight up disrespectful.

Six-oh-five. *Come on, sis.*

I promised Bri, just about the only friend I have at my new "home," I'd get in, leave Tasha's gift, see her off to school, and get out of here. She protested, but she made me this dope watch to get here and back—*without magic*—undetected. She'd just finished it days ago and was nervous it might not work. A pulsing dot shifts on its screen, zeroing in on Tasha's location when I tap. Works just fine. Bri is smart as hell, I swear.

As long as I lay low, no one will even know I'm gone.

A frayed purple necklace dangles from my neck. I roll the thread back and forth between my fingers. The last time I saw Tasha, she wore a matching one. The sparrow charm that used to hang from it broke off months ago. Tasha's got a thing for birds. Something about flying mesmerizes her. She was always back and forth between Moms's and her dad's grandma's house. She's like a bird, even if she can't fly. Little bones, light, so small. Always flitting between fam's houses. A bird with many nests. When I last saw her, she was going on about some new species she'd learned about in school. I smirk. She loves school. A trait we don't share. Tasha musta got that from her pop's side of the family.

I didn't have a dad, so home for me didn't change every weekend. I pull the knot in the charmless necklace, making sure it's tight. As ratty as it is, it's mine, my sister's—ours. One of the few things I was able to hold on to from this place when I left. My only real keepsake from home.

Tasha's glittery pink Converses catch the sunlight as the door opens, and I gasp. She's taller than before. How she grow that fast? The door fully opens and I'm up on my feet. I lighten my pace across the street, careful to stick to the shadows. I can see her, love her from a distance, be here, but I can't touch her. Touching her is the one rule I can't break.

Something changed when I was bound to magic in Ghizon, the place I live now. I rub the onyx lump fused to my wrist and it warms. Having magic is cool, but it isn't worth the cost. If I'd had the choice, I'd have chosen Tasha and life here on the block.

A message on my watch shakes my wrist and I ignore it, eyes fixed on my sis.

I skip across the street to get closer, careful to keep my hood up.

Shade swallows me on her side of the street. She pops in earbuds before locking the door and slipping her string straps on her shoulders. That faded-ass tie-dye. I told her that went out in the seventies, but she loves it. She was never one to follow what everyone else is doing. She's always been like that though—cool doing her own thing. Like me. That we musta both got from Moms.

Come on, Tash. Look down. Neon braids dangle from her cornrows, dancing across her scalp in zigzags. Her hair is always tight. Her nails probably match. That's my sis. Nail polish isn't my thing. Chips too easy. I keep my fresh white 1s clean though. Toothbrush in my pocket at all times. Tash ain't leaving the house without the dopest 'do and flyest nails. Period. Twelve years old and stuntin'.

I slick down my edges, grinning . . . remembering. On the stoop, Moms used to rip through our heads, braiding ours and half the neighborhood's with a piece of cigarette dangling on her lip. Took the whole Saturday, I swear. She'd smack the hell out of my hand with a rattail comb if I moved too much.

"You got too much damn hair to be tender-headed," she'd say.

I flick away hot tears. Moms is gone and crying never solved shit.

Glasses perched on Tasha's beautifully wide nose hide her dark eyes. Her shoe nudges the wrapped box I left on her bottom step and my heart skips a beat. She grabs it and looks around. I press into the neighbor's brick. She *cannot* see me. How would I explain that? Where do I say I've been? What do I do if she wants to come back with me? She wouldn't understand. And what if she tries to touch me? Patrol back in Ghizon says touching humans gives them memories of all your feelings and experiences. She'd know everything about the secret place I live and the magic they gave me. I

5

can't. Ghizon exists in secret and they intend to keep it that way. Just being here for a few is enough. It *has* to be enough.

Chin up, I pretend the dull ache in my chest isn't there. Lines riddle Tash's forehead.

The paper, look at the wrapping paper.

She rips the side open, then stops. She brings it closer to her face and tiny craters dent her cheeks. She holds the package there, staring, smiling. A priceless smile, worth every bit of trouble I could get into for this. I wasn't sure what to wrap it with. They don't exactly have a mini-mart with wrapping paper where I'm living. They'd probably magic some shit together, but I don't know those spells yet. So I took pages from Moms's old journal and wrapped the box, like an extra gift in addition to what's inside.

Tasha peers closer at the paper and gasps. *Moms's words, she's reading them.* Her fingertips find the corners of her eyes. I stay on her six as she walks with quick steps toward her bus stop, opening the package. *I can't see her face.* I wanna see that big-ass grin when she actually opens it up.

We round the corner, head down Fischer Street and turn into Moms's complex. A square block of row-style brown brick apartments with a basketball court in the center. My old spot. The janky-ass hoop still hangs there with a piece of plywood for a backboard. The smell of bay leaves, onions, and garlic curl my toes. *Somebody's grandma is cooking gumbo.* I haven't set foot in my old stomping grounds since I left. Seeing the backside from across the street wasn't easy. But walking into my neighborhood is . . . hard.

The block's lit like it's a Saturday night. People are everywhere, spilling out of their homes. Moms's old door is still coated in chipped green paint. The number nine dangles there like it always did, perpetrating as a six. My fingers twitch to fix it out of habit. Tufts of weeds peek through cracks on the stoop where I spent summers drinking Kool-Cups, gossiping with my girls, hollering at dudes.

I walk along the shade. Tasha's digging into the box now. The playground swings shuffle in the wind, creaking. They're like a clock, reminding me I shouldn't be here.

Tick tock. Tick tock.

Maybe a little closer. Just a little.

I stroll down a broken concrete path alongside the swing set, carefully cloaked in darkness, but closer to her now. She cracks a smile and I'm warm all over.

She rounds a corner up ahead and I follow as a pair of six-foot-two somethings walk by. Baggy jeans, another face I don't know, says, "What's up." I do the same. Their bling dangles and clinks above zip-ups and long sleeves. It's not cold enough for all that. Like most winters in Houston, it's muggy as hell.

My watch vibrates. Another message. Ignored.

Just a few more minutes. A chance to see her face light up at what's inside that box. Something to let her know that today of all days, I am still thinking of her.

Around the corner is Tasha's school bus stop. Six-nineteen. On time. She rips off the last piece of paper and pulls out a golden trinket from inside the box.

It was a little pendant Moms gave me. The last thing I had from her. She put the heart-shaped pendant in my hand three weeks before she died. Told me she worked a double shift for months to afford it. That didn't mean I needed to feel bad, she'd said. Just that my ass better not lose it because she can't afford another one. Tash used to ask me to play with it. I wouldn't even let her breathe on it. Now it's hers. I'm the oldest, which means I have to be the strongest. She needs it more than me.

My watch pings. I swipe right. A new message and all the ignored older ones scroll up the screen.

Bri: You okay?

Bri: It's been a long time. I'm getting worried.

Bri: Rue?

An old-school Cadillac with a rattling trunk steals my attention as its shiny chrome wheels slide to a stop. His black-tinted windows crack and kids at the bus stop rush over. Two kids about Tasha's age hop out. Nosey, like Moms always said I was, I crane my neck trying to see.

Tasha looks in my direction. Like, dead at me. I can't move. Does she see me? *Shit. Shit. Shit.* She waves at me, but she's looking past me. I spin on my heels. Some dude's hanging out a car across the intersection, waving back at her.

I exhale.

"Aye, yo, T," he yells. The dude's white button-up is tucked neatly into a pair of faded jeans. His face—do I know him?

"Sup!" Even her voice sounds older. She puts the heart-shaped pendant in her pocket and jets his way. I squint, hunching beside a dumpster. Who is this dude? And why the hell is whatever he wants so damn important she has to leave her stop to cross the street to come *to him.* You want something, you come here. My sister won't be running after no one.

She looks both ways and he does too, beckoning her closer. She's all smiles. Her bus. She's going to miss her bus. Uneasiness coils in my gut.

She knows this dude. And by the way she's grinning, she knows him *well*. I'm on my feet, keeping her in my sights. I don't like this. She darts across the first half of the street as the sound of a horn zips by.

"Hurry up, girl," he says with a smile, his pasty skin reflecting the morning sun.

"Aye, wait up," she answers. "I'm coming."

Coming where? Where the hell we going? I need to be closer. I'm not feeling this, any of this. Not with my sister. Not while I'm here. I creep so close, the scent of her vanilla hair puddin' swirls in my nose. I'm so close. So very close. If she turns around she *will* see me. Then what?

As she checks both ways again, tires peel out in the distance. Burnt rubber stings my nostrils. The dude's now in his Impala—dark blue with glistening wheels. My heart won't slow and I no longer expect it to. Tasha dips across the rest of the intersection and hops in his passenger seat. He pulls off the curb and she turns my way.

Our eyes lock.

She sees me.

SHIT!

I'm no expert on the ins and outs of Ghizon—the magic world—but one thing I know for sure: Magic folks, like these Laws here, do *not* like broken rules. What does a slap on the wrist even look like there?

Tash knowing I'm here is a problem. A big-ass problem.

Her mouth is hanging wide open in utter shock. She grabs the dude's shoulder to slow down. He throws me a glance, black ink peeking at me from the collar of his shirt. His eyes burn into mine and he doesn't smile . . . doesn't stop . . . just slows, approaching a yellow light. My excitement shatters.

Tires screech far off in the distance. The tatted driver runs the red and keeps rolling across the intersection . . . staring at me instead of the road. A white sedan dents my peripheral, racing toward them. The skin on my back bristles like icy hot knives.

Th-they're going to get hit.

The sedan driver's eyes bulge as he slams on the brakes.

No. No. No.

Rubber screams and skids against pavement. *My magic.* I close the distance between us and raise my hands, fingers spread wide. I tug all my focus to the center of my wrists. Energy like heat rushes through me, pooling in the balls of onyx glowing at my wrists. Waiting, ready.

The time spell. The damn words. What are the damn words?

"Tind na yo wevee." Magic rips from my hands like branches, blinding and hot.

Everything stills.

Time stops.

The nose of the white car is frozen in motion, kissing the passenger side door—Tasha's door. The face of the guy driving the white car is scrunched in pain, frozen and unmoving. Tasha's arms are all I see, stilled in a wave. The entire scene is frozen like figures of glass, pupils dilated with fear. Wind whips around us feverishly.

"I'm here," I say. Her eyes are wide and still. She probably can't hear me, but I whisper all the same. "You're going to be okay."

The guy in the driver's seat next to her is still as ice, hand on the door handle, a twisted grin glued on his face. A big-ass coiled snake tattoo is on his neck. I move around the car and tug at the back door. Locked. With no one conscious watching, I press my palms together, conjuring a force of energy between them. I thrust it at the rear window. It shatters in a sea of chimes.

"Feey'l." Flames ignite from my fingertips. The smell of burned chemicals fills my nostrils as I scorch through her seat belt as quickly as I can.

Magic bearers should never touch humans.

The damn rule plays on repeat in my head.

Frantic, I wrap my shaking hands around her and a tingling sensation moves through me. I bite down, ignoring it, and pull harder, her warm skin against mine. Singed but hanging on by a thread, the seat belt still doesn't let go of her legs. The time spell will wear off any second, and this car crash will crunch back into motion. I tug and bite the belt, pulling as coppery liquid fills my mouth.

It won't relent. *Shit!* She will not die here. She won't! I clamp my teeth and yank again. The belt releases.

Magic bearers should never touch humans.

The rules. The stupid rules. This is my sister, not just *anyone.* They can do their worst to me, I'm not losing her. I pull her petite frame onto the asphalt.

The streetlights are flashing now and the colors shift from green, to yellow, to red, and back to green. I glance over my shoulders and check my watch. How long does the time spell last? I bite my lip. Bri would know. I fidget with my watch to send her a message as the sound of crunching glass splits the air.

I raise a hand, trying to keep the spell intact. *Hold. Please hold!* My hand shakes more violently and the air itself seems to tremble. It's not going to hold. She's like a cinder block, but with one arm I drag her toward the sidewalk, away from the crash.

"Wake up, Tash. Come on, wake up."

She bats her eyes. Sounds of crumpling fiberglass crack through the air. My spell is buckling. My hand trembles, the heat from my wrists simmers.

"I-I can't hold it." *Oof.* A jolt of pain radiates through me and chaos erupts in blurred motion. The car she was just in skids across the intersection and plants into a pole.

But the driver . . . the driver *just* inside is gone.

Wait . . . what . . . but how?

The driver of the white car hangs out the window, neck crooked backward and streaked with blood. I turn my face away. Tasha pulls herself up on shaky elbows, blinking in my direction.

"R-Rue?" She looks at me and I cover the warm stones in my wrists.

"*Rue!*" Her voice cracks and nothing matters anymore.

I pull her in to me. "It's okay. You're okay."

Cars swerve to a stop, narrowly missing the pile of crushed metal. A man in a navy windbreaker emerges with a phone to his ear.

"Help will be here soon," I say. She weeps against my chest, a gash on her forehead crying tears of blood. I hold her tight—tight like Moms would do.

"It's over," I whisper, refusing tears trying to break free. "You're okay. I'm here. Everything's okay."

The crowd nearby clamors over one another for a look at the wreck, when a sweet chemical scent wafts past. Gasoline.

No. Shit. No!

"W-we have to move." Even on the sidewalk we're too close. I fumble for her arm, pulling it over my shoulder. She's heavy. So much heavier than I remember. "We have to get up." The gasoline smell stings my nostrils and words stick to the roof of my mouth.

"Tash, we have to get farther away!" Her head bobs like she's woozy, her forehead wound gushing faster.

Magic. Move her with magic.

A cluster of eyes cling to us; everybody's watching, recording. I-I can't. The time spell wore off. People are watching! I can't use magic with them all looking. I—

The chemical smell grows stronger and a flicker of fire dents my periphery.

Do something!

B-but people are around . . .

I-I . . . I have to. I can't lose her.

The words are fuzzy in my head, and the black stones fused to my wrists swirl with warmth, but nothing sputters from my hand. *Focus.* What are the words? I can't think. I pull hard from my center and my wrists glow hot as the black balls fused to my skin heat like a skillet. My words are muddled, but I feel it. I feel my magic. Energy rushes through me, ripping from my palms, a light sprouting like rays of sun.

"Shee'ye ya fuste." The light shifts into a wall transparent as glass between us and the crash, rippling like droplets of water. The ground shudders and clouds of orange blaze explode, slamming against the invisible barrier. Jolts of pain pinch my spine, but I keep my hands still. If I let go, the flames will swallow us. She moans.

"Tash? Stay with me. I'm here. It's going to be okay."

She hugs me, nestling her fingers against my skin. I close my eyes and focus on the rhythm of her heartbeat pressed to my chest. Moms used to rock me back and forth and hum when I was little and scared. So I rock.

Holding her stirs a heat inside of me, brighter and fiercer than the sizzling flames popping just a ways away. Sirens moan in the backdrop and orange light colors my eyelids. I don't want to open them. Not yet. My wrists chill as the fire and magic around us fizzles out and a gust of smoke assaults my head.

She's okay. We're okay.

My wristwatch buzzes. It's Bri.

Bri: What did you do?! Patrol is coming. Run!

CHAPTER 2

WHEN I WAS LITTLE, I got caught stuffing some cookie bars in my pocket at the corner store. A man with an overgrown beard posted up outside the store had asked me if I had any change so he could get something to eat. I didn't. And he looked hungry, *real real* hungry. So I slipped inside LuLu's, giving my usual wave. Lu didn't even look up from his paper as I stuffed some Fig Newtons, the little snack-size ones, in my pocket. Seconds from the door, Lu's voice stopped me dead in my tracks. "I'm calling the cops if you don't put that back."

I cried, begging him not to say nothing. I put it back, but he called Moms anyway. She whooped my ass into next week.

I kept thinking, *I was trying to help*.

But it didn't matter. The law is the law.

All that mattered is I bucked up against the rules. And for that, I had hell to pay.

Déjà vu.

My head swims. Everything's hazed and cloudy. The eyes—so many eyes. They're all staring from the sidewalk. Everyone's whispering to each other, their phones out, mouths open.

What have I done?

They saw me. *Shit.* I gotta get the hell out of here.

Tasha's leaning in to me and I hold on tighter. Someone pulls my arm and I jerk away. No one's taking her from me. Not now that she knows I'm here, alive and okay. Not today. They pull harder and wailing sirens scratch my ears.

She lets go first, carried off by someone in a uniform.

"No," I say, reaching. "Tash, come back." The words are heavy on my tongue and jumbled in my head. "I can take you home. I gotta tak—" I stagger to my feet, an earthquake rattling inside my skull.

What the hell is wrong with me? Why am I so woozy? "T-Tash—"

"Ma'am?" A firm hand grabs my arm and I pull away. Hard.

"Don't touch me."

"I'm here to help, ma'am." His pale cheeks crack a smile, spreading his oversize mustache. "Listen, ma'am. Could you step over here and tell us what you saw?"

Cops. My neck stiffens. He pulls harder and I come, staggering.

"Have you been drinking, miss?" he asks.

"No!" Flames erupt from my fingertips. I shove them in my pocket. My wrists flash, from searing hot to ice cold a second later and back again. What's wrong with me? My magic is out of control!

"Miss. Cooperate." The cop shakes my arm, harder this time. I try to pull away, to say something, but I can't think. I can hardly speak. Tasha. Where's Tasha? And the guy in the car? I glance at the wreck and the driver's side of the car Tasha was just in is smashed to pieces—the driver, nowhere to be found. I grip the officer's arms, more to hold myself up than anything else. I have to make him understand.

"There was a guy." The words are like chalk on my tongue. "Faded jeans. Tucked white button-up. H-he . . . knew somehow. Like he was trying to get her—" Sounds fade into a loud buzzing and everything's black. My heaving breaths resound like a gong in my head.

Gong.

Gong.

Then a flood of color rushes at me as the world blinks back into focus. Something is wrong. I've done magic a hundred times since living in Ghizon. The only difference today was . . . I gape at my hands. Touching her did this? What else could explain it?

"You were saying?" The cop widens his stance, folding his arms.

"I—" *Gong. Gong.*

My knees wobble, but I lock them in place as a stranger's raspy voice rings in my ear. "Lot of funny stories from the witnesses. Stuff you wouldn't believe." She points at me. "What's the story with this one?"

Voices. *Gong. Gong.* So many voices.

I rake my fingers through my scalp. It stings like fire. "Listen to me!" I pull the officer's sleeves to mine and his back straightens. *Careful. Don't piss him off.*

I squeeze my eyes shut and I can see the man from the car in my mind's eye. His pale skin and crisp ironed shirt. He wore faded black jeans and hair pulled back in a ponytail. His eyes were light-colored and tats peeked from the collar of his shirt. And his car. The way he angled it in the intersection and stopped, a surly grin on his face when he looked my way.

"There was a man. A-a man in a car." I point. "O-over there. He was *right* there! He lured my sister to his car and h-he knew somehow that something bad was going to happen. H-he—"

The cop turns to Miss Raspy Voice. "I don't know. Around these parts, no telling what she's on." He turns to me. "There's no man in the car over there, ma'am."

He's not listening. Why am I even trying?

"He was just there, I swear." *Water. I need water.*

"Get her seen over there." He points toward an ambulance. "Run her prints, too." He lets me go and I stumble. *I need to get out of here.* Tasha's perched on the edge of the ambulance talking to a blond paramedic with a clipboard. I will myself over, one foot in front of the other. The gash on her head isn't gushing anymore. She's sitting up, eyes open, talking, a cup in her hands. She spots me and her eyes say more than any words could.

She knows. Memory transference.

She knows everything.

I plow into her legs more roughly than I intend to and Blondie gives me a look.

"Sorry," I manage. "I—this is my sister."

Tasha nods and Blondie gestures for me to go ahead.

"T, are you okay?"

She nods. "All this time I thought you were dead. Gone. I don't know." Her finger traces the rim of her water cup. "I . . . you . . ."

I reach for her cup and she lets me take it. The water is cool going down my throat. I blink; her face is clearer, in focus. Not one hundred percent, but better.

She whispers. "The place you live . . . it's—"

"I'm sorry to break this up," Blondie says. "We need to get her back to be seen. She looks alright but we'll want to run some tests. Are you able to ride with?"

"I-I can't ride." I tug at my sleeves, suddenly hyper aware of my secret. "I—I gotta go."

Each word curves my sister's lips farther downward.

I hug her, squeezing harder than life itself. "I'll be back to check on you."

"When?" Tears dangle on her lashes.

The hole in my chest shudders with pain. "Soon." I don't know if it's true. I want it to be. I'll do my damndest to make sure it is. "I—please, please just lay low." I hold her face in my hands. "No strangers. Fam only."

She nods and flicks away a tear.

"Moms raised a diamond." I lace my fingers between hers.

She squeezes. "And diamonds don't crack."

The paramedic pulls her backward, breaking our grasp. Leaving her here like this isn't how I imagined today going. As the doors close, she opens her palm and the heart pendant shines. She smirks, holding it to her heart as the doors click shut. A tinge of warmth fills the hole inside my heart. *I knew she'd love it.*

Around us, flocks of police officers flit back and forth around the crumpled metal car, checking on bystanders, jotting down notes, talking into their walkie-talkies. *They saw me . . . what I did to save Tasha.* Men, women, kids are staring from every corner of the block, pointing, talking, as the City Laws take notes.

"Miss, I'm going to need you to come with me to answer some questions." The fingers cupped around my shoulder are firm. Almost painful. The warmth I just felt dissolves at the familiar sight. I'm face to face with the man's telltale grayish pale skin; he almost looks like some white dude in need of a tan. But I know that complexion.

Patrol—from Ghizon.

Here.

In my world.

On my block.

"You'll need to come with me. Now." It's not a request. My fingers twitch for my watch. Maybe I can flick it on fast enough to zap back "home." Veins pulse at the corners of his eyes. I don't know his face, but he's Ghizoni. They're all the same, with their pallid skin. I can't see it, but he has a secret fused to his wrists—circles of onyx embedded in his flesh.

"I . . ."

"Sir, do you have clearance to be here?" The city cop pops a notebook closed.

A plastic smile splits the Ghizoni's face as he greets the cop. "No problem, officer. Special unit investigating what happened here. Just a few questions for the young lady."

"You got a badge?"

"Of course." He turns toward me like he's reaching into his back pocket. If looks could kill, start typing my eulogy now. "Shut up," he mouths, waving one hand in front of the other. There, in the palm of his hand, where there was just air, a black leather rectangle adorned with a gold crest glints in the sun. I bite my tongue to keep from gasping.

The cop nods. "Very good. We'll need a few words with her when you're done." He ventures off, and I don't know if I feel relieved or more panicked.

Patrol turns to me. "Where were we?"

Definitely more panicked.

"You're in violation of using magic outside Ghizoni borders." He slips a silver restraint from his pocket and leans in for a whisper. "Not to mention illegal use of a transport spell to the human world in the first place."

I hide my wristwatch arm behind me. Bri won't take the fall for this too.

"Come along without making a scene or this will get far worse. For you. For everyone."

There's no way out of this. No way good.

"I'm not going anywhere with you." Darkness creeps at the edges of my vision and I sway. But blinking quickly seems to help. I think. I hope.

Patrolman tilts his head. *He noticed.*

He pulls down his shades. "Who did you touch?" He spits words like they're laced with poison.

"I—I don't know what you're talking about. I ain't do nothing." Do I have rights in Ghizon like here? Not that that shit matters half the time.

He glances both ways. "I *said*—"

If Patrol in Ghizon are anything like the Laws here, talking won't do shit.

He reaches for me.

And I run.

My feet fly across the pavement, my block a blur of color. I dart across the street, hiking over a garbage can, knocking it down behind me. My heart pounds faster than my feet. Footsteps echo at my back.

An alleyway between the laundromat and Klassy Kuts barber

shop opens up ahead and I pound the ground harder. I saved my sister's life and somehow that's a crime. My lungs burn and my thighs cry in pain as I run. Because that's just what you do when Laws are after you. Guilty or not, you just run.

My wrist vibrates and I can't manage a look. Maybe I can lose them, get back to Ghizon, act like I've been there the whole time. They don't have shit on me. They can't prove anything. *Would they even have to?*

The sound of my heaving breaths echo off the towering apartments around me. I chance a glance over my shoulder and all is clear. So I stop to catch my breath and check my watch.

Bri: Dorms are closed. Meet at my house?

I try to shoot off a reply when a hand as cold as death clamps around my wrist.

"I *said* come with me." His silver restraints coil around my wrists like a braided rope, then harden into shiny metal. "The Chancellor intends to see you. Now." Patrolman lifts his sleeves, and the orb in his wrist glows. With a winding swish of his hand, the cuffs on my wrists cinch tight. I hold my chin up. He won't see me struggle.

"Fine, take me to see him. I did the *right* thing. I *saved* someone's life."

"A *human* life." He chortles. "And you think that matters?"

CHAPTER 3

I'S CALLED A CHASER. What you're feeling." Patrolman leads me, cuffs first, down the alley, deeper into the shadows. "The lightheadedness, dry mouth. Happens because you're Bound. The first time you touch a human." He loops his arm into mine and presses his hands together and I stare confused.

"Don't you read? Go to class?"

Yeah, asshat, I do. "Uh, a year of magic school doesn't make me an expert on the topic." *Excuse me for missing out on the last century of how shit works.*

He ignores the snide remark. His fingers tremble as a ball of light sparks between them, unsettling the dust in the alleyway around us. "When one of the Sacred Statutes is broken the first time," he says, raising his voice over the rumbling vortex in his hands, "touching humans being the most serious of them . . . the perp's magic back-fires, almost like a poison emitted into your bloodstream."

A perp? Is that what I am now?

"Unless you get an antidote." Something he does with the corners of his mouth makes me doubt an antidote is in my future. They would let me die for touching someone? My own sister?

"It's supposed to slow the perp down until we find them."

"And then what?"

"And then"—the alley glows blinding white, his magic dissolving the faded brick walls around us—"you reap what you sow."

I part my lips to speak, but he mutters the transport spell. The air swallows us, and in a blip, we're gone.

Over the Ethiopian highlands, south of the Serengeti, thousands of nautical miles off the coast of Madagascar, where the Atlantic and Indian Oceans meet is a hidden land I ain't never seen on a map or in some history book. But I've slipped beyond that invisible curtain of open ocean before, to a hidden place nestled at the base of Yiyo Peak, a mountain so tall it kisses the afternoon sun. It is Ghizon, home to a clan of magic-wielders. Self-proclaimed gods. Their magic gives them that stink of uppity.

For several moments I feel squished all over, like I've forced my entire body into skinny jeans several sizes too small. Waves of memories of being whisked away to Ghizon the first time, when Moms's blood was barely cold, threaten to drown me. The pops of gunshots, her open-eyed stare . . . it all comes rushing back. I don't want to relive it.

As my feet set on the ground in Ghizon, the past calls to me. And I give in.

CHAPTER 4

Eleven Months Ago

THE SUN SHOULDN'T BE allowed to shine every day. Some days it needs to sit its ass down somewhere and let it be gray.

In my pocket, I roll the worn edge of a photograph of Moms—one of the few things I had time to grab—back and forth between my fingers. I tug my jacket tighter over me and take an incremental step forward. The line for Sorting and Binding—finding out which caste I'm assigned to and having magic fused to my skin—isn't super long, but waiting isn't my idea of fun. Not ever, but especially not now.

Pop.

Pop.

I shake off the memory of Moms hitting the ground and swallow my lunch back down, taking another tiny step forward.

Celebratory banners in deep purples and jade sway in the breeze and a band of Ghizoni play curved horns that look like elongated elephant tusks onstage. The crowd moves to the rhythm, waiting for the designations to begin.

Steel and glass buildings tower around me. New Ghizon's

Central District is full of cloud-blocking buildings tucked tight together with narrow alleyways between. Giant screens hang from the glassy skyscrapers and the words DESIGNATION DAY dance on their glass. The words dissolve every few seconds, replaced by flashes of the crowd waving, fingers twisted into what looks like a knot held over their hearts.

Bursts of sparkle erupt over the crowd, glittering in the high sun. At first, seeing people conjure things out of thin air, bend animals to their will, shift and move and change things with magic wowed.

Now, it just annoys.

I'm not one of them.

Patrol lines the outskirts of the audience, their fingers glued to their chests too. No idea what the gesture means, but judging by their reverent stares, it's some allegiance type shit.

The only other brown face in this place . . . in this world . . . is on the corner of the amphitheater stage in a too-small chair. The man I basically *just* met. The one Moms laid up with to make me: Aasim.

I don't want to do this. I don't want to do any of this, but he didn't make it sound like I had a choice. He looks at me and his lips crack a weak smile.

I look away.

I told him not to bring me to this place.

I told him I don't want their gift of magic or whatever.

I told him, let me go to Moms's funeral *at least*.

And yet, here I am.

"We have to go now," he'd said, like I'd asked for his help. Like I needed him.

I didn't and I don't.

Now, barely a month here and I'm obligated to participate in this "honor" held twice a year. "To help you get acquainted with your new home," he'd said. Like, what does that even mean? I'm not one of these people and won't ever be.

Behind me a buzzing line of sixteen-year-olds chirp like prating birds. They don't say anything to me and I say nothing to them. What's the point? The only one here who's half-human ... who I'ma talk to? About what? From my room, to class to meals I can barely stomach and back home again. This is my new life. *Thanks, Aasim.*

On stage, a musician with a braid that dangles all the way to the floor plucks strings on a bowl covered with what looks like animal hide. Peering closer, I realize there are no strings. Just his fingers dancing across the leather daintily, somehow filling the air with a tune. His head sways, the balls of onyx in his wrists shining. The sweet lilt of his voice isn't lost on me. Tasha loves birds and his melody would put a lark to shame. *She'd love to see this.* For a moment my baby sister's face is all I see.

The music livens, yanking me back to the present and the twenty or so giddy Ghizoni in line with me, constantly glancing at me when they think I'm not looking. I shrink a little. I should have stayed in my room. Anywhere but here. Under all these eyes. Strange, curious eyes.

It's not just their gaping that makes me uneasy, it's the tilted stares and whispered words on my way here from the dorm. Any time I pass, really. It's not just the buzzing magical energy pumping through this place like electricity. It's not just that *no one* here looks like me—but *him.*

It's that this is not my home.

These ain't my people.

And after seeing Moms's blood bathe our stoop, home is the only place I wanna be. In my bed, wrapped up in the blanket Moms found for me at that garage sale that one time, hugged up in her smell, on her pillow. The thoughts of her used to make me sad, bring tears. Now . . . I don't know what I feel.

Nothing. Is that a feeling?

A horn sounds and at the entrance to the Amphitheater, in the very back, a burly man appears. His head of wispy white hair folds upward like a crown, then cascades down his back in knots. Golden ornaments in his hair jingle with each of his steps.

The Chancellor—the guy who runs Ghizon.

He descends the steps, Patrol clinging to his sides like he's royalty. I met him once when Aasim's secret of being laid up with Moms first got out. He was an asshole, real condescending like. And not just with his words. Something about the way he held his chin, the way he looked at me when Aasim admitted his crime: making me.

The Chancellor waves to the crowd and the edges of the aisles pull to him like magnets, grasping for any piece of him within reach. An exuberant few kiss his robes. Gems hug his knuckles and he smiles, cupping the face of some lady's baby. She about faints. He climbs the stage with one more wave and it's then I notice the screens are all his face. He holds his arms wide and everyone, literally everyone in the arena, stands, hands over their chest.

Around me the jitters have quieted and every student waiting to be Sorted is rigid, fingers knotted with a glaze of adoration in their eyes. The Chancellor stops in front of a chair inlaid with gems larger than the rocks on his fingers. He surveys the crowd, a warm smile on his lips. *Ugh.*

His eyes land on mine and with each breath his smile thins.

I dig my hands into my pockets. He still stares expressionless, and yet I feel like maybe he's trying to say something by not saying anything at all. This is weird. Really weird. *I—I . . . what do I do?* I peer around at the knotted fingers thing and try twisting mine, but before I can actually move, he gestures for everyone to sit, his gaze still on me as he plants in his chair.

Another horn sounds, this time twice, and the girl first in line is two heads in front of me. She steps up on the stage platform, her red hair blowing, where an old woman greets her with a grimace. I don't know what exactly happens when you're Sorted, but I'm near the front so this is almost over.

The music quiets and the old lady, who's the Sorter by the looks of it, is hunched over, waiting. But not like she means to be; like she just walks that way permanently. A million creases fold her sienna skin, tanned from the sun. Without it, she'd be white or gray or whatever like everybody else here.

I don't know what she's 'bout to do or how she's going to do it, but whatever it is, it ends in being assigned to a group. Curiosity has me craning my neck harder to see. Aasim mentioned something about it determining my job, how I'll contribute to Ghizon society. I don't wanna work here. I don't even wanna *be* here.

Her chin bounces, up and down, up and down, as she mutters something under her breath, her dark linen shift fluttering at her feet. I can't make out the words, but every eye in the place is on her. Including the Chancellor's. Two beaming faces from the front row of the amphitheater appear frozen in time, staring. I'm not even sure they're breathing. Must be the girl's parents. They catch me looking and their smiles fade to disgust.

Sigh. The sun beats down, but I slip my hoodie over my head anyway, my hair wilding out from each side. A stick bangs the concrete, popping like gunshots, and gooseprickled memories dance up my skin. The Sorter circles the red-headed girl, tapping a knobby stick taller than the both of them, so thick her hand barely wraps around it. She *tap tap taps* the ground. You could cut the silence in the arena with a knife.

I crane my neck farther.

The Sorter lady waves her free hand around the girl like she's feeling the air.

"She's checking her energy, the vibe she gives off," someone whispers behind me, but I don't turn around.

The air itself seems to ripple at the Sorter's hand movements, the black stones on her wrists glowing orange. Redhead swallows and shrieks as flames ignite from the woman's fingertips. She waves and waves some more, the fire coming within inches of the girl's face.

I squint. That lady ain't bringing no fire anywhere near me. She wanna know my energy? I can just tell her—it's annoyed, like the rest of me. Is it too late to get out of line? Aasim didn't say nothing about any of this.

"Hmph." Old Lady makes a fist and her flames snuff out. Well, that's a relief she isn't going to burn her skin off. Stick Lady circles again, her gummy bite bouncing like she's thinking. Sizing up this girl like I would if I was 'bout to square up.

"Mo'ya na na." She raises her stick and holds it high before slamming into the back of the girl's thighs. She groans in pain.

Oh heeeeellllll no.

The stick whirs through the air again and slaps the girl in the stomach. She grunts. I know one thing, that lady or nobody else is hitting *me* with no damn stick.

I can *feel* the girls behind me staring, hard, like this is the most entrancing shit they've ever seen. Something they've fantasized about their whole lives: the day they get magic.

After a few more swats with the stick, the Sorter seems satisfied she's found whatever she was looking for. Then she shoves a thumb into the side of girl's mouth, pulling it open and looking at the girl's teeth.

What the hell is this, an auction?! I cannot. She's not touching my teeth. She's not touching me period. I'm not being paraded on stage like property. Hell, the fuck, no. I have half a mind to leave. I look around; Patrol is everywhere. Would they even let me?

"Hmph." The Sorter grunts, but it's, like, an approving grunt, if there is such a thing. She mutters more words I've never heard and I could swear someone behind me snorts. A few more seconds pass, and then she faces the crowd. "*Zruki.*"

Zruki? The hell is a Zruki?

A burst of applause rings out from the front row and a woman with her hair in an unkempt bun clutches her chest in relief. The man next to her with black-stained fingers presses his forehead to hers. They smile. Must be something good, I guess.

Sorter Lady points a bony finger toward the sign that says BINDING and the girl's pallor returns. It's only then that I notice the old woman *only has* a thumb and a pointing finger. I gulp. I probably should have asked who all these people are, what being Sorted and Bound entails, *something*. But that would have required talking to *him*.

We ain't talked my entire life. Why start now?

Been figuring shit out on my own all this time.

This ain't no different.

Sorter Lady gestures for the next person in line and the girl in front of me disappears toward the platform. She's wearing a crimson dress in a shiny material. Taffeta? Silk? Some shit. She sashays on stage like it's a dance and the crowd *ooohs* and *ahhhhs*. The elder woman taps her stick at the spot where Crimson Girl is supposed to stand, apparently unimpressed with the flashy entrance. Crimson Girl blushes and hurries to her place, but not before fanning out her arms. Gilded peacock feathers sprout from her collar like her head is set on a pedestal shrouded in gold.

I'm next in line and my sperm donor's full on smiling now. I don't want his smiles. I don't want anything from him . . . I don't want . . .

"Next, daughter of Aasim," Aasim says.

I *don't* want to be called that.

Aasim says his piece then sits, pride alight in his eyes. The Chancellor's stare is on me like dead weight. Standing on the platform, I can really see just how wide and deep the theater seating goes. A collage of bright blues, deep rusty oranges, and every hue in the rainbow colors the crowd's made-up faces and matching ornate hairstyles. My heart flutters a million miles a minute. A woman in the audience with rose-shaped hair folds her arms and I can practically feel the chill from her shade. Glittered strands of hair hang in tendrils around her face, a sharp contrast to the stank eye she's giving me. Deep red stain colors her lips, dark and glossy . . . probably sticky . . .

Sticky like . . .

Red like . . .

My throat constricts and a stubby forefinger and thumb beckon me onto the stage. Sorter Lady's looking away from me as she gestures. I come. My feet are lead, but I come.

Our eyes meet and the chill I felt from Red Lips is as warm as a summer day compared to the ice of this old lady's stare.

"Na!" She bangs the ground, her eyes as wide as the moon on a cloudless night.

"Uhhh?"

"Na! Y'gi na." She scowls, blocking the path between her evaluation deck and the BINDING sign where Redhead and Crimson Girl exited to be Bound to magic.

"Na, Zruki. Na, Dwegini." She turns to the Chancellor and her nostrils flare. "*Na!*"

She's not feeling me. At all.

"*Naaaa!*" She hisses like a snake. I back up several steps and the crowd erupts in chatter. I can leave. I don't wanna be here no way. Be sorted Zruki or whatever the hell the other option is. I spot my wannabe kin on the far end of the stage and he doesn't move or speak, just chews his bottom lip.

The Chancellor's eyes haven't moved.

Still on me as he strokes his chin.

Stick Lady points at me like she did the others, but she points toward the exit. As in *leave*. I don't get to be Bound, apparently. Does that mean I get to go home? Because that'd be great.

The crowd is harder to see as I descend the steps from the platform, backing up until I bump into something. "Oops," I say. "Sorry."

Papers spill on the ground and the noise on the platform dies down. The Sorter woman is in a tizzy, arguing with some military-type dude with a scar under his eye. He doesn't look like he's playing, but the way she's shouting, she ain't playing either. I turn my back on the commotion to a smiling face covered in freckles, unruly blond hair, and red square glasses.

"It's fine." She reshuffles the papers in her hand.

Was I supposed to bring paperwork to this thing?

"Don't mind her," she says, pointing at Stick Lady. "People say she smokes jpango leaves all day. Pretty sure her brain's fried at this point. They say the only words she knows are 'Zruki' and 'Dwegini.' Which, for her job, covers it. So!" She snorts.

I look back at the old woman and needles prick my spine. "Nah, something tells me she knows much more than that."

The girl shrugs. "Maybe. But don't let her get to you. Even if she won't sort you, you can probably still be Bound. You're Ruler Aasim's *daughter.*"

Her words are sandpaper on my skin. "Oh no, it's cool. I mean . . . wait, ruler?"

"I know you're new around here," she says. "Half-human and all. Gossip mill spreads fast. But you *want* to be Bound. Trust me."

"I mean, not really. For what? To play dress-up every day? What's the point?"

She laughs, then stops when she realizes I'm foreal. "It's so much more than that. The capabilities are wild. You'll see." She gestures at the air like she's grasping for my name.

I let her.

I don't know this girl.

She sticks out a hand. "Ajebria."

Well, shoot . . . she's being friendly as hell. "Ah-juh, what?"

"Just call me Bri. It's what everyone calls me. If I had friends, that is . . . I mean . . ." She facepalms. "I prefer Bri. Sorry for being weird. I don't talk to many . . . I mean I don't have . . ."

"I'm Rue." I offer dap and she stares, confused. I take her hand, ball it into a fist, and pound it on mine. "Dap."

"Dap." She slow nods.

"Dap."

We laugh. "You said *Ruler* Aasim . . . is he like . . ."

"You're not serious. You have to be kiddi—" She must read my face because she changes her tone, quick. "Yeah." She bats flyaways out of her face like they're a flock of gnats. "Third in command around here. So not like *ruler*, ruler, but like real close to the top ruler. He works right under the Chancellor."

Aasim works right under the boss man? That why he on stage in that little bitty chair?

"The Chancellor," Bri continues. "He doesn't want to be called by name because that's too personal. He founded this place and essentially *owns* Ghizon. He united the islands' native tribes and shared his magic with all of them, and he gives it to all of us, too, so, hello Binding!" She leans in for a whisper. "No one knows where he got it from, but rumor has it he laid with a goddess who desperately wanted a son and he wagered she'd give him magic in exchange. Only thing is, she didn't conceive so he had to get away by the skin of his teeth with magic. Apparently there's a veil of protection over the island so she can never find us."

She squints up at the sky as if she really believes this shit. "But who knows? There's no shortage of rumors around here. Usually they have a seed of truth, I always say. I digress. But yes . . ." She does that thing with her fingers and lays them over her heart. "The Great and Generous Chancellor. Seyeen."

Now I want to know what *she's* smoking.

"You have a lot to learn about this place. Sounds like your da—"

"Aasim," I say, interrupting. She gotta stop with that father shit.

She studies my face for several moments. "Your . . . *Aasim* didn't tell you much about this place."

I gave him all of forty-five seconds to talk to me before my AirPods were in. "Very little."

"Well, not to worry. I'll get you up to speed." She nudges me with her elbow and I force a smile. I should try to be more friendly. She really is nice.

"Th-thanks." And I mean, having someone to actually *ask* questions probably is a good idea.

The commotion behind us has stopped and it's Bri's turn for Sorting on the platform. But Stick Lady joins us on the far end of the stage and her watery eyes burn into me like frost.

"Hmph." She points toward BINDING before huffing and storming off. I guess Bri was right: I do get to be Bound. Bri holds two fingers to her lips like she's blowing a blunt and winks. I laugh.

"Meet you on the other side," she says.

"Bet."

The other side is off the platform, thankfully, in a nearby building. The Binding building. No more crowds, no more stares. Just white walls, sterile like a hospital with a giant floor-to-ceiling picture of the Chancellor. His white eyebrows are slicked down, shiny, and his thinning white hair looks much fuller. His skin is still overly pinkish like he spends too much time in the sun or he's really embarrassed permanently. Or both.

Aside from the portrait, the walls are bare. Thin, long benches line the hallway and lockers are on the opposing side. Two swinging metal doors have STAY OUT written in bold blue letters. A pencil-thin woman with a literal nest of violet hair on her head scans a card on some sort of pad near the door and pushes through. Before her, Redheaded Girl went inside, and I could swear seconds later I heard screaming under the elevatorish music they have playing. Maybe I'm hearing things.

I pound my head back on the wall. The rattling in my brain is calming in a way. What is Tasha doing? Where did that CPS lady even take her? Darkness wraps around me and I see my sister's face on the back of my eyelids. She's smiling, then crying. Her mouth widens and her nose thins. Her eyes stretch a little as her features morph into Moms's. I roll my purple frayed necklace between my fingers.

I catch sight of Bri strolling up, fidgeting with some metal gadget I can't quite make out. But the way she's biting her tongue, it seems dire.

"You survive?" I ask.

"Oh yeah, Zruki for sure. My build, my genes, it's mine work for me. Plus, my parents are Zruki and it usually follows genealogy."

"So what do non-mine-working-Zrukis do?"

"Those . . . would be . . ." She grunts, pushing one end of the metal into the other. "Ugh! Sorry, my PRI Modifier is out of whack.

37

They're Dwegini." She shoves the metal thing in her pocket and I catch a half glance at it. It's squarish with red buttons and a blue light on top. But one end is dangling and I don't think it is supposed to be.

"Dwegini?"

"The others. They're not built for mine work. They do administrative stuff, they're entertainers, armed guards, they do medical stuff, research. *Lots* of magic theory research. Chancellor's really into that. He keeps his supple-bodied folks working in the mines. That's where the onyx comes from, for binding. My parents are both mine workers. Dad's working on a side job to get us a bit more rations, and maybe even move to a larger unit. I think you call it a house? But my dad's efforts haven't really gone anywhere. I don't mind sharing a room with my parents, and my brothers are so little, they don't seem to care."

One bedroom? For all five (maybe more) of them?

"And the floor really does feel good to my back . . . after a while. Plus, it's free. Can't complain too much."

The floor? Now, *that* I didn't expect. "I don't understand. People seemed relieved to be Zrukis. But you laid up in government-sanctioned housing?"

"I mean, Zrukis may sound like the lower ranking in the hierarchy work-wise because its manual labor, but it's an honorable trade, Rue." She stands up straighter. "It's critical to the function of Ghizon. Sure, it's charmed dresses and artsy makeup, but it's also rapid cell regeneration, cloaking, which has all kinds of uses, growth serums. I mean . . . this magic the Chancellor unearthed is brilliant."

I hadn't thought about that.

"All our protections here, the weapons Patrol use . . . all magic."

"Protection?"

"Yep."

I sit up taller. "Tell me more."

"Oh man, there's so much. And our magic only grows more functional as we continue to study it," she explains, her eyes lit up. "Onyx is everything here. Can't Bind people without onyx. And *we* do that. *Zrukis*. We're kind of a big deal." She bats another flyaway hair. "And at least we *get* Bound. There's one more word in that old woman's vocabulary." She shudders. "Macazi. That means you're casteless, not worthy of either and not fit to bear magic at all. They don't even get units. It's community housing for them, until they die off or who knows what. Rumor is they use them for"—she whispers—"trials . . . like for research. *Zruki* is not at all a bad gig."

The way she's looking at me, I think I'm supposed to marvel at her designation. And because I want to try to be a decent friend to this chick, I do. "Oh wow, my bad. Well, congrats."

"Thanks. Our units are decent, too. Being only one room means less time cleaning, and it's easier to heat and cool with Memi's magic. The floor *isn't* as bad as it sounds."

"No, y-yeah. I didn't mean anything by that." I'm just surprised that in a world with magic, people would live like they broke. Why does the Chancellor need a grip on things like that? Why not let people live freely, earning their way? What does he gain by giving them magic but controlling how they use it, where they work, their quality of living, making them work their way up the chain in their free time, on the slim chance they can find free time? I seen that before and that . . . that ain't admirable.

That's suspect.

"I know what you mean. Been there," I say. "Moms's mattress got bedbugs once and we had to save up for four months to replace it."

She stares a second, confused. "I can't imagine Aasim's daughter sleeping on the floor, but—"

"Let's be clear. I *just* met him. I don't know him. So . . . just . . . chill out with all that mentioning him, please. My Moms raised me. *Alone.* And it's not like this back home. It's . . ." I gaze out a nearby window. The banners from the ceremony still flutter in the wind. A juggler flips colorful balls in the air using one hand and they burst into birds in every color and flutter off, while a crowd of admirers throws coins at him. "It's just different."

"Well, it doesn't matter because once we're Bound, it's off to the dorm for a year of training. With our own beds!" She dances in place. "Oo! Maybe we can room?"

"Maybe." The thought of not seeing Tasha or home or anyone I actually know for an *entire* year makes me sick.

She throws a salty look at her pocket and I know that noncompliant gadget is still under her skin. "What's wrong with your thing?"

"Oh my PRI Mod? It's nothing."

"Rule number one of friends—no lies. Just keep it real."

She turns beet red. "Wait, friends? I . . . we . . . really? O-okay." She pulls it out of her pocket. "I don't usually get to show anyone because, well, it's not magicked or anything. My parents think it's stupid. Just some dumb particle rearranger I made."

It's clunky and cold and I can clearly see the spot where one piece is refusing to slide into the other. I give it a push, just in case. No luck.

"What does it do?" I ask.

"It takes apart molecules and places them somewhere else."

"In English?"

"My bag with my books is so heavy."

"*Okay . . .*"

"I didn't want to walk all the way from the quad, the dorm, back home just to drop them off between classes. So I made this thing. It shrinks the particles into tiny molecules, transports them through the air, and makes them reappear in my room."

"Uh, Bri that's not at all dumb. That's the coolest shit I've ever heard."

"Wait until I'm Bound," she says.

Another faint scream plays under the music.

"I'm going to add some cloaking and locator spells to it so I can send and retrieve stuff any time I want." She wears a silly grin. "I've been studying magic and more complex spells since I was eight, years before I could even think about being Bound." She pats her stack of papers. "I'm ready."

Good, because the shit sounds painful. Am *I* ready?

"Yo, foreal foreal. You're smart. People back home get paid a lot of money to pop off some dope shit like this."

She narrows her eyes like she's deciphering a code.

Translation. "You're really smart, Bri. This is impressive. And bump anyone who says different."

She chews her lip, then smiles. "Y-yeah. B-bump?"

"Bump."

"Bump them!"

I smile. Can't even help it. I turn the gadget over and over in my hands. "You can make anything? Like, *anything* anything?"

"I'll put it like this: I've never *not* been able to make something I tried to make."

"How long does it take you to make stuff like this?"

"Depends. Why, what are you thinking?"

Tasha's face ripples in my memory. Her tears, the screaming when the CPS lady came and took her away. I rub the edges of Moms's photo in my pocket.

Travel. I wanna go home.

CHAPTER 5

THE EARTHY SCENT OF Ghizon hits me like a slap. Slate walls surround me, and a draft creeps through my cotton hoodie, chilling my bones. I land on the metal deck at the south end of New Ghizon's Central District, staggering as I try to catch my balance. My head's swimming. That transport spell makes light rail travel feel like snail speed.

Great, I'm "home."

Patrol pulls me upright by my throbbing wrists. Sickness sloshes in my gut and breathing takes more concentration. I wish I could just explain why I did what I did. Get them to understand. But that's foolish. My best bet is to get away from them first chance I get.

Creaky aluminum lights bob overhead, swaying in the humid island air. An array of metals clank, suspended in the air, snapping and shifting together piece by piece, assembling themselves. The warehouse? They're taking me through the warehouse? We push our way through the room, which feels like an auto hobby shop, buzzing with magic mechanics and maintenance crews. Patrol's heels *clack clack clack* on the floor and my heart echoes their beat.

The sounds of tinkering dissolve into a silence that would freeze a pot of boiling blood.

Bystanders pause. Work halts.

Despite my hazy vision, it's clear: All eyes are on me. I want to ask what the hell they're looking at, but I keep my head down, focusing on the woozy pulsing, which, thanks to Tasha's water, is a bit better. Shouldn't they be in class? Or somewhere besides here, gossiping, gawking? You'd think I'd be used to it by now. People tripped when I first showed up. A Ghizoni girl being Bound the same day as me even asked to *touch* my skin. Like, what?

"Where to, Keef?" A pair of Patrolmen fall in line behind me, one at each side.

"Straight to the Chancellor with this one." Three guards escort me. Three.

For saving someone's life.

Muted pounding beats in the distance. We push open the steel doors at the back of the warehouse and a dusky sky greets us. Outside, a cemented path twists and turns around the tall steel and glass buildings that make up the Central District of New Ghizon. It's weird that they call it *new* Ghizon, when there is no *old* Ghizon. Colorful tents and food and craft vendors line the walkway as far as I can see.

I scan for red square frames and unruly blond flyaways. No luck. She has to know my lack of a response means I got caught up . . . I hope. Where is she?

Crowds of people move through the street dancing, arms and legs covered in multicolored stripes, while the *ting* of plucked strings ring in the air. Celebrating. Happy. Oblivious to the fact that my sister almost died today.

Buildings as tall as skyscrapers loom on either side of the crowd.

Their lacquered walls dotted with rows of windows stare like hundreds of peering eyes. The farthest building in New Ghizon's Central District is my dorm-style hall. Oversized screens hang outside the residence dorms, the Infirm Ward, almost every tall building in the District, playing the usual images of the Chancellor, smiling and waving, on repeat.

Always on repeat.

To the west, Yiyo Peak, jagged and dotted with specks of glass, kisses the fading sun. Even its radiance annoys me. Thousands of homes shine like squares of polished glass dug into its jagged surface. Twinkling lights grow brighter, like a night sky plastered onto a mountainside. The brilliance should mesmerize, but each flicker is as comforting as candles on a grave.

Banners slung from one end to the other without strings read ABDU YOI'FURI—DAY OF THE FOUNDERS. That's right. That *is* today. Of course, of all days I could be arrested, I'm snatched up just as half of Ghizon takes to the streets to herald its founder. Their glasses clink, overflowing with fizzing drinks. "J'syon hi!" Good health.

Today brings Ghizonis so much joy.

Today brings me so much pain.

According to Ghizoni history books, seventy or so years ago the Chancellor unearthed a glassy black stone in the isle's fertile mountain, Yiyo Peak. He mined it for its "molecular properties" that make it "the perfect binder for magic," whatever that means, and used the promise of magic to unite the isolated tribes living here. According to the two days of Ancient History class I actually attended, the clans jumped at the chance, sealing the Chancellor's diehard loyalty from these people. They worship him for it.

He was an asshole the first time he spoke to me, so magic or not, I can't stand him.

Random bouts of wooziness assault me. The effect of the chaser isn't hitting me as strongly, or I'm getting used to it . . . I hope that's not a bad thing. Patrol tugs again and reluctantly, I follow. Wherever they think they're taking me . . . I have no intention of going. Running from Laws ain't nothing new. I just need to get a moment of distraction—a second so I can get away. Where is Bri?

She would be here, right? If she knows I'm in trouble, she'd come. I reach for my watch but the handcuffs are blocking it.

Bu-Bu-Bum. Bum. Bum.

Each pound of the drum sloshes my insides. The farther we go, the louder the music pounds. Each beat of celebration wedges the dagger deeper. I want to snatch those damn sticks out of the drummer's hand and beat him with them.

I catch his eye and the drumming stutters, then fades. With the sudden absence of music, heads turn my way in waves, a few at first, then more. The celebration comes to a near silent halt as I'm led through the crowd, hands bound. Like the entire city was waiting, eager for a glimpse of the brown girl who broke the rules. The crowd, a sea of faces with colorful hairstyles contorted in twisted shapes, whispers and points at me. Several have magicked faces and enhanced animal features. With magic at your disposal, I guess you get bored after a while and start experimenting.

My feet are rigid as Patrol practically drags me. My mouth is chalky. Water. I still need more water. Patrolman tugs for me to walk faster and needling pain pricks my wrists.

Moms raised a diamond. I straighten up and keep moving.

The festival hums around us, the music pounding once again. The path ahead snakes between a short building with slate walls, the Amphitheater, where I was sorted—or not sorted, actually—and behind it, the Binding Ward, where they gave me my magic. I rub a thumb over my wrist, remembering. All this magic and power could do so *much* good back home, but they want to hole up here. It's just so messed up.

Justice Compound, the place where they take lawbreakers, looms ahead. They're not putting me in some cell. Nope. Not happening. "Where is—" I say under my breath when a familiar face jets through the crowd, glasses perched on her pointy nose.

There she is.

Bri keeps pace with the guards, but she's far back, so far it's hard to see. She's gonna flip when she hears her techy contraption on my wrist didn't fail, and that aside from delivering the gift I was able to *save my sister's life*. We knew a transport spell would tip the authorities. So being the smarty-pants she is, she hacked the mainframe and found some code for human geolocation that was already in there. It took a long minute, months actually, but she wrote it into a wristwatch. So I could be there for Tash. That's what real friends do.

Ride or die.

Before I can tell her anything, first I need out of this sitch.

As if Bri read my mind, she flips a silvery something high in the air and it dissolves, like it was never there. Seconds later, cold metal presses against my palm. P-R-I-modifier or whatever she calls it for the win! Knew she'd come through.

I fall back so the guards are walking in front of me and wiggle the key-shaped metal into my restraints. It's awkward, but after a few tries the key slips into a hole and clicks.

I keep my hands still. I have *one* shot to get away from under these idiots. I look for Bri in the crowd to give her a sign it worked. A smirk or something. But a myriad of disinterested faces is all I see. She's gone. My wrist vibrates, but I can't look. Not yet.

I need a distrac—

"Ling ling ling, ya'ling ling." N'we dancers shimmy our way. The ringleader wears sapphire chiffon low on her waist and golden bells *ting* with each step. Coins fly at them from the crowd and Patrol's practically salivating as the dancers rotate their hips, jiggling all the jiggly places.

My chance.

I drop the cuffs and jet, running like my life depends on it. And I mean, it might. My only hope is that I can get off these streets and hide away at Bri's. Her parents are practically model citizens. Hiding away there, Patrol would never expect to find me. How long that'll last, I can't say. Long enough for me to figure out a way to get back to Tasha, hopefully.

I breeze by a little too close to a merchant futzing with a tent and the whole thing collapses.

"Shoot, sorry!" I don't look back, hoping they heard me. I disrupt a line of feather trainers—animal masters who can compel birds to obey—around a huddle of people with fists full of coins, my kicks eating the cobblestone. Everything's a bit hazy, but I push through it.

"V'ja! V'ja!" Patrol shouts for me and I pound the dirt harder. Wedged between the slick buildings is a crumbling stone shanty that looks older than everything around it. It's set back on the lot, with cracked walls and a roof half caved in. I slip into the narrow alley between it and the building next to it and crouch down low. Patrol's voices grow louder, and I lean back, fully in shadow.

"Which way? Did you see the girl? The human girl?"

"I—I, no," says a man sauntering by with a cane. "I didn't see anyone."

"Ja! Ja!" An elderly woman with a head wrap around her head like a crown butts in. "Y'pwe onja. Onja meese."

My Ghizonian isn't that great, but I'm pretty sure that lady just dimed me out. She points in my direction. *Shit.* I duck down lower. Patrol hands the woman a coin and she disappears toward the festival.

I press back into the shade as far as I can, stone scraping my cheek. Seconds pass like days, but Patrol stomps past without a glance my way.

I exhale and check my watch. Bri's message from a bit ago is still blinking on the screen.

Bri: I knew the key would work! Eeeee!

Me: Like a charm.

The music from the festival a block over plays in the background. Bri's house is through Market Street, which is off the main square. I should be able to get over there unnoticed if I—

Curious little eyes staring at me from the far end of the alleyway snatch my attention. I can barely make out the features on his tiny face, but his sooty, tattered clothes are a giveaway. His face is thin and where his cheeks should be plump and smooth, they sink in.

Macazi.

The magicless.

They live in sanctioned housing if they're lucky, but with no magic—no way to contribute to Ghizon—they're treated like litter society hopes will just blow away.

"Hi," I say, but he turns to run away.

"No, I'm not gonna hurt—Listen, I have something for you. Can you wait right here? I'll go get it." His expression doesn't change. I *really* don't have time for this. Patrol could come back any moment.

"It's a gift. Uh—pris!"

His face lights up at that word and I promise to be right back. I skip over a few blocks and keep my head down. Last thing I need is for the Patrol I *just* lost to catch sight of me. But what am I supposed to do? Let him starve in an alleyway?

I jet across an intersection that veers off to the eastern side of the island where tightly knitted rows of units sit, their roof tiles staggered like steps. The east side's where Bri and most Zrukis live. As the perimeter of the festival comes back in view, scents of qui, something like a turnip with the flavor of garlic, wafts past and my stomach churns. Meatmen hover slabs of dripping carcasses overhead, searing them with flames from their fingertips. The really talented ones can sear it with breaths of fire.

I stick to the shadows close to the buildings and wait. A boy no older than Tasha grins at the crowd, offering skewered samples. The clink of coins changing hands slices through the melodious backdrop.

Meatman sets down his slab to talk to a customer and the little boy is absorbed in serving an eager group of samplers. I slip my hand around the metal skewer and snatch the entire slab of meat, woodsy spices dancing under my nose as I hurry back to the alley with hot juices dripping down my arm. "V'ja, maca," someone shouts. I don't look back.

Little Guy is still there and his mouth falls open at the sight of the savory meal.

"Take it to your mom. Quick, hurry."

His brows meet.

I fold his little arms around the skewer, grease running down his arm. "Take *this*"—I point—"to your *mom*." I cradle my arms, then give him a gentle shove. "Hurry. Fast."

He just stands there staring. Why didn't I pay more attention in Language class? I sigh. How do I say, "go" or "mom?" I don't have a clue. "Listen, kid. You gotta get the hell—I mean, you gotta get moving." I rip off a piece of meat and hold it to my lips. He watches me chew and something clicks; he understands. He runs off hugging the slab of meat, which is as big as he is.

If that were Tasha, I'd want someone to make sure her belly was full. It's only one meal, but it's something. Angry voices grow louder. Meatman's coming around that corner any second. I take off in the opposite direction, toward Bri's, when my wrist shakes.

Bri: You close?

Me: Sorry, detour. Yeah, Why?

Bri: It's your father. He's on his way here.

I *hate* the man who calls himself—my father.

For bringing me here. For leaving Tasha there. For coming to the block to "change my life," but not coming back to save Moms. For being a stranger my *entire* life. I *hate* that I wear his nose and our shoulders hang the same way.

So grateful Tasha didn't grow up with that BS. Her pops was around, offering to take us places, apologizing for my pops being MIA. Said he knew him for a bit before he got snatched up by the cops. That's what folks assume happens when you ain't been seen around the way—either locked up for ten or carried by six.

But that wasn't true in my father's case. He wasn't behind bars or in the ground. He *chose* to leave before I was even out the womb. Moms would make excuses, but I stopped caring around Tasha's age. By then, I figured if that nigga ain't want nothing to do with me, I didn't want nothing to do with his coward ass either.

"Rue?" Bri asks, holding her front door wide open. "You listening? Where'd you go?"

"Me first. Why's Aasim coming here? Like, how'd he know I would be here?" And what's he even gonna do?

Bri gestures for me to come inside. I've only been to Bri's once before. She doesn't like being here, so I don't get an invite often. The whole house is just like everyone else's: a concrete box with two small square windows. Near the front door are two other doors, one for the bedroom they all sleep in, and the other for the bathroom. I sit on wide, pillowed cushions on the floor next to a table covered in metal pieces and wires. Bri's stuff, no doubt.

In the corner, Bri's mom is folded over a pile of colorful strings that look like yarn but not nearly as fuzzy. Her fingers move a mile a minute like she's conducting a yarn orchestra and a beautiful tapestry of colors interlace and knot, weaving itself across her lap. She doesn't say a word to me, but cuts me a look and mutters something to Bri in Ghizonian.

"Ya, Memi." Bri rolls her eyes but doesn't explain.

"So, Aasim . . ." I tap my foot. "I'm listening. How'd he know I'd be here?"

She shrugs. "He just sent a message that said he'd be here. He assumed you were with me, which isn't that far-fetched."

He's literally the *last* person I want to see. "Ugh."

Bri's mother glances at me, shifting in her seat. I don't think she likes the sound of Third in Command coming to her house, and she probably isn't all that happy about harboring a fugitive, either.

"Na'yoo zechka." She stares a moment then gets back to her work, looping a purple strand around a line of rainbow-colored ones.

"How did you even get her to agree to let me be here?"

"I sort of told her Aasim *asked* that I bring you here."

I've never heard her mother speak anything but Ghizonian. Bri says she knows English but doesn't approve of using a western language just because it's widely popular. The western world is near idolized here. Without contact, it's like forbidden fruit, making it all the more alluring. Fashion magazines are about all the insight anyone has, and even those are contraband. No idea how they get them, but never fails that at a party, someone's passing around a very worn, out-of-date copy of *Teen Vogue* or something.

"She's just really old-fashioned," Bri had explained. "She doesn't think we need English since we have no contact with any other countries. It feels like treachery a bit to use anything but the native tongue."

I didn't say anything else about it, but that didn't sound like the whole story.

"What took so long to get here?" Bri asks.

"Just got caught up with some Macazi."

She laughs. I don't.

"Oh man, you're serious?"

"Quintomae," her mother mutters under her breath.

"What she say?"

Bri rolls her eyes. "Quintomae. It's nothing." She looks from her mom to my blank stare and back to her mom. "You've *never* heard The Myth of Quintomae? Like, really?"

"Nope," I say. "Didn't grow up here, remember?"

Her mother mutters something under her breath again, this time too faint to hear. Maybe hiding here wasn't the best idea.

Bri pulls a pillow into her lap. "So, legends tell of a man who was half man, half lizard. He thought he was invincible because of his impenetrable scaled skin. So when J'hymus, the Sea Monster, appeared off the northern coast and the king himself couldn't fend off the beast from terrorizing his people, Quintomae saw a chance to make a name for himself. He—"

"He pleaded with the king to let him fight the beast," a baritone voice cuts in. Bri's father is home from the mines. "And the king said no. But he ignored the king's edict and marched into the sea with only a bewitched javelin to take on the sea creature. Quintomae was never seen again." Bri's father loosens the ties on his shoes. "Ya'weshna e verzee. Disobedience is death."

"Lo viz. Ajebria v'ja, Quol Aasim . . . e *maca*," her mother says, helping him peel off the soiled clothes stuck to his arms. Whatever she said, he doesn't like, because he gives Bri a look of disapproval. White bandages dotted with red spots wrap around three of his fingers. And what looks like burn marks mar his forearms. The clothes tug at his skin, but he doesn't wince.

"Did the monster keep terrorizing the people?" I ask, and he studies me a moment.

"No," he says, untying the robes cinched at his neck.

Sounds more like victory in sacrifice. He wanted to kill the monster and make a name for himself. . . . I mean, we still talking about him, ain't we? I'd say he succeeded on both fronts. But I keep my mouth shut.

"Quinto." Bri winks. "Your new nickname." She laughs. "Daring." She makes a dramatic gesture with her hands. "Fearless Rue."

I laugh at her teasing, but squirm when I find Bri's father's gaze fixed on me. Her mother takes his outer robes, leaving him in a soot-covered shirt and stained pants. She moves around the kitchen and in minutes there are drinks in our hands.

Water. I gulp it down and the wooziness I'd been feeling since the car wreck is finally almost unnoticeable.

"Thanks," I say, but instead of, "You're welcome," she whispers to her husband.

"Let's go in the room," Bri pulls me by the arm.

"Bri." Her father gestures at the table, his tone laced with irritation. "Kwi lithia a'si swera." He brandishes his hands and Bri's mom looks like she's sweating bricks. "*Swera. Swera.*"

Swera? Trash?

"Sorry, Dad." Bri grabs an armful of metal contraptions from the center table and takes them with us into the bedroom.

"I wish she spent more time refining her magic than making those useless—" The door creaks closed, drowning out her father's words.

"Hey." I set my hand on hers. "Your contraptions are *not* trash. You're brilliant, Bri."

She covers my hand with hers. "It's fine. And I'm sorry about them."

"Hey, I didn't understand half of what she was saying, so I'm good. Are *you* good?"

"I'm fine. That stuff doesn't make any money, so it's useless as far as they're concerned. I get it. And Dad's always extra stressed when he gets home from the mines anyway. It takes a lot out of him, and seeing my junk everywhere doesn't help. I should have known better." She dumps her gadgets in a pile in the corner.

I want to tell her to tell her dad where to stick it, but that's not Bri. She walks the line. Her bits of defiance, like making my watch, are always undercover. I want to tell her to be as bold as her inventions around her parents and in the world—to be who she is, who *I* see in her. But that's easier said than done. I shove all the very imperfect things I want to say back down in case they come out wrong or aren't sensitive enough, and I just throw an arm around her instead.

"My mom hasn't been back to the mines since she hurt her foot. But she earned a good bit of coin with her last tapestry, so that'll cheer him," she says perking up. "But enough about me. Tell me all about Tasha! What happened?"

"Oh man, where do I start?"

A pound at the door startles us as it flies open.

"In here, Bri. Come." Her dad's face has changed, his features softer, more . . . submissive.

Bri's brothers apparently got home from lessons at the same time that Aasim arrived. *Great. Just effing great.* Bri's father pulls his family in tight beside him, dusting off his boys' hair and making them stand up straight.

"Ruler Aasim," Bri's father says, "I just want to assure you we had *nothing* to do with any trouble that may have been—"

"It's fine." Aasim waves a hand. "I'm not here to get anyone in trouble. I just came to get Rue. I figured she'd be with Bri. When are these two not together?" He says it like he knows me, knows my friends. Bri's father's shoulders relax.

"Rue?" Aasim adjusts the lapel of his charcoal tailored suit, his peppered pencil-thin dreads tucked neatly behind his back.

I look away from him for a couple of beats. Intentionally. "Aasim."

"I have to take you in. Chancellor's waiting. It'll be easier that way. Trust me."

Trust him? I cut Bri a look and she mouths, "I'm sorry." I saved my sister's life today. Nobody needs to apologize for that. I smile back and wink to try to assure her everything's going to be okay, even though I have no idea how. I have to make them see I had no choice.

Aasim thanks Bri's family and turns toward the door.

"I did what I had to do," I say, pushing past him. "And I'd do it again."

CHAPTER 6

THE JOURNEY BACK TO the Central District takes forever. Thankfully, Aasim doesn't try talking to me. I can tell he wants to. He keeps opening his mouth, then shutting it. Hoping the trend continues.

I don't know what the Chancellor's going to make of what I did. But I'll make him understand. And if he doesn't, I'll bear the consequence. I saved Tasha's life.

Patrol meets us at the building entrance. Stone pillars tower on either side of the guards, making them somehow seem taller.

"Ruler Aasim, you've found her. I can take her from here, sir."

"I'm handling it," Aasim says, pushing past him and gesturing for me to follow.

"But sir, I have strict orders to—"

"And I've changed them." Aasim's nostrils flare, the same way I imagine mine do. "Dismissed."

The Patrolman walks off muttering something under his breath. Inside the lobby, guards line the corridor. Ten? Twelve? I can't keep count.

"I'll get her booked." Aasim waves off the two uniforms at my back. Booked? Like a criminal? It was just one "offense."

He swirls one hand around the other and a frosted cup appears. "Drink more water. It'll help." He walks off and I follow. Annoyed, I take a sip and the dregs of my wooziness abate. Glass elevators float at the end of the hall, bobbing up and down.

"After you." He steps aside and I roll my eyes. The moment the doors shut us inside, he turns to me. "Tell me who you touched."

What about my face says *talk to me*? "I did what I had to do. Your people *have to* be able to understand that. They have loved ones too."

"I couldn't risk anyone overhearing me on the way here. But in here it's just us. Listen to me, Rue." He rests a palm on my shoulder. "Ghizon is not like your world. They don't value human life the same."

And you're one of them. That why Moms died back home and you ain't do shit? I pull away and put my earbuds in. I'm not trusting him to help me. I'll figure this out myself. My flattened cheeks are heavy as the glass box whisks upward through the levels. He pulls my music out of my ear. He's lost his mind, clearly.

"Don't touch my—"

"Rue, please, there isn't much time. If you tell me I can try to figure out a way to help them."

No matter how high I roll the volume, his tenor voice breaks through the melody flowing into my ears. This is *the* slowest elevator I've ever been in, I swear.

"Rue, you can't just come here and disregard the way things are done. That has consequences."

Disregard?! "I didn't *ask* to come here, remember? And since I've been here I haven't done anything but play by these people's dumb-ass rules." Moms would be on my ass if she heard me talking to an adult like this.

"But you're here now," he says. "Look at your wrists. Rue, you're Bound. That means you have to play by the rules or . . ." He sighs. "Just please let me help you." His words are like tiny needles pricking every part of my body. "This pains me too, very deeply."

This pains him? Really? I pull the lone earbud out of my ear. "You? You're hurt? I don't see you in cuffs. I don't see you forced to live away from everything and everyone you've ever known. I don't see your little sister crying herself to sleep at night because the only person in the world that understands her pain after Moms died disappeared with no explanation. No. That's me and Tasha."

Shit, I just told him her name.

A chime says we've reached floor 429. I step toward the elevator doors. *Come the hell on. Open.*

He sighs. "So that's who it is, your half sister?"

"My *sister.*"

"I—I should've . . . too late for that. They *will* find out, Rue. They won't stop until they hunt her down and—" He chews his lip deep in thought. The doors slide open and I can't get out of the glass box fast enough. Hunt her down? I—they can't touch her. It's not right. They wouldn't. She's no harm to anyone.

Overhead, the ceiling towers with a glittery night sky. I don't know how they do it, but the effect soothes. Across the fake starlit room is a single glass door. I start toward it, Aasim on my heels.

The handle chills my palm as I pull open the door.

"Wait." Aasim's eyes soften, but even deeper lines course his face. "I can try to explain to the Chancellor that you don't have a single blemish on your record and that you'll take ownership for what you've done and apologize for breaking the rules. But . . ."

The sound of "but" makes me queasy. I try to speak, but the only words that come to mind sound desperate, weak. I won't be weak in front of him.

"I-I promise I'll do *anything* in my power to help, Rue."

"I don't need your help. And I never will."

He cups my shoulder. "In the meantime, just—just *try* to adhere to the rules."

"When people we love are in danger and we have the means to stop it—we *do* something. Even if it's against the rules . . . Aasim."

He pinches the bridge of his nose. "Where's the girl?"

"Probably at her grandmother's." I let go of the door handle.

"Has her memory been wiped?"

That's a thing? I must have skipped that day. "N-no. I-I . . . there was no time for any of that. My magic got weird and . . ." *That guy with the tattoo disappearing from the car . . .*

"The first time you touch them they see everything. Your strongest memories—usually the most recent ones—become theirs. Like a stock of photos tucked away without sound or meaning. But even a human *seeing* could be enough to out that Ghizon exists. That's not a risk the Chancellor will be inclined to take."

What risk is Tasha? "She's a kid! And doesn't everyone around here say he's so generous and kind? He—"

"Rue, I *know* him. I've known him my *entire* life. He basically raised me, remember? He's calculating. Clever. And careful. Very careful. This is *not* a risk he's going to take."

"H-h-how much does he know?" I ask.

"For now, he doesn't know *who* you touched, but I assure you, he will find out."

I stumble for words. "He won't hurt her. I'll kill him."

"Well—"

The glass door thrusts open and a guard with a familiar face—a friendly familiar face—peeks through. I muffle a gasp and the knot between my shoulders eases. Some.

"Good day, ma'am," he says. Recognition flashes in his eyes, but his tone is stilted. "Follow me, your cell is ready." He turns to Aasim. "The Chancellor and his general are inside waiting for you, sir. They're ready to begin."

Luke, Bri's green-haired, green-eyed boyfriend, chances a wink as he escorts us inside.

CHAPTER 7

THE DETAINMENT ROOM IS a concrete box with a rectangular window on the far end. On the other side of the window is another room with three pairs of eyes fixed on me: the Chancellor, Aasim, and a man with a scar under his eye: the General, the Chancellor's dawg. He wears a tunic the color of ice, and his eyes are even colder.

"Over here, Rue," Luke calls. I back away from the window feeling sick. The way the Chancellor and his scar-faced errand boy are staring at me, I could be in deep shit.

A rancid smell like crayons stings my nose as I move to the center of the room, past a small cot and a single metal chair.

"If you'll sit."

"Nope, I'll stand." Something about standing makes me feel more . . . ready, more . . . in control.

"O-okay. Th-that's fine." Luke plucks a syringe from a metal tray. "This might hurt a little bit." He cranes his neck for a good angle. "Could you lift up your . . ."

I grab my nest of curls and hold it off my neck.

"Yep, perfect. Just like that."

My neck stings a moment before a tingling sensation takes over like ice water seeping into my veins.

"Another second. Almost done."

"What exactly is this?" I ask, grimacing. A question you ask *before* you let someone cut your skin open.

Luke resurfaces, a silver disc the size of a penny floating above his palm. "A tracker," he says discreetly. "The General told me to. But don't sweat it," he says, leaning in, a satisfied smile on his face. "Bri can deactivate it if you want. Just tell her it's the Z300 model. She'll know what I mean."

"Slow down, techie. Why do I need a tracker?" I whisper.

"They told me to do it," he says, leaning his head toward a tinted two-way window. "I'm just following orders."

"I see."

Next, he hands me a cup. "Drink up."

The liquid is bitter on my tongue and I gag.

"It's an antidote for the chaser. Water will only get you so far . . . and it'll wear off eventually."

I take another sip. It's like drinking perfume. I clamp my mouth shut so I don't spit it back out. The men behind the glass beside Aasim still stare, arms folded.

The Chancellor moves closer to the window like he's studying me, and I bristle at his stare. He's 'bout my height with a boxy frame and chiseled cheeks. His eyes have dark circles around them, and something about his RBF says he's always thinking . . . plotting . . . planning.

The General joins the Chancellor at his side. This one I don't know as well. Only seen him a few times. He's taller than the others, built like some sort of commando, but older. His hair is grayish white with a giant bald spot in the middle. His arms are like boulders—like he spends the whole day bench pressing. A deep scar in the shape of a dagger runs beneath his left eye. His stare is like acid on my skin.

As much as I loathe Aasim, he's probably the only one in there trying to do right by me.

"Am I able to talk to any of them?" I ask Luke.

Again, he gestures for me to sit, and this time I do. "I'm sorry. They said full booking. I'm going to have to take your things."

I sigh, nodding.

"And no, you don't get to talk to them. I mean, unless they want to. Shoes?"

I hand them over, nerves twisting my insides. "So how does this work? When do I get to explain myself?"

"Socks too. And I'm going to need that watch." He peeps over his shoulder and whispers. "I promised Bri I'd make sure you keep this. I'll get it back to you." Luke clears his throat, pretending to check my tracker. "She said they have no way of knowing you used it. You set off the signal using your magic among humans."

"So my watch is safe?" I ask, as low as I can, handing over my things.

"Completely. They have no idea it even exists."

That's some small relief, I suppose. That, and Luke on my side. Bri picked a real one. He and Bri have been together for *months*. Seems like a straight up nice guy. They geek out and shit. She likes him. So I like him. He breaks her heart though? I'll break his face. He knows it too.

"Looks like your tracker's in and working properly." He clears his throat again as if doing that repeatedly sounds natural. "If you have a shirt under the hoodie, I'll take the outer layer too. Any hair accessories, other jewelry?"

What is this? Why am I giving up all my stuff before I can even make my case, explain myself?

"That necklace."

"You're not getting my necklace. Period." I tuck the purple thread around my neck into my collar. "If they want it that badly, they can cut it off my corpse."

He gives a sympathetic smile and doesn't push it.

Behind the glass, the men's gestures grow increasingly animated. Aasim's talking—fast, from what I can tell. The Chancellor's rubbing his chin. The General I can't read as well. He's standing there, face plain, lips forming a thin, straight line. Low-cut gray hair fades to white around his temples. He doesn't move. Doesn't speak. The Chancellor turns to him a second, whispering something. And Aasim keeps talking, but no one appears to be listening.

"What do you know about the General?" I ask Luke.

His eyes meet mine and the color drains from his already gray complexion. "General Deo? He—"

The door clicks open and Luke hops to attention, back straight, eyes dead ahead.

"Sir," he says.

The General, so tall he nearly ducks beneath the doorframe, steps inside.

"Excuse me," I turn to him, trying to sift the pissiness from my voice. "What's going on in there? Am I able to speak to you or the Chancellor directly? Explain myself?"

His voice is gruff and the lines on his face don't move when he speaks. "Tracker in. Good work, recruit."

Ignored. Completely.

Luke motions for me to drink up the last of the perfume drink. I throw it back and the General's attention shifts my way.

He glares at me. "Who did she touch?"

Me? He's not even asking me directly?

"This recruit does not know, sir." Luke's hands are glued to his side, rigid as a board. "This recruit can ask, sir."

"Aye, yo." I wave, resisting the urge to roll my eyes *deep* in my head. "I have a mouth. I know how to speak. The hell?" The sass slips out my mouth before I can call it back. *Shit.*

Shock is written all over Luke's face. And some other emotion I can't quite read.... "You won't speak to the General that way again." His brows dent ever so slightly, like he feels guilty for his tone and detached posture in the General's presence. I forgive him. I get it. Bossman's watching. Last thing I want is him or anyone else to get in trouble.

"Well, please let the General know I am perfectly fine speaking for my—"

"Who did you touch?" he asks, his gaze a cold dead hand wrapped around my throat.

I search for words but only sputters come out. "I ... I ... ahem. I don't know what you're talking about."

His lips straighten again. Behind the glass, Aasim's talking with his hands, veins popping out his temple. He's pissed. So that's where I get my temper from. The Chancellor's listening, it appears, still drawing circles on his chin.

"Get her ready for Unbinding," says the General. "Chancellor's orders."

Okay. Okay. Losing my magic. I can handle that. And then what? Luke meets my eyes and I practically will him to know what I'm thinking.

"This recruit will do as you've said, sir. And after?"

The General's stare leaves mine and I can finally breathe again.

"She's to be banished, so you'll need to prep for a memory sweep as well."

Banished, as in I can go home? I won't have magic, but that's okay. And Bri, I'll miss her. But I'll still have my watch. I cup my wrist. My watch. Luke has it.

General Deo turns and my pulse begins to settle. The door clicks open and I catch a glimpse of Aasim still arguing and now pacing. Back and forth. Back and forth. What's he trippin' about? He's got to know I'm fine peacing outta this place. The General's clacking steps halt. He turns.

"And recruit?"

"Sir?"

"Use this vial of truth serum if you must." A stoppered vial appears in his hands. "I want to know who she touched."

Luke takes the vial with a nod.

Wait, what? "I'm not taking anything." My hands shake, but I force the words out. "I didn't do anything wrong."

"According to whom?" His words slice like daggers. "You will do as you're told willingly, or you'll be *forced* to do as you're told." His lips crack a smile that doesn't reach his eyes. "Chancellor's orders. Recruit, get me that name."

Words claw their way up my throat, coming out weak and desperate. "Why? For what?"

He stares a moment, unmoved. Then steps closer, my forehead warming under his breath. "Don't you know? They're to be killed."

For several moments the world spins. This is not possible. He won't. He can't. He hovers there, glassy eyes transfixed on mine.

"Chancellor's orders." He paints on a smile, one that touches his eyes this time, before turning on his heels. The door clicks shut behind him.

I pound my fists on the door. My knuckles cry in pain, but I pound harder. I won't cry. I won't. They won't see me that way. *Moms raised a diamond.*

"Rue." Luke's bottom lip trembles as he sets the truth serum down. I stare at the vial. It's clear as water with bubbly fizzes at the bottom. I'm not taking that. They won't make me. He drags a chair across the room and I seize the moment, slipping the vial in my pocket while his back is turned. The three behind the window are still talking. No one sees.

"I-I'm so sorry," he gestures at the chair. "I don't know what to say. Whoever you touched, I-I'm so sorry. Can you sit? The serum can make the lower limbs unstable; works better secured in a seat."

"No!" I'm hollow and my chest is heavy. Everything's so heavy. I gape at the door. This is some cruel dream. He didn't mean that. He's coming back. This isn't real.

He lowers his voice to a whisper. "I promised Bri I'd do what I can to help." Luke shuffles through his pocket, his back to the window. "Can you pretend to go along with it?" Clearly, Luke's scared of the General. "T-tell me what I can do. A-anything? I'm so sorry."

I should answer, but I have no words. There's nothing he can do. I'm not letting him get caught up trying to help me. Who knows what they'd do to him or Bri? This is my burden to carry and I'll carry it alone.

"I'm going to figure this out." I sit in the chair.

"H-how?" He pats his pockets and looks around for the missing vial, genuinely confused. Back behind the glass, Aasim is silent. Does that mean he won? Or gave up? The General leans in to the Chancellor's gaze locked on mine.

The first time I met the Chancellor, he told me I shouldn't exist.

"We don't lie with humans," he had said. "It's beneath us." I remember how he stood there, arms folded with hostile judgment in his eyes. He wore a jade-colored coat, and stubble dotted his chin. He smelled of earthy spices that burned my nose. I should have clawed his eyes out that very moment and cut out his tongue. If I had, maybe he wouldn't be contorting his twisted mouth right now to condemn my sister to death.

A twelve-year-old who's nothing to him and everything to me.

"Humans are underdeveloped as a species," he had said two seconds after our first hello. "They tote around unchecked emotion without any sort of self-control. We are *gods*. Though your father breeding you was a grave crime, I'm a reasonable man." His words sear my memory like a fresh-inked tat. "Show your loyalty is *here*," he'd said. "That you're more *us* than *them*." Then he turned to Aasim and said the four words that changed everything. "She may be Bound."

Aasim was pleased. Said it was a real mark of trust. "It's the only way I can keep you safe," he'd said.

The Chancellor moves closer to the window, not even a nose length from the glass. His stare pierces like needles, eyes as still as death. There's no sympathy in them. No warmth. No understanding. Only judgment.

Something inside me snaps. I'm up and nose to the window too. My wrists are scorching hot and I let my anger burn like fuel. Everyone around here plays fiddle to his pompous ass. If the streets taught me anything, it's to see through the Laws bullshit.

Moms raised a diamond. He won't break me.

I slap the window; it vibrates and he slow shakes his head in disdain.

"You don't scare me!" Anger swirls in my head, throbbing. Magic surges through me like lightening and the glass between us shatters in a shower of chimes. The Chancellor flinches, his stone exterior cracking for a second. The glint in his eye . . . is that anger? Fear?

Face to face with the man condemning my sister to die, I don't feel regret or sadness. Only rage.

"You shouldn't have brought her here." He looks at Aasim. "She's far more like them than us."

CHAPTER 8

B EING BOUND TO MAGIC was by far *the* most painful experience I've *ever* endured. And I've had a hot comb too close to my scalp. I don't know if Unbinding hurts as much as Binding. And I have no intention of finding out.

Lights creak overhead as I stand near the door in the concrete box, waiting to be taken to Unbinding. Warm fingers shove cold metal into my grasp. *My watch.* I curl my hands around it and stick it out of sight. Luke nods without a word and I hope he knows how thankful I am. His shift is done and the new guards taking over are complete strangers. He tugs the restraints on my wrist gently.

"She's all ready to go, sir." He snaps to attention.

"Get her to the Infirm Ward afterward. She'll be out of sorts." The General's voice is firm and his men obey without question. The guards drag me along more roughly than needed, but I stay compliant. I'm the unpredictable human, the emotional creature they don't understand.

And I'm wounded. This makes them fear me.

We head back down the glass elevator and into a breezeway that bridges over a courtyard to the Binding building. Inside, the halls are just as I remember, blinding white. Hollow footsteps echo around me and orbs float overhead, lighting the corridor. People in lab coats walk to and fro, scribbling on clipboards.

I keep my head down on my hands bound in front of me, magic subdued by the restraints. He's going to have to take them off to access the onyx on my wrists for Unbinding. Even if for only a second. That's my chance.

Maybe my only chance.

We stop at a carved opening at the end of the hall with a sign over it that reads RECEIVING WINDOW. A woman with curly teal hair sits, typing. She points to a circular gadget sitting on the ledge without a word or a glance at me.

"Your thumb." The Patrol at my right nudges my elbow and I press my thumb to the scanner.

"And one more print here," she says, moving her hands back quickly, I guess to avoid touching my skin. Humans disgust many of them. Especially the older ones, I've noticed.

I press the other thumb on the scanner as the Chancellor's words sizzle in my memory. He sees my humanity as weakness, a threat to his superior way of life. He's arrogant, self-important, a coward. But Moms taught me to grind, to find a way when there is none.

I haven't forgotten who I am. Who Moms raised me to be.

"That'll do it," she says in some fake chipper tone, and we scoot farther down the hall. We turn two corners and enter a familiar room. It's windowless and tiny, like a patient room at the doctor. It's white, pristine, and cabinets line the back, just as sterile as it was eleven months ago. The door clamps shut and my heart rattles in my chest.

This is it.

When they remove the cuffs, that's my chance.

A tech with a dusty blond hair enters the room and the door clanks behind him, locked. He sets down his clipboard.

"Officers." He nods at both of them. "This won't take long, Rue." He says my name like he knows me. He don't know anything about me. I loosen my hoodie around my neck.

Tech Dude hovers over a tray of assorted syringes, a tiny bowl, and instruments that look way too sharp to touch living flesh. "If you'll assist me, sirs. Help hold her still."

The taller Patrolman joins the tech over the instruments, their backs turned.

"We'll knock her out for the most of it," he says to Patrol, holding a syringe. The rest of his words are a dull buzzing in my ear as his buddy reaches for the cuffs on my wrists.

Seconds. You will have seconds.

He slides the key into the restraints. "Now, hold still. Don't make this more painful than it needs to be."

Any second.

There's a *clink* and my hands are free.

Onyx tingles against my wrists and my insides swell with heat. I can feel my magic gathering, pooling, growing, the deeper I dig. My fingertips prickle.

Now.

I knock Patrol's hand away and whip open my palms, wisps of energy thrashing there. He reaches for me, but I dart sideways, scorching his fingers with my magic. He groans in pain and falls back. The tech yelps, backing away as the other guard hustles toward me.

Focus.

The flames flickering in Tasha's wide eyes, her tears when I said goodbye, the General's smug grin, the Chancellor's condescending stare—all of those moments play on repeat in my head. Heat torches my veins as I *pull* all that anger to the balls fused to my wrist.

The sphere of lightning in my hands rips and crackles, doubling in size. I slam the magic together and thrust at the door. The walls shudder and the door pops off its hinges, clanging on the floor. I dodge sideways, missing Patrolman's garb by inches, and stumble into the hallway.

Four guards are at my back as I book it down the corridor, latching my watch back on my wrist. They're fast but my feet fly with passion. The watch uses a synthesized signal from something, Bri'd said. However she designed it, it only works outside.

I need to get out of this building and fast.

Streaks of light shoot past me as they throw one curse after another. I run harder, bobbing and weaving before swinging around the corner. A pair of techs huddled over a cart of elixir vials shout as I pass. I ignore them and push through a set of glass doors. The halls all look the same. Which way do I go?

A steady beat of footsteps squeak against the polished floor behind me.

"Hey!" Shouts stab my ears as I dash through the next set of doors, down a hall chock full of people milling about. The courtyard's on the north end of the building, so surely that's the way out of here. I charge through, barreling toward the north stairs.

In the stairwell, there are no echoes of footsteps behind me, only nosy folks and confused stares. I slip through the double steel doors, booking it down a few flights of stairs. When I spill out of the stair-well I glance over my shoulder, but they're gone. I listen.

Silence.

I really lost them! For now.

I turn back. What are the words? How does it go? Uhh . . . yo, something . . . ah! "Yo'lum k'dex nae." My wrists warm and sparks shoot from my palms. The stairs groan, swelling and twisting to twice their size. The metal creaks to a stop and what were just stairs are now a pile of crumpled metal wedged between concrete walls. Let's see them get past that.

Up ahead, the lengthy corridor opens up. I run until a familiar voice jerks me to a halt.

"Rue?" A deep line is nestled between Bri's brows, her blond braid dangling. "I was so worried. So I decided to come down here and wait. Are you—"

Apparently my face says more than my words can. She grips my shoulders and pulls me into a hug, squeezing tight. Bri is one of the nicest people I've ever met. She'd never last a day where I'm from, but she has a heart of gold.

"Where will you go?"

"The Chancellor plans to *kill* whoever I touched." I don't say my sister's name because even muttering those words makes my hair stand tall. Bri knows. She knows all of it. She gasps, barring her mouth shut.

"I can't let him hurt her."

"Your watch."

"I have it. Luke."

She pulls me to her, crashing against my chest. Tears slip between her lashes. This isn't how I imagined saying goodbye either. For just a moment, I rest my chin on her shoulder—the shoulder of the only friend I've made in this lonely place. I want to say so many things. *See ya later* doesn't do it justice.

Other kids were straight up rude when I showed up, talking down to me when they'd explain spells, assuming I'm stupid and shit. Because just like back home, people think different means less. Less capable. Less competent.

"That girl gon' over-enunciate one more damn time, and I'ma pop her ass in the mouth," I had said under my breath during a spell-casting class.

Bri had laughed. "I'll put a sticky spell on her feet so you can get away." That's when I knew we'd be inseparable.

"She's not a native?" one bouje girl had asked the teacher, *literally* in front of my face! "How do we know she's not lying about who she is, where she's from?"

Because here, like back home, different also means untrustworthy.

Some days it was easier to shrug off, other days I wanted to claw my eyeballs out. When it gets like that, though, Bri's always there to distract me from wallowing, pull me into studying, or just make me laugh.

And that makes her as good as family.

I want to tell her all she means to me, but the words are jumbled when I try to speak. I squeeze her back and break the hug, hoping she can feel all my love, all my thanks for making this place semi-tolerable.

"Get outside," she sniffles. "The coordinates are still in there. Don't waste a second."

I tap my wrist and the screen glows blue.

Her voice cracks. "When you're ready, press and hold the button down for—"

"Three seconds, I remember," I say. "This isn't goodbye forever. I promise."

She nods, tears streaked across her lips. "Be careful, Rue."

After one last firm hand squeeze, I jet off, scanning for a red EXIT sign and keep running down the hall. North, just head north. I know the doors to this building face north. I round another corner and *finally* spot them.

Cool air whips around me when I burst through and my stomach plummets at the 400-something-foot drop below. I lift my sleeves, finger hovering over my watch, when a door clicks behind me. Aasim stands in the doorway, wind wrestling his garb.

For a second I want to go to him. *Stupid.* What am I thinking? The feeling confuses me. Angers me. He says nothing, just stares.

He's letting me go.

"Not going to say goodbye?" he asks, breaking the silence.

I study my feet, guilt wedging a hole in my resolve. I don't owe him a goodbye. I don't owe him or anyone a damned thing. Armed guards burst through the door at his back, weapons raised. Aasim raises a hand and they halt.

"But, sir, the Chancellor said—"

"I don't care what the Chancellor said, stand down!" His words crack like a whip and the guards retreat inside. That was nice of him. More than nice. Fatherly.

What do I say . . . thanks? I really don't have time for this. Words flood my mind, but I press my lips tight. My attention for these few seconds is all I have right now; the best I can give.

"Rue, this won't work. The Chancellor is too powerful. Too—"

"I'd prefer to die trying than not try at all."

With guards several paces away, he whispers. "There's so much I want to tell you. So much you don't know. I-I might even have a way to help." He looks over his shoulder. "What happens if you go out there and lose? What happens to her if you get in trouble or hurt?"

I can't think like that. *Moms raised a diamond.* My sister needs me. My watch face warms to my thumb.

"Rue, please. Stay, let me help you."

Three . . .

"When you were born I promised your mother I'd keep you both safe."

Two . . .

I meet his eyes. "You shouldn't make promises you can't keep."

One . . .

I turn, and in a blip, I'm gone.

CHAPTER 9

T
ASHA LOVES THE CARAMEL java at Joe's Joe, a coffee shop
and bookstore that's about a twenty-minute bus ride from
where she lives. I hate that it's so far, but it is what it is: You
gotta leave the hood to find a library or bookstore.

Metal industrial-style tables fill the space in neat rows. Matching
chairs cluster around them like people have been in and out all day.
A velvet plum sofa sits on the far end of the shop against an exposed
brick wall, near the ordering counter. Just past that is a doorway
that leads to the book area. A barista with full lips and a long, dark
ponytail taps her phone, smacking on a piece of gum. Customer
line's empty, but the tables are practically full.

No Ghizonis on my tail.

Yet.

I had $3.84 in my pocket when I left this place a year ago. Dollars
are no use in Ghizon, so I dig it out to grab T her favorite drink
from her favorite spot while I tell her the *second* worst news she'll
ever hear: People from Ghizon—people she doesn't even know—
want her dead.

I shift in my seat and I check my watch.

3:17 p.m.

She should be here any second. My phone still works on Wi-Fi and thankfully had a bit of juice left even though it hasn't been turned on in a minute. I told Tash to come here straight after school. She was so happy to hear from me so soon that she didn't even ask any questions.

I don't have a plan besides running. I didn't learn any spells back in Ghizon that could help us stay hidden. And then there's the problem of her grandma 'nem finding out. We can't have them thinking she disappeared. I don't want them to worry. I just wanna keep us safe.

Chatter buzzes above me like a cloud. Every close of the register or chair sliding across the floor makes my heart jump in my chest.

3:18 p.m.

I drum my fingers on the table. Somehow I'll find a way out of this. It's not even a choice, really. If we have to, we'll run. No one is touching her. She has her dad's people and grandma, but they can't protect her from the Chancellor. At least I have magic. They have . . . the police? That's a joke.

I thumb the glassy ball fused to my wrist. As awful as Ghizon was, I did get magic out of it, which will come in handy. But shoot, if I use it, they can trace it. *Hmm.* Maybe Bri can help. She has a tech solution to everything.

3:19 p.m.

News headlines roll across a TV screen mounted to the wall overhead. Images of yellow police tape and red and blue lights flash next to some news lady talking. Green letters in the corner spell MUTE. I don't need sound to know someone's been shot up.

A bell chimes and the door swishes open. Tasha steps inside, peering in every direction. Somehow, laying my eyes on her again makes me feel a little better. I hate that we couldn't talk after everything went down. I couldn't explain more about Ghizon. I'm not even sure what she's thinking.

I pull down my hood and blow the steaming mug as she walks over. Dark circles hug her eyes, which turn down at the corners. She weaves between tables and I take another glance around.

"T." I greet her with a tight squeeze. She smells like honey and jasmine. Like everything that is sweet in the world.

"You came back," she says.

"Of course, and I won't be leaving you ever again." I reach to squeeze her hand. But she pulls away.

"Your favorite." I slide the mug across the table a little too eagerly, leaving a trail of spills behind it. "With extra caramel and whipped cream, just like you like it."

"You doing okay?" I ask, ready for her questions.

She shrugs. "I guess. I—I just don't understand . . . why you had to leave, why you couldn't stay, how you're here. . . ."

"Sometimes people think they know better." I wish I had a better answer. "You know how it is. Moms was gone and Aasim figured he'd snatch me up instead of letting CPS get me or whatever."

She folds her arms.

"I *told* him I wanted to take you with me, T." I reach across the table for her fingers.

She doesn't take them.

"I *told* him but he didn't listen."

"Aasim?" She cups the mug in her hands but doesn't take a sip. "That your dad?"

"*Aasim.* The dude Moms was laid up with." My fingers hang there, grasping at air.

She purses her lips. "So what makes this time different, Rooty?"

Damn. Ain't been called that in a minute. Moms started calling me that because my favorite cereal was Rooty Roo's. I'd eat it for breakfast, lunch, and dinner some days. I don't even know if I liked it that much or if that's just all we had. I chuckle. Moms would buy boxes in epic proportion whenever Bulk Buy had a sale. Feels like a lifetime ago.

"*This* time I'm not letting them take me back. No one's gonna break us up again." I reach harder. "Tash, I won't leave you again. I promise."

She looks out the window instead of at me and it's like the air in Joe's Joe turns frigidly cold. She has Moms's profile. Those same high cheekbones and naturally long lashes. Her lips purse like Moms's too. But her nose, that's all her dad's people. I have Moms's nose and her sable complexion. She's so beautiful. A ghost of sadness haunts Tasha's expression, but her eyes don't drop a single tear. She's tough like Moms too. Like me.

"Okay," she says, finally meeting my eyes.

"Okay?"

"Okay." She blows and takes a cautious sip from the mug.

She needs to know everything. So she gets how serious this is. "There's more I need to tell you."

I reach for her and to my relief we lock fingers. I explain everything that just transpired in Ghizon. She gasps and her mouth falls open lower and lower with every passing second.

She snatches her hand away, eyes wide with fear. "I . . . he . . ."

"Listen to me. I will *never* let them touch you. *And* they don't even know it's you."

Yet.

She nods like she's trying to believe me.

"Tasha, it's always been us. When Moms was working all night, when she was doing a triple shift on the weekends, every day after school. We always gonna be alright. As long as we stick together." I lean in for a whisper. "*And* with this magic, I can make sure we stay safe."

I want to believe it even if it isn't true. I have to believe it. I'm the only one who can protect us.

"There's all sorts of stuff I can do because of these." I flash her a quick peek at the onyx bubbles on my wrists. "And if something goes down, you saw how I handled it the other day."

She smooths her cheeks clean, nodding.

"I *will* fix this. *Nobody* is hurting my family."

She sniffles and chuckles all at the same time and my chest is a little lighter. "It's ironic, isn't it? You never even wanted to know anything about your dad's side of the family."

I bristle at the word "dad."

"And yet it's the magic from the family you have *no* love for that'll protect the family you *do* love."

For a second words don't come and a bitter taste spreads on my tongue. "They're the enemy, T. Don't make it more than it is. Finish up that drink and let's get out of here."

She takes a sip, wrapping her long fingers around the cracked porcelain. Moms said we could play piano with our long fingers. Never tried, but I bet Tash'd be good. In another life. Or maybe a different time.

Life will be different for us.

I'll make sure of it.

The line at the register has lengthened and Full Lips is blushing at someone placing an order. Next to the trash can a pair of guys wait in line for the restroom.

"So I-I mean I-I saw things when you touched me by the car, but, like . . . what is it like there?" Tasha reaches for my wrist, rubbing the onyx beneath my sleeve. "Does it hurt?"

"Getting it fused to my skin hurt like a bitch."

She snorts. "Does everyone there have that?"

"Mostly, yep. They call it being Bound . . . like bound to magic. The Chancellor calls it an 'act of benevolence.'" I add air quotes to the last part.

"Which one was the Chancellor?"

"He's basically like the president in Ghizon. He runs everything, and his right-hand man—the General—does his dirty work."

"So Mr. Magic Giver is a jerk behind the scenes but puts on a nice face in front of the people? Doesn't sound much different from here."

I snort. "Exactly. You get it."

"Where does the stone come from?" She studies my wrist. "Like, could I get one? Maybe if there were two of us with magic . . ."

My stomach sinks. It's only normal she'd wonder, but we can't even start thinking like that. Going back to Ghizon is like a brutha in baggy clothes walking into a police station. I'm trying to keep us *alive*.

"No, there's no way. They don't want my Black ass with magic, you think they gon' hand it out to you, too?"

She laughs and I feel a smidge better. She's right: Two of us with magic would probably be smarter, but there's no way that can happen so I don't even want to get her hopes up.

The taller man waiting to get into the restroom still hovers near the trash station. We meet eyes. He darts his gaze in another direction a bit too quickly.

"So, I mean, what do they look like when they come here?" she asks. "Patrol, or whatever they're called. If they're going to be after us I should at least know what to look out for."

The restroom door opens and the sound of flushing grows faint as it clicks closed. Vacant. The man near the trash can doesn't move. I *think* he's waiting on the restroom. I mean, he's been there for a minute . . . what else could he . . .

"Rue?" Tasha pokes me, but my eyes are fixed on the empty restroom and the man who's been waiting outside of it as long as I've been here. I don't like this. Maybe I'm being paranoid?

"I was just asking what they look like, if they all wear the same thing or. . . ." Her words trail off as old dude's eyes find mine again. His jacket shifts and metal glints from his belt.

"Get up," I say.

Tasha looks confused, but she stands. "What are . . ."

I shush her. "Act calm and just follow me. We're fine."

I think.

I move toward the opposite end of the shop and pull Tasha in front of me, gently pushing her toward the door. I don't know who he is or why he keeps staring, but he's carrying a gun and that's enough for me to get out of here. I take one more long look at him. He's white, I think. His dark hair is long but tidy, hanging just past his collar. Bet no one would guess Mister Buttoned-Up Shirt Tucked in His Slacks is packing heat.

His head is swiveling back around my way when I slip through the door.

"What happened?" Tasha looks over her shoulder as I push her to keep it moving.

"Nothing. I don't know. Just got a bad feeling in there." My breath picks up with our pace. I'm probably being paranoid. Texas is an open carry state. "Some dude in khakis was looking at us one too many times."

"Khakis and a button-up?" she asks. "Dark jacket?" She must have seen him too.

"Yeah, I—"

"Uhh, him?" She throws a glance over her shoulder and my heart stops.

The coffee shop door gives a faint chime as it closes behind us and there he is, taking a stroll in our direction.

"Faster." I pull her by the elbow and cross the street, walk-running. *It's just a coincidence. It's just a coincidence.* I don't know if that's the truth or if I'm praying it is.

He crosses the street too.

Shit! Shit! Shit!

What does this dude want with us? His complexion says he ain't Ghizoni. At least I don't think he is, but he *is* a ways away.

We turn another corner.

A few minutes later, he does too.

"Aunt Melba's old house is 'round here. We need to get off these streets." I cut a left, picking up my pace, and Tasha keeps up. He rounds the corner behind us and I pick up even more speed. I can hardly get a word out from being out of breath.

"Aunt Melba dead, Rue."

"I know, but Neesha 'nem ain't done nothing with the house." A good amount of distance is between us and him now, but still my knees shake. He is *definitely* following us. Too many twists and turns for this to be happenstance.

We gotta lose him before getting close to Aunt Melba's.

"This way." I turn down an alley, heart hammering in my chest. The sun disappears. Brick towers on either side of us and the backs of shops stretch ahead as far as I can see. Pairs of dumpsters every couple of buildings send a smell of rotten raw meat to my nose. As much as I hate wedging there, hiding between those two dumpsters is probably our best bet.

"Down here." I crouch low, pulling Tasha to join me. She crouches beside me and I shove her behind me a bit.

A door claps shut and Tasha yelps.

I wrap a hand over her mouth. "Quiet," I whisper.

Footsteps patter in our direction. A dumpster creaks open and a soft voice mutters something, then grunts, and the metal box clangs in response. Just someone throwing away trash, thank goodness.

Done, the stranger turns to go back inside I guess, because the sound of footsteps grows faint. But a deep voice cuts in.

"You see some girls come this way?"

It's him.

"N-no, I-I s-sure didn't. I-I was just taking out my trash. I own that there salon."

I pull Tasha in to me, her eyes wide as saucers.

"You don't sound real sure," he says.

"I-I—" Her voice cracks.

"You, you, what?" His steps grow louder. Closer.

I have to do something.

"I-I don't want no trouble now with you folks. Can you just put the gun down?"

Gun?!

"Let me go inside," she asks. "I ain't seen nothing. I ain't gon' see nothing. Just p-please let me get back inside."

Tasha's whole body is trembling against me.

Think, Rue. "Stay here. Don't say a word."

The lines worrying Tasha's face beg me not to move. But it's not even really a choice. I can't let this lady get hurt.

I step out and the old woman's legit surprised. I mouth, "It's going to be okay," and she looks from the gun to me and back to the gun.

The shock on the gunman's face turns to a smile quick, and the barrel of his 9mm points my way. Cars whip by on the street at the end of the alleyway. I have half a mind to scream for someone to help, but moving cars don't have ears. Pedestrians barely do.

"Hands up."

I put my hands up, studying this guy's face. Moms always said to study the face of someone who attacks you. Walking home from school, she was always worrying we'd get messed with.

"Let it burn into your memory," she'd said.

Gunman's brows are bushy, eyes blue. His skin is pale, but scorched, like he tans too much. He's definitely not Ghizoni. He has a mole near his left ear and the head of a snake tattoo peeking at me from the collar of his shirt. An eerie feeling settles on my shoulders.

I've seen that mark before ... somewhere.

He spots me staring and tugs at his collar, raising his gun arm higher. "Eyes to the ground. Where's the other one? The girl."

"She ran off. I stopped to hide."

Cold metal chills my forehead as the gun barrel presses into me. The old lady whimpers, but I don't flinch.

"It would be stupid to lie to me." He tryin' to scare me. It's not like I haven't seen heat before. Felt it against my skin. Like I ain't watch bullets fly through the air like arrows stealing mommas from their kids. Robbing sons of their dreams.

I've seen worse than the likes of him.

I lift my sleeves. "She gone."

If he doesn't back down, I'ma have to use magic. . . .

But it'll set off Patrol. . . .

His fingers move to the trigger.

I have no choice. I have to. "Feey'l," I mutter, reaching for the familiar burning sensation in my wrists. For a second my wrists flicker with warmth.

Then my arms go cold all over.

Wait, what?

Again, I dig for that tingle of magic fused to my wrists, to lay this dude flat on his back.

Nothing.

My magic? It's not answering.

Again, dammit!

The orbs on my wrists don't even warm this time.

Oh my god, we're gonna die. I bite down, bracing for his wrath.

He tilts the gun sideways. "You . . ."

Police sirens *woop* and my heart stutters.

The walls around us flicker from red to blue and back to red. I don't know whether to be relieved or scared. Sirens *woop* again and someone shouts, "FREEZE!"

Gunman's blue eyes burn into mine for a split second longer, full of a fire I don't understand. He takes off, knocking over the old salon lady as he sprints down the alleyway. A cop takes off past us, chasing him down. I brace for the sound of bullets, but they don't come.

I guess they don't shoot first ask questions later for everyone.

His partner walks up, her dark pixie cut rustled by a gust of wind. The badge on her chest is hard to read in the shade. I squint. Resendiz.

"Are you okay?" she asks.

I nod, my whole body shivering. My magic isn't working, but I can't tell this lady that.

"Was anyone hurt?" she asks.

"No."

Her eyes pinch together. "Are you *sure* you're okay?"

"Y-yeah. Just shaken up." I call for Tasha and she joins my side. I hope she didn't see me saying that spell. I can't tell her I'm broken. Magic is my *entire* plan. The weight on my chest is heavy, so heavy, each breath is a fight. How do I save us without magic? How do I protect us from Ghizon or just any ole creep trying to do us harm?

I don't know.

FUCK.

We explain everything from the coffee shop to him following us into the alley. We tell her about the way he almost hurt the salon owner lady. I give the best damn physical description possible. Officer Resendiz writes it all down and asks me if I'm okay ten more times at least.

"These last several weeks the crime—especially in East Row ..."

That's where I grew up. That's home.

"... has been *bad*. Multiple shootings, robberies, every other week." She looks between us. "And don't get me started on cartel arrests. You two should get home. It'll be dark soon. Can I give you a ride?"

She's nice and all, for a cop, but that's a bit too far. "Nah, we're good."

"Okay." She tucks away her tablet and smiles. "I mean it, off these streets, right now. It's not safe out here—worse than I've ever seen it."

"Yeah, okay. My aunt lives just up the road." A half lie. Aunt Melba's been dead, but her house *is* 'round the corner. I'm anxious to get there. I need some time to think. Who was that guy? And what's wrong with my magic?

I gotta figure this shit out before we both end up dead.

CHAPTER 10

L AST TIME I SAW Moms, she was slipping on a white lab coat. She'd said something about a new job down at the Medical Center. Some kind of way this job was supposed to make it so that she could eventually drop her weekend hustle. Tasha had a fever that night.

Moms didn't want to leave, but she also wanted us to eat.

If she'd stayed home, maybe she'd still be alive.

One Year Ago

"Now, don't you answer the door for nobody even if you know 'em," she'd said, slipping her arm into the second sleeve. "That door stays closed. Any trouble out there, you just mind ya' business."

"Not even the cops?"

"*Damn sho'* not the cops." She pulls me into a hug. "You crazy? Can't nobody know y'all up in here all night without me. That'd get us in so much trouble, get y'all taken away. You need anything, Ms. Leola's phone number on the fridge."

The door clicks shut.

I hate doing overnights without Moms, but it's so normal these days. I set out Tasha's medicine. She needs another dose in an hour, then a different one a couple of hours after that. Alternating the medicine, careful to give her the exact amount, no mistakes.

I set my phone alarm to wake me up every few hours through the night. My study notes for my test tomorrow glare at me from the table. Studying ain't happening. Not tonight. Maybe in the morning. I keep moving down the hallway.

Tasha's curled up on Moms's bed under a yellow blanket. The ratty collar of her favorite T-shirt peeks from under her chin. It's one of Moms's old ones; used to be orange, now it's peach. It's worn out, but Tasha loves it. And any time she's sick she *has* to wear it until she's well again.

I chuckle, sliding in bed beside her. The sheets are chilly and gooseprickles dance on my skin. I shimmy closer to her warmth. She's so hot, but it's almost cozy.

Before Tasha came along, when I was sick like this, I would lie here *wishing* Moms could be here, clutching the phone, scared to death of being home alone. I slip an arm around Tasha's head and stroke a few soaked strands of hair. Moms always preaching about how building a future requires sacrifice and sacrifice ain't never easy.

Shit, sacrifice hurts.

Sacrifice kills.

But it's what you do with the pain, Moms would say.

Tasha nestles in to me and I hug around her tighter. "Momma should be off work for good on the weekends soon," I whisper in her ear. She groans. "Maybe we can go to the mall, walk around or something. All three of us."

Her eyes roll in their sockets, but she doesn't speak. Is the medicine even working? The damp towel across her forehead is 'bout hot as her head. Probably should change it. I step into the hallway and turn toward the bathroom.

That's when it happens.

"R-rooty!" The front door bursts open and Moms's voice is strained, higher pitched than it should be.

"Momma?" I step into the hallway and catch a glimpse of her coming inside. It's dark, but I can make out her earrings and necklace, the same ones she always wears, and her eyes—wide. So wide—nearly double in size. A chill ripples through me like ice fills my bones.

"Y-you forget something, Ma?" *Moms isn't forgetful.*

That's when I hear it.

Pop.

My knees pound the floor, crawling back to the room.

I know that sound. Everyone 'round here knows that sound.

Pop.

"T, wake up!" I pull her awake and snatch her to the floor, hands glued around her mouth. *Oof.* She's so heavy and out of it. I pull hard, tugging, dragging with every bit of my strength.

Pop. Pop.

The shots are fainter, clouded by muffled voices. My hands are shaking, but I can't feel them. I can't feel anything.

Wedged in Moms's closet around piles of junk, I fold my knees against my thudding chest, straining to shut the closet door. A hook and padlock hangs on the inside of the door frame. Never noticed that before. My clumsy hands work it closed and click it to lock.

Tasha's burning against my chest, and I squeeze her. I tell her everything will be okay. I tell her Moms will be fine. I tell her not to worry, I'll keep her safe.

I tell her every lie I wish was true.

Next time we saw Moms, she was in a body bag. I'm not letting my sister go through pain like that again. At least one of us should have a childhood . . . a real one.

Two more city blocks and Aunt Melba's street sign comes into view. I bolt toward it, pulling Tasha along. Auntie's been dead five years at least, but no matter, spare key was always under the aloe vera plant 'round back.

"You sure about this?" she asks.

I'm not sure about anything at this point. Why my magic doesn't work, who that guy was, if the Chancellor has found out who I touched, where we're gonna sleep. My head's going to explode. "We need off these streets so I can think." I walk faster, more like a light jog. Tasha keeps pace as a rusted green carport comes into view. Sun-drenched siding covers most of the house, the parts that aren't patched in graffiti'd wood. Chipped yellow trim frames the windows and door. No one's visited here in a minute. Knew it'd be abandoned, boarded up still. Empty houses where I'm from just sit ignored for years, generations, forgotten by the city—just like the people who live here.

I cut a sharp glance around. "Come on, while the coast is clear."

Tasha moves ahead of me and we cut across Auntie's overgrown lawn. I pry open the side gate and it creaks in greeting. Tasha slips through first, then me. She's so tall. Damn near my height and thin lines already dent her young face.

"Keep an eye out," I say. "I'ma get the key."

She shoves her hands in her pockets, teetering on her feet.

The porcelain planter is still in the spot I remember, dusty and sun scorched.

"You get it?" she yells, voice riddled with cracks.

I shove the weighty pot aside and a brass key glimmers from underneath. "Yeah, we good. Come around back."

We follow the jagged concrete walk that wraps around the back of the house, making sure I step around the cracks littered with dead grass. *Habit.* A pair of metal chairs and a sun-scorched card table are piled against the back door, half-ripped cardboard boxes on top.

"Help me clear this."

"I don't feel good about holing up in Aunt Melba's old house. Can't we just go somewhere else? To my grandma's? My pop's cool, I swear."

"T, *please* with the questions. It's just for a minute. You heard the cop, we need off these streets. I need a second t-to . . ." *Figure out what the hell is wrong with my magic.* ". . . to plan. We got the Chancellor after you and now whoever these dudes you are mixed up with here."

"I ain't mixed—" Her volume is 'bout three octaves too high.

"Tash, we are not talking about this out here. I . . . I . . . Just help me push this table."

"You what? Tell me." She folds her arms. "What's wrong?"

"Nothing's wrong!" I really shouldn't yell. She's just worried. I still my shaky hands and try for a calm, level tone. "I'm sorry. Can you just grab that end? I need a minute to regroup, figure out what's next." I hoist up my end of the table and she helps.

We *could* go to her people's house, but the questions. Oh, the questions. Where am I supposed to say I've been the past year? Everybody knows Moms got shot up and I just vanished. And even if I could come up with a convincing enough lie, I can't have every nigga out there just know I'm back, hugging and touching on me, asking me why I keep my sleeves pulled down and never take my hoodie off.

I need a spot *without* questions, a space to breathe, to figure out what's wrong with my onyx, and decide where the hell we're gonna go. I chew my lip. I probably need to check in with Bri, too.

The sun burns my hands as we move the last bits of trash, making more noise than I intend to. Moments later, I'm slipping the key in the door. *Please don't let nobody be up in here.* The brass slips smoothly in the hole and I blow a quick breath and push the door open.

Shadows retreat as sunlight rushes in. Hazy air, heavy with dust, makes me squint and cough. Something reminiscent of cat piss fills my nostrils. *Ugh.* My stomach hovers in the back of my throat as we step deeper inside.

Aunt Melba's old flowered couch rests beneath the boarded-up windows in what used to be her living room. I move closer and a furry head pops out of a pile of blankets.

"Meow."

I jump back. I *don't* do cats. It apparently feels the same way, because bells jingle as it darts off.

"Aww, it's so cute." Tasha takes off down the hall, trying to call it back. She always did love cats. They lick their own asses. That shit's nasty.

With Tasha out of sight, I try again to summon my magic, muttering a spell under my breath.

Nothing.

Then another.

Still nothing.

Don't panic. Think.

Tasha's voice rings down the hall, trying to coax the cat.

I can't go back to Ghizon. I can't go to Tasha's family. At the moment I have an abandoned house and no magic. Back against the cracked yellow walls, I dig circles into my temples. This shit's gonna get us killed. This is too much. It's all just too much.

"You aight?" Her voice rings from the hall.

"Y-yeah!" I scramble up. "I'm good. J-just thinking." I turn away from her approaching footsteps.

Across the room is the kitchen and Aunt Melba's round table sits undisturbed at the center, coated in a layer of dust. A splintered crack runs through its middle, along with an overturned box of Fruity O's and a dirty butter knife.

Think, Rue. Can't go back to Ghizon. But I need answers about magic that can only come from Ghizon. Bri has an invention for literally everything, maybe she'll have some ideas. I run my fingers across the table and it rocks on uneven legs.

I pace, raking my hands through my scalp, and feel a piece of metal in the back of my neck. The tracker Luke put in! I grab the butter knife. Too dull. I flip through the drawers and cabinets, loosing clouds of dust. Mail, napkins, soy sauce packets. I close that one and open another. Nestled between more to-go spork packages than a person could use in a lifetime is a burgundy pocket knife.

I flick it open and clamp my lip between my teeth.

Do it.

I suck in a breath and dig the knife into my flesh. *Agh, it hurts!*

I dig around the tracker's metal rim, then slip the knife

underneath it. Everything's slippery with blood and my neck burns like a ring of fire. I bite down harder and ease the blade a millimeter deeper. A scream claws at my throat, but I swallow it back down and in one smooth motion, tilt my wrist up.

The tracker slips out, slimy and coated in red. A white light blinks from its top. Shoot, it's still active. I toss it on the ground and it crunches under my shoe. The room sways a moment.

"Find me now, asshole," I say under my breath, pressing my sleeve hard against the wound.

"Boo!" A paw touches my back.

"Ah!" I snatch up the butter knife and whip around. Best I got at the moment.

Tasha laughs. "OMG, the cat's not gonna hurt you. A-and . . . is that . . . blood?"

"Meow."

"Get that thing away from me." I toss the knife. My nerves are shot. "It's nothing. I-I'm fine."

She looks at me weird a second, then rolls her eyes, stroking the cat's head. "If you say so. And whatever, he's cute. The rooms are empty, by the way. Looks like kitty lives here by his lonesome."

I exhale. Across the length of the room and back, I pace over and over. Tasha's on my heels going on about how she's always wanted a cat, but it was always a no growing up because it was another mouth to feed. Her mouth is moving but I barely hear the words.

How do I get us out of this? Moms always said we *make a way out of no way*. She said it's not a choice, it's required for anyone growing up in her household.

How do I make a way, Momma? How? When there really is no

way. I have no weapon, no magic. People in Ghizon chasing us, some dude here after her ...

Oh shit.

The guy from her bus stop.

She was grinning and *got in his car!* And he fled. Who doesn't stay to see if the person in the car with you during a wreck is okay? That doesn't add up.

"I need to know who that guy was, T."

Her brows cinch and she strokes the fur cradled in her arms. "I have no idea, Rue." She looks away. Like she usually does when she's lying.

"You cannot be serious right now. You lying?"

"I swear I do *not* know that dude. I thought he was from that place—Gize."

"Ghizon. And no, from far away they sorta look like white folks but their skin has a grayish tint. Hard to explain. They sort of look sickly."

"All of 'em? What about the Black folks?"

"What Black folks?"

"I don't know. I didn't see any in your memories, but I figured there'd be some. I mean, that's weird, right?"

What is she talking about? How is that important? "Listen, I can protect us from the Chancellor"—*I hope*—"because I know what I'm looking out for. But whoever these dudes you got looking for you, I can't protect you from them if I don't know who they are." I grip her shoulders. "I need the truth. All of it."

"Who is *they?*"

"Tasha!" Full on yelling at this point. "You saw some buttoned-up white dude at your bus stop the morning everything went down!"

Her mouth falls open.

"You were grinning your ass off to go talk to him. He had dark pants, a white shirt. You got in his car. *Who is he?*"

"Oooooh. I didn't know you meant *him*. I thought we were talking about coffee shop dude." She twists the end of her shirt. "He's one of the guys from the Community Center. He told me he'd drop me off so I didn't have to take the bus. Said we would get donuts on the way." She screws up her mouth like I'm making a big deal out of nothing.

Who gets up that damn early in the morning to take some random kid for donuts from her bus stop? He ain't pick her up from home. I don't buy it. "So, you think you know him?"

"I mean, yeah, I see him after school most days." She pulls out her phone and swipes up. "He's cool. He plays basketball with us and stuff." She swipes past images on her Instagram and double taps. "There he is, Chad."

Chad's surrounded by a group of kids about Tasha's age, with a basketball under his arm and a giant snake tattoo on his neck.

I've seen that same tattoo somewhere before....

My stomach drops.

... on the guy at the coffee shop.

CHAPTER 11

W AIT. SO YOU THINK the coffee shop dude and Chad know each other?"

"Either that or they coincidentally have the same tattoo in the same spot and a strange interest in you." I swipe through a few more pictures on her phone. That's definitely the guy from the bus stop. "You wanna explain now? I'm listening?"

"I swear to God I do not know that man from the coffee shop." Her eyes water and she looks like she did curled up in Moms's closet. So small, so scared. She's not lying. "I-I swear, Rue." She's full on crying now and it hurts. She ain't ask for any of this, neither of us did. And yet this is what it is, this is our life.

I pull her in to me. "I believe you, okay. It's going to be alright. I'm sorry if I scared you."

She smooths away her tears. "So, what now?"

"Well first, I need to figure out"—*why my magic won't work*— "how Chad and coffee shop dude are affiliated."

"It's a tattoo. A lot of people have those."

"Yeah, but these are in the *same* shape and in the *same* spot— down the side of the neck. That ain't coincidence, T. Ink ain't cheap, either. My ex, you remember Julius?"

She nods.

"He was tatted up and down both arms, all across his chest and back, collecting art from all these dope artists in town."

Julius was always skipping to hang at Dezignz, this ink spot in Houston that don't care about age long as you got an ID that says what it needs to say. At first he was getting tats for free in exchange for "favors" to the dude who runs the place. But when Julius's grandma got sick he started pushing his own weight to make bills. That's when he changed, started dressing nice, hair always fresh. So, of course, THOTs start coming around. I'm not 'bout that life. I'm *the only* one or *not one* at all. I was good to him too. Kept a scrapbook of our dates. I ain't care what he dressed like, either. He was always cute to me and smart as hell. That's how we got close, studying for a Geometry test. But the money got to him, or maybe it was the ass thrown his way, because I sure wasn't ready for all that. I don't know. Either way, he started acting dumb, so I dumped him. His loss.

I chew my lip. He *would* probably know something about the snake tattoo though. *Ugh.* The last thing I need is a reason for one more person to be sniffing around us. No, I'm not reaching out to him. Not a good idea.

Hmmm, but the scrapbook . . .

"Tash, where's all Moms's old stuff? My stuff?" The scrapbook I kept when we were boo'd up was full of pictures, ticket stubs. The first test we studied for together I got an A, so I put that in there too. So lame in hindsight. He added pics of each of his tattoos, signed by the artist, hoping it'd be worth something someday. If I get my hands on my scrapbook, maybe I can find out who did the tats to see if there's a connection or something.

"Ms. Leola's, I think." She nuzzles the cat cradled in her arms and he purrs. "That's what my daddy said. But I haven't been over there since the CPS lady came and got me."

"Then that's where we're going—to Ms. Leola's." She's everybody's grandma in East Row. Whatever's going down, you can count on some pound cake from Ms. Leola and tea so sweet it's like instant diabetes. "The bus stop's right on the corner. Don't even need a transfer. We should hurry up."

She hands me her bus pass and some spare change in her pocket as we make our way to the door. The cat's under her arm nibbling on one of her fingers.

"You gotta leave that thing here, you know that, right?"

"His name is Cupcake." She smiles big and her eyes do too. "We can't just leave him here all alone. That's so sad. Everybody should have somebody."

"Tash, we don't even know if we can feed ourselves. How the hell are . . ."

Her expression droops.

"Don't look at me like that." I cannot believe this shit. "*Fiinnnne*. Tuck his ass away so we don't get kicked off the bus."

She grins bigger and hurries past me out the door. Out of sight, I tap my watch.

Me: Bri, can we talk? In person. It's urgent!

Two taps and the geolocation for Ms. Leola's house sends with a swish.

◆　◆　◆

Ms. Leola came over first that night, even before the cops. Cops ain't stay long. Didn't write shit down. I ain't never been more scared in my life.

But Ms. Leola fed us, had us come to her house, and even let us stay home from school the next day. That morning, though, some lady came from CPS and took Tasha. She told Ms. Leola someone else would be coming for me. But I don't have family like Tasha. Ms. Leola's the closest thing I have to a grandma. I didn't understand why I had to leave at all.

Ms. Leola argued with the CPS lady for me to just stay there. It didn't go well because she slammed the door when she left. Hours passed and I just sat there by the door, hoping it was a mistake. Hoping somehow Moms was actually at the hospital and she'd be okay. Ms. Leola tried to feed me, tell me somehow it would be okay, but I refused to move from that door. I just knew Moms was coming back. Tash too. That it was all some bad dream.

I waited so long that I dozed off.

Next thing I knew, I was in Ghizon with Aasim standing over me, introducing himself as my father.

Haven't seen Ms. Leola since.

Going back to her house feels like walking into the past, about to relive that night and morning all over again.

I'm not ready for this.

As if that matters.

I have to be.

I give Tasha a reassuring nod as we step onto the bus. My watch screen's black. No response from Bri yet. The front of the bus is empty, so I fall in a seat and tuck my face deep in my hood. Tasha sits next to me talking into her jacket, *because that's not suspicious.*

Two elder ladies sit in the front row, giggling over an issue of *O* magazine. A boy no taller than the seat, with earbuds, sits near the back, nose in a book. No one else. Bus is empty otherwise.

I hunch down in my seat as we roar into motion. Buildings and blocks move past in a blur and I almost nod off when my watch buzzes.

Bri: What's wrong? Are you okay? You mean you want me to leave? Like leave Ghizon and come there? It's been crazy here since you left. Security is insane.

Bri's a rule follower. Hacking is her one vice, which is I think is actually a useful skill. She always makes the best grades. A model student. And the irony is she ended up with me as a best friend. But she's my only access to information in Ghizon and I need answers.

Me: Yeah, pls! Something's wrong

Everything's wrong.

Bri: I could get in HUGE trouble for that. Can you talk?

I cut a glance at Tasha, still grinning with Cupcake, and hide my watch arm a bit more.

Me: No, I can't talk. My onyx won't work! My magic isn't responding.

My watch suddenly vibrates in short pulses, her name flashing on the screen. *Shoot, she's calling!*

I tap. "Bri?"

"What do you mean it won't work?" Her voice comes through like a loudspeaker and I almost stumble out my seat. I *tap tap tap* the volume *wayyyy* down.

Tasha gives me a weird look and I play it cool. I stand and put as much distance between my mouth and her ears as I can.

"That's not possible," Bri says, this time only loud enough for me to hear.

You can't tell Bri something she doesn't already know.

"I'm telling you, it's broken."

"Have you reached out to Aasim? Surely he can help."

I grind my teeth and resist the urge to roll my eyes.

"No," I yell a little too emphatically.

The driver glances my way a second but quickly moves on back to his phone playing some soap opera.

"Bri, I'm not comfortable with that. I don't know him like that."

"Comfortable? Rue! You're asking me to sneak out of Ghizon. Fourteenth Law, Clause B, states . . .

Oh god, do not recite.

"Departing Ghizon territory—"

She's reciting.

"—without express consent from the Chancellor is strictly forbidden."

I massage my temples. "I know what the law says. I just . . . someone's after us . . . someone *here*."

She gasps.

"Without magic I don't have a way to watch out for us, keep us safe. Please meet me, bring whatever books you can find and all your lab stuff. So we can figure this out."

Silence. She's considering it.

"You won't need to do any magic here, so they'll never know. And you can zap here undetected because of this bomb-ass watch."

"The watch doesn't have weapon capabilities."

"OMG, for the hundredth time, bomb doesn't actually mean . . ." I sigh. "I just meant the watch is really cool because you can get here undetected like I did."

She tsks. "I mean, that's true and the probability of the watch not working with the amount of testing I put it through is . . . about .00008 percent."

That's probably a literal calculation.

"See! No issues. No risk."

"It really is a fine product. The frequencies are synthesized to optimal levels. I even engineered duplicate sound waves to mimic the ones in the air, but affixed a cloaking spell to it at the *molecular* level." She's grinning, I can tell. "I mean there's really no risk, y—"

"Bri?"

"Ya?"

"You're geeking out on me again. So, is that a yes?"

For several moments, nothing.

"I can't believe I'm actually thinking about doing this! What's that thing you always say about friends dying together?"

"Ride or die?"

"Yep, that's the one. I hope that's metaphorical. I'll be there soon."

"You da real MVP."

"I'm really not." She chuckles. "There's, like, *no* chance I'd get caught if I use the watch. So I'm going to try to be a proper ride or die."

I laugh. "Aight, see you soon!"

Ride or die is a code. Means friends—the real ones, not the fake-ass flaky ones—are always there for the good and the bad, even when shit gets real.

And right now, shit's real AF.

CHAPTER 12

EVERY NIGHT IT'S THE same.

Darkness hangs in the sky like a guillotine. A thick nest of forest hugs around me, frigid air rustling the thinner branches. Trees like I've never seen with black bark and wide leaves twist, bent like a leg with several knees, out of sight. Goose bumps prick my skin and I shiver, standing there.

I always stand there, heart thumping.

Like I'm waiting for someone.

And he always shows up.

Like he knew I was coming.

The whites of his eyes are beacons in the night as his tiny fingers wrap around my wrist. How old is he? Like, three? He presses a finger to his lips and worry knits his tiny brow. He pulls me along and my heart races as fast as my feet. Leaves crunch under us, cracking through the air, and my breath comes quicker. I duck under a bristly branch with fuzzy crimson flowers and step over several fallen ones.

Something cracks.

I don't breathe.

He stops and squeezes my hand, listening. The fear in his eyes is thick like the night.

"*Where . . . ,*" *I start.*

Then I wake up.

I gasp and blink the world back into focus. The hum of the bus settles my nerves. Some.

"Rue?" Tasha asks, smoothing her hair down from resting her head against the window. "You okay?"

"I dozed off. I'm sorry. I-I'm fine."

Outside, the sun dips below a tall brick building and darkness sets on us.

"You don't look fine. You're panting like a racehorse and your lips have, like, no color."

"I said I'm fine." I hop up for a better view. "That's our stop up there. Come on."

Familiar buildings of East Row slink into view, orange in the streetlight. I sit up, soaking in the sight of home. My insides twist like a knot, half nerves, half anticipation. I know I'm asking Bri to risk a lot. The last thing I'd want is to get her in trouble over something I had her do. But I had to ask. I need answers from Ghizon.

The streets are full of people coming and going. Buses roaring past, construction forever ongoing, and cars with rattling trunks cruising past at 'bout two miles an hour so everyone sees them. No tall suits, strange tattoos, or people on our trail so far.

Keeping my eyes peeled.

Trying to not think about the fact that if someone does spot us, I can't do shit.

We step off at the bus stop in front of my old high school behind King Patty and Shipley Do-Nuts. Brown sugar and cinnamon swims in the air and my stomach churns. My school building's still there with the same faded brick and broke gym windows. The detached trailers running along the side of the auditorium where I took Spanish and AP Lit are still there. Funny how they call 'em "temporary buildings," but they been there as long as I can remember.

Tasha and I cross the street, walking alongside the chain-link fence outside Jameson High. The tar-top track is purple with white stripes, school colors. Saturdays in winter, or Houston's version of it, with flyaway pants and spikes, flood my memory. I first met Julius freshman year running the hundred-meter dash. He was there "making moves," as he'd say, and I caught his eye.

Memories of the old building hold me there, staring. Funny how leaving and coming back after so long feels like a lifetime's passed. I'd expected something to be different, but nothing's really changed. Same shit, just a different day.

I grab Tasha's hand as we cross another busy street as if she's little, like *little little*. Habit, I guess. But she doesn't pull away.

"Who was that you called earlier, anyway?" she asks.

"Bri, my girl from Ghizon. She's gonna come through, help us figure this out."

"Figure what out?"

Careful. Uhhhh. "This tattoo thing." I twist the end of my shirt. "She's on some next-level engineering type shit. Trust me, she's great to have around. We'll put our heads together on this."

She looks at me funny, but she doesn't say anything else about it.

The green-trimmed row-style buildings I used to call home grow larger in the distance and heaviness moves in like a cloud. Being back here to see T was hard enough, but actually *facing* Ms. Leola, the last person I saw before being snatched from everything I knew, is . . .

My heart stutters in my chest.

A lot.

I blow out air and my pulse slows a little.

As we get closer, the steady rhythm of rope thwacking the concrete and chants of double-dutch ring in my ear. Colorful beads dangle from the ends of the girl's braids, flapping with each jump. The two ropes swish past each other, slapping the pavement. *Thwack.* Her friend on the side chants between licks on her blue Kool-Cup. *Thwack.* She keeps hopping, faster each time. She's pretty good. I smile, smoothing my sweaty palms on my pants.

The numbers on the houses get smaller as we walk past. Until we spot the one that used to be ours. *Keep moving.* Ms. Leola's is a few stoops down.

My feet stick to the ground.

Broken steps at the foot of my old home torment me with a flood of memories.

Keep moving, Rue.

I can't.

It almost feels disrespectful not to stop and sit in the moment. Moms died there. *Right* there. I can't just walk by, I can't just pretend . . .

A lump rises in my throat. *I won't break.* Tasha's feet don't move either. Her eyes are glued to the door and her arm to my side. I should leave, stop staring. Stop twisting the dagger, dancing with the pain.

I can't. I'm fixated on the door, the stoop that used to be mine.

I step closer. Sounds fade and motion slows. My fingers find the rail leading up the step. A step I walked up to come home millions of times. Its chipped paint is coarse against my palm. I rub my hands, expecting to see red. When the paramedics and Ms. Leola pulled us out Moms's house, I refused to go, and held on to this rail. But my hand slipped because it was slick—slick with Moms's blood. There was so much, I remember that. My chest is heavy—my tongue, thick.

The door bursts open and a woman I don't recognize stares at me. "Can I help you?"

"N-no." I stumble backward. "I-I'm sorry." My cheeks burn with shame. What was I thinking walking up these steps like it's still my place? Another step backward and the stranger slams the door of my home shut. Tasha stands there still staring, tears twinkling on her cheeks.

I turn to comfort her and . . .

"Rue, baby? That you?" Her voice is gentle and aged. I'd know its ring anywhere.

Ms. Leola.

I turn and she gasps, fragile fingers covering her mouth. She looks the absolute same in her flowy house dress—like an African queen. It's deep green, bright blue, and a rich purpley-pink with a head wrap to match. Dry coils of white hair peek beneath its edge.

Tasha hovers behind me, eyes still glued to Moms's old door.

I get it, looking away is like saying goodbye all over again.

Ms. Leola makes her way down her stoop with shaky steps.

I rush to help her down, but stop myself. She takes each step careful, trembling that way some older folks do. Ms. Leola kept me every day after school. Once Moms got over Aasim leaving, she hustled hard—three jobs and weekend classes. She was gone *a lot*. Then Tasha came along, so she worked even more.

Those years Ms. Leola made sure we ate. T was younger so she may not remember as much, but *Sesame Street* on Ms. Leola's plastic-covered couch was my every morning till I was old enough for school. And even after that I lived at her house basically every weekend until I was old enough to stay alone.

"I don't believe my eyes, Che." Closer now, she reaches to caress my cheek, but I pull my face away. *Touch. She can't touch me.* She doesn't seem to notice because her smile deepens. Scents of gardenia potpourri wrap around me like a blanket.

"These old eyes must be broken. I can't belie—Rue?"

I nod, grinning. I'm a child again.

Ms. Leola wraps a fragile arm around me and squeezes. My hoodie keeps our skin from touching, so I lean into her comfort, like a fire in the middle of a winter storm. Her hug is strong and everything comes back in a rush.

The lady ripping Tasha from my arms . . .

Hearing my little sis plead for me to go with her . . .

Ms. Leola holding me, rocking back and forth, when the pain was so sharp all I could do was scream.

Her arms are walls around me, holding me together. Being here again, seeing that stranger on the stoop where Moms should be, it's all too much.

I can't do this. I'm not strong enough.

I'm limp in her arms, so fragile the wind could *whoosh* and shatter me into pieces.

"It's alright, child." She pats my back and I nestle into that nook between her jaw and shoulder, careful to keep our skin from touching.

"Oh baby, just let it all out."

I do.

Hot tears coat my face, soaking her collar. I weep for Moms. I weep for the friends I left here. For time I can never get back. I weep for Tasha. I weep for Aasim. It's like someone's ripped out stitches from a gushing wound.

It hurts.

So bad.

Her brown eyes are cloudy, wrinkled and old like her cocoa skin. "Now, now, Che. It's gon' be alright. You're a survivor. A fighter. The strongest person I know, ya hear?"

I'm supposed to be the strong one, the one who holds it down when Moms is away. I weep and weep some more.

I smooth my cheeks clean.

She pets my head. "My Jelani."

No one, literally no one but Ms. Leola, calls me by my middle name.

"And besides," she winks, "I knew you'd be back."

"Y-you did?"

"These old eyes done seen more than you think. Knew you wouldn't be 'round them magic folks forever."

I gasp. *Did she say magic? So she knew? I thought . . .*

She laughs and wrinkles hug her eyes. "Been waiting on this day, baby. And I been holding on to something to give you!"

My mouth dangles on its hinges.

She chuckles, ushering me toward her house. "But we got time to talk about all that." She pats my tummy. "Let's get inside and get y'all something to eat."

CHAPTER 13

MS. LEOLA WILL STUFF you if you let her.

I let her.

Not even five minutes after sitting on the couch to finish my plate of greens, oxtails, cornbread, and *wayyyy* too much cobbler, Tasha and I were *out*. Food coma like a MF. I stretch my sore neck and the spot where Tasha slept beside me is still warm.

Sunlight floods the living room and I tug the drapes closed. But not before taking a quick peek around. Block's quiet. Must be early. Notifications from Bri flick on my watch screen.

Bri: Trying to get out of here. Something popped up with the parents. Ugh. Be there soon. Sorry!

Bri: Hello?

Bri: You still want me to come, right?

Bri: What time is it there?

Bri: Rue????

Bri: UHH I'm on my way. Hope that's still ok?? See you soon.

Bacon and Ms. Leola's fresh biscuits waft through the air.

"Well, good morning," Ms. Leola says.

"Ah, you ain't have to make us breakfast," I say. "Putting us up was enough."

She laughs. "Girl, sit down so I can fix you a plate."

My stomach growls and I thank her as I join Tasha at the table.

Me: Passed out. Sorry. Get here as soon as you can.

Bri: Mhmm. Worried sick over here. Setting up my alibi (Luke). Leaving soon.

Tasha burps and I give her the stank eye. Moms taught us table manners; she better act like it.

"Can I get you another plate, baby?" Ms. Leola asks from the kitchen. She's sweet and moves like someone generations younger.

"I can't eat another bite, but thank you," Tasha says.

I scarf down my food in seven point three seconds. And I'm so full, I'll puke if I move. I'm sure of it. She's banging around in the kitchen. I tell myself to go help, but my feet straight up ignore me.

The night's events replay in my mind like a horror flick. I can't believe Ms. Leola knows about "those magic folks." How long has she known? And what does she have to give me? From who? I have so many questions. It's odd knowing that someone from back home has even the slightest whiff of my life in Ghizon. It's like my two worlds are crashing together and I don't know if I need a helmet. And if I do, where to find one.

Tasha's fork is still scraping her plate as if she can really grab every last crumb if she angles the fork just right.

"Now I know you two got some room for *this!*" Ms. Leola's got a plate in each hand with a wedge of pound cake on top dripping with a lemon glaze, her signature dish. Yes, cake . . . after breakfast.

I don't know where I'ma put it, but I'ma put it somewhere. Lemon swirls in my mouth as the cake melts on my tongue. So dense, yet so moist.

"Eat on up and there's plenty more. Now that you rested, I'ma find this box I have for you." She smiles. "When yo daddy gave it to me he said to make *sure* I ain't lose it."

I choke, coughing. "Aasim? It's from Aasim?"

"I guess that's his name. Tall chocolate thang, thin dreads? Good looking, always wore a tailored suit, looking like a young Idris."

Oh god. "I guess."

"Look, I don't know the man. But I did know yo momma. She was like a daughter to me and she loved him and trusted him an—"

"—and she's dead."

Ms. Leola exhales and it's heavy. "I don't know why things happened the way they did. I'm so sorry, baby, and I know ain't nothing I can say gon' make it right. That kind of pain don't get better. You just sort of learn to live with it. Be stronger because of it." She wags a finger. "But what I *do* know is that your momma made me promise if something ever happened to her, I was to find your father, so I did."

I shove the scraps of food on my plate away, appetite gone. "S-so, it was you?"

"Hear me out, now. Yo momma came in here 'bout a week before she died. Something had her real upset, now. She'd been crying. I could tell, but you know how she is. She acted like she was just fine, like she had it all together. She gave me these coins, look like pure gold. She looked me dead in the eye and told me if anything ever happened to her, to take those two and press 'em together and it would summon yo' daddy. Now, I ain't know nothing about no magic or who he was, but you best believe when I saw her body"—her voice cracks—"lying in that doorway like that"—she sniffles—"I came here and did *exactly* what she asked."

I don't know what to say. She's not lying. She wouldn't do that. This, I guess, was my mom's dying wish. That I go to Ghizon, ripped from my sister, taken from everything I know. I hate it. Even now, knowing it's what she wanted, I still hate it.

"I don't know what to say. . . ."

She rests a hand on my shoulder and I go warm all over. This is the closest thing I have to a mom at this point, and even if I don't get it, she honored Moms's words. Can't fault her for that.

"It's always gon' be things in this world we just don't understand. And baby, for me, that was one of 'em." She walks off into the kitchen and her voice is dimmer. "Now, when yo daddy came and got you that next morning, he told me to *make sure* I give you this here. Now, I *know* I put it in here somewhere."

A chair screeches across the floor.

I dash into the kitchen. "Please don't climb on nothing, Ms. Leola. Can I help reach something?"

"Child, I got this." She steps up on the chair and my heart about stops. I hover there spotting the chair like the base in a cheer squad pyramid.

She strains, reaching, and her robe hangs long from her arms, colors swishing in the air like a goddess. She reaches from one too-high shelf to the other. "I had some boys from the neighborhood move y'alls stuff into that back room, but this here was different. Had to go through *so much* trouble to get it, too. But I gave your daddy my word and I intend to keep it."

She plants both hands on her hips. "Not up there. Where did I . . . ? If I can't find it, them boys coming to do some housework for me today. They probably seen it." She bites her tongue. "Oh, maybe I put it . . . give me a second." She steps down from the chair and finally my pulse returns.

She leaves the kitchen, heading down the hall. "Yep. It's back here."

Tasha comes in the kitchen and sets her plate by the sink.

"Ahem."

She looks at me and without a word collects all the dishes and starts washing.

"We ain't 'bout to start embarrassing Moms just because she ain't here no more."

"Yeah, yeah. I'm just so full." She chuckles. "I *just* woke up and I already wanna nap." The cat purrs at her ankles but catches a splash of sudsy water and runs off. Fine by me. The way Ms. Leola is 'bout her furniture, I'm surprised she let Cupcake come inside at all.

The doorbell chimes.

"Tasha, get down the hall in a bedroom," I say. I don't know who it is but I ain't taking no chances. "Shut the door and lock it."

She goes. I duck into the kitchen, close enough to see but not be seen. Ms. Leola comes back from the hall, dusting off her clothes.

"Now who in creation is ringing my bell this early?" She peeps through the door hole. There stands Bri, glasses pressed to her freckled face, wearing 'bout five pounds of makeup.

"Uhm, hi!" she says before Ms. Leola can get the door open good. She sticks out a hand and the onyx fused to her wrist glistens in the sun. "Oh, uhh . . ." She jerks it back, blushing. "Sorry! I . . . uh . . . forgot to wash my hands. You don't want to touch these." She nervous laughs. "I-I'm looking for—"

"Bri!" I rush to help Ms. Leola with the door before they

accidentally touch. "It's fine, she's a friend." Closer now, Bri's cheeks are Pepto pink and her lips are bright red. "Where did you look up your makeup tutorial? Barnum & Bailey?"

"This is me blending in." She raises her chin, knowingly.

You really can't tell her nothing sometimes. "I guess. Try YouTube next time."

"You what?"

"Nothing."

"Well come on in before y'all let out all my AC," Ms. Leola says.

It takes only about two and a half minutes for Ms. Leola to sit Bri down to two plates of food and her own wedge of pound cake. Bri has no idea what she's dealing with, by the looks of it.

"I don't think I can actually eat all of this."

"You betta try." I wink. Nothing ruder than refusing a plate from somebody's grandma. I catch Bri up on the coffee shop dude, the run-in with the cop, and the snake tattoo. Since we are in front of Tasha, I make a point to *not* mention reaching for my magic. She isn't nearly as alarmed as I was, but she's doubly curious about the tattoo. She also apparently loves cats, which make her and Tasha immediate best friends.

"We'll bring you over to our side." Tasha nudges me with her elbow.

"Cupcake'll win you over."

"Wouldn't count on it," I say. "Dogs? Sure. Cats . . . *nah.*"

"So, Ghizon . . . Rue, things are *bad.* Like, bad, bad. The Chancellor posted pictures of your face in the dorm halls and told students if anyone hears from you we're supposed to report it. He even reprimanded your da—Aasim."

"What do you mean, reprimanded?" I ask.

"I don't know. That's just what I heard. Something about his magic is restricted. Like he can't do anything. He's a straight up turd—that's what we call kids who get their magic suspended for a period."

Why would they do that? He didn't have anything to do with me leaving. I catch myself: What does it matter anyway? I got ninety-nine problems, but Aasim's ain't gon' be one of 'em. I shrug. "Good luck with that."

"So did you find the tattoo in the scrapbook?" Bri asks.

Moms's things are in piles of boxes in one of Ms. Leola's spare bedrooms. Most of the boxes are half taped together and falling apart. Nothing's labeled. But the scrapbook was in my room under my bed so it should be with my stuff. Tasha and I couldn't get two boxes open before Ms. Leola had us at the table eating dinner last night.

"Not yet, still looking," I say.

"Y'all catch up." Tasha hops up. "I'll keep looking for it. Nice meeting you, Bri."

"You too."

"What does it look like again?" Tasha asks, heading into the hall.

"It's a book covered in pink heart stickers. Hard to mistake for anything else."

She teases me and disappears down the hall.

Bri sighs when Tasha rounds the corner. "When all this is said and done, I need to update you on boy drama."

"Boy drama? I need to lay Luke out? Because I will."

She laughs "No. I don't know. Maybe. He's being dumb. Let's talk about it later."

I give her the look that says, *Say the word and it's a done deal. I'll handle his ass.*

"It's fine. We're fine. It's just little stuff. I'll give you all the details later. I promise!"

"Aight, holding you to it."

"So back to the tattoo." She grabs a bag of gadgets she brought with her. "We can probably do an image scan. That way we can see all the locations where that same snake image appears. Depending on the technological advancements here, of course."

"I mean, we just Google everything," I say.

"What's a google?" she asks.

"That's actually a good question. No idea, but it's where—"

"Found it!" A box lands on the table with a *thunk*. Ms. Leola wipes her forehead with a satisfied smile. "Tucked it away real good, apparently. Almost put my back out on that one. Take a look, baby. I'ma get my peach cobbler out the oven."

Bri lifts an eyebrow, so I catch her up to speed on all Ms. Leola told me. The coins intrigue her the most, but Ms. Leola said they disintegrated into thin air after she used them.

"It's dagvaar."

"A what?"

"Dagvaar. A one-use sort of magical ritual. It's usually attached to an object that ties the giver to the receiver in some sort of pact. It's supposed to notify the owner when activated and self-destruct moments later. So it can only be used once and never be traced."

"So it's a device that summons its creator?"

"Exactly," she says. "I wish I could've seen it." She rests her chin in her hands. "I've only read about them and they're *hard* to make.

That's really complex old magic, Rue. Like, how would Aasim even . . . ? It takes an old type of Ghizoni magic that they don't teach anymore." She taps her lip. "Actually, I don't know if they ever taught it. And of course all the books on ancient Ghizon were lost when the Chancellor took ru—" She's such a magpie, I swear.

"Bri, back to Earth, we don't have a lot of time to figure this out."

Had I not skipped History class back in Ghizon so much, maybe I'd have some idea of what Bri is talking about. Girl's easily distracted, but a walking talking Ghizon encyclopedia.

"You know you're the shit, you know that?"

She appears flabbergasted.

"Girl, get up on some slang. It's a compliment." I slap her shoulder. "To be so book smart, when it comes to some things, you dingy as hell."

I laugh. She laughs too. "Well, that's probably true."

I nudge her. "You're still a keeper though."

"I think I'll keep you, too. If only so I can eat Ms. Leola's food again."

"Deal." We laugh and do our special handshake thing.

"So your mother gave Ms. Leola dagvaar, which she got from your dad—"

"Aasim."

"Sorry . . . she got them from *Aasim* to notify him if something ever happened to her."

"I mean yeah, that's what it sounds like."

"So he wanted to keep an eye on things here? Hmm."

I guess. I dig my toe into the carpet.

She chews her lip, piecing together clues of a puzzle I'm not interested in. "It makes sense. I mean, coming here, touching people, let alone having a full-blown relationship, a kid . . . I mean that's, like, super risky."

You shouldn't have brought her here. The Chancellor's words are a broken record in my head. *She's far more like them than us.*

"And then?" she asks.

"And then he apparently came to get me and told Ms. Leola to give me *this*"—I point to the box—"if she ever saw me again."

"Well open it! I'm dying to know what's inside."

My stomach flips. Why am I nervous? It's just Aasim. Probably some kind of *Oh, I wish I was a better dad* gift. I resist the urge to roll my eyes, and click the latch on the box open.

There, against a bed of black velvet, sparkles a single golden cuff and a thin golden necklace with a curvy pendant dangling from its end.

I stumble up from the table. "N-no, i-it can't be!" I back away.

Impossible words claw their way up my throat. "That's the necklace Moms was buried in."

CHAPTER 14

MOMS'S FAVORITE COLOR WAS yellow.

The sheets on her bed were the color of fading sunshine and she had a pair of yellow and black high-top J's she'd wear when she was trying to do it up. Her lucky sneakers, she'd called them. Bright yellow, soft grayish yellow, browner yellow like deep mustard, and even greenish yellow like chartreuse—she loved every shade. She even had a yellow striped coffee mug with a chip on the handle that made holding it sort of awkward. Coffee stains on the bottom were so bad you never knew if it was clean or dirty. But that's the only mug she'd have her morning coffee in. You'd never catch her in silver jewelry either, because gold is its own shade of yellow. She thought being around the color yellow brought happiness—luck even. She could be superstitious like that sometimes.

The yellowish gold necklace glimmers in the dim light against the velvet box.

And this necklace, this very one, she never *ever* took off. Not when she showered, not when she went to work. It never left her chest.

It was her way of sportin' something yellow every day.

Or so I thought.

"G-go ahead, p-pick it up." Tasha had heard the commotion, saw the necklace, and flipped out too.

"I-I just don't understand," I say, hesitant to move. "She wore it the last time I saw her. A picture from the day of her funeral (which Aasim made sure I got a copy of) showed her wearing it then too. Which is normal because—"

Tasha loops into my arm. "Because she never took it off."

Exactly. "Ms. Leola, how'd you get this?"

Ms. Leola fidgets her earring. "Now, I never want it to be repeated beyond this room." She lifts her chin. "I only did what I did because I had to." She sighs. "I-I kissed her goodbye one last time before they closed the casket and plucked it from her neck. Nobody saw me, of course. Tucked it right in my fist with my Kleenex."

Wow.

Bri peers closer at the bauble with narrowed eyes.

"Ms. Leola robbing a casket?" Tash whispers. "Now *that* I didn't see coming."

Worry lines dent Ms. Leola's brow. "All I know is she was gone and lord knows I ain't want nothing to happen to you, too. Your daddy said to make sure you wore it. So I did what I had to do to get it."

Make a way out of no way. It's our way of life.

I hug her. "It's okay, Ms. Leola. Your secret is safe with us."

Bri is still tapping her foot, silent.

"So you're not mad?" Ms. Leola asks.

How could I be mad? Shocked, sure. But mad, no. "You just did what you thought was best. It's like we have a piece of her—"

"Sorry," Bri cuts in. "Not trying to be rude, but can I see that?"

"The bracelet or . . . ?"

"Both."

I grab the necklace from the box on the table and it's like touching Moms all over again. I'm actually grateful to have this bit of her. "Here you go." I drop it in Bri's palm.

She pulls a gadget from her pocket.

"What in the—?"

"I can't use magic without setting off Patrol, but give me a sec."

"Huh?"

"Just watch." She presses a button on the top of the gadget and it whirs in midair a moment. Then, like a magnet, the device snaps to the stone fused to Bri's wrist. "Ugh." She pulls it free, covers her own wrists with her sleeves. "Press the button again for me. It's sensing my stones."

I press and it fans over my wrists, like a crab floating in midair with a suction cup under the bottom. I brace for impact as it brushes past my onyx stones. Nothing happens.

"It only clings to magic," Bri whispers. Of course. And my magic is dead as a doornail. The gadget hovers, scanning past other surfaces. I dangle the necklace near its sensor and like a vacuum attacking a Lego, it clamps to the necklace and won't let go.

She snatches the sensor and reads the numbers flashing on the top. "Just as I thought."

"And that means . . . ?"

"This is from Ghizon, Rue. And that"—she shows me the numbers on top of the device: 356103—"is the code for a cloaking protection spell. Rue, this necklace makes whoever is wearing it invisible to . . ."

"To anyone in Ghizon," I say.

The weight of both my worlds comes crashing down at once. The epiphany fumbles from my lips before I even fully understand the words. "This necklace kept her off the radar all these years. Kept her invisible to them—all of them. Including . . ."

Ms. Leola's hand warms my back.

". . . Aasim," I say, under my breath.

The world's spinning and I plop in the nearest chair. He gave her this, put it on her to keep her safe, knowing he'd never be able to even find her again? Th-that's not quite the asshole picture of him I'd had.

The thoughts roll around in my head, slamming into and cracking walls I'd erected.

He wanted to protect her. And me.

Still, all those years of struggling with Moms working trying to make ends meet. How much more good could he have done if he'd stayed here? Protected us *here*? Leaving . . . I'll never forgive him for that. There had to be another way.

And if there wasn't, he should've made one.

"What about that?" Tasha points at the cuff, resting inside one of two impressions the box.

"Was there another one?" I ask. The velvet is soft, dotted with a few specks of dust. "Looks like there's space for two here."

"I don't know nothing about the bracelet, baby. That was already in your mom's things. It looked expensive so I put the necklace with it to keep both of 'em safe."

"Definitely Ghizoni metal, I'd bet." Bri grabs the cuffs edge. "Ahhhh!" It *thunks* to the carpet and she sucks the tip of her finger. "It burned me!"

Burned you? I squat, studying the bracelet. "It doesn't look hot."

"Well it is."

"Let me get some ice on that, honey." Ms. Leola scoots into the kitchen with Bri on her heels.

I press a fingertip to the edge of the golden metal and remove it quickly. Definitely warm to the touch. I scoop it up and its warmth coats my hands like I dipped them in chocolate—warm, but in a homey sort of way.

Its heat travels through my wrists and strange voices swirl in my ear.

Huh? I strain to hear as the heat creeps farther up my arm.

What's happening?

I grip the metal tighter.

Louder now, the voices speak a tangle of sounds I can't make out.

Everything's still, so still, as I sit there listening, my heart in my throat.

The doorbell startles me, and the cuff hits the floor.

"Get that, would you?" Ms. Leola shouts from the kitchen. "Probably them boys from 'round the corner coming to help with some housework."

I can't take my eyes off the cuff. What *was* that?

Tasha moves toward the door and I scoop up the cuff, zipping it up in my hoodie pocket. The door swings open and my stomach drops. Standing there in Ms. Leola's doorway, in ripped jeans and a white tee, covered in tats with a blingy smile that makes my knees weak, is my first boyfriend, the first lips I ever kissed and only boy I ever loved. . . .

Julius.

CHAPTER 15

H E STEPS INSIDE AND all the air in the room leaves. *What's wrong with me? I'm over him.*

Tasha gives me a look. *The* look. "I'ma get back to looking for that book." She tiptoes off, mouthing the words "He is fiiiinnneeeee" as she heads back to dig for the scrapbook.

"Rue?" He steps inside and licks his lips.

"Julius? Demarcus? That you, baby?" Ms. Leola returns from the kitchen with Bri on her heels, holding an ice pack on her hand.

"Yes, ma'am. Just me today. Demarcus couldn't make it." The bass in his voice does something to my insides and I suck in a deep breath.

"Ain't seen you in a minute, girl." He smiles and dimples split his cheeks in that perfect way that always made me melt. "How you been?"

"I-I'm good." A lie. "Just back for a visit. See my sister, the old crew."

"There's a plate." Ms. Leola stacks a few Styrofoam containers next to a plate piled with food with a wedge of pound cake twice the size of the one I had. "And be sure you take that back to yo momma 'nem. There's a plate for Demarcus, too."

"Thank you, Ms. Thomas. And yes, ma'am." He plants a kiss on her cheek before settling at the table. Ms. Leola leaves us to catch up, and I guess even Bri senses the tension because she joins Tasha in the back to look for the scrapbook.

"I thought you came to work?" I joke.

"You know she ain't gonna let me do nothing before making sure I eat."

"True." I laugh, trying to look at something besides his umber eyes. I don't know what I expected him to be like after a year, but it's like a lifetime has passed. Staring at him now, the drama and how everything ended is a faint memory. Funny how time does that— makes some things feel smaller than they used to. We shared a lot of good times, even though he was acting dumb at the end.

"You looking good, as usual." He flashes a gold smile and shifts his posture, his shirt clinging to the rounded muscles rippling beneath. "What you been up to?"

"Just hanging tight, handling business. You know." That's code for *I can't tell you* or *I don't wanna tell you, or both.*

"That's wassup. You been aight since everything went down? I been thinking 'bout you. Came by here a few times, hoping to catch you. I didn't know where you went. No one on the block did. Shit, had me thinking the worst, you know?"

"I'm managing." I pull my hoodie tighter over my shoulders, trying to ignore my burning cheeks. So much history with him. So many feelings. He was my person—the person I went to.

"You always been tough as nails, girl." He playfully shoves my shoulder and his touch, even through my hoodie, sends a jolt through me.

I loved him. Like, really loved him.

"Like a diamond," I say. "So, what's good with you?"

"Been working a lot. Got this gig at the car parts store I been holding down, then helping Ms. Leola around here. Graduating in a few weeks, too."

I don't know what I thought he'd be doing, but this ain't it. "So you ain't kicking it at Dezignz no more?"

"*Nahh*, done with that whole crew. Not trying to get caught up. Ain't 'bout that life anymore. Trying to own mine, not let these streets own me. Plus, my moms got a good job downtown so we ain't hurting for the cash like we was."

I'm smiling. "Proud of you."

He nudges me with his shoulder. I shift, careful to keep his skin away from mine.

"Proud of me too."

Our eyes lock and time zaps backward. I'm in high school again and it's just me and him. I feel funny all over and I scoot my seat backward. When did our faces get so close?

"The fam, good?" I ask. His little brother was like a brother to me. Smart like him too. High cheekbones sit beneath his deep-set eyes and his teeth glisten when he smiles.

"Yeah, we good, everybody's good." He tries to tuck a strand behind my ear, but I pull my skin away as I breathe in his scent. Notes of vanilla and cedar make gooseprickles dance on my skin.

"It's really good to see you," he says.

I pretend not to notice the way his tongue runs across those plump lips I used to kiss. "Good to see you, too."

"Am I interrupting?" It's Tasha with a giant heart-covered book cradled in her arms and a kitty circling her feet.

Oh god, could she have worse timing?

He looks at me and the book and grins, huge. "Wait, wait, wait." His chest muscles clench as he chuckles. "Is that what I think it is?"

Tasha sets the book between us and I am mortified. She flips open the page, past pictures and tests and movie ticket stubs, and I am *dying* inside. He's getting a kick out of this, grinning and looking at me like I been sitting here this whole time pouring over our relationship, reminiscing.

"This is *not* what it looks like, I swear."

"Aye, yo. It's cool. You ain't gotta front. I missed you, too." He laughs into his fist, trying to slow down the page turns. "Remember this?" He points to a frayed red ribbon from our first Valentine's Day. He allegedly brought me these "pretty flowers" and wrapped them up in this ribbon. Even tried to tie a bow. Well, windy-ass Houston. By the time he made it to my door, all that was left was the ribbon and a few stems. We laughed to tears and he never lived that one down.

"OMG, *staahhhhp*." I swear if I was white my cheeks would be beet red. "Tasha, what did you find? Anything useful?"

"No, that's what I was gonna say. There's plenty of pictures of his tattoos in here."

He looks between us, confused.

"But there's no artist names, like you thought."

I swear, common sense ain't common. "Girl, take them out." I reach inside the plastic cover and pull out a picture of a tribal tattoo he got done on his biceps. "Turn them around." I flip over the picture and, sure enough, scribbled there is the tattoo artist's name. "See!"

"No, but foreal, what are you doing?" Julius asks.

Do I tell him? Or rather, how much do I tell him?

I tug my sleeves down for good measure. "So, I saw a tattoo on these two dudes getting away with some foul shit. I think it's weird they have the same exact tattoo in the same spot, so I wanted to find out who did them. It's super detailed, looks real top-notch, so I figured your old pieces could point me in the direction of an artist's name."

"Show me the ink."

Tasha hands him her phone with a picture of bus stop guy, and Julius squints. He stretches his fingers, swipes a few times, and leans in again. "You're sure this is the tattoo?"

"Yeah."

"How sure?" He looks at me and everything that's warm in his eyes grows cold.

I sit up straight. "*Very* sure."

"That's Litto's crew, Rue."

"Who?"

He snatches up Ms. Leola's TV remote from a side table and turns on the TV. "Litto's crew." His deadpan tone sends a ripple of fear through me. He flips to a news channel. Headlines run across the screen.

Another arrest in the recent shooting of . . .

Double homicides in the neighborhood of East Row in broad daylight have detectives . . .

He flips to a different news station.

The mayor is recommending an early curfew . . .

Gang violence this last year is double that of the last ten years . . .

He flips again.

More murder.

And again.

More violence. More crime.

One thread in common—the victims are all young and Black or brown-skinned.

"I don't understand," I say.

"Rue, Litto's crew *owns* the city, all the drugs. He dominates the cartels feeding this side of the Row. No one's packing heat or pushing weight without their say-so."

I can't breathe.

"I don't know why you're looking into them"—the fear in his eyes cuts like a blade—"but stop, *please,* unless you got a death wish."

CHAPTER 16

"NO, RUE!" TASHA'S VOICE is strained.

"Yes." I slip the protection necklace over Tasha's neck and fasten it. "This will keep you invisible and safe from the Chancellor and his General while I go figure out what Litto's crew wants with you."

Julius is pacing the room back and forth, hands running through his low top. He stops and looks at us, confused. If I told him about Ghizon, would he even believe me? Without seeing it, it's unbelievable.

Tasha grabs my wrist. "You can't just go off looking for these gang people or whoever they are." Her lip quivers in that way I know if it doesn't stop, tears will soon follow. "What if . . . what if something happens? Y-you promised you'd always be here."

I'm a ball of confusion, somewhere between agreeing with T and the urge to do what I know I gotta do. Was this what it was like when Aasim said goodbye to Moms? I pick at a rogue thread on my shirt harder than I mean to and a hole appears. He never came back. Not that I even wanted him to, but I can't, under any circumstance, do that to T.

But what choice do I have? Running from folks on the street catches up with you. If Litto's dudes are after T, I need to know why.

And from there we can figure out what to do. At least for now, the Chancellor's off her tail.

"T, I *have* to do something. We can't just sit here and live our lives running from everybody. What kind of life is that?"

"At least it's *life*."

I press my forehead to hers. "I'm going to be alright."

That's what you tell your little sister when she's scared, even if you're not sure it's true. When you stepping in to protect them because ain't nobody else around going to do it.

Julius stops pacing. "I agree with fam on this one, Rue. You can't do this."

It's almost cute that he cares, but he doesn't understand who he's dealing with. What I could do if my magic would answer. I reach beneath my sleeve and thumb the onyx fused to my wrist.

"I agree." Bri folds her arms. "It's too risky. And with—"

I cut her a look and she snaps her mouth shut. I know what she's thinking. Without magic, what am I going to do? And truth is, I don't know.

But not knowing how to fix something isn't an excuse not to try.

Can't they see, if *we* don't do something, who will?

"I—just," Bri stutters, tapping her foot like she's had twelve cups of caffeine. She does that when she's really worked up. "The odds don't look good, is all I was going to say."

"We don't even know what these people want," Tasha says.

"They want you dead," Julius adds. "And they wouldn't flinch at snatching Rue's ass too."

"But *whyyy?*" Hearing my sister's voice crack wedges a knot deep in my chest.

"Look, I appreciate the concern," I interrupt. "I feel what you're saying and I'm not stupid. I'm not trying to walk up in there and demand answers, but I *can* check out the spot they hang at. Try to figure out what the hell they're after, *why* they're looking for my sister and me, specifically. Pick up some intel."

Bri sighs, foot tapping a million miles a minute. "Is there a Patrol here? Or someone you can talk to and tell them what's going on?"

Julius laughs under his breath.

I get it. She's trying to help. Bri looks between us and the pained expression she wears says everything her words do not: If she stays with me in case I need magic, and ends up using it, Patrol will be here in a heartbeat and have all our asses hemmed up. If I go find these people on my own and end up in danger, I won't be able to protect myself.

Patrol *cannot* find out our location. So her using magic, even if it's dire, is *out!* Then all this would be for nothing. She needs to get back to Ghizon and do what we agreed on. That's best-case scenario at this point.

"I'm *just* going to collect info. I'll be fine. And you should get going, Bri. See about that thing we talked about." I flash her an expression I hope isn't too obvious. Before the commotion started about me going to scope out Litto's crew, I had pulled her aside. She'd said before she came to Ms. Leola's that she looked me up in the Ghizon mainframe and there it was, plain as day: *Rue Jelani Akintola . . . deceased.*

"The listing is really clever because it automatically deactivates your onyx, like powering down your magic. There were lots of cases of corpse robbing decades ago, so they added in that coding."

"So that's it?" I had gestured to my wrist. "My magic is dead? This is basically some kind of weird wrist jewelry at this point?"

"Pretty much."

Not the answer I had hoped for.

The best thing she could try to do, she'd said, was hack the mainframe and change the listing to *alive*. "There has to be an incidental procedure in case some dude spills Juva Juice on a key map or enters it in wrong. Me trying to hack the system is probably our best bet."

I'd agreed.

But now she's looking at me crazy, like I was just gonna sit back here and play hopscotch while she's gone.

"But . . . ," she says.

"There are no buts." I face her. "That's not how things work, Bri. Not here." No one's coming to fix this for us.

"Rue, I know odds and these aren't good. I'm telling you . . ."

She knows everything, I swear. But life here ain't like it is back there. Can't she see that?

"Get going, Bri, please. We talked about this."

"I mean, if the cops had a handle on Litto's crew," Julius chimes in, "they wouldn't be all over the damn news. I'm not saying do this, Rue. But I get it. If you go, I'm going too."

Ride or die. Universal code 'round here.

"Then it's settled," I say, meeting Bri's eyes. She nods, barely.

Tasha weeps into her hands. Cupcake purrs, pushing up against her ankles. I scoop him up, holding in the urge to vomit, and place him in her arms. I kiss her forehead and hold it there, savoring the moment, in case it's the last one I ever give her.

Bri's right. This is risky. But so is doing nothing.

"Moms raised a diamond," Tasha says sticking out her pinky. She doesn't like it, but she knows this is for her, for us. I twist mine around hers and a single tear threatens to fall.

I let it. "And diamonds don't crack."

CHAPTER 17

THE CUFF IS WEIGHTY in my hands, like it's made of solid gold. Its warmth is entrancing. Muffled whispers swim in my ear every time I touch it, no clearer than before. Julius clicks his seat belt as his car rumbles into motion. He can't hear them. Bri couldn't hear them. No one could.

No one but me.

The warmth creeps into my chest and I feel light, like I'm floating. It crawls around inside me in a wave of motion, swelling in my rib cage, swishing from side to side. Like it's searching for something in my very bones.

"You listening?" Julius's voice slips through the haze of thoughts and I stick the cuff in my pocket.

"Yeah, sorry." I angle the vents, AC blasting a different way. "What you say?"

"I was asking if you heard about Kid and his folks?"

Kid was this little boy who used to live across the complex. His momma is a known crack head, his daddy too. They would just disappear for days sometimes. Their house didn't have running water, I guess, because at night you'd find him filling up water jugs from Moms's spigot. She knew he was doing it. The whole block did. But nobody ever said nothing. Moms would say kids that are hurting don't need judgment, they need lots of love and kindness.

Kid would come by during the day sometimes, offering to help do some chores around the house. Ms. Leola always gave him a task and put a little change in his pocket and food in his hand. Ms. Aretha on the back side of the Row always made sure he had fresh clothes when school started. Kid didn't have parents around all the time that he could rely on, but he had the block and we take care of our own.

"Nah. Haven't had my ear to the street in a while."

"Somebody called the people. CPS picked him up."

"*Damn.* Foreal?" I mean, that's good for him I guess, but I don't know how to feel. "I just hope he's with people that's gon' do right by him."

"What you mean?"

"Just that all that glitters ain't gold. Being snatched up from home ain't guaranteed sunshine and rainbows."

"Kid gon' be aight," he says, shifting the car. "He's bred from 'round here."

Diamonds. "You right."

We zoom past several more complexes and down past the older houses in the neighborhood; every other block there's one boarded up with overgrown grass. Litto runs his stuff through Dezignz, according to Julius, so that's where we are going. We pass Ole Jesse pushing his grocery cart of soda cans. He walks back and forth across these streets all day and I'm pretty sure he sleeps in one of those abandoned houses. Three or four clear trash bags spill over the cart's edge as he rolls down the side of the street. I'd tell him to get on the sidewalk, but there isn't one. His cart's real full; he must be about to turn them in, put some change in his pocket. He tilts his chin as we roll past, saying *what's up*. We say *what's up* back.

People spill out of LuLu's Corner Store up ahead as we roll up to a red light and stop.

"So, tell me about Litto, everything you know," I say. The crowd piles into an unmarked SUV with windows so tinted it looks painted black.

"What's there to say? His boys are everywhere."

"What do you know about Litto himself?"

"To be honest, nothing. Just heard the name. When I was *working* at Dezignz . . ."

"Uh-huh." I smirk and he does too.

"When that was my spot, I never saw him. But the guy who owns the shop made it seem like he worked directly under him. Rue, I gotta say this, even though I know your stubborn ass ain't gon' listen."

"I'm listening."

"You a badass, and I know you aren't going to let anybody come for you or your family, but this is out of your league. Trust me on that." He cares, still. It's sweet.

"How you know I don't have some tricks up my sleeve?" *Literally.*

"Unless you hiding some Feds special ops type shit under your sleeve, you out of your league."

We laugh. A gust of wind from his cracked window flutters the du-rag hanging down his neck.

"I'm just getting information. I know how to lay low. You act like these streets ain't raise me too. I'm not stupid."

"I know."

"Aight then."

Silence hangs in the air for several moments as we zip past more older houses, and they get newer and nicer the farther we go. Every few blocks is a cluster of brick two-story houses with columns and half-circle drives. Something about the outside of the houses looks old but the insides are brand new—not just the walls and floors, but the people too. We roll past the gentrified area. Dezignz is on the edge of the East Side and a solid half hour away if we catch the lights right.

Cop sirens blare in the background and my hands dig into the door handle. The cop car speeds past and I exhale. The streets are full of people walking to and from the bus stop. But something's different. There's more people than I remember, standing around loitering. Every bus stop bench is piled with people rolled up in blankets sleeping.

"I don't remember it being quite like this," I say. "Was it always so many people?"

"The crew's stepped up the game on this side. You got people losing houses trying to make money any way they can, and trouble is as easy to find as a gas station 'round here. Litto keeps what he calls stations on damn near every corner."

"Stations?"

"Yeah, there's one." He points at a white woman standing outside a weave shop tapping her phone.

"She's white."

"Yep. Cops ain't bothering her."

"What's a station? What does she do?"

"What you think she do, Rue?" He laughs at me.

"She look like some fancy developer type, just sitting there on the phone."

"Nah, the stations serve the area over here. They're eyes and ears. Suppliers."

The light turns green and we jerk into motion, but I can't take my eyes off the lady. I crane my neck over my shoulder to see if she has a tattoo.

She meets my eyes and my stomach flutters. She doesn't look away. No expression. Just eyes, on me. Like she knows I'm staring, like she sees through me. We roll past and she grows smaller in the distance.

"I didn't see a tat on her neck," I say.

"And you wouldn't. She ain't busting in doors, shooting up folks. She's the silencer on the gun, the enemy you don't hear or see."

"So the snake tattoo?" I ask.

"I heard only Litto's dawgs get that. His inner circle, most trusted crew. You not gon' see them standing on corners. Shit, you not gon' see them at all."

But I have seen them.

Twice.

I try to swallow the lump in my throat, but it won't go down.

Julius plants his hands at ten and two, his sleeve of tats flashing. Colorful feathers from the tail of a phoenix wrap around his forearm. His grandma's face and name stare from his shoulder, with the year she died underneath. "Since I'm clearly not going to be able to talk you out of this, it's my turn to ask a question."

I chuckle. "Sure, what you wanna know?"

"I missed a lot of the shit y'all were talking about back at the house."
Uh-oh.

"What was the necklace about? And, like, where the hell you been? Something happen?"

Sigh.

"You know I got you. I'm just trying to figure out what's up with you? The truth."

I shift in my seat. What do I say? How much? Does him knowing put him in danger too? The questions got my head spinning.

"Rue?"

"Someone's after my sister—someone besides Litto." That's pretty much the whole truth.

"Who? Why?"

The General's pallid face and thin lips swirl in my memory. "Nobody you would know," I say.

"Uhm, okay. That ain't a real answer though. Do you know why? What they want?"

The General's stern complexion and dead slate eyes are frozen in my mind. The scar under his eye moved when he spoke. *Get me that name, recruit.*

"I felt cold all over when he looked at me."

"When *who* looked at you? Rue, you not making no sense."

Did I say that out loud? "Just this guy. He's the boss's right hand at this place I used to work and I broke the rules. So the boss told him I had to be . . ."

Get her ready for Unbinding. His words play on repeat in my head. *Recruit, get me that name.* Luke scrambling to slip me my watch back. *That name.* Tasha's name. *They're to be killed.*

Words slip from my lips in barely a whisper. "He was practically smiling when he told me my punishment."

"What punishment? Like he fired you?"

Julius's words fade and bile hovers at the back of my throat. *She has the necklace. It's okay. He won't find her.* My knee's bouncing as thoughts of the General's threats and the Chancellor's cold stare wrap around my throat . . .

They're to be killed.

Tighter.

Chancellor's orders.

Tighter still.

I gasp, fanning myself for air. "A-air. I need . . ."

"Rue!" The car jerks to a halt and I roll my window down. Humid air washes over me. *Inhale.* Tasha is safe. I'm still public enemy number one, but at least my sister is safe. *Exhale.*

"You okay?"

"I'm okay." I would touch his hand, reassure him, but touching is out of the question. Dezignz, written in swirly silver letters against a slate charcoal wall, sits outside my window.

"Well, we're here. Figured I'd just drive us around this area, scope out things. If we . . ."

Oh, he clearly doesn't understand how this is going down. "I appreciate you. I really do. But I gotta do this on my own." I click the door handle open. "Thanks for the ride. I can catch the bus back."

"Rue!" He's all shock and stutters as he unbuckles. "I'm not leaving you here!"

"Fine, stay in the car. If you hear anything, call the police and get out of here. *Period.*"

"If I hear anything, I'm coming inside. *Period.*" He folds his arms. He isn't going to back down, so I don't even try.

"What's your plan?"

"Sneak in, snag some intel, and get out. Making sure no one I love gets killed." I step out and the entrance to Dezignz tattoo shop—Litto territory—hangs above me.

Julius shouts at my back. "I hope that plan includes *you!*"

Me too.

I slip past the entrance and down the side alley of Dezignz. Two side doors and a lot of shiny cars hide back here. I check the first door with a gentle pull. Locked. The second door opens.

I listen through the crack. Nothing. Pulling it open wider, cool air brushes against my face. The dark room is a storage closet, by the looks of it. Rows of racks line the walls. In the center, pallet wood crates are stacked with packages covered with plastic wrap. Drugs.

Still no sound or sight of anyone as I slip inside. The strip of outside light shrinks and disappears. The storage closet is bigger than I thought, and dark. More like a small warehouse. A ceiling towers overhead and the hum of an air conditioner muffles my steps. A beacon of red flickering overhead reads EXIT. There's another exit sign in the corner to my far right. And another door without an exit sign on my far left. That one must lead to the inside of the shop.

I get closer, pressing against the wood door. Its knob is warm. Someone was just here. I listen.

Arguing voices.

Something's wrong.

Footsteps. Lots of footsteps.

There's several of them.

A door closes and the muffled shouts continue, escalating, when something metal bangs into the wall. In the hallway I catch a glimpse of the front entrance waiting area. Black walls dotted with glow-in-the-dark everything make it look like the middle of the night. Cameras peek at me from either corner behind the desk and I jump backward.

Shit. I pull my hood tighter over my head.

I slip past the entry to the shop and move closer to the door where the voices are coming from. The closer I get, the harder my heart thumps. Men's voices shout back and forth so loud I expect the door to rattle. I press my ear to it.

If they open this door, I'm dead.

"What you mean he *didn't* show?"

"The hell you think I mean? Blow didn't show his face."

Blow? Is that someone's name?

"So when D says do a thing, Blow thinks that shit's optional?"

"I guess so. You know how niggas act when they get a little cash flow."

Ah, so Blow is like an errand boy? But who is D?

"I told you 'bout trusting these boys. Keep yo shit tight. You the boss, D."

Boss? Shit.

D is Litto.

I-I didn't expect Litto himself to be here.

"How we moving to the West Side and you got Blow getting sloppy with shit over here? That ain't gon' work."

The guy at the coffee shop? Could that be Blow? Or the guy at the bus stop? I need to get a look at faces.

"Litto?"

Silence.

An eerily familiar voice splits the air and my blood runs cold. "Where's Blow now?"

Sweat soaks the back of my neck. *I know that voice.*

"He ain't answering."

Silence.

Metal clicks. The sound of the gun takes me back to Moms's closet. *Breathe.*

"Get his people here," Litto says, his voice so familiar I have chills. "Then he'll come."

His people? Like his family. That voice. Where do I know that voice from?

"What else?" asks Litto. "How are the numbers?"

"Aside from Blow's bullshit, it's looking good. Got the Laws where we need 'em. The new commissioner owes me a favor."

"And the schools?" Litto asks.

"We got hands and feet in most. Working on some of the others. That prep school is hard as shit to get into. Kids there act like they too good to fuck with strangers."

Hands and feet? Drug pushing?

"I'm not as concerned about the prep school. It's the ones along East Row that you need to focus on."

"Oh, we got those on lock. Pushing at least a key through the Jameson High every month."

Whoa. Drugs ain't new around here, but targeting a high school?

My high school?

What.

The.

Fuck!

"Good, very good," Litto says.

"One kid, though. He ain't cooperating. Brought him in today to level with his ass."

"Explain." A chair swivels then squeaks like someone's stood up.

"I give 'em the choice, like I always do—make money or spend it. This little nigga don't want neither."

"Sounds like he's made his choice," Litto says. "You know what to do. Get it handled, now."

Handled? As in? I gasp, stumbling away from the door, and throw myself into a hall closet.

They're going to kill a kid because he doesn't want to sell drugs or do them? What the fuck? *Out of your league.* Julius's warning plays on repeat in my head.

The door to their meeting room opens and through the crack of the closet door I can see a sliver of their faces as they exit the room. I crane for a better glimpse of the men talking. The first one out is pale-faced with a long ponytail and a Glock in his hand. I'd know his face anywhere—the man from the coffee shop.

I can't move.

Behind him two more dudes come out the room, both with loose-fitting shirts and big-ass snake tattoos on their necks. I don't recognize one, but the other is definitely Chad, the community center guy who "picked up" Tasha from her bus stop.

I'd lay their asses out right now if I could.

"Litto, you want to talk to this kid?" The last guy turns back to the meeting room, a gun the size of his arm clutched in his grip.

"I'll take a look, but you just handle it. I should be getting back." Litto steps out and I can see him—like, fully see him.

Thin lips, grayish pale skin, and a scar below his right eye.

My blood turns to ice.

Litto is the General—General Deo from Ghizon.

CHAPTER 18

Y SHAKY FINGERS FIND my wristwatch. The pitch-black closet glows blue. I can hardly type, my mind and heart racing each other.

Me: Bri!!!!! I need my onyx to work!!!! NOW!

Ghizoni don't come here. Period, at all. It's forbidden.

Footsteps pass the closet and I suck in a breath. *Don't move. Don't even breathe.* The General and his crew exit the hallway and I ease out of the closet, on their heels.

They're going to kill somebody. Some kid!

My watch vibrates.

Bri: Are you okay??? I'm still trying!!

Me: It's the General.

How does he get away with this? His disgusting condescending smile haunts me. *Chancellor's orders*, he'd said. Could Aasim know?

Bri: What?? What's the general?

Me: General Deo is HERE with the guys with the snake tattoo! I saw him! I need my magic Bri, now!!

I slip around the corner and they are heading back toward the warehouse I came out of. He's here. They said the kid is here. I can't just leave him. *Shit!* I look around for anything—a gun, knife, some-thing.

Nothing.

Shit. Shit. Shit.

The warehouse door closes and my foot nudges a pipe. Not my first choice, but it's something. The rusted metal scratches my palm as I tighten my grip.

Bri: GENERAL DEO?! RUE, GET OUT OF THERE NOW!!

She doesn't understand.

This is a ride or die moment. I can't.

I push open the warehouse door and slip inside. This time the lights are on and shouts bounce off the walls. I duck behind a tower of pallet wood crates for a better view. There's three of them and a boy who looks about my age sitting tied to a chair. His mouth's gagged and blood drips from his brow down onto his mahogany skin. I recognize him from Homecoming Court. It's Brian, quarter-back at Jameson High.

My heart ticks faster and I thumb the cold onyx fused to my wrist. *Come on, Bri.*

I turn the metal in my clammy hands. Maybe if I can clock one from behind, then I can snatch his gun and drag me and Brian out of here. Maybe.

Bri: RUE???

Me: I can't leave. Activate my stones.

Bri: TRYING!!!

"Answer me, Brian!" The commotion grows louder and I swallow a gasp. It *is* Brian. I didn't know him really well, but he was popular, from East Row. That makes him fam.

"Say something," the taller of two pops him upside the head with the butt of the gun. The General watches, unmoved.

Brian lifts his head and blood glazes his busted lip. "I . . . I told you. I don't fool with that stuff."

The General gets close to him. "And what would you have us do?" His voice is eerily soft. "You've seen our faces, know our spot, you even know how we run our routes."

"I didn't ask for none of that, man."

"You acted cool," the guy from the coffee shop chimes in. "Like you were looking for work. So Litto"—he gestures at the General—"being the generous man he is, had us show you the ropes."

This isn't right. Brian was set to be valedictorian, and sickly talented on the football field. He didn't screw with drugs. His auntie woulda whooped his ass up and down Homecoming in front of everyone. Literally.

"*Nahhh*, not like that," Brian says through swollen lips. "I was just trying to get a job. I like the ink y'all do. That's it! P-please l-let m-me g-go. I ain't no snitch, I swear I won't say nothing."

"What do you think *we* think when we see a nigger come in here?" Deo asks.

I dig my nails into the lead in my hand, rage bubbling beneath my skin. I'm going to bash his face in.

"You've seen everything. What would you have us do with you, Brian?"

No. No, no, no!

Brian's eyes grow wide. He knows. He knows they're going to kill him.

My magic. Everything in me digs for that familiar warmth,

clinging to the hope that maybe it'll work. I chew my bottom lip and concentrate. There's a warmth inside me, an energy I can't grasp. I strain harder.

I reach. It shifts.

I grasp. It wiggles away.

My magic is there. But it's not.

"Get up," the man shoves Brian. "Go out like a man." They unloose his ties and one dude grabs the metal chair Brian was sitting in. The General sighs, picking dirt from his nails.

This is a game to them. I'm going to be sick.

My watch vibrates and I creep closer. *How do I make a way?* If I step out there, they'll kill me. Then Tasha? And what about the rest of East Row?

Brian holds up his fists, unsteady on his feet as the guys circle. The shorter guy swings the metal chair and Brian tries to dodge. But he's woozy. It slams across his head with a rattling clang and blood spews from his mouth, splattering the ground.

No! My hands are soaked with tears. *Brian. His name is Brian.* I say it over and over again, letting his face burn in my mind.

I sneak a few steps closer, still not close enough to swing and hit.

Another blow flies. Brian buckles over, hands slapping the concrete. The General's shoulders rise and fall in a sigh as the men kick him.

I hate him. I'm going to pluck his eyes out of his skull.

Brian hunches over tucking his head, boots slamming into his ribs.

"Brian," I whisper, clawing at my scalp.

"You think you one of them smart boys? Too good or some shit?" The coffee shop dude points the gun at him.

"Nah. I-I just I don't wanna sell that shit. It's not for me!" Brian weeps, hugging his knees, and they mutter something I can't make out. I ease past a tower of discarded crates to get even closer and my shoes squeak. *Shit!*

The General looks in my direction. I press against the stack and freeze.

Easy, Rue.

What can I do? What can I really do? I peek. Everything that comes to mind seems equally stupid. The one from the coffee shop fires a pop in the air and slams his foot down again, this time on Brian's head.

Brian. His name is Brian.

He shudders on the ground and the lump in my throat grows.

He was seventeen and in a band.

And again, Gun Holder's sneakers skid the slick red ground. More punches. Brian moves less. I slide down to the floor and hug my knees.

He had a full scholarship to that H.B.C.U. in D.C. I remember people talking about it.

"This is a waste of my time. Finish this," the General says, before muttering the transport spell and dissolving on the spot like a ghost.

Then the gunshot comes. *Pop.*

I cry harder and louder as more shots pop in my ears. I rake my fingers through my hair. I want to run out and stop them. I glare at my broken wrists and bite back a scream.

He was in the National Honor Society, going to walk across the stage in a few months.

Vomit hovers at the back of my throat.

Brian's feet don't twitch. His hands don't move. Tears slop over my fingers and I try to stop them, but they just come harder. More shots split the air.

"Stop," I whisper, rocking back and forth. "Just stop, please."

A car alarm wails outside and someone's knocking at the shop entrance. All of a sudden the warehouse is still. Someone's coming. They look at one another and I duck down as they rush past. The warehouse door creaks shut and I let out the scream I've been holding in.

Brian lies there, swimming in a growing pool of blood. I hurry over to him and throw myself down at his side. Blood, there's so much blood. A flash of Moms's stoop haunts me a second before I blink it away. He's bleeding out, dying alone with no one but me to weep for him. I press the cotton of his hoodie to my face.

Brian. His name is Brian.

His chest is soaked from my salty tears. My phone. I fumble it from my pocket, looking around, and punch in nine-one-one.

"Jus—just hold on." Tears gush from my eyes. I don't know if he can hear my words, but I say them anyway. I take his hands in mine. "Someone, please please hurry please!" The cry scorches my throat.

"Ma'am I need your address." The emergency responder's voice blasts in my ear.

My mind's fuzzy, but I manage to tell them where we're at. Sirens sound far off and I shake Brian's shoulders, my nose a congested mess of sniffles. "A little longer." I shake harder. *Please, don't go.* "Just hang on a minute longer."

His skin grows colder with his every breath. Until, his eyes still. I hunch over him, ear pressed to his chest.

Nothing.

I grab his sleeves and tug, willing him to move, desperate for some sign of life. His mouth hangs sideways.

It's too late.

He's gone.

"Ahhhh!" I cry until my chest aches and my throat burns. Everything's blurred and foggy. He can't be gone. Just a little more time is all he needs. He can't—I pound my fists on his chest. I was here, right here, and couldn't do shit but watch them hurt him.

Sirens whoop so loud I expect to hear people come in any moment. Brian still stares up, so I brush his eyelids closed.

I have to go.

The paramedics should be almost here.

Brian. His name is Brian.

I fire off a text to Tash without details, telling her to stay put, then, swipe up on my watch and my missed messages from Bri pop up.

Bri: Rue??? You ok??? Hello??? I can't hack it!!!! Rue??? I'm so scared!! Rue???

Me: Ready my watch signal with a cloaking spell. I'm coming back to Ghizon.

Bri: OMG I was so worried. Okay! Ready in 5 . . .

I've already called nine-one-one. Avenging Brian, protecting us—all of us—is the best I can do now.

Bri: 4 . . .

I need my magic back. Whatever it takes.

Bri: 3 . . .

I grit my teeth, anger dancing with my sadness.

Bri: 2 . . .

There *is* one Ghizoni who might be willing to help.

Bri: 1 . . .

My father, Aasim.

CHAPTER 19

Four Months Ago

THE FOOD IN GHIZON is probably the most tolerable part. It doesn't taste too bad. It needs some seasoning, and by that I don't mean salt and pepper. That's a given. It's what you add after that, Ms. Leola would say, that gives it flavor.

Aasim sits across from me in the kostarum, which is basically like a cafeteria ("food room" is the literal translation, I think) for all Bound students in training. Most give my table a wide berth, but it doesn't faze me at this point.

I scoop the leez, a creamy puréed-looking substance, and take a bite, intent on not looking straight ahead. It's savory-sweet on my tongue, like garlic when it's been roasted awhile. These weekly lunches were not my idea. They were his. Avoiding him is easy enough on a regular day, between dorm, class, eating, and hanging with Bri (and Luke, the latest development in our posse, a.k.a Bri's new boyfriend).

But here, when he's sitting across from me, it's *the* most annoying part of my week. Bri sits a few tables over hugged up with Luke. I told her to come get me in ten. Act like it was some urgent study thing. She winks at me, Luke's arm snaked around her neck.

I don't even understand them. How you just met but you in love?

Bri ain't even social like that. But Luke came checking for her, showering her with attention, and of course she didn't know how to act. So now I guess we're a posse of three.

"How were classes?" Aasim asks and I catch sight of the disappointment in his face.

"Fine." I take another bite of meat, watching food trays whisk through the air to self-sudsing cleaning stations.

"That's it?" He folds his arms, sitting back. "Which class is your favorite?"

I don't understand what he wants from me. He's never once apologized for not being there. Not like I wanted him to. But, just saying, he never even acknowledged it. He acts like this fifteen minutes of face-to-face time each week can make it like he was there. He wasn't.

I chew.

He waits.

I chew some more. (I probably could have swallowed a while ago.)

"History."

"Oh yeah?" He perks up, intrigued. "I liked History too. Found it . . . eye-opening."

I just made that up. I haven't been to my actual History class in months. But I do find the history books at Totsi's Texts interesting. Ms. Totsi's a real nice Zruki lady. She lives a few streets over from Bri actually.

When she wasn't working at the mines, Ms. Totsi apparently developed her magic to be able to transcribe spoken words to text. Like she could just say words and they'd appear written on the page. The Chancellor was impressed, so he took her out the mines and put her in charge of all Ghizon's historical texts.

But, I'm not telling Aasim all that. I pick at a scab on my skin until it hurts. He ain't even come back when Moms needed him most. Mr. Magic's Third in Command, but when yo baby momma have bullets flying at her head where was your magic then? *Ugh.* Is lunch over yet?

Six minutes left.

"Rue, I know you—"

Say we don't have to do this. Say this is the last instance of this torture.

"I know this isn't your favorite thing. But I wanna get to know you. You're my . . ."

Don't say it.

". . . daughter."

I dig my nails into the underside of the table.

"I don't even know, like . . . what kind of music do you like? Trap? R&V?"

He knows about that? We usually just sit here talking about my classes or some stupid Ghizon thing. "It's R&B and y-you've never asked that. . . ." Or anything about my life before here. About *me.*

"I'm all ears. I want to know."

He won't know any of the artists even if I name them. I have some on my old phone I could let him hear if . . . "You really want to know about music?"

"I do. Your mom was into music. Figured you might be too."

She was. Moms used to have tunes blasting every time she cleaned. Said it calmed her nerves. What was she like with him, I wonder?

I sit up. "I like a lot of types, but mainly I—"

"Aasim," the General joins our tableside, his lips in a permanent scowl like they're glued on his face that way. "The Chancellor wants to see you. Now."

Aasim sighs. He's gotta go, *of course*. It was stupid anyway.

"I really wanna hear this, Rue. But I need to—"

The scar under the General's eye twitches. "You hear me, boy?"

Boy? Oh shit, nah! Aasim doesn't even flinch. I push my tray aside. Not hungry anymore. "I was about to leave anyway."

Aasim says something as I leave but I don't hear it. Across the cafeteria, Bri's tray is pretty much still full. She's too busy keke-ing with Luke. (Or Lateef, I should say. He hates when I call him by his real name. He prefers the western variation he made up.)

"You gon' eat that?" I ask, sticking my finger in her leez before she can respond. Luke snorts and we do a handshake thing I taught him. He's slow on the uptake, but I don't drag him for it.

"Uhh, not anymore," Bri says, pretending to be annoyed.

"How's the watch coming, by the way?"

"It's coming. Haven't had time to work on it in a bit." She blushes and I know what that means.

I muss her hair. "Just don't forget. One year is coming up soon."

"I know, I know. I try to work at night, but *someone* talks in their sleep." She smirks.

Here she go with that again. She says I wake up asking about some little boy. I know the dream she's talking about, but I don't talk in my sleep. "Not true, Bri. I don't even snore."

"You *doooooo*." She turns to Luke. "She does, right?

"Hey, I slept over *one* time. Don't get me in the middle of that. . . ."

"Wrong answer."

"I mean, of course, babe," he says. "Rue, you talk in your sleep."

"This is an attack and I don't appreciate it," I say, a laugh tickling my throat.

"No, but really," Bri says. "I'm tracking the timeline. I got this, trust me. Ride or death. The watch will be ready."

"Die, Bri. Ride or die."

She my girl, that was her point. We do our handshake thing that's three steps more complicated than me and Luke's.

"By the way, what was all that about?" Luke asks, nodding at where the General just was.

"*Ugh*," I say. "I don't see how you work for him."

Luke's been interning with the General, trying to get promoted to Patrol. That would take him out of mine work and get his family a bit bigger unit. Luke has no siblings or anything. He's just not 'bout that soot-covered, long hours, manual labor, mine-worker life.

"Guy's a jerk," he says. "But hey, if it gets me a better gig, I'll do what I have to do."

"I mean, I get what you saying. Hustle mentality for life. But that dude . . . nah. Just, nah."

"What did he do to you?"

"Let's just say I don't like his vocabulary."

CHAPTER 20

THE SCENTS OF GHIZON hit me before the sights do. Iron striking stone clatters as my feet touch the ground. Bri's coordinates put me on Market Street. The street runs through the Commercial District of Ghizon, which is basically their version of an outside shopping mall, and empties into Bri's neighborhood.

Close storefronts stuck together like narrow townhouses line the street ahead, some towering, some in odd topsy-turvy shapes, others short and squat. Like the Central District, large screens hang outside the windows of storefronts; Benevolence, Duty, Fidelity appear and disappear on them.

In, around, and between the stores, crowds hustle from one place to the next, yapping to their friends, carrying bunches of bags. Dwegini. Only they'd have the time (and money) to spend a leisurely day out and about. Zrukis work sun up to sun down.

Careful to keep my head down, I rush past Peekey's, a store in the shape of a giant O, like a donut—or lekerae, as they call it here. You can tell what's inside the store by how the outside is done up. The screen on their shop window flashes images of icing drizzling on knotted pieces of dough, on repeat. Sugary sweetness fills the air as I hurry past, when the screen changes to an image of the

Chancellor waving and smiling. The General is behind him and the wafting cinnamon smell turns to sulfur. I keep moving.

I have to stop him.

"And how do you do today, mais?"

My heart jumps at the voice as the doors to a gadget shop swish open. I exhale. *It's only a spell.* I rush past, ignoring the talking doors trying to lure me back with a two-for-one sale.

"Oh, excuse me," someone says, but I don't look up. I hurry, faster. Not so fast that I look suspicious, but much faster than a normal stroll. The center of the street opens up and I hang a left at Befuddled, an herb shop with elixirs and remedies that's basically a giant tree with floors upon floors of shopping built into its branches. I hop over a protruding root eating into the cobbled street as I spot the entrance to Bri's neighborhood, a dot in the distance. Almost there. Once I pass a few pet stores, a jewelry shop, Muses and Mixes, a spot to buy music and even take lessons, and countless odds and end boutiques, Bri's block is easier to see.

Suddenly, an elder man with a cane stops mid-street and stares at me. I pull my hoodie on tighter and try to get lost in the chattering crowd. It's only then I notice the screens lining the stores up and down Market Street have changed.

Images of the Chancellor's mug have been replaced—with mine. SHIT.

The screens are silent, but words run along the bottom of the screen.

IF SPOTTED, INFORM PATROL IMMEDIATELY.

CONSIDERED DANGEROUS AND UNPREDICTABLE.

REWARD.

I break into a run as more onlookers stare from me to the screen and back to me.

"Get her," someone shouts, but I don't look back. The street is a mosaic of color as I run past. Chilled air burns my throat but the thought of what could happen if I slow down threatens to choke me. I have to get to Bri's. I have to get off this street. But with people watching now, is going to her place even smart? What if they follow me? Assume her family's involved?

A cold hand wraps around my wrist and everything goes black.

The inside of Totsi's Texts is piled with books. Books stacked in corners, books on top of books lining shelves. Towers of books like pillars on either side of the door. I crouch in the shadowed hallway from the alley-access door Ms. Totsi used to bring me inside. The bell chimed the minute she brought me in.

"Wait here, I'll get rid of them," she'd said before sauntering off in that way elderly people do even when it's urgent.

I met Ms. Totsi looking for Bri once and found reading books in her shop was way more interesting than actual History class. She gave me my own reading room and let me stay as long as I wanted. Eventually, I stopped most lessons altogether and just holed up here.

She and the customer walk past looking for some specific text. I press back, deeper into the shadow. Their voices fade and after a few moments, the coins clink, changing hands, and her door chimes. He's gone.

"You can come out now dear," she says. "Straight to the room you usually use."

We tuck inside the corner room in the back of her store and the familiar lumpy maroon couch I usually plop on is almost a comfort.

"I didn't mean to scare you, dear." She presses thin frames to her nose. "People are vultures at the sound of a little change."

"Th-thank you." I twist the end of my shirt. "I-I need to get to Bri's house just down there on Moit Road."

"Well you can't very well walk there. Not with your face all over the place. What were you thinking? He's been playing your face on that screen over and over, night and day, child. No way you could've missed it. I'd assumed you were hiding out somewhere and good on you. Hide, because whatever that man wants"—she looks over her shoulder—"he takes."

"I didn't know." Actually, I forgot. Bri did mention it. "I-I haven't been around, exactly."

"Well now's not the time to start being around, you hear me?" Her eyes are as wide as orbs.

I nod.

She sits on the sofa next to me and exhales. "It hasn't been good, dear. Not good at all since you've last been by." Whispering a spell, she swivels one frail hand over another, her fingers calloused and stubby from years in the mines. A square pastry appears in her palm. "Your favorite, with the tem tem berries you like so much."

I take it and even though nothing inside me wants to eat right now, I bite. "Thank you, Ms. Totsi."

It's somewhere between Ms. Leola's pound cake and a cheese-cake with a flaky crust and purple berries inside. And it's everything I needed. A taste of happy. A mouthful of love.

"Can you help me?" I ask.

She stares a moment and there's more behind her pondering

expression than she lets on. Like the answer to my question is a weight heavier than she's sure she can bear.

"If we had the time, my dear, I'd tell you a story of how I founded this shop. And why." She pats my hands. "But alas, time is very rarely on one's side. Eighty years I've seen and time . . . no, it's never on our side, is it?" She stares off like there's more she wants to say.

I wait.

But she snaps out of it. "And yes, dear, I can help you get to Bri's undetected. But you must promise me something."

"Yeah?"

"If you ever find you've nowhere else to go, you come here to these books and find yourself." She gestures around us. "I may be gone, but a friendly face will always greet you."

"O-okay." I don't know what that means, but I'm not in a position to say no.

"Now," she hops up and her voice trails down the hall. I'm on her heels trying to keep up when she pulls open a closet with a stack of ornate trunks piled one on top of the other. In the corner sits a burgundy one with fleur-shaped etchings and a cluster of locks. I tug on one of the gold fasteners and Ms. Totsi pulls my hand away.

"No." Her expression is as rigid as steel. "Not that one. Not yet."

I let go.

"Now, where was I?" She's all smiles again, pulling down a plum-colored box with a single gold belt around it. "Oh yes, we can't magick you *into* the neighborhood because that's, of course, prohibited. But you can magick *yourself* and slip past the lot of them." She digs through the chest, folds of fabric flying in every direction. "Ah! This one's perfect." She tosses it to me.

"A costume?" It looks like a bodysuit in all black with gold thread sewn into the seams. Costumes are pricey here. It's not like running through Walmart around Halloween and grabbing something on sale. Ghizonis pay solid gold for costumes, because they're *magic*.

Slipping into a costume is like slipping on a new layer of skin. They wear off after a while, but when you're wearing it you literally look like something or someone else.

"You ever try one?"

"Once." At a party with Bri. I don't know how I let her talk me into going. Everyone still knew it was me with Bri. I was there all of five minutes before I'd had enough with the whispers and stares and insisted we leave.

"Pays to know the best costume designers in all of Ghizon, my dear. Don't let the caste fool you. Zrukis are brilliant. Go ahead, try it on."

I hustle open the legs of the costume. The bunched-up black fabric is tough to get into. I slip one leg inside and then the other and zip up the fabric. The gold cuff in my pocket digs into my side as the fabric cinches around me. The zipper clicks in place and the tingling starts to sting. I bite down, trying to ignore the fact that my entire body feels like it fell asleep.

"Now walk a bit, go on," she says.

I pace. And with each step, the fabric melts into my skin, meshing to conceal my hoodie and jeans. I catch a glimpse of myself in a mirror and I'm covered in an all-in-one bodysuit that looks like it's made of black scales with tips dipped in gold. And my face is all made up, exotic looking, with smoky eye shadow and sculpted hair. Gold filigree is woven into a headpiece resting on my hair like a crown.

"You look fearsome, dear," she purrs. "And completely unrecognizable."

She's right. The mirror agrees. You'd never know who's under here. This costume is really dope. And probably super expensive.

"I-I can't take this. I don't have the money to—"

"Don't be silly child. Helping you is . . . my civic duty."

"What does that—"

"You best get going." She shoos me toward the door. "You have everything you brought with you, dear?" She looks toward where my pocket should be.

I pat and the cuff is still there. "Y-yes." When did I mention the cuff? I didn't.

"Good luck," she whispers as I slip out the door. Back on the street, the crowd has settled and I walk by another screen with my face big as day. And this time people pass without a second glance my way.

My watch vibrates.

Bri: You almost here? Aasim is on his way. You okay?

Me: Yeah

I silently mourn Ms. Totsi's with one more glance back. Outside of her bookstore, I didn't have a place to just *be* in Ghizon.

I didn't have a place here, because I don't have a people here.

That's what it boils down to. Now, I'm the unruly creature they don't understand. The girl who won't be confined by their rules about what I do, how I should act.

Now, I'm a threat—more of an outsider than ever.

Sprawling trees from the edge of Bri's street peek at me from up ahead. My calves burn and my soles ache.

I'm *so* close to Bri's.

So close to getting answers about how to fix my magic.

So close to making a way out of no way.

I pick up speed as the last words I heard the Chancellor say sludge through my memory. *You shouldn't have brought her here. She's far more like them than us.*

He's right.

I'm not Ghizoni.

This won't ever be home to me.

I'm here for magic and vengeance. Then I'm taking my Black ass home.

CHAPTER 21

BRI'S HOME IS AS quaint as it was the last time I was here, but the concrete walls never quite put me at ease. Where are the pictures? Doodles her little brothers make? Or prizes from school contests she won? Do they even do that here? There is one portrait on the wall in a gilded frame. The Chancellor's face is on the wall of every building, every place I've ever seen. I'm not sure if that's a rule or the people just like it that way. Or both.

I toss my costume in the corner of the room and make my way past Bri's brothers in a full on fight over a wooden doll. Luke's in the one chair so I settle on the floor. He is *always* around, I swear.

"I'm so sorry, Rue," Luke says.

She called Luke to update him on everything? I mean, I know him, but I don't *know* him, know him. "Thanks," I say.

Sunlight flitters through the single window in the main room of the house until Bri pins a dark cloth over it. "The sun's a nuisance in here this time of day." She winks.

"Good thinking." Luke grabs the other end of the cloth and pins it.

Stacks of self-folding towels bob through the air and a kitchen drawer flies open to receive them.

"Thanks for letting me just pop up," I say to Bri's mother. She doesn't respond, buzzing around the kitchen, which is steps away. I know she heard me. Flames dance on her fingers as she brings a pot of water to a boil, mumbling something to herself.

"It-it's fine, really," I say. "You don't need to go out your way to make—"

"Ya," she says, flashing a tight smile.

"She says she insists," Bri translates.

"No'yee dja Zruki. Mwepa kindazi."

"She says it would be rude to not offer," Bri says. "And that Zruki are not rude people."

"O-okay," I say. "Well, thanks."

"You sure your momma cool with this?" I cut a glance at Bri, whose arm is twisted around Luke's.

"Yeah, it's fine. I'm sure," Bri says, tapping her foot. Something 'bout the way her momma keeps looking over her shoulder at me makes her seem nervous.

And her being nervous makes me nervous.

"Cute outfit." Bri picks up my costume, inspecting it. "Felt like a little shopping on the way? What are you, queen of the fire-breathing lizards now, or however you say it there?"

"Dragon. And whatever, it got me here unrecognized, didn't it?"

She laughs. My watch says I've been here three minutes and it feels like three minutes too long. I'm hoping between Cupcake and Ms. Leola, Tasha's okay. The text I sent before I left the General's warehouse forbid her to go anywhere. Not even school. Cops don't go looking for truant kids in the 'hood. Praying she listens.

"Aasim told me he'd be here real soon," says Bri.

I wipe my clammy hands on my pants, pull out the cuff digging into my side, and set it on the table. Its hue and brilliance matches the necklace I left on Tasha; it's also obviously Ghizoni gold. Going to ask Aasim about that, too. I want answers. All the answers. And I'm going to have them.

"What's with the—" Luke unlaces his fingers from Bri's and picks up the cuff.

"Don't—" *Too late.*

"What the hell? It burned me."

"Yep. I don't know." I scoop up the cuff and the whispers start, but louder this time.

And clearer.

I strain to listen, but it sounds like a mix of stutters and hisses. I turn the metal in my hands. *What are you trying to tell me?*

"It doesn't burn you?" Luke asks, rubbing a pink spot on his thumb.

"Nah."

"It's gotta be full of some kind of dark power." Bri leans over it. "I don't get it. Never seen anything like it. But you can sense it, you know?"

I sense something, that's for sure. Is it darkness? Some malicious, angry magic trying to hurt me? Maybe I should tell Bri about the whispers, see what she thinks.

The cuff grows hotter.

On second thought, I won't tell her. She'd freak out.

The cuff cools, like it heard me.

I slip it back inside my pocket and zip it up, ignoring the bulge in my side.

Bri's mom hands me a mug of gri, which is like hot chocolate but sweeter. I don't want it, but I was raised right so I smile and say thank you. She looks away.

I don't like this.

Bri's about to take a sip, but her mother claps. "A-ah! Seyeen."

The Ghizoni prayer of thanks. I'm not praying thanks to the damn Chancellor. I look down and keep my mouth shut to be respectful of this lady letting me up in her house. Bri and Luke bow their heads.

She gestures for Bri to pray in English, I guess so I can participate.

"Thank you, good Chancellor, for your kind generosity," Bri says. "Thank you for the magic with which you entrust us and the station you have given us. May we wear it with honor and use it with integrity. To the great and generous Chancellor, long life and good health. Seyeen."

Long life? Good health?

I sip my drink.

They all mumble, "Seyeen."

"So what did you tell Aasim?" I ask. *And* Luke apparently.

"Everything. Well, everything that happened at the coffee shop. About the tattoo."

"And?" I ask.

"And he just said he'd meet us here at sundown and hung up."

Hmmm. Coming here to talk to him is the *last* thing I wanted to do. But he's a higher-up in Ghizon and probably my only shot at reactivating my onyx.

I don't know what to make of him.

The necklace he left Moms kept her safe all those years, sure. But what kind of nigga just lay up with they girl, knock them up, and bounce? What am I supposed to say, thanks? Thanks for risking Moms's life by getting involved in the first place? But, I mean, without the necklace would Moms's life have ended even sooner? Ugh. My head hurts.

"I-is everything okay back at your home, Rue?" Luke wraps his arm back around Bri and she nestles in to him. "I-I don't know much about what's been going on with you," he says. "Bri doesn't tell me much."

"Oh? I thought . . . ," I start.

"Uhh, no. You know me better than that. He happened to be here when you buzzed me, that's all. He could tell something was wrong." She shrugs him off playfully. "One, that isn't my business to share. And two, Rue's my girl. That's like ride or death code one-oh-one."

Because she'd know. I snort a laugh, almost spitting out my drink. She really going in on this ride or die thing.

Lines dent Luke's brow. "Ride or what?"

"Yup," I say. "She's right."

We do our special handshake thing and Luke rolls his eyes.

"Women are so complicated, I swear." He grabs a cup and takes a sip. "No, but really. Whoever is in trouble, are they okay? I was worried. Is it your mom or family or something?"

She *really* ain't tell him shit about me.

"Nah, my mom is dead."

"Wow, sorry," he says without a flinch.

"It is family though," I whisper out of earshot of Bri's mom. "I have a little sister back home in East Row."

He takes another sip. "That's terrible. You must be so worried."

"'Preciate it."

"Well, I hope your sister is okay," he says.

I'm about to say thanks but the door clicks open.

Aasim.

Everyone stands, except me, and Bri's mother is visibly sweating now. She bows her head several times, muttering things under her breath.

"Thank you, *Maim* Zoryn. There's really no need for that. I-I . . . that's more the Chancellor's thing." He clasps her hands. "Thank you for allowing my daughter . . ."

I catch a chill.

". . . in your home with such discretion."

She bows again and offers him a mug.

"Luke, good to see you," Aasim says.

They sure are friendly as hell. What happened since I left? Aasim shakes his hand.

"Again, I appreciate all your help. I know it's no easy task keeping eyes on the man you work for."

The General? Luke's been spying on his boss for Aasim?

"Of course, sir."

"Bri, thanks so much for calling me."

Bri nods but she doesn't offer a hand. She's not overly friendly with him and I appreciate that.

He turns to me. "You're not wearing it?" He reaches for his own neck.

The necklace? That's really his first words to me?

"Are you hurt?" he asks as a follow-up. "You doing okay?" The concern and fatherly vibe is weird from him.

"I'd like to talk business." I toss Bri a look and she nods, pulling Luke along behind her as they leave the room. Her mother follows suit.

"Good luck with Tasha, Rue," Luke says. "Hope it all works out." The bedroom door clicks shut.

When did I tell Luke my sister's name?

"Rue, I—" Aasim snatches my attention away.

"Stop." I put up a hand. "Let me say this and get it out of the way. I'm not here to be friends. I'm here to find out what you know about the General's dealings back in East Row and get my onyx fixed. I don't know what's involved in all that, but it's the least you could do." I fold my arms. "Your turn, go ahead."

"Rue, there's so much you don't know. So much I have to tell you, show you. I'm sorry about Tasha. Is that where the necklace is?"

"Yeah, when *I* left family back home I actually planned to come back."

He sighs. "Rue, it's not that simple. I loved your mother very much, *and* you. We've never been able to talk about her. I—"

"No. Don't do that." Not now. Not with everything else going on. "Magic. The General. What do you know?"

"Rue, I'm your father . . ."

Oh, now he's my father.

"I know you must be . . ." He searches the air for words. "What I'm trying to say is . . . there's so much I'm sure you're dealing with. . . . Just tell me what you're holding in."

"I'm not holding in anything." How can he possibly think now is the time to bring up Moms? He doesn't get to do that. He doesn't get to just bring her up . . . and force me to remember . . . and especially not when Tasha and East Row—

"Rue—"

"STOP. *Please!*" I won't cry. I won't. "I'm not doing this with you here or now. You happen to be in a position to fix my magic. That's the *only* reason I'm standing here talking to you."

His eyes grow wide.

I don't care. "You're not gonna force me to talk about stuff I'm not ready to." A brick sits on my chest. "Answer my questions. Tell me everything you know and fix my magic. I have people relying on me. And I"—*unlike you*—"am not gonna let them down."

He stares at me, a pained look on his face. Like I hurt him or something. I mean sure, he did something by leaving the necklace, but he still left. He still put everything on Moms's shoulders for seventeen years. And for that he'll always be a stranger to me. We can figure out this magic thing together, then I'm out. I don't need his help to protect Tasha or back home. I'ma make a way and do this shit on my own.

Just like Moms taught me.

Just like I've always done.

"I've clearly hurt you, very deeply. I'm sor—"

"I'm not hurt, I'm impatient. They're *killing* my people, my home. They tried to kill my sister—twice!"

"I'm so sorry, Rue. You're right. This isn't the time, forgive me. And okay, okay. Let's get your magic back. Even if we can't fix us, I know we can fix your magic. So you can protect East Row."

Finally, he gets it. "Th-thank you. That's *all* that matters to me. Protecting *my* people is the only thing I care about."

He nods solemnly, but the glimmer in his eye is more pride than sorrow.

I straighten up to speak, but the words come out cracked. "I-I'm g-going to destroy them for what they're doing to my home." Tears streak my cheeks, but I smudge them away, quick.

He clasps my shoulder. "You *will* have justice."

I want to pull away from his touch, but I don't.

His breath warms my ear. "But, Jelani . . ."

No one calls me by my middle name.

I face him, my insides tingling.

". . . first you need to understand where you came from."

CHAPTER 22

YIYO PEAK IS WHERE the onyx stones are mined. The transport pod hums toward it, the sun growing smaller behind its highest tip. Honey-colored earth wisps by in a blur, like smeared pastels. Land like I've never seen surrounds me. All my time in Ghizon I've never explored the rural parts. Mahogany and sable earth rise and dip for miles, forming white-tipped peaks that kiss the clouds and craters like valleys covered in thin grass.

The sea of field hugging the peak stretches high and low to the edges of the earth, swallowed by the sun on the horizon. I check my watch. No news from Bri. I told her to use the homing tracker on our watches to keep an eye on Ms. Leola's and buzz me if anything goes down.

"What is this place?" I ask.

"The rest of Ghizon." Aasim smiles.

I don't smile back. "I don't understand. Where are we going?"

"The onyx mines."

"But why? I wasn't born in a mountain. Like, how is this relevant? Also, why couldn't Bri come?"

Bri wasn't happy to be left behind, but Aasim made it seem like this was something only he and I should do.

"You need to see it for yourself, first."

I tap my foot. "I'm not going to be out here for long."

"I know." He squeezes my shoulder and I roll away from his grip.

"We're going to get your magic fixed, Rue. You have my word."

I bite back the first snide remark that comes to mind. And the three after it. The ordeal at Dezignz flashes in my memory and I feel sick all over again.

Brian, his name is Brian.

Holding on to his name makes me feel like I'm holding on to him. I tug my hoodie tighter around my shoulders. My foot taps faster and I check my watch again. It's been an hour, maybe two since we left Bri's and it feels like it's been days. I don't know how this trip into the wilderness is going to fix my magic, but it better happen fast.

Fields of thin golden grass billow like fine hairs in wind. The trail beneath us snakes through, winding toward a colorful entrance jutting from the center of the mountain. Tree trunks with knobs like knees twist and wind up and out of sight. Leaves fan out from their upper branches in shades of green. Light flashes like a pulse inside the transport as we pass in and out of their shadow.

"These trees . . . I—" I've seen them before. *The dream.* I gnaw at my lip.

"Jpango trees." Aasim's beaming grows. "You'll only find them out here."

There's so much foliage in odd shapes and sizes like I've never seen. I assumed it'd be all dry mountainous desert. I had no idea there was lush life out here.

A thin barrier as transparent as glass flickers into view. The transport halts, shudders a moment, and like an air pocket through a bubble, pushes through. I whip around but only find the trail we've passed as if the barrier isn't there.

"For protection," he says. We slow, then jerk to a stop.

Protection from what? Yiyo Peak towers ahead, rays dancing around its edges. We sit in its shadow, waiting. For what I'm not sure.

A rounded patch of dirt skirts the edges of our destination. Closer to the carved mountain entrance now, towering stone columns that look as if they were chiseled by hand stand around the mine's entrance.

"Is anyone in there working now?" Zrukis work the mines overnight when it's coolest out. Sun'll be down soon, which means people showing up would see us, right?

"The mine's closed all week in observance of A'bdu Yoi' furi."

Ah, of course, the "oh so wonderful" Chancellor strikes again.

"You ready?"

Brian, his name is Brian. "Yes."

Something about the way Aasim stares at me makes butterflies flutter in my tummy. What are we about to walk into? We hop out and my shoes scrape the gravelly ground. Silence sits on us like a blanket. No wind, no rustle from the trees. Aasim leads the way to the carved doors at the entrance to Yiyo Peak. They're stories tall, higher than any door I've ever seen. Higher than Moms's entire apartment building. And their markings coil and twist in a familiar pattern. Dug into their surface are flecks of gold.

"It's so beautiful," I say, the wind around us picking up. "I've never seen black wood like this before."

"Jpango," he says. "The doors are hand carved and painted. This door is generations old. Older than New Ghizon."

"How do you know all that?"

"Ancient history."

They ain't teach none of that in any Ghizoni book I got. The doors' carvings are smooth against my fingertips, and a warm sensation moves through me. The spot where the cuff is dug into my side burns hot.

What the—*ow.* I snatch my hand from the door and the heat evaporates.

The heat.

The scrollwork pattern on the doors.

That's where I've seen it . . . the cuff!

I pull it out, ignoring the whispers, and compare the two.

Aasim gasps. "She kept it." His eyes dance with a fire I've never seen—a fire reminiscent of the one burning inside of me. I'm warm deep down into my bones, but I hardly notice it.

"It speaks to me," I say, knowing how that must sound.

His eyes grow wider, awe written in lines on his face. "A-and what does it say?" He's practically salivating. Clearly, I'm missing something here.

"I don't know what it's saying, what it's trying to tell me. Can you hear it?"

He shakes his head no, but his smile grows. It's like there's something he's not telling me. Something hanging on his tongue he's hungry for me to see.

I don't see it. "What do you think it means? I don—"

He presses a finger to my lips. "You just have to *see.*"

He pushes Yiyo's carved doors open and a searing heat washes over me like I've stepped into a flame.

CHAPTER 23

Seven Months Ago

"SO, MISS?" I HAD asked in my Ghizon History class.

The teacher had tugged on her robe and turned to face me, her lips pencil thin. "You have a question, Miss Akintola?"

I'd sat up, trying to make sure I catch every word outta this lady's mouth. I'd known they worship the Chancellor, but I never understood why. He's this frumpy, pot-bellied guy with an angry mug and very little hair on his head. All the pictures of him are always the same, too. Him staring with those steel eyes and lips so tight I'm not even sure they know how to smile.

What do they see in him? I don't get it.

"Yeah, so you're saying the Chancellor just showed up and united all these different tribes on the island of Ghizon by offering them magic?"

"Humans . . . idiots," someone says and the students around me had snickered but I ignored it.

The teacher had given me this look, like talking about this was some sort of crime. "If you'd read the text, you'd know that answer." Somehow, her nose rose higher in the air, her dark curls bouncing. "We are studious here, Miss Akintola. I suggest you try harder to keep up."

She's lying. I read that shit. That's not in the book.

"Actually, the text *starts* with commencement of Founder's Day. I *did* read it."

"A-ah, mind your tone."

My tone is fine, but I change it up anyway. "I just meant that the book you gave us doesn't go into detail about what Ghizon was like before the Chancellor united the clans. It doesn't even say how many there were, where they were, wha—"

"And why would it?" She interrupts. "This isn't the History of the Four Indigenous Tribes on the Isle of Ghizon class. This is the—"

"So it's *not* in the text. How am I not keeping up?"

All eyes on me.

She crossed the room, a wild look in her eye, and got real close to my face.

"This is History of New Ghizon, the Ghizon full of *magic* and *wonder*. . . ." Her arms swept in the air in grand gestures. "A peaceful land of magical innovation. Thanks to the Chancellor's incredible ability to engineer raw magic with his *bare* hands." She was so exhilarated she almost ran out of breath. So dramatic, I swear.

"And to take that power and so kindly share it with us. I just . . ." She closed her eyes, holding her palm to her chest. A few people clapped. Someone give this woman an Emmy.

"Benevolence. Duty. Fidelity. *That* is what we are learning about, Miss Akintola."

"So, it was four tribes then?"

She turned pink and pointed to the door. I'd become used to that. I packed my stuff, and when I reached the door, I turned back. "It's messed up that *you* know what Ghizon was like before the

Chancellor, but *we* can't." I got a few lingering stares as I left. Didn't go to History class or any class much longer after that. Ms. Totsi's selection of books was a little better. I learned about the village Aasim is from. How they were dying out years before the Chancellor swept in. And sadly, even the Chancellor's magic couldn't save them.

But nothing—absolutely nothing—in Ms. Totsi's old books could have prepared me for the inside of Yiyo Peak.

CHAPTER 24

Y SIDE BURNS. My eyes too. Inside the cave, the heat clings to my skin and I scream. I scream until my throat burns.

I'm on fire. I have to be.

I blink several times.

My hands appear fine. My clothes feel the same.

It's hot. So hot. But *inside* me somehow, not out, like my very bones are made of flames.

I stagger.

"Rue, you okay?" Aasim reaches to steady me and I use his arm to get my bearings.

"I . . . I'm fine." I think. After a few moments, the heat settles— not like it's gone, but like it's at home inside me.

Flames dance in oblong stone bowls hovering overhead. Everything grows brighter as my eyes adjust to the dim orange light. A rocky cavernous ceiling twinkles above us like a sky dotted with stars made of smoky glass.

Onyx.

Humid air clings to my skin and a thick, industrial stench burns my nose. On my right a path deeper into the cave extends under a low ceiling held up by wooden beams. To my left are carts piled high with black stone discs, spilling over their edges in heaps on the ground. Flickers of orange lick their surface, reflecting the firelight hanging from the jagged ceiling.

"Th-there's so much of it." I grab a piece of onyx and it's cold. I don't know why I'm whispering, but I have the distinct feeling someone is watching me. Someone other than Aasim.

"This way." He gestures for me to walk toward the narrow tunnel. It looks like a partially collapsed construction zone, only without hard hats.

But the onyx is just sitting here, out in the open.

Why does he want to go *the other way?*

He gestures again, more urgently this time. I slip the hard stone in my pocket and follow.

The tunnel's ceiling is so low, my breath shortens with each step. I run my hands along the jagged surface made of bits of brittle rock and glassy stone. The firelight from Yiyo's entrance fades the deeper we go, but there's a faint light up ahead. The ceiling is lowering. Walls tighten. Finding even ground for each step is harder than the one before it. Where are we going? This is madness. We pass a sign plastered with stamped letters that reads STOP.

We keep on going.

Everything's hard to see the darker it gets. Light glimmers on the edge of Aasim's frame hunched over ahead of me. The tunnel narrows even more and I bend deeper, my back aching. My hair grazes the top of the cave and Aasim reaches back for my hand to lead the way. I don't take it, but I stay on his six.

My pulse *tap tap taps* faster in my veins. I ease out a breath hoping to slow my heart rate. How much deeper? What's back here?

Several more steps and my neck aches from being stuck sideways.

Crash.

I yelp, my heart punching my chest.

My lungs burn.

I'm coughing.

Everything's a cloud of dust and a portion of the ceiling is a heap of rubble at my feet.

"It's okay," he says, coughing. "Come on. Not much farther."

Behind us the entrance to the cave is small in the distance. I squint through the haze, another cough tugging at my throat.

"Where . . ." The rest of my words come out a squeak when a ray of sun cuts through the darkness. Someone's opened Yiyo's doors.

Footsteps.

Shit, we're being followed.

Backtracking a few steps, I crane around the twisted tunnel for a glimpse at Yiyo's entrance. There is a tall frame, rigid in stature, looking both ways. A wisp of light sweeps over his face. I'd know that steel mug anywhere.

The General.

My heart lodges in my throat. "Aasim," I whisper.

He turns back and sees what I see.

"With me, *now*," he whispers back, but his words ripple like waves and the General's head turns our way. *Shit!*

Bang. Streaks of light dart past my face like an arrow, shattering the rubble at my feet. I scramble up and stumble forward, faintly aware of the back of Aasim's shirt up ahead. *Run.* Another bang and more rock crumbles.

"Hurry, come on," Aasim says. My steps are clunky over the craggy tunnel floor.

"Run all you want, Aasim, Rue," the General's voice echoes off the walls, turning my blood to ice. "There's no way out of here."

The General's steps are louder. He's so close I can hear his raspy breath. A dagger of light, as lethal as a live wire, swooshes past. I press the stinging spot on my face and blood trickles between my fingers. *He hit me!*

I urge my feet faster.

Don't think. Don't breathe. Just run.

I'm hunched over so much I'm practically crawling, grabbing, pulling, shoving myself forward any way I can. My foot catches and I'm on the ground, my knee pulsing with pain.

"I . . ." Aching rips through me. The walls close in around me and I'm dizzy. *It's no use. I can't—*

"Rue!" Aasim's high pitch slaps me to my senses.

I have to keep going.

His hand wiggles for my reach.

This time, I take it.

"A little farther," he says, looping my arm over his shoulder. A swirl of fire slams into the wall, its heat licking my neck.

The General laughs, his voice not nearly far enough away as I'd like it to be. "I love a good chase," he says. The space between the echo of his footsteps grows shorter. My side throbs, but I ignore it and push, limping as fast as I can.

I refuse to die in this cave.

The cuff burns hotter, like fire itself is in my pocket. Several more feet of hazy dust. My neck aches and my thighs are crying for me to stand up straight.

Then we stop.

Just stop at what looks like a dead end, a solid stone wall inches from my nose.

"Put your hand here." Aasim places my hand on the scratchy stone. The wall's chill pulses through me. "Push," Aasim says.

Push a stone wall? Is he serious?

"She's quite the nosy one, Aasim. Been meddling in all my business." The General's voice reverberates down the cave. He's close, so close. Another flash of magic explodes rocks behind us. Aasim ducks and presses my hand to the wall harder.

My hand shakes.

I can't think.

"Rue, push, NOW!" I push the stone wall with every bit of strength I can muster. It ripples like quicksand and he shoves me forward.

"Go."

"Wh-what?"

"Go, hurry!"

Through the wall? This is absurd! I suck in a breath and step into the rippling wall. Cool washes over me like I've stepped through a waterfall and for a moment the raging fire in my bones is gone. I step out on the other side and air assaults my head.

Streams of magic and the General's shouts dissolve into the solid stone wall behind us.

"He can't get through there, can he?" I ask, panting.

"Shouldn't be able to." Aasim's behind me and I blink several times, adjusting to the light. Whispers from my pocket burn my ears and the rock wall behind us glows a moment like it's dotted with a thousand fissures, then shifts. The stone wall buckles and cracks, folding in on itself, loosing clouds of dust, doubling in thickness . . . like it's protecting itself. *Whoa.*

Where there was just a layer of stone wall is a packed stack of boulders layered on one another. It looks secure.

I hope it's enough.

The space around us is tall and towering again, much like the entrance to the mountain. No piles of onyx in the corners. No sooty smell. Just empty, open air. I smooth my bloody hands on my hoodie and the wound on my cheek stings.

"He knows the way through the tunnel now," I say. "This place was secret before, right?"

"It was." Aasim pats the wall. "He still has to get through there to reach us." He reaches for my face. "You're hurt."

I jerk back out of habit. "S-sorry."

He nods in understanding and I feel bad. "I-I never said thanks, by the way." I study my feet because that's easier than looking at him. "F-for the necklace you gave Moms. I-I should have at least said thank you. For that."

He doesn't say anything, just nods, a solemn look in his eye.

"So, wh-what is this place?" My voice echoes as clacking footsteps grow louder our way. Out of the haze of dimness comes an older man with brown skin as rich as sable, his arms held wide with a smile to match.

H-he's Black?

What's he doing here? Inside this cave?

Creases hug his eyes like we've known each other for years. His floor-length robes are trimmed in black and gold and two leather belts wrap around him, one at his waist, another on his chest.

"Welcome, Jelani." He bows, then glances at the gash on my cheek. "I am Bati."

How does he know my name? *That* name? I flash a nervous smile and wave.

"We were followed," Aasim says, embracing Bati in a hug.

"Aasim, good to see you." Bati glances at the wall a moment, worry knitting his brow. "I am sorry to hear it." He studies the wall. "Strong enchantments seal that wall," Bati says. "They should not be able to pass."

His smile dissolves and I swear I hear him whisper, "I hope." He gestures for us to follow, but my heart's still thumping in my throat.

"Please, come," he says, clasping his hands. "We have refris prepared. And let's get that gash patched up."

Aasim follows without question. *It's going to be okay.* We're out of death tunnel, so anything is an improvement from that. I fall in line behind them.

We pass beneath a wooden archway carved into the onyx walls and come to a large room filled with wooden chairs and low tables. Golden light seeps between rectangular slits cut into the stone walls, like there's fire hidden behind there. Wide bowls full of flames hang from chains anchored in the ceiling swaying gently.

A brown-skinned heavyset woman with hair tied in a colorful

head wrap lights lanterns along the perimeter with her finger; a tiny girl with braided hair follows close at her feet.

What is this place? Who are these people?

"This way," a young guy with velvety umber skin says, gesturing toward an oblong table lined with chairs. Ornamented dishes piled with meats, fruits, and grains line its center. Eating? We don't have time to eat. What are we doing? Why are we here? I don't wanna be rude, so I keep my mouth shut, but Aasim has about five minutes to let me know what's up.

I take a seat.

"Is everyone here . . . like us?" I whisper to Aasim.

He nods and I settle into the back of my chair, a bit more relaxed. Around the room lines of people shuffle through, glancing our way. Some look and smile, others stare.

All these people—brown-skinned people—in Ghizon?

Why are they here, hiding?

I have so many questions.

I crane around and small faces with curious eyes peer at me from the shadows. I squint and they scatter. Aasim is deep in a whispered conversation I can't make out.

"Refris?" asks the guy who showed us to our seats.

"Uhhhh." I glance at our greeter, Bati. He's busy whispering in someone's ear, his narrowed eyes full of concern.

"He says, do you like something to drink?" Bati catches me staring. "A refreshment? If you're not hungry for supper we also have lots of treats." He gestures at a table at his rear smothered in cakes in a pool of glaze, braided chunks of dough, pies with crumbled topping, and chunky squares of what looks like fudge.

"Oh." I shake my head, my stomach churning. "It looks tasty, but nah, I'm good." I don't eat just everybody's cooking. Been in one too many questionable potluck situations.

"Thank you for such welcome," my father cuts in. Everyone digs in and I pause, expecting to hear Seyeen, the prayer of thanks to the Chancellor.

It doesn't come.

Tiny fingers touch my shoulder. The little girl's no longer hanging on her mother and instead is hanging on me. Neon beads *ting* at the ends of her braids. Her ebony skin, as smooth as silk, almost glows it's so radiant. She's so beautiful. A little goddess.

She cups her empty hands together, smiling so wide I can count every single tooth in her grin. Her hands open and where there was just air, a tiny purple flower is blooming. *Magic.*

"For me?"

She nods.

Wait. She's so young. How is she Bound?

I take the flower by the stem with a smile, shifting in my seat. How does she have onyx? At what, five years old? The Chancellor doesn't bind until seventeen.

Uneasiness churns inside.

The larger woman, her mother I think, mutters something and swats the girl's hand.

"Oh no, it's fine. She's not bugging me," I say, but my words dissolve in a buzz of excitement over the food the woman has. A tray piled with sautéed qui, crusted ksi ksi, which are like sweet collard greens, chunky kwello root, which are kind of like sweet potatoes but red instead of orange and savory instead of sweet. In the center of the bed of vegetables is a chunk of glazed meat. With a flick of her wrist, the hovering tray moves to the table in one smooth motion. I salivate. Maybe I could take a small taste. She smooths her hands on her apron and pulls the little girl away. She waves, running off.

Wait.

Her wrists, that little girl's wrists . . .

There's nothing on them.

I break my neck for a glance at the mother, but she's already too far to see. Aasim clears his throat and it takes all the focus I can muster not to watch where they rush off to. The guy who ushered us to our table is across the room fussing over a stone bowl that won't stay lit, the flames from his fingertips barely there. I tilt my head for a better view of his onyx. Maybe theirs are different?

His wrists . . . there's no onyx on his wrists either.

My thoughts are a haze of confusion. "I-I d-don't understand," I say, louder than I intend to. All heads turn my way. The scrape of utensils and chairs halts and dead silence hangs in the air.

Bati smiles. "Your father hasn't told you much, I see."

"I didn't know if she'd listen," he says.

That stings. But I guess . . . I guess it's true.

"And besides," he says, "she needed to see . . . for herself."

"All these people here"—I don't remember standing, but I am—"I . . . I don't see onyx on anyone here."

Bati and Aasim's eyes stay on me. But everyone else glances at one another, like my words don't make sense. Like it's not weird for people to be walking around Ghizon, even if it is in a mountain, floating platters, making flames, growing flowers—*without* onyx infused with the Chancellor's magic.

"Does she have it?" Bati asks.

"Do I have what?"

"She does," says Aasim. "In her pocket, I believe."

"If I may . . ." Bati clasps his hands, but only I look his way. He rises from the table, holding up his hands. My pocket jerks every which way.

What is he—? I tug my hoodie still, but it squirms more violently. His hands tremble and his face is all determination like this pains him or is hard for him . . . or something. The cuff rips open my zipped pocket and snaps to his hand like a magnet.

No onyx on his wrists either.

WHAT IS GOING ON?!

My stomach plummets, like I'm standing on the edge of some cliff I'm supposed to jump off, teetering on the edge of a truth I can't make sense of.

Bati rotates my cuff in his hands. "*Ooo*, hot." He switches the finger he's holding it with. "Jelani, you don't need onyx to get your magic back."

When did I tell him my magic was broken?

"You never lost it. Nor have you ever really *used* it—not truly." He walks toward me and all I can hear are his footsteps and my heartbeat. "Those few spells they teach are useful, sure." He chuckles. "But you, my dear, are of the oldest blood of ancient Ghizon. *Your* magic is within."

The heat on my neck rises.

Say something. Stop staring like an idiot.

"Everyone has some form of magic here." He hesitates at that last part. "And not a single one of us has onyx." He glances at Aasim and he nods. "Jelani, Ghizoni magic was birthed by your ancestors, passed down to their children and their children's children, breathed into us—and *only* us—by the gods themselves."

"But," I start, "the Chancellor, he . . ."

"Those stones are a child's toy compared to the power your ancestors could wield. A *stolen* child's toy."

"So . . . I don't . . . wait . . . you mean . . ." Words are a jumbled mess in my head. "You're saying *all* magic . . . the onyx that the Chancellor gifts everyone . . . the power that's here on the island . . . it's . . ."

Bati nods, handing me back my cuff.

No, it can't be.

The chilling realization washes over me and I bar my mouth shut, as if my hands can hold in the truth and everything it means.

I never liked the Chancellor, but this? This!

"It's not possible . . . he . . ." I stutter.

"Yes, Rue." Aasim turns to me. "Magic was never the Chancellor's to give."

I meet his stare and finally understand the fire that burns there.

"It was ours."

CHAPTER 25

Eleven Months Ago

THE HALLWAY IS BARREN by the time they call my name for Binding.

The revelry and thump of the drums outside have faded and only scraps of streamers and confetti remain. Sorting is done for everyone, and except for me, Binding is done too. Each person before me, including Bri, disappeared behind the chrome swinging doors and came out sniffly with bandaged wrists.

"Come," a gruff voice says. The lady who called everyone else must be gone, because the man standing at the door is only vaguely familiar. His hair is cut low, very neat. He has a shadow of a beard on his face, white like his low top. And a mean gash beneath his eye. He doesn't wear a lab coat like she did or even have a clipboard.

I don't like this. "Where's the nurse lady?"

He turns his back without an answer. I'm here, it's finally my turn. I've been waiting all day for this. I need to just go through with it. Get it over with. Push comes to shove, I can throw some hands if I need to. He look old as hell.

I follow him from a distance. The hallway through the silver doors reminds me of the clinic Moms used to take me to. Sterile rooms, like patient rooms without windows, line both sides of the lengthy corridor. Except here there are no nurses, doctors, or people moving from room to room. This hallway is as silent as it is stark white.

The only bit of color is a painting of the Chancellor's head on display at the end of the hallway. We hang a left. Then a right and two more lefts. I keep track. *Just in case.*

The room we slip into is like the others except cabinets line one wall and there's a black door at the back of the room.

"Sit," my escort says, pointing at a metal table in the center of the room.

I swallow the lump in my throat and take a seat. The metal chills my legs, even through my jeans, and I hug around myself. "So you doing this or what?"

He doesn't laugh at my obvious attempt at sarcasm or even comment. Instead, he grimaces and posts up on the wall in the farthest corner of the room. His gaze never leaves me and I feel icky. Ten showers with screaming hot water are in my near future.

The door clicks open. "Oh, there you guys are." A dusty brown-haired man sticks out his hand. "I'm Twan, the tech that'll be doing your binding attachment today."

"Uhm, okay," I shake the tip of his hand.

"So first I need you to take off this outer robe you have." He pinches my hoodie.

"I'm not taking off my hoodie." I roll up my sleeves. "This will have to work."

He smiles apologetically. "O . . . of course, sorry. I just would hate to get any blood or anything on it."

Blood? What am I in for? "I'm good. Go ahead."

"I'll need you to lie back and uh, sir . . ." he turns to the man on the wall. "You said the Chan—"

"All ready to begin then?" The Chancellor's voice booms as he enters the room. "Rue Jelani Akintola, daughter of Aasim Amare Akintola." His voice is more lively than his expression, none of its warmth quite meeting his eyes. "General, good afternoon," he says, and the man on the wall—apparently a General—softens.

"Afternoon, sir."

"Now if you'll lie down." The tech pulls on gloves and I ease back onto my elbows. I don't like this. Lying down in here with all the strange vibes in this place. Where's Aasim? Stupid question. Why do I even care?

"Ah, ah, not so fast," the Chancellor says. "This one's going to stand first."

The tech's brows meet. "Stand, sir, but . . ."

"You heard the Chancellor," the General spits. "Do as you're told." He looks to me. "Stand, girl."

"Rue. I don't answer to girl."

"Rue, if you would?" the Chancellor cuts in, gesturing for me to stand in front of him. I glance at the exit, to keep it in my sights. *Just in case.*

Once I'm in front of the Chancellor I can see him more properly. He's much older than his portrait lets on. Some of his hairs are pale gray and his eyes are a frigid shade of blue.

"The stones," he says. The tech holds two black circles about the size of a half dollar.

"Wh-what are those?" I ask.

"Just rocks, well stones, really," Tech says. "Onyx mined from Yiyo. It's a great conduit for the magic. It binds really well to it, we've found. We tried obsidian and it was downright awful. I mean, you couldn't even—"

The Chancellor clears his throat.

"Sorry, sir." Tech hands him the onyx.

I swallow. This shit is gonna hurt. I know for a fact I heard them girls screaming.

The Chancellor holds the balls of onyx in one hand and shoots a stream of magic like a fuzzy strand of electricity from his fingertip. The stones glow orange and it's only then I notice the Chancellor's gaze isn't on what he's doing.

It's on me.

Tech stands next to me as the Chancellor fills the stones with remnants of his magic. I don't know this tech guy, but he's the only one in this room who hasn't looked at me like they despise me. That alone makes his presence comforting.

The stones' brilliance grows brighter and brighter and with each lumen, the General is more visibly irritated.

"Sir," he says, "forgive me but this is a mistake. I—"

The Chancellor's eye twitches. "General."

He snaps his mouth shut.

Giving the half-human who isn't Ghizoni magic? Yeah, I bet plenty of folks here wouldn't be a fan of this, actually. Their problem. Not mine.

"About ready," the Chancellor says. "Tech?"

Tech moves into place like he's done this a hundred times. His slips protective frames over his eyes and the Chancellor drops the stones in his hands, steam rising from them.

"This part is gonna sting a bit." Tech meets my gaze. "But it'll cool down quickly."

A response sticks in my throat and all I can manage is another swallow.

"First, repeat after me." The Chancellor takes my hands and everyone's heads turn his way. In expectation or confusion, I'm not sure.

"With this Bind, I eternally vow," he says.

I look to tech and he shrugs, nodding at me. "W-with this Bind, I eternally vow."

"To mind my work with fervor and allegiance."

"T-to mind my work with fervor and allegiance."

"And whatever cause thine Wisest might deem."

I don't even know this man?! "I . . ." Tech nods for me to go on. "A-and whatever cause thine Wisest might deem," I say, shoving the words between my teeth.

"To uphold the pillars upon which we've been built."

"To uphold the pillars upon which we've been built."

"Benevolence. Generosity is quite important here."

"Benevolence," I say.

"Duty. We Ghizoni do what's required of us." He levels his gaze at me. "*Whatever* is required . . . for the good of Ghizon."

I nod. "D-duty."

"And fidelity." He lifts his chin, eyes glaring down at me. "And we are *unyieldingly* . . . loyal."

"F-fidelity."

He studies me for a moment. "Tech, you may initiate the bond."

The next few minutes are a haze of agony. One minute I'm sitting while Tech's holding the hot stones to the insides of my wrists, apologizing every few seconds. And the next minute my insides are a crescendo of sharp pangs.

"AH!" My skin screams like it's being fried in hot grease. Everything's black, there's so much pain I can't see. "Make it stop!"

"Almost, Rue. Hang in there." Tech presses harder and the skin underneath splits open. I gasp and brace for the pain of my wrists splitting open, but it never comes. A swell of cool seeps into my veins, winding its way through me like it's looking, searching for something. Within seconds, the magic douses every simmering part of me like sand tossed on a fire.

I blink the world back into focus and sit up straighter.

I don't know if my skin feels better or if I'm just numb. But the burning has stopped, and my wrists are sore but normal. Round stones sit fused to the insides of my wrists like little half moons. The edges around the onyx where my skin meets the stones are swollen and puckered like stitches that've come out too soon. I rub a thumb across one but it doesn't hurt. Thank goodness.

Tech offers me a hand to steady myself, but I don't need it so I don't take it. On my feet, everyone's staring at me, their expressions haunted with disbelief.

"What?" I ask.

"Y-your bandages … I-I … y-you …" Tech points at my wrists, his arms full of bandages I apparently don't need. "Th-there's no blood."

The puckering that was just there is gone, and smooth skin meets the onyx. *Wow, he wasn't kidding.*

"I don't . . . it's not even irritated." He stares half flabbergasted, half intrigued. "I've never seen skin take to magic so quickly."

The Chancellor storms out.

What's his problem?

"H-how do you feel?" Tech asks. The General rubs his thin layer of beard, studying me. How *do* I feel? I can feel a hum of the magic nestled inside me comfortably, like it's sitting there waiting . . . listening . . . ready. I crack my neck.

"Fine," I say. "Better than I have in a while actually. Thanks." I pat Tech on the shoulder and see myself out.

It's been a couple of weeks since the Chancellor affixed onyx to my wrists, and between getting moved into Bri's dorm, learning the ropes here—basic stuff, like where to eat, finding a place to shower—I'm just now picking up my books. My arms are heavy like I'm carrying a pile of bricks as I push open my room door.

"That took *foreeever*, geez," Bri says, huddled over a book snuggled in a chair. The space isn't huge, with two beds and a small table in the middle, but she has a dedicated chair in a corner that's for her studying. Which basically means she lives in it. "What took so long?"

"Long line. Guess everyone waited until the last minute to get their texts."

"Not everyone," she says, hopping up to study my stack of titles.

Of course. Bri's apparently been checking out how-to-textbooks from a local bookshop since she was old enough to read. I empty my hands on the bed. My arm muscles thank me, and light from the tiny window in our room catches my stones. They've been almost unnoticeable these last couple weeks, just ornaments occasionally warming time to time.

"So . . ." The onyx glistens like a bubble of blackness. "How do these things even work?"

"It's like invisible momentum, an energy that you can use to move things. It can't be made or snuffed out. Just transferred or change form."

She's gotta see the confusion on my face.

"Just focus on the stone in your wrists and point where you want it to go."

"Focus and point?"

"Focus and point," she says. "Okay, well, it's more complicated than that if you want to distort or bewitch something, conjure fire, that sort of thing. But just moving something around? Focus and point."

Focus and point. I think I can do that.

She examines my arms.

"Ow, it actually has been sore the last few days"

"Sorry! It should wear off soon. Sucking on some meekle can help."

"Ugh, no thanks." I don't know what the heck that is. Trying weird food is more than I have in me today. I've been sticking to the two dishes I halfway recognize: a potato looking thing stuffed with what I keep telling myself is cheese, and a dark meat that looks like fish but has a Mongolian beef chewiness to it. Bri tried to explain what meat it is, but I really just need to live in my taste bud oblivion, right now.

Bri shrugs. "Probably smart. Last time I tasted that I felt loopy for, like, a week. Though, I think that might have been the point." She considers the thought a moment, then moves on, plopping down on her bed. "Well come on, let's see what you can do!" Her book's still open.

Advanced Spells
Now with a Bonus Enunciation Guide

"Bri, I'm barely through the door." I close it at my back. "And I haven't even cracked open any of my books. Like, damn, gimme a minute." I do wanna see if I can actually do something. See what all this pomp and circumstance around being Bound is.

She rolls her eyes deep in her head and I laugh. I pull out my spell book from the bag on my back. Bri's back in her chair in the zone, three books open and deep lines dug into her forehead.

The writing on the page is painfully small. I squint. Moms always said I needed glasses. But glasses ain't cheap and squinting is free.

> Magic wielders can usually transfer magic fairly easily with only a basic understanding of the skill, because a lot of energy transference is felt. A humming in your veins, a warming of your wrists, you can feel the magic gathering and point it with your hands where you want it to go, silently. Though, depending on the strength and relative exhaustion of a person's magic, a spell may be used to increase chance of success. (If the spell cast doesn't respond, a cool-down period of three to five seconds may be needed.)
>
> See *Advanced Magic Transference Appendix A.*

I focus and my wrists warm. A heaviness sets on them like my onyx has turned to lead.

And point.

The stack of books on the table tumbles off the side into a pile on the floor.

"You did it!" Bri shouts.

I didn't even know she was paying attention anymore. That's much simpler than I thought it'd be.

"Rue, that's great."

"Thanks." I glance at the text open on my lap. "What about, like, spells?"

"That's way more difficult, don't even worry about that now." She flaps a hand in the air. "It's all about enunciation and timing, commanding your magic at its strongest point as it wells up inside you."

Commanding at its strongest point. "Command, like, say?"

"Yeah, aloud. It's super prickly though and complex. Takes lots of practice. I've been studying spells for *years* just to get ahead, and I can't get the stupid things to work. But I'm hoping to have a breakthrough now that I'm officially in training."

I don't know if she's talking to herself or me. Bri does that, gets off on brainiac tangents. I slide a finger down my spell-casting page. The cover reads *Beginner* and I double take at Bri's. Definitely different.

Magic can also transfer from you *to* an object you'd like to control. That's how magicked objects work on their own, such as dishes self-washing. *Transferring* magic is a temporary spell that transfers to the object for a time. Some spells will need maintenance after a while. Self-washing dishes, for example, after several months, may not wash as well, or the water may not get as sudsy. This means the spell is weakening and could use a little boost. A simple refresh spell will do the trick.

NOTE: *This is temporary magic, different from imbuing. [See restrictions on imbuing in the next chapter.]*

I turn the page. Why would imbuing or whatever it's called specifically be restricted?

RESTRICTION: *Imbuing*, specifically depositing or storing one's magic into inanimate objects without express written consent from the Chancellor, is strictly prohibited. To inquire if an object may be imbued, complete Form IXII on page 793 of this manual. Allow eight to twelve weeks for processing.

I turn a few more pages to a picture of a man with a prominent nose and a warm smile. "Where did all this knowledge about magic come from?"

"Right? It's so interesting discovering new ways the magic works. Research is really important to the Chancellor," Bri says. "But it's a Dwegini duty, so . . ."

Hmm. Interesting. I turn the page to a section titled "Lead Researchers" and scan.

Mr. Jon'ye, after which the Jon'ye Lo'Quiim Award is named, is heralded as the greatest mind in Magical Molecular Anatomy since Ghizon's colonization. His discovery of how to alter the physical manifestation of magic into fire and electrically charged energy, like man-made lightening, is the single greatest advancement of our time and an invaluable asset to Ghizoni law enforcement.

Thanks to Jon'ye, the "feey'l" spell can conjure spheres of tangible energy or give your fingertips flames—a great convenience for practical tasks such as cooking, space heating, seasonal decor; and even more broad benefits such as self-defense, late night travel, and illuminating mass spaces.

Okay Mr. Jon'ye, let's see. I bite my tongue from sheer nervousness.

Focus—my wrists warm and grow heavy, like before.

Command at its strongest point.

I close my eyes and center my thoughts on the swell of heat coiling around my hands.

"Feey'l"—and point.

Sparks like splintered pieces of wood fly from my fingertips and slam into a purple Blob-O lamp. "Sorry! I didn't mean to—"

"You—you did it?"

If she means breaking Bri's lamp, yes, yes I did. If she means having some sense of control over the daggers flying from my hands, that'd be a no.

She's up on her feet. "H-how'd you do that?"

"I . . ."

"I've been studying these spells books for so long, I could recite the book cover to cover." A nest of flyways brush her forehead and she shoves them back. "I—I don't understand, how you just . . ."

"Are you done flipping out? How about you keep trying?"

Her mouth hangs open like there's more she wants to say. "Bri, you're smart as hell. Keep trying."

She tucks back in her chair with a deep sigh. That girl needs a study break. She's losing it. I turn back to the book in my lap.

> A plaque in Mr. Jon'ye's honor can be found in the research
> wing of the Museum of Magical Advancement, resurrected
> after his untimely death shortly after his discovery.

Dude died after his big discovery? That's sad.

> Magic wielders are encouraged to practice spells in an envi-
> ronment with flame-resistant, incombustible, etc. walls, as
> misfiring a spell often ends up in literal fire (a translation
> complication between the close meaning of the words). Do
> not attempt new spells in the vicinity of precious objects.

Oh, now they tell me.

"Ah!!" Flames dance from Bri's fingertips and she's beaming. She wiggles her fingers. "I did it. Jon'ye's spell!"

"Told you!" We do a handshake thing I've been teaching her.

"I mean, I knew it," she says.

"Knew what?"

"If you could do it, of course I could."

Huh? I mean, I *am* new here. Maybe that's what she means. I wait for her to say more, but she's back eyeballs deep in studying.

CHAPTER 26

ASIM IS AHEAD OF me following Bati deeper into the mountain, down a set of stairs carved into the rock. The farther we go the colder it gets. I told Bati on the way here that the cuff speaks to me, like it has something to say, and he didn't laugh, actually. He had said two cuffs, a pair, were forged by the village Elders.

"But to hear their message, you may need both together," Bati had said. "And we have its pair in the bowels of our lair."

"The Chancellor is the 'magic-giver,' I say. "Zrukis and Dweginis worship and follow him because of it. And the magic was never his?" This is still so hard to believe.

"Never," Aasim says, firelight casting an orange glow on the silver in his locs. "He took it from us . . . somehow . . ."

He and Bati share a look, but I miss what it means.

"And then he stored it in the onyx he found here. Onyx sticks to magic really well. One thing's for sure, as much magic as he expends imbuing onyx on Designation Days, he has to be refilling it somehow. No way anyone uses magic—"

"*Stolen* magic." Bati chimes in.

"Exactly—that often without a problem."

They share that look again and I shift on my feet. There's something I'm missing. "But h-how did he do it? Was your history written down anywhere? As proof to show people?"

"Our complete history, I'm afraid, we do not know in great detail," Bati says. "Only what those of us who made it here can remember. And no, it wouldn't be written, would it? Who expects their history to be erased?" Our procession deeper into the cave halts and Bati has a far-off look. "I do recall pieces of conversations I picked up from my own father when I was a boy."

Aasim sets a hand on his shoulder.

"He was not one of the lucky ones," Bati continues. "He was too old to run and never made it here. The Elders, though, they knew much, but many of them perished of the Sickness before the Chancellor even came."

"And the ones who didn't?" I ask.

Bati glances at my cuff. "That's a whole other story for another time, I'm afraid. Why don't we keep going, shall we?"

So many questions. So many things I don't understand. I can see words are on the tip of Bati's tongue, like he's wondering how much to say. What to tell me and when.

"Please go on. I want to understand," I say.

He looks to Aasim, who nods in response. "Understand me now, child, I was very young. The wisps of what I remember being told are no more than cobwebs pulled to pieces over the years." He sighs. "We grew up in secret. Not here of course. Out there on our land, where the stars shone down on us at night and the sun coated our backs in sweat during the day. Our tribe was small but advanced, gifted with magic of the gods themselves. We knew there were others on the island, but we kept away from them so they wouldn't know about our abilities, what we could do. Wars have been fought for less. We cloaked our piece of the land in a veil of protection, making it impossible to find us unless you knew we were there. And no one did. For generations. Until . . ." He steadies himself on the rocky stairwell.

This memory unsettles him. Scares him even.

He goes on. "The other tribes on the island had heard whispers of a brown-skinned magical people, I would bet. But no more than a myth, lore to lull children to sleep at night. But when the humans came from th-that place you are from . . ."

"America?"

"Sure. Strange objects floated in the sky at times late at night. And one day a group of men showed up scouting, hunger in their eyes. We came out from our veil and banded together with the other tribes on the island to get rid of the scouts. But by then the damage had been done. The human visitors were gone, but the other tribes saw we were no myth, saw what we could do. As a gesture of peace and friendship, we extended our cloaking veil to shield the entire island, so no one—unless they'd already been here—could find us again.

"That was nice."

"Nice, but foolish. We had peace, trade even, with the other tribes for a time. Until one day the Chancellor showed up from the Moyechi tribe, known for their craftiness and ambition, saying he'd grown up hearing about our majestic people and wanted to see us himself. He could see the Sickness was eating our people away from the inside, stifling our magic, like a poison in our blood. It was no secret at that point we were weak. He offered us unification under him as Chancellor, saying he'd unearthed his own magic and would gift it to all who followed him." He gestures at both Aasim's wrist and mine. "He flashed those black beads on the insides of his wrists." He scowls. "I overheard my father tell my mother that very night how the Chancellor's eyes glittered with dark ambition, the kind that festers like rot in the bones. The Elders of our tribe knew we were the only ones marked with magic, so if the Chancellor boasted of magic . . . he was either a liar or a thief.

"We fled here. As many of us who could, that is. Many were too old, too sick. The Sickness had cut our tribe in half in just a few moons. The village Elders stayed behind and filled those cuffs with their collective power. I was but a boy when my father handed them off to me, told me to run like my life depended on it and make sure those cuffs make it here. He said no one would ever suspect a child to be carrying something so valuable. I ran faster than I knew my feet could go. The smattering that did make it here used the remnants of magic they had left to enchant that wall you passed through. That took a toll on everyone, weakened us even more."

"Th-the Sickness? Wh-where did it come from?"

"I don't know. But I do know from the moment the Grays knew of the power we possessed, their eyes dazzled with envy."

Grays?

"People in New Ghizon," Aasim whispers to me, apparently sensing my confusion. "And I have my own theories."

"The Chancellor?" I ask.

"The Chancellor was ambitious, my father told me," Aasim says. "He started showing people what he could do with the black stones fused to his wrists, telling them to follow him and he would share. Our people were taken with sudden Sickness, dying out, and coincidentally he's full of magic to give? *Pfft.* I'm not naive. That is no coincidence." He looks away. "Besides, my grandfather never trusted him."

"Oh?"

Sadness shadows his stare. "That is definitely a story we will save for another day."

My mind is blown. The Chancellor united the entire island around this lie. He sits up in his high office in New Ghizon living and breathing this lie. He condemns *my* sister to death for outing something that doesn't even belong to him.

"And everyone from Ghizon with brown skin has some remnants of this raw magic?" I ask.

"It is very weak, but yes," Bati says. "You have it too. You must only reach it. Lean into it. Let it be a part of you."

I don't know what kind of magic he *thinks* I have because I'm technically related to Aasim. But I don't feel anything. Besides my hip being seared alive by the cuff in my pocket the deeper we go into this cave. And I did try. I tried to reach for magic to save Brian. And nothing. My chest aches and images of blood spatter settle over me like a storm cloud.

"I-I don't know what to say. That's messed up that he's out there living a lie and all these people are forced to live their truth in here. Hidden, tucked away."

"I have a feeling it won't be that way much longer." Aasim gestures for me to catch up to Bati, who's much faster over these narrow steps than either of us. He snakes us deeper into the mountain and for several moments we walk in silence. So much to digest.

Warmth swims through my wrists, up my arms, dancing with the sleeping heat in my bones. I turn the cuff in my hand around and around, the deeper we go. I squint into the metal's radiance and my heart flutters. It has a message, something it wants me to hear. I can feel it.

We descend steeper steps and now everyone's chilly but me. The staircase grows darker the deeper we go.

"Bati," a voice echoes from above us, followed by hurried steps.

The messenger looks toward me, but past me to Bati. "Grays, sir. A large group has been spotted kilometers from here."

"Mine workers?" Bati asks.

"I am not sure. The leader does not look like the mine worker type."

"No, the mines are closed today." I look between them, fear coiling in my gut.

"What does he look like?" Aasim asks.

"Well dressed, tall, cruel jaw, mark below his eye."

The General. I dig my nails into the craggy wall. He's back with more people. He's really throwing all he's got to come for me.

"He won't be able to get back here, will he, Bati?" asks Aasim.

"Not as long as the enchantments hold," he says before dismissing the messenger. "But let us hurry, see what the Ancestors are trying to tell Jelani. We may not have much time." He ushers us back down the stairs, faster this time.

At the bottom of the staircase is an iron door. It clanks open with Bati's wave and we step inside. Darkness, so thick I can't see my hand in front of my face, lies on us like a blanket.

Bati clears his throat. "Aasim, if you would, light please?"

"I-I'm not able to . . . uh."

Despite the darkness, I can see Bati's eyes turn Aasim's way. "Oh, oh okay. Not to worry." A flash of light sparks and weak flames dance from Bati's fingers to stone bowls hanging over head. Aasim fidgets, tossing me a glance.

Why couldn't he conjure a fire? He didn't fire back at the General either when he was chasing us. Is his magic weakened too? But he has onyx . . .

The walls of the room are covered in shelves on one side, lined with tomes with spines inlaid with gold. Symbols I don't understand are etched into their edges.

"Our history," Bati says. "Or what I've been able to record of it since being holed up here."

I slide one off the shelf and the leather is dry in my grip.

"Spells, elixirs, the bones of our language . . . it's all in there." The spell book we got in training was pencil thin. There were more pages of instructions and restrictions than actual incantations. How much does the Chancellor even know about the magic he stole? The paper is gravelly against my fingers. "Could I take a closer look at this please? Hold on to it for a bit?"

"Yes, of course, Jelani," Bati says, and I catch Aasim's smile.

The other side of the room is covered in markings carved into the stonework, but in neat clusters, like parts of a story being pieced together.

"These are the pieces of our history we are still putting together," Aasim says. "Done by your ancestors. Yiyo was a sacred meeting place for them."

My ancestors? But I'm not Ghizoni. I mean, not really.

In the center of the room is a single box on a pedestal I only just noticed. "The cuff's pair . . . i-is it in there?"

"It is." Bati steps back almost reverently, and suddenly my hands are shaking. It's so, so hot again.

"Go ahead," he says. "Please, open it."

"O-okay." I hand off the tome and smooth my sweaty palms clean. I can sense its warmth from just touching the box. It creaks open, and a golden cuff stares back at me. I hold the other beside it. Twins. Identical.

"Why didn't you keep both here?" I ask.

"Aasim stumbled on evidence the Chancellor knew the cuffs might be more than folklore. He was trying to find them, so Aasim warned us." He makes a gesture of thanks toward Aasim. "We agreed it would be wise to separate them for safety. So he stored one in the human world where he met your mother, I gather."

Aasim nods, a soft smile on his lips.

"The other stayed here, with us." Bati steps closer to me and scents of earthiness swirl in my nose. "They were made to be a sort of fail-safe . . . for protection. With everyone fleeing, the Elders didn't want us overcome, our magic lost forever. We were already weak. The wisest, most practiced minds of magic in our village imbued those two cuffs with every wisp of their combined power." He beams. "I can't even fathom the unshakable power these things have."

A chill washes over me. "What do they want to say, you think?"

"I could guess, but that remains to be seen. Put them on, child."

I slip them on my wrists and the whispers are louder than they've ever been. Aasim starts saying something, but Bati's hand silences him. The gold metal calls to me like a longtime friend.

I'm listening.

Firelight dances on the cuffs' surfaces and their swirly patterns twist and shift before my very eyes. I gasp. The patterns coil and shift again, writhing like they're agitated, unsettled.

"D-do you see that?" I ask Aasim. His eyes grow wide. He can see it. Thank goodness, I was beginning to think I was losing it.

"What's it saying?" Bati asks. "What do you hear now?"

"Uhhm, I don't know." I close my eyes, focusing on the whispers, straining to make sense of them.

O'yatsa ki'nyokoo.

"I can't . . ."

O'yatsa do'vexi.

"I don't know what it means."

"Say it," Bati says. "Tell it to me."

"Uhhm, okay." My mouth is dry. "Let's see . . ."

O'yatsa ki'nyokoo. "O-oh-yah-s-see-key-yoki," I say.

His brows cinch. "Again?"

"Oh-yatsa-key-nuh-yo-coo," I say.

"Blood of the ancient," Bati translates.

O'yatsa do'vexi. "Oh-yatsa-doe-vex-see."

"Blood of the future."

Yoo yoo e grizz. Yoo yoo e n'sh'kva. "You-you-e-grease-you-you-e-neesh-k-va."

"Daughter of rage, daughter of truth."

KeeI'i! Da'ya e kees'i n'boo. "Kee-e-die-yah-e-kees-e-nuh-boo."

"Burn! Ashes of old. Fire forges the new." Flames flicker in Bati's eyes. "The cuffs have chosen a wearer, Jelani. You."

My heart stops. Me? Why?

I am not even Ghizoni.

Apparently Bati can read the expression on my face. "You see, Jelani, magic is a living thing with a will to survive, like anything else. The Elders knew if our magic was at risk the cuffs would call to someone to bear them—to wield their power."

What does that even mean?

This is too much.

"Rue," Aasim's hand warms my back. "You're more than a stubborn girl from a poor neighborhood. You're *my* daughter, blood of the ancient gods of this land. Before the Chancellor united the tribes, before onyx ever existed, *we* dominated this land in all our glorious majesty." He pulls my face to his. "Our people—*your* people—possessed a magic beyond your wildest dreams."

My insides scream as he tiptoes around a truth I'm not ready to see.

"You have that *same* magic inside you, and with these cuffs you can access it. Use it to restore Ghizon."

No, there's a mistake.

This isn't . . . I'm not . . .

I can't breathe. I can't think.

"You are Ghizoni," Aasim says.

I'm not. Words lodge in my throat.

He really believes this. That I'm . . . no, he has it wrong. Somehow, this is all wrong. I don't even know these people. I hardly know *him.*

I'm just Rue—Rue from East Row.

The world spins and my chest tightens. The cuffs dangle from my wrists. Their burning swallows me and I can't look away. I'm transfixed, the whispers as clear as day, and yet still a tangled mess in my head.

"Th-these cuffs ... I ... I thought they just had s-something to tell me...."

"They do," Bati says. "Our Ancestors, our Elders, are saying they stand with you. With these cuffs, you have not only your own magic but theirs, too."

"I ... I don't ... but ..." My words and thoughts are all stutters. Bad-ass magic *would* come in handy right about now.

"Rue, with this power, you'd be ..."

"Unstoppable," I say.

CHAPTER 27

A PASSAGEWAY AT THE REAR end of the cave opens up to the very edge of the island, hugged by jungle foliage and cricket-chirping darkness. A stone path cuts through the trees to a cluster of short huts—chakusas—with cone roofs and woven doors. Bati showed me back here to a spacious room where I could have just a minute, a second to breathe.

I appreciate that.

My Air Maxes are caked in dirt. Shit's going to take forever to clean, if I can even clean them at all. I nudge a loose stone in the dusty floor with my shoe and glare at the woven ceiling, thoughts racing through my mind. I can hardly focus on any of them.

A mix of anger laced with frustration burns through me. I'm not some wielder of the Ancestors' magic, like they're making me out to be. I can't even get this "inner magic" I'm supposed to have to work. I'm no one's avenger. Ain't nothing special about my blood. I'm just me.

But can I really just walk away and leave things like this?

They're basically kin, brown-skinned like me.

I've never felt a connection to this place, but this . . . this is wrong.

I pull at the ends of my hair, which are crying for some coconut oil. Taking down the General and the Chancellor will do a lot of good for a lot of people. Maybe I can help that way? Not as Jelani, or whatever they think that means. But as me, as Rue.

But how would I even do that? Ugh, the million-dollar question. My head hurts. I'll figure this out. Somehow, I'll make a way. I always do.

I slip the cuffs on my wrists and they dangle there. The heat from them has all but died out, now that they're united. I can sense them, but it's not the same. It's like they were using me to get back together. But now that I have them both, they have nothing to say. I don't get it.

I close my eyes and search for that warmth, that familiar wiggle and twinge.

Nothing.

Focus.

I bite down, my nails digging into the straw arms of my seat. *Ow!* My tongue. I rake my hands through my hair. If they have an instruction manual on how to access this raw magic inside me, there because Aasim was my sperm donor, that would be helpful right about now.

"Jelani?" Aasim and Bati appear in the doorway. I wish they'd stop calling me that. I stand up and dust off my clothes. I can at least appear as if I have my shit together.

"Yeah? In here," I say.

"Everything alright?"

"I'm fine. Just thinking . . . figuring out my next move."

"You're not in this alone," says Bati.

I am. Protecting East Row, Tasha, taking down the General, the

Chancellor. I don't see a line of people trying to hop back to my block and throw down. I *am* in this by myself. But that's why Moms raised a diamond.

"I appreciate it," I say. Trying to work on my sass around these Ghizoni who *look* like me. "Thanks."

Speaking of East Row . . . I pull out my phone. Eight percent battery, but no signal, of course. "I need to check on my sister." How long have I been gone? No sunlight in the cave, so it was impossible to tell. And now it's pitch black outside.

I tap my watch and buzz Bri. Maybe she can figure out a way I can talk to Tasha. "I'm asking Bri to come here."

Aasim fidgets.

"That a problem?"

"Who is this Bri?" Bati asks Aasim.

"A Gray," Aasim says, and Bati frowns.

"Why do they look like that anyway?"

"The grayish skin? Something about the UVB rays and the veil over the island turns pale skin that grayish color." He turns back to Bati, whose frown has deepened. "Bri is her bes—"

"She's my best friend here. The only Ghizo—I-I mean, G-Gray—I trust." No shade to Aasim, but Bri's my girl. I pretty much just started talking to him. "I-I don't mean to say I don't trust you all here, I mean the only one I trust *of them.*"

Bati nods. "I understood what you said." He purses his lips.

This idea doesn't please him. Why?

"It is not for me to criticize. The Ancestors trust your judgment, as should I. Do as you wish." He turns to go. *Shit, did I offend him?*

Aasim watches him leave then turns to me. "It's a sensitive topic."

"But, Bri—"

"I know. But look at it from where they're standing. Everyone out there is the enemy. The Chancellor's brainwashed the people out there into worshipping him. Those outsiders in New Ghizon wield magic, thanks to him. You think they'd give that up? You think they'd see him the way we do?"

We.

I mean, he's right. People do get comfortable in their ways, like a favorite pair of jeans. Hell or high water, no matter how tight they get, they ain't throwing them out. Will it be the same with this?

"Bri would." *I think.* "I mean, I hope she would." My insides flip. Would she see what the Chancellor's done? Why it's wrong? Would she get it? "Well, I'm bringing her here, so I guess we'll find out."

"And if she doesn't see things our way?" he asks.

Our.

"Then what?" There's something in his gaze that makes me uneasy.

"I-I'll deal with it. With her." What does that even mean? I don't know. And I don't want to find out.

Like clockwork, my wrist vibrates. I'd told her I need to check on Tasha, and asked her to get here right away, alone and undetected.

Bri: K, send me the coordinates.

I shoot her our location.

Bri: Luke's keeping an eye on the General. Any movement in or out of Ghizon, he'll let us know.

Me: Thanks. Y'all still good?

Bri: Eh. I guess.

Me: See you soon. I want all the deets.

Bri will understand. She *has* to. She's always been my girl and she won't let me down in this. She usually recognizes messed-up shit when she sees it. She'll see this for what it is.

My insides are a bed of eels.

He tugs my hand harder and I follow as fast as I can. As if this time we might actually get out of this forest. As if this time we might finally make it to where he's leading me. My kicks skid clumsily over the damp forest floor. I hook an arm around the black bark of a tree and it's smooth to the touch, like polished ebony. Faster. He tugs, hands wrapped tight around my wrist. I'm breathless. I push, even though I know the crack is coming.

My hand hurts under the pressure of his squeeze. Fear does that— makes you stronger than you should be. His nails dig into my skin and I hop over a branch I know is coming before I even see it.

"A'ja! A'ja, do'vexi," he says.

He's talking to me?! He never talks.

"A'ja! A'ja, do'vexi!" His nails dig into my arm.

"I don't understand," I tell him, searching his expression for some indication of where we are and where he's trying to take me. But I find only panic.

Something cracks and in seconds I'm awake and panting. The thatched roof solidifies in focus and I can breathe again.

Aasim let me be after our exchange and I was thankful for it. My mind had been racing since our conversation about Bri. A moment to rest my eyes is what I thought I needed.

He spoke.

The boy in the dream *spoke* to me.

Like he knew I was there. And those trees—jpango, like the ones around here. I swallow to force myself to inhale.

It's just a dream.

It's not real.

I exhale and it turns into a yawn and I spot tiny red craters—fingernail wounds—dug into my wrist. They sting like a fresh wound.

I still my shaky hands. *A-a dream. Just a dream.*

Before I dozed off, the little girl with the colorful beads brought me a tray of refris. Maybe I should eat. Its fragrance washes over me like Ms. Leola's kitchen on Easter Sunday. Lemony, sugary, and sweet, but one bite in and I can't stomach anymore of it. Not when so much hangs in the balance. So much pressure.

I slip on the cuffs again and try to feel something.

Nothing.

No whispers, no flicker of feeling, no heat.

Everything's silent. Cold. So frustrating. I slide them off and set them on the bedside table.

Air. I need air.

And Bri should be here any moment. Matter of fact, it's taking her much longer than I'd expected.

I step out beneath the speckled sky painted with a strip of crimson. Bendy jpango trees cluster around one another overhead. Their leaves flutter in the wind, starlight twinkling between them. That's one thing about the nights in Ghizon, they're beautiful. And out here in the wilderness, even more so. Never seen views like this from my square of concrete back home.

I stick to the stone path, the sound of waves lapping the side of the cliff lulling me toward it. Bet I could see more of the stars from there.

I like staring up at the stars. Something about them feels so far and yet so close. I imagine Moms is up there watching over me, reminding me to make sure I shine.

She took me to the country once, just me and her. Tasha was at her Dad's grandma's. It was really odd that Moms had time off work and even more odd that she wanted to spend it in the boonies so far outside Houston you could see more cows than people.

"Where we going, Ma?" I had asked.

"Oh, you know, just felt like driving."

A lie. Moms ain't wasting gas money. I gave her side-eyes and noticed a giant bag in the back seat, a bunch of clothes spilling between its busted zipper. I felt weird in that moment. Moms always kept it one hundred with me, or so I thought, but in that moment something told me I didn't know everything she was thinking—and I wasn't going to.

"Well, wherever we going, do they have food? I'm hungry."

She had laughed and pulled out a turkey sandwich and hot chips, my favorite. "With extra mayo, no lettuce, and a thin slice of tomato, just like you like it." She'd gripped the steering wheel with a heavy sigh. "I just feel so free out here."

"Free?" I had asked. I never knew Moms felt chained. Now, I guess I get what she meant.

"Yeah, like out here it's just me and the stars. Nothing in between. I could just reach out and touch one if I wanted. Or be up there with them if I wanted."

"Ma, dancing with the stars is a TV show, I don't think you can actually do it." I'd laughed so hard at my own joke, my ribs hurt.

She'd joined in. "You a mess. I just mean that when I look up at the night sky, there's no distraction, no noise," she'd said. "I feel like if I reach high enough I can *actually* touch them. Back at home . . . when things are busy, you know . . . and work . . . I just. It's easier to see that the sky's the limit out here. There's nothing between you and the stars, you hear me? Nothing." She had squeezed my hand. "You just reach. Whatever it is, you make—"

"—a way, I know, Ma." I'd squeezed back.

I imagine Moms up there dancing with the twinkling specks overhead. And she could renegade and bop better than a DaBaby music video, so if she is dancing up there, she showing out f'sho.

The sound of lapping waves snatch me from my daydream. The farther the path goes, the denser the foliage. Trees rustle between my steps and I glance backward, but there's no one there. The path curves between another patch of bendy, crooked trees with familiar red flowers.

I know this nest of tangled branches, that crimson bloom.

The dream.

CHAPTER 28

I SHOVE PAST THE BRANCHES and over several fallen ones, the sound of the ocean growing louder. The knot of branches from my dream is real. I'm trudging through it, my heart in my throat. The constant feeling someone's watching cloaks my shoulders, but I keep walking toward the way the boy always leads me. Wisps of sounds like soft footsteps tickle my ear.

Crack.

"H-hello? Someone there?"

Silence.

The stone path turns to dirt and a layer of dead leaves. Trees close in around me, knitted tighter together, moonlight hiding behind wide, towering leaves.

I know this place.

I brush a finger across a black bark tree with deep red flowers.

Smooth to the touch, just like I thought it'd be.

A flicker of golden light flashes in the distance. I creep toward it, half curious, half terrified. The forest comes to an abrupt end up ahead. And there, on the literal edge of the mountain, is a ring of fire hissing like a snake around the perimeter of a pit.

And someone's inside it.

I squint, half expecting to see the little boy, his tiny hands and moon-like eyes. I peer between tangled branches, coarse bark scraping my knees.

In the center of the flames, a guy much too old to be the little boy pivots and thrusts like he's fighting an invisible enemy. He bounces back and forth on his feet, thighs like boulders clenching with each shift in stance. He moves like music, circling, slower at first, then faster. A staff made of orange wood—no, orange *light*—sparks as he slashes and twirls.

I gasp. I've seen flames from fingers, transport spells, hovering dishes, but this—a weapon made from magic?

I gape at my hands. *C-can I do that?*

Behind me, murmuring voices whisper. I *knew* someone else was out here. I peer backward, but darkness hugs my vision. The fire pit lights are dying out. But the guy? There's no one in the center. I looked away for a split second. He was *just* there. The hair on my back stands up. Am I'm seeing things? No, light, fire, or whatever it was, was *just* there.

The fire ring is a rusty glow of embers. Maybe he left. Maybe I'm losing my mind. Someone clears their throat.

"Who's there? Show yourself."

"It's not polite to spy on people." The guy from the clearing steps from the shadows, his angular jaw pulsing. Black fabric wraps around his legs, his torso, and his folded arms. He's a lot bigger in person, with thighs like drums and thick leather straps hugging his chest in an X. His deep-set dark eyes burn into mine and I ball my fists.

My magic might be broke, but these hands ain't.

"Creeping up on someone in the dark is a way to get an ass beating," I say.

He steps closer and moonlight illuminates his face. His features are softer than I thought. His dark eyes are set back beneath a prominent brow, but they're not stern; they're soft, slanted at the corners.

"I'm sorry." His voice is deep, but his hands fidget and his tone is cautious. *He's nervous!* "D-did I scare you? I-I didn't mean to. I would never—"

"It's all good." I offer a hand. "I'm Rue."

Closer now, I recognize him as the guy who helped us to our seats when we first arrived. The one frustrated with the flame staying lit in the stone bowl. But judging by his ass-whooping practice or whatever that was, it looks like his magic is working *just* fine.

Now *mine* on the other hand . . .

"Jhamal." He bows, raising my knuckles to his pillow-soft lips, and kisses. "My pleasure, Jelani, my Queen."

I swallow a laugh. He already feels bad and I'm trying to be polite. "I'm not a queen."

"You're daughter of Aasim. He works with the Grays in New Ghizon, their third in command." He grimaces. "I don't respect the other two. Thieves. Aasim is as good as a ruler to me. Which would make you"—he bows again—"my queen."

I laugh; can't even help it. He can't be serious. Is this game? If so, it's some weak-ass lines he spitting. He smiles and I chew my lip.

"Okay then, well, how do they say it where you are from?" he asks.

"What do you mean?" I want to be annoyed, but a smile tugs at my lips. I keep walking toward the pit, now barely distinguishable in the darkness.

He follows. "What do the gents from where you are from call you?"

"I don't know what you mean by *gents*. But I guess they'd call me . . ." I try to think of something that doesn't sound completely ridiculous to someone who's lived on an island that, technically speaking, doesn't exist—for his entire life. "Guys usually say girl, woman, even chick."

"Like with feathers, chick?" He tucks his hands under his armpits and pops out his neck.

"No." I sigh. "Not—"

He sputters a moment like his mouth's full of air, then bursts out laughing.

"You playing me?!" I shove his shoulder and he laughs harder. "You are *totally* playing me!"

"No, no, only kidding." He snorts, laughing. The definition in his jaw pulses when he laughs, and my toes are suddenly prickling. The dirt path ends and we keep walking on the rugged mountainscape, the salty air growing colder.

His chuckle settles down as we approach the pit he was training in. "I swear I only know a little. It sounds like a very different sort of place than here."

"It is."

"No magic?"

"None. Well, besides me."

The light above glitters in his eyes like diamonds against black velvet. "I could not imagine a world without magic."

"I couldn't imagine one with," I say, stepping into the pit, still shivering.

He conjures a flame and brushes the rim of the pit with his hands. "Some heat." It catches, circling us. "But to be the first is amazing," he says.

Fire dances around us, and our skin glows orange. He continues, "Your people back in your hoodhome, how do you say?"

"My hood."

"Your hood. The people there must think you very special. They must marvel at your gift."

"You would think, huh?"

"Now it is you who's telling jokes." His sleek cheekbones rise tight under his eyes as he laughs. A heat washes over me and I'm not sure if it's from the flames popping around us, or how close he's standing to me. I hug myself and find something other than his lips to stare at.

"Where I come from our people aren't treated special because of where we live, how we dress," I say. "Turn on the news and they say we're violent or criminal. Even lowlifes."

"What is it you mean *because* of where you live?"

"People where I'm from don't have a lot of money. Our houses aren't big and fancy." I face him. How do I make him understand? He's never seen my home. "Most cars—the things we use to get around—aren't shiny and new. Shit, if the fridge is full, we're doing good. Some dope slinging, too. But cops see that and think we're all that way. They see brown skin walking my block and assume hustlin' means we're bad and have no future. Like we can't come up from that shit."

"So they see your house and think you are what you live around?"

"Pretty much."

He jerks back, alarmed. "I would not do well in this hood. They would see my home and it would be very bad."

"Why is that?"

"Because our walls are woven together by horse shit."

I laugh so hard my cheeks burn. He smiles that twinkling grin of his and I'm almost woozy. His bare chest tenses and relaxes with his every move. Suddenly it feels more like midday instead of midnight.

"I have someone coming to visit, I should say good night. We'll be out of here soon."

"Ah. That's too bad. You come back, yes?"

I shrug. "I don't think so. But who knows?"

"And if I don't like this idea?" His plump lips spread and even his teeth sparkle.

I tuck a hair behind my ear, studying cracks in the ground beneath my toes. Maybe I can chat a little longer.

"How did you do that thing with the weapon earlier?" I ask, twisting the end of my hoodie.

"Oh, that trick is very easy." He squats, brushing the dusty floor of the pit with his fingertips. "But only one I can do here, I'm afraid. I am sure you can do much more than my silly tricks."

I laugh. "You'd think. What do you mean you can only do it *here*? Here in this pit?"

"Yes, come. I'll try to explain." He gestures for me to join him on the ground.

"I was born here," he says. "But from what I learned, Jelani, our people used to command the winds and the rain, brighten the luminance of the stars themselves. The very sea followed our Ancestors' commands. We were gods. We ruled this land. Now, sure"—he twists one hand over another and a tiny dish appears—"I can float a plate . . ."

He rubs two fingers together and a red long-stem rose appears between them. "Or conjure a rose for a queen . . ."

He hands it to me, our fingertips brushing, and I'm warm all over.

"But we will never be what we once were as long as the Grays wield our magic."

That explains why he was so frustrated trying to keep the flame lit in the dining hall. Their magic is there, but small, stunted.

Is that my problem too? I'm not even Ghizoni, not really. So if *his* magic is subdued, mine *must* be no more than an ember. I'm inches from the flames, but chilly all over when the realization washes over me.

I *have* to get the cuffs to work.

Without them I won't be able to wield magic ever again—at all.

And where would that leave Tasha? Where would that leave East Row?

Puke burns its way up and I hunch over, leaving a pool of bile at my feet. Jhamal's hand is on my back as I heave again. Nothing but spit this time.

"Jelani, are you okay?"

I clean my mouth with my sleeve. "I-I just have to figure this out th-these cuffs. O-or my sister . . . my home . . ."

"Just them, my Queen? The spirit of our Ancestors remains alive in those cuffs. A relic that's been in our tribe since the clouds were hung in the sky. And they chose to call to someone . . . for protection."

Someone . . . *me.*

I'm tingly all over. "Your magic seems to be working okay out here. I mean, that weapon was wild." Couldn't they use that to defend themselves? Fight back?

He brushes the dirt around us. "This is where the Elders were buried, next to the Ancestors. When I am here, I am closest to my roots. When I am here, my magic moves in me fiercely. But beyond this pit, simple spells are my limit, I'm afraid."

Wind unsettles the dusty pit floor and I can't look away.

"Can you feel them here, my Queen? Do they speak to you?"

I press a palm to the dirt and close my eyes. At first the dirt is gritty between my fingers, then everything goes dark. Bursts of light swirl in my mind's eye like someone turned on a TV in my head. Images of the forest—the familiar forest—and my little friend pull me in. The heat from his hand causes mine to sweat and we run. Over and under brush, around jpango trunks wider than I've ever seen. I'm dripping with sweat, my hands, my hair, my face.

We run and this time there's no crack.

He takes me through the entire forest until I'm panting and breathless. No tall towers or steel buildings in sight. A tall peak swallowed by dense foliage is up ahead, so tall it nuzzles the clouds. Yiyo.

Is this the before?

Little Man pulls me toward the mountain and I can't follow fast enough. Closer to the mountain I can make out Yiyo's carved doors, but it doesn't smell of oil and smut. Whiffs of rosemary and jasmine fill the air.

This *is* the before.

I can feel this place. It's as real as the wind in my lungs, like the cool air sifting through my roots. Whispers play from the forest behind us, as if the trees themselves can talk, and they're urging us on. The vision shakes like this might be the end. Like I might be pulled away.

I'm not leaving. I focus hard on the scene. "What is it you want me to see?" I whisper to him, and we stop.

"Where are we?" I ask Little Man, but he just stares at me. I reach for Yiyo's door, but it escapes like sand between my fingers. The world around us shifts, obscuring everything. The trees lift, Yiyo dissolves into thin air and the forest behind us bleeds into the sea.

Now a village surrounds us. A crowd of people sway in a circle, arm in arm, singing, celebrating. Music pounds like thunder and a sea of bells *ting-ling*. Gravel crackles under my feet. No one in the crowd even flinches, as if we're not there.

They're wrapped in robes of purples and blues with threads in gold and bright pinks. Thin belts loop their waists and golden rings adorn their hair. More gold ornaments hug their knuckles, crown their heads, coil up their arms. Even their sandals are adorned with gilded beads between their toes.

The Ghizoni, in all their glory.

Before the Sickness, before the Chancellor.

Clusters of cone huts are in the backdrop, their doors fashioned with hair-like fibers and dotted with flecks of gold. Wide smiles warm me up inside and laughter rings so loud it rattles in my head.

I start to latch on to some sort of meaning, but the setting switches again in a dust storm of colors. Little Man holds fiercely to me this time as the people depart like dust on the wind. The next scene settles around us and Little Man digs his hands into me.

I hold him tighter. "I-it's okay. I-it's just a dream. We're gonna be okay." I think.

The wind picks up as the darkness lifts, like someone's fast-forwarded to sunrise. It's dawn and the gusts settle. My little friend buries his face deeper into my hoodie. He won't even look?

I gulp. What's coming?

Sunlight peeks over the horizon and a man in a golden breast-plate, looking like an older version of Aasim, storms past us thrashing his hands.

An Elder?

With each swipe of his arm, trees are uprooted and flung through the air, out of his way in a blur of black and green. The ground trembles as a trunk rips from the earth, leaving a giant crater in its wake.

I gasp and the man turns and stares right at me.

I take several shaky steps backward.

He still comes.

H-he sees me? And hears me?

I shove Little Man completely behind me when the Elder raises his hands like he's pulling down the very sky from overhead. Light dims and a loud clap rips through the air. He mutters something I can't understand and fear pricks my insides like daggers.

I want to run, to move. But I'm stuck, frozen a few feet from him.

The Elder stares, but instead of malice in his gaze . . . there's . . . is that . . . fear? He panics, and I tremble too. "I c-can feel it," I say to Little Man, but he keeps his face tucked away. I can feel what the Elder's feeling. Fear, worry, pain.

He clenches his jaw and pulls harder. The sky blackens like an afternoon storm. Violent. Dark. Sudden. Cold rain pelts down on me, thumping on my head. Malice fills his eyes.

He's going to attack me.

L-like I'm the—

My throat constricts. *I'm* the enemy in this vision? Oh my god, I am. *I'm* the enemy here. Th-the Elder wants me to feel what he felt. He's showing me . . . letting me see for myself what it was like when the Chancellor came for them. When he fled for his life.

A young child cries in the distance and the Elder flinches. Aasim? I-it's Aasim. The Elder's hands twitch and the weight of his sadness pangs through me.

He has to decide: Go for the baby or fight the enemy?

As if he can read my mind, he twists in the air and thrusts at us. I brace for the blow, holding Little Man tight behind me.

Something slams into my chest and I fly backward, hitting the ground with a thud.

I'm panting and Jhamal stands over me.

"My Queen? Are you okay?"

"The boy . . . I . . ."

"What boy?"

"I have to . . . he . . ." I pat the ground and realize I'm back in the pit. My next breath comes a little easier. I'm back on the cliff with Jhamal; dying flames crackle around us now. My clothes are wet . . . like rain-soaked, wet.

I'm okay. It's okay. It's over. The dream or vision or whatever it was is over.

"Did you feel them? The Ancestors?" he asks again.

"Y-yes, I-I can feel them," I say to Jhamal.

And they can feel me.

I dust myself off. "I-I saw them. O-or was with them . . . o-or I *was* them. I don't know."

"Saw who?"

"The Elder? H-he could uproot trees, warp the sky, command the rain, move the air like ripples of water. He shoved them at me."

I sound delusional. This sounds completely delusional.

Jhamal smiles and our fingers brush each other again. This time we hold them there.

"That sort of magic hasn't been seen in my lifetime," he says, his breath so close it's warm on my ear. "But, yes, my Queen—*that* is the sort of power our people used to have."

I don't have words.

To hear it is one thing. But to *see* a single man move the earth with a slight movement of his hands. To watch him choose to fight, but know it ended in his death. I graze Jhamal's arm; its warmth draws me to him.

"It's so terrible. All of it is so terrible. I'm so sorry." Thoughts race in my head, but shouts from beyond the fire snatch me away from the edge I'm teetering on—the edge of freaking TF out.

"Rue!"

I yelp.

Aasim's running full speed toward me. Jhamal throws sand on the fire and we dash toward him.

"Been looking all over for you." Aasim does a double take from me to Jhamal and back to me.

"You scared the mess out of me," I say. "What's up?"

Aasim's stare is laced with worry.

"What's wrong?" I ask.

"Bri's here."

Over Aasim's shoulder in the distance is a narrow, fair-skinned figure also running toward us, waving her arms. I push past him, eager to hug my girl, but angst is all over her face.

Something's up. "What happened?"

She catches up to us, out of breath. "I-I wanted to synthesize a satellite signal with the hologram feature on my watch and try to connect it to a cell phone. A long shot but . . ."

"Bri, English."

"I tried to reach Tasha on the way here to see if it'd even work." She fidgets. Aasim paces in the backdrop.

"And?"

"Rue, there's been another shooting in East Row."

CHAPTER 29

B ACK INSIDE MY CHAKUSA, Tasha's face flickers into view, the hologram hovering there above my watch.

"Tasha," I say. Her mouth is moving but the image comes and goes, glitching.

"Can you hear me?" Her voice comes through choppy.

"It's connected securely," Bri says, tapping a giant screen on her lap. "I can't see her, but you should be able to. Hold on . . . two more seconds . . . *annnnnd* now. She should be able to hear you."

The image sharpens and Tasha's face comes through clearer. Her cheeks are puffed, eyelashes wet. "Rue?"

Just hearing her voice is like wedging a dagger into an open wound. The necklace sits on her neck and my pulse ticks a little slower.

"T, you okay?" I reach for her face, but my fingers flutter through the orangey hue. My heart sinks. *I wish she was here.*

"I'm okay, but Demarcus . . ." Her voice trails off. Demarcus is like a nephew to Ms. Leola. The same Demarcus who comes around from time to time with Julius to help her around the house. He worked at Ole Man Stan's Meat Market and went to college at night.

"How's Ms. Leola doing?" I ask.

Tasha glances over her shoulder. "She's okay I guess. Just trying to get in touch with her sister. She's working on a few cakes to take over there this evening." Body ain't even cold and Ms. Leola already cooking up love in the midst of her own pain.

"Hug her real tight for me, T."

She nods, smoothing a tear from her cheek.

"Did the cops have any more information?"

"Nah," she says. "They didn't even come tell us. We found out on the news. They saying he might have been mixed up in drugs."

Bullshit, not Demarcus. That's, like, their default excuse.

"They blaming Litto's crew. The mayor put a curfew in effect. It's bad, Rue."

My nails dig into my palm until it bleeds.

Multiple shootings, robberies, every other week. The cop's words from the alleyway swirl in my memory. *It's not safe out here—worse than I've ever seen it.*

"Isn't Litto's crew the same people you went looking into at the tattoo shop?"

"Don't you worry about that. I got caught up here trying to figure out something . . . it's . . . I've almost got it figured out. I'll be home real soon."

She nods and silence hangs between us. There aren't words that feel right to fill the space. But the thought of ending the call makes my knees shake. So we just hold the call. She seems older somehow in these last few days. Like we've lived years in the span of a week. Holding her here, where I can see her, makes me feel like she's safer somehow.

The image of her head flickers. "T, you still there?" I glance at Bri, studying her flat glass screen. She gives me a thumbs-up. The image stutters back into view. "Don't take that necklace off, sis. Not even when you wash your butt."

"I won't. I promise." She laughs, her voice boxy from the connection. "I like wearing it, kinda feels like Mama is watching over me." She strokes the thin golden chain at her neck.

"Give Aunt Bertha and them my love."

"Okay."

"And *no* leaving the house. Get the damned groceries delivered, something. I'll pay you back for it. Just keep yo behind inside."

"Okay, okay, I get it."

"I *will* see you soon, T."

"Please just get back here. I feel safer when you're close."

"Me too."

"See you soon," she says.

Bri gives me a raised brow, asking if the call is done. I nod yes, and blow a kiss at Tasha's fading face.

Bri's hand warms my back and I flinch.

"You okay?" she asks.

"Yeah." A lie. I picture my fist kissing the General's face. But I will be.

I kicked Aasim out of the hut for some privacy for the call to Tasha. Truth be told, after the call, I wanted to break the news to Bri first about everything I'm about to tell her. Not because I have to, but because it seems like the kind thing to do, considering how tight we've been. Bri has no idea the truth she walked into. And for her sake, for our friendship's sake, I hope she came here with eyes wide open.

"You're pacing," she says, setting her screen aside. "You're obviously not okay. Rue, talk to me."

I'm going to. But where to start?

"I'm sorry about Demarcus." She's standing up now, the lightness gone from her voice.

I don't want to do this. I don't want to throw away a year of friendship. But if she can't see how fucked up this is, can we even really be friends?

"Please?" She steps to me, bright green eyes behind those red-rimmed glasses. "Whatever it is, you know you can tell me."

I still my shaking hands and scoop up the cuffs.

"Rue?" Her voice is strained.

Stop putting it off. Talk. "Bri, what did you see when you came through Yiyo Peak?"

"Huh?" Her brows cinch. "Is that a real question?"

"Real as a heartbeat, yep."

"Okay, uhm, let's see." She chews her lip. "I saw piles and piles of onyx. Then Aasim took me through this long, caved-in tunnel to a wall, which we walked through. Somehow! And it opened up to more mountain. There were tables and chairs. Uhhmm, what else . . . ?" She glances around the room. "That's pretty much it. Aasim didn't let me stop and sightsee. He just took me through the mountain and out back here."

So Bati and everyone are tucked away? They really don't trust anyone from the District.

"So you didn't see anyone? Not a single person?"

"No, why? What am I missing? Just tell me."

"There's an entire people living in secret here, Bri."

The lines on her brow deepen.

I slip the cuffs on to keep my hands busy. "An entire tribe of magical people who look like *me*."

She shakes her head no, like what I'm saying don't make sense.

"And no one here has onyx bound to their wrists. *None* have the 'great Chancellor's gift.'" I use air quotes on that last part.

"What? I don't understand. What do you mean *magical* people, Rue?"

"I mean fire-wielding, matter-shifting, *magical* brown-skinned people. People like me."

"That means—" She settles onto the bed. "Wait, what *does* that mean?"

Aasim's warning haunts me. "It means magic was never the Chancellor's to give. He stole it. It was . . . theirs."

Bri parts her lips to speak, then closes them, looking hella confused. Maybe I'm not explaining it well. If I had an accurate history book, I'd give her that. Maybe that'd make it easier for her to see. Or maybe her confusion is rooted in something else. I gotta keep trying. Surely she'll see.

"When the Chancellor showed up to unite all the tribes," I say, "Aasim's people fled here in secret."

"You can't be serious," she says, an incredulous look on her face. "This is a joke."

Does my face look like I'm joking? What about any of this sounds like I'd be joking? I *woosah* for some patience.

"Rue, that was, like, over sixty years ago," she rolls her eyes. "And I've never even read anything like that. How do you even know for sure?"

My pressure rises. "You think I'd make this up?"

"No, I—that's not what I meant. I just—this is a lot to digest."

"A whole lot," I agree.

She pulls her sweater tighter around herself. "I know you wouldn't lie. I know that, Rue. I-I just don't understand."

"I wasn't done. Maybe if you knew more you'd understand more. Can you just listen?"

"I'm sorry, go ahead." She pretends to zip her lip with a finger.

I continue. "Aasim's village was dying out of some Sickness when he was born. In fact, his mother died of the Sickness when she had him. So Aasim only had his dad when he was small."

"Your grandfather?" She presses her glasses to her nose.

I shift on my feet. "Sure, m-my grandfather."

"Oops. Sorry, I'll shut up, I swear."

"Thanks." I offer a half smile, hoping she means it this time. I tell her everything, how Aasim's ancestors got magic from the gods, how a Sickness killed almost everyone in their tribe, how the Chancellor found Aasim amidst the fleeing and raised him like a son, imagining his only memories and allegiance would be to him. And how his people have been living in secret, biding their time.

"Biding their time for what?"

An unsettled feeling clinches my insides. "That's for them to answer, not me."

"I-is there any proof of this?" Her words sting. *Denial.*

"My word. The people here. That's proof enough . . . for me."

She takes a deep breath.

"Plus I saw it . . . sort of."

"Saw it how?" She's pacing. She says she don't think I'm lying but she ain't acting like I'm telling the truth.

"In a vision . . . or something."

"A vision? Rue, that's nonsensical talk."

I am silent. And clearly irritated.

"I know you wouldn't just lie, Rue. I'm not saying that. But maybe you don't know what you saw?"

Wow. "Uhm, I was wide awake." Now *I'm* pacing. I expected this to shake her, but this? Maybe Aasim was right.

More silence.

She mutters to herself like she's replaying everything I just said. She's blinked practically twelve times in the last second. She looks every which way but at me. There's something in her eyes I can't place. Curiosity, yes, but something else. She stares at her wrists, thumbing her finger over the onyx.

"Stolen." Her words come out a mere whisper, like she's talking to herself.

"Stolen." My pulse quickens.

Her chin touches her chest and I can't tell if she's sad or pissed. I take a step back.

"Every . . ." She shakes her head no. Her eyes are glued to the floor even though I'm two feet in front of her. She won't look at me.

Silence.

I could say something, fill the space with words. But is it my job to make her feel better about the stolen magic on her wrists? I didn't do this. Aasim's people didn't do this. The Chancellor did. I told her the truth, that's all I can do. She's gotta decide what to do with it.

That's on her. Not me.

She picks up her chin and her green eyes are glassy. "S-so e-everything I-I've ever known is a lie? That's what you're saying to me, Rue?!"

"I-I know this ain't easy to hear. But, I mean, it's the truth." Around truth, some people act like roaches when the lights come on. They scatter, trying to not hear it. But Bri wouldn't be like that. Would she?

She mutters something I can't hear.

"Sorry, what?"

"I-I believe you. I'm just—" A tear rolls down her cheek. "So angry. That everything I was taught wasn't true. That I've been walking around here like . . . like all this knowledge, my grades . . . being the top of my class . . . as if any of this really matters. Everything I've learned. All the practice I've done. I worked so hard to be the smartest. As Zruki, I'll be doing mostly mine work. I probably won't ever get a big fancy job. But I still wanted to be smart. Like, real smart. You know? Even if others look down on me, I'd know that I'm *just* as capable as they are."

I've never heard Bri talk about being Zruki before. Not like this.

"Being born to Zruki parents and designated it's like no matter what you do, you're still Zruki. You can't get rid of that title. It's like a stain."

"Like people only see the box they put you in," I say. "They don't see what you're really capable of, what you *could* do." *My entire life back home.*

"Exactly! So I worked really hard to blow people away, prove them wrong," she says.

"Me too, I—"

She cuts me off. "Be the smartest Zruki in all of Ghizon."

I get it. Make a way out of no way.

She turns to me, pain written on her face. "But you're telling me none of that work matters. Not anymore." She cleans more tears with the back of her hand. "Like, every single thing I've done was pointless because it was all built on a lie. And I'm just *so* angry he would do this!"

This is messed up on so many levels. But why we still talking about her? I mean, she didn't really get the shortest end of the stick here. Did she even hear what I said? I stuff my hands in my pocket and stare at my shoes.

"I just . . . ugh!" She growls in frustration, tossing her red frames on the bed. "I *knew* I shouldn't have made that watch," she whispers under her breath. "Then none of this would have ever happened."

Did she just . . . ? "*What* did you just say?"

She sighs. "I just mean—"

"Nah, don't backtrack. You regret making me this watch? The watch that let me visit my sister without setting off Patrol? The watch that lets me go back and forth between here and there to protect her and figure this magic shit out without getting hemmed up by the Laws?"

"The who? No—I . . ." She rubs her temples. "I just meant all this trouble started with that. I should have known that chances are this would snowball." She paces faster. "You'd see your sister. Miss being home. Of course it would be hard to not touch her, she's your family."

"I TOUCHED HER TO SAVE HER FROM BEING KILLED IN A CAR WRECK!" Is she serious? "That's what you do when you *care*, Bri—you take risks."

"Rue, I've been there for you since day one. Don't even act like that!"

"I'm not acting like anything. You were my girl, true, when it didn't cost you nothing. And sure you're angry now, but what you gon' do? Anything?"

"Rue, this is not my fault and I came to Ms. Leola's at my own personal risk."

"You know damn well this watch makes travel undetectable. You said it yourself. What risk? And no, this isn't your fault. I've said that a thousand times, even though you're not listening! But what do we do now, Bri? You still sportin' my people's *stolen* magic on your wrist."

She holds her arm to her chest, aghast. "What, you expect me to get rid of it? I *earned* this!"

You can't earn something that's stolen. But I let her talk. That's what people do when they can't hear.

She goes on. "I'll have you know that hacking is very dangerous and—"

"—it's encrypted so no one knows it was you. You cover your tracks well."

"So you're saying I'm not a real friend."

"I don't know what you are anymore. First thing out your mouth is how you the victim. And I mean, sure, believe that. But eventually I hope you realize this is bigger than your straight A's not meaning anything. At the end of the day you still have all that knowledge you stacked up. You got freedom. What they got, Bri?"

She looks shocked, like I slapped her. Like she gotta choose to mourn the shit she lost *or feel* for me.

"An entire people's culture was ripped away, their right to live taken, the gifts that make them special used and perpetrated by someone else. Bri, people are dying. Fuck your straight A's."

She's beet red. "Rue, I didn't know!"

"No, you didn't know. But now that you do . . . what? You *regret* even making my watch in the first place? *That's* your takeaway?" *This is so fucked up.*

This is getting way out of control. I grab my cuffs from the table. "I need some air."

She glances around nervously.

"Don't be ridiculous. Ain't nobody gon' hurt you here"—*without my say*—"so you can wipe that look off your face."

"Rue—"

I walk out. I can't make somebody see something they ain't ready to. Maybe with time she'll come around. It's not my job to unpack that for her. I'm unpacking my own shit, thank you very much.

And besides, I have bigger things to worry about. Like keeping my people alive when it feels like everyone, everywhere wants to see us dead.

CHAPTER 30

THE DINING AREA IS a chatter of conversations over breakfast, but I'm distracted by the scrape of my fork on my plate.
I push the food around, as if that'll make it smaller, and flex
my wrists.

Late last night, word arrived that the General's men left and
came back with twice the numbers. And now they're inside the
mountain tunnel trying to force their way through the wall. I *really*
hope the enchantment holds. Everyone here is oddly calm, trusting
that it will, but as a precaution, every person, men and women alike,
is covered in plated armor with war-painted faces. With their magic
so weak and the cuffs not responding to me . . . I can't even think
about what'll happen if the General manages to break through.

The cuffs stuffed in my hoodie taunt me. I was up until damn
near sunrise trying to spark some sort of magic. At times, I could
feel a tug, like the magic's there. But the cuffs don't answer. It's like
they chose me, then changed their mind. How many more people
are going to die before I can figure this out?

I shove my plate away. A chunk of glazed dough plops in Bri's bowl.
She works her fingers around the two-prong sticks they gave her. I know
they have forks back there because they offered me a fork yesterday.

"You need a hand?" I ask her.

"No, I got it." We haven't spoken since the argument. I don't know what to say to her. She keeps getting side-eyes from everyone, a few whispers here and there. But she keeps her head down, eating. She sighs, exasperated, storming up from the table.

I love her, but she's going to have to work through this on her own.

Aasim is across from me, neck deep in his fille—which is like rice, but purple. I'd told him earlier this morning that I wanted to leave today.

"Not yet! Let me look into something first, then we can get out of here," he'd said.

"Today though, right?" I'd pressed.

"Hopefully. But *really* soon." He'd said he has a plan to share with me, but the Chancellor fell off his radar, so he wanted to square that up before we get moving.

I want to get back to Tasha and take care of the General from there, meet him off his turf. Basic squabble rules: jump somebody on their home turf, end up outnumbered. I'ma start at Dezignz, taking his boys out one by one. Make them summon him. Draw him out. Assuming I can get these damn cuffs to work.

But how will I even get out of here with the General supposedly in the mountain trying to break through? I make a point to ask Aasim about that later and rub my temples, trying to ignore the nagging feeling things are spinning out of control. I chew my lip a little *too* hard. *Ow.*

"Your mother did that." Aasim tears a bite from a buttered roll. "She would bite her bottom lip whenever she was nervous."

"I'm not nervous."

He laughs. "She would lie about it, too."

I roll my eyes. My father's nose is wide and his jaw angular, like mine. His long fingers wrap around his spoon as he slurps another bite. My "piano" fingers are oddly long, too. Moms used to joke about getting us one, knowing damn well we ain't have room or money for that. I let silence hang there a minute, massaging my wrists, sore from the weight of the cuffs I'd worn for hours last night.

"So, how . . . uhm . . . how'd you meet Moms?"

He looks up all too eager, smiling. "You really want to know?"

Gah. Don't make this more awkward than it already is. "Uhhh, yeah. I asked didn't I?" I swear I don't mean for it to come out that way. It just does. "S-sorry. I-I mean, yes, I'd like to know. Please."

"Your mom had a smart mouth, too. Couldn't tell her anything. That's actually how it started."

"Oh yeah?" I settle back against my chair, trying to stop grinning like a little kid. I can't remember the last time I smiled like this. And with everything going on, I could use a smile.

"I was there, scouting the place. Thinking about storing the cuff somewhere in the human land, so I'd slip over time to time and just observe. Anyway, this one time I visited a spot I liked. They had a guy there who played jazz like velvet. I'd never heard anything like it. So I snuck in and there she was. It was speakeasy night and she took the mic. When she opened her mouth, it was over. I knew, Ghizoni or not, I never wanted to leave her sight."

"So . . . ?"

"So, I didn't leave." He laughs. "I stayed there and tried talking to her. She was all attitude at first. But I really liked that jazz style so I'd been reading up on it and she was impressed I knew a thing or two."

Imagining Moms doing anything but working is sort of weird. "Moms sees straight through BS. Can't get one past her."

"Yes, she does." His shoulders slump. "Did."

He really misses her.

I miss her too.

"After that I asked her out. It didn't take long for me to decide I wasn't coming back anytime soon, if ever. She had the most beautiful smile. She . . ." His eyes glaze over. ". . . I'd just never met anyone like her. So I stayed. I told her I'd figure out how to make it work. I told her . . ." His words trail off and he stares at nothing.

"It's fine. I get it. I don't usually talk about her either." *Hurts too much.*

He says nothing for several moments. Then takes another bite and blots his mouth with his napkin. "Alaya nah, ick e'bah."

"Alaya, *what?*"

"Alaya nah, ick e'bah—grow stronger in the pain. You need to study up on your Ancestors' language."

Alaya nah, ick e'bah.

Grow stronger in the pain.

Sounds like something Moms would say.

"Where would I even find a book like that?"

"I can get you one, if you're really interested."

"I might be; I'll let you know."

His lips curl the way mine do. I wonder how much he told Moms about this place. "So, uhm . . . did you and Moms . . ." I draw circles on the table with my finger.

He leans on his elbows on the table, smiling. "I'm listening."

I draw more circles. "Nothing. Never mind. Tell me about the General."

"You sure?"

"I'm sure. Another time."

"Fair enough." He winks, pushing his bowl aside. "So, the General. I'm thinking the safest place for you is here. He's not getting through that wall."

This dude, I swear. Three steps forward, two back. And if everyone here really believed that, why they walking around suited up in armor? That's just Aasim trying to keep me close. Which is . . . kind. But nope. That's not how it's going down.

"I'm not staying here. No disrespect, but this isn't my home. I'm not Ghizoni."

He glances at the cuff I'm turning in my hand. "You are."

Even if I was . . . how am I worthy of all *this*? All they think I'm supposed to be able to do? "No. I'm not. Look, no use in us arguing. I have my sister, Ms. Leola . . ."

"Bring them here."

He really doesn't get it. "It's not just one or two people. When you from where I'm from, the whole place is family. I told you that when you made me leave. I'm not leaving East Row. Who's going to protect folks back home if I come here?"

"Who's going to avenge the Ghizoni if you don't?"

Sigh.

"I'm going home. You're just gonna have to trust me on this. I need to be there with my sis. And besides, if I can draw him out to my neighborhood, that takes the heat off here."

"Alright, well." Aasim throws his hands up in surrender. "I'll let it go for now, but your people here need you too."

My people are in East Row.

"So what's your plan?" I ask. "What you been working on?"

"I'm trying to find hard evidence that the General is taking his orders from the Chancellor. That this whole street gang thing has to ultimately be his doing. And *why.* No way the General's doing all this under the Chancellor's nose." He strokes his chin. "I put a few feelers out, waiting to hear back."

"I still want the General's head."

"And you'll have it. He's going to tire of trying to break through that enchanted wall. And when he does, he's going to look to other means. We can do this one of two ways: Try to pit the General and the Chancellor against each other or take them both head on." He picks a shred of meat from his teeth. "Still sorting that out."

"Shoot, I was just hoping to bust up in his tattoo shop Scarface style. Tell 'em say hello to my little friend . . . ." I set the cuffs on the table. "When I get these bad boys working, that is."

"You will. Keep trying. It's in you, Rue."

"And, uhm, is it just us? Can you even help?" I don't mean it to sound rude. It sort of does. "I mean, Bri mentioned something about your magic being reprimanded because I left, or whatever."

He wipes his face. "The Chancellor poisoned my magic. Much like the chaser you felt after using magic to save your sister. Without the antidote, you would have—"

"Died."

"Yep, mine's just a bit more severe. And the Chancellor's the only one who can undo it." He's staring off in the distance. This isn't something he's trying to talk about. I can respect that.

"My bad. I didn't know he'd do that to you when I left. I—"

"Don't be. He actually did this to me when he found out about your mother. When I brought you here a year ago, he'd said he'd never trust me with magic again. None of that is your fault. All my own doing."

"It's fear. He's just scared of you because you don't need his stupid onyx."

"He's scared of you, too, trust me. With your Ancestors' magic and your mother's hard head . . . he's *smart* to be scared."

I laugh.

"And I *can* use magic, Rue, it just has a steep price. He hasn't taken my powers. He can't do that and he knows it. But he's attached a death toll on it that'll trigger if I use a spell. If I transport to your home, I die. If I strike someone with magic, I die."

I shift in my seat, cuffs clinking in my zipped pocket.

"In many ways," he says, grimacing, "I'm not much use at all."

"Not true. I have these cuffs because of you." I nudge his shoulder. "I'm going to destroy them. All of them. And I wouldn't be able to do that without your help. Moms used to say ain't nobody gonna do for you what—"

He finishes my sentence "—what you won't do for yourself." Our eyes meet and his droop. He throws an arm around my shoulder. I let him.

"I loved her, Rue. More than life itself."

Something about the solemn look in his eye, or maybe it's the way his shoulders slump, makes me believe him.

"Jelani?" The familiar voice makes my toes curl. "Excuse me, I'm sorry. I was wondering if I could have a word with you?" I don't even have to turn around to know Jhamal's behind me. I chance a look at my father, who pauses chewing, eyes on our visitor.

This is awkward. *Please* don't say anything to embarrass me. He looks between us several times, but says nothing, thankfully.

Jhamal bows, half his chest covered in a gold breastplate. "Ruler Aasim."

"No need for all that." My father waves a hand as he finishes his bite and stands. "I was just, uh—finishing up. Rue, if I could see you over here a second?"

I resist rolling my eyes as Jhamal dips his chin.

"What's that about?" my father asks, pulling me to the side.

"Nothing," I say, pushing him to walk away. "Weren't you just leaving?"

"No, really. Who's that?" He points back, craning his neck.

I shove him along harder. "No one."

"Do you like him?" he whispers, lips twisted in a suggestive smile.

"OMG. I'm not doing this with you. Go. Shoo. Don't you have some recon to do? I'll see you later so we can get out of here."

He steps outside but turns back, a whimsical look in his eye. "I'm just saying, a Ghizoni boy paired with our blood could ma—"

"*Dadddd!*" I cover my ears, cheeks burning. "*Stahhhp.*"

"Too soon?" He throws his hands up in surrender. It's actually kind of cute.

"Bye!" I can't stop smiling as my dad disappears around the corner. I blow a quick breath before turning around.

"Shall we walk?" Jhamal's voice rolls off his tongue like honey and I bite my lip. *Ow.*

Fire flickers in crescent-shaped bowls, warming the craggy corridor. Outside the dining hall, a path leads us to an opening, brimming with sunlight. We walk toward it, the clang of his armor echoing our steps.

"I heard you are really leaving soon. I just wanted to say goodbye." His eyes twinkle and soft impressions dent his perfect cheeks. *What is it* with me and dimples? I friggin' love them. I'm warm all over. Much warmer than before.

"I'm sad to see you go, but you have monsters to fight," he adds.

Sunlight washes over us and the stuffy air evaporates. I dig the toe of my shoe in the ground. "No one else can fix this. I will."

"I am a good fighter. If you're ever in need of extra hands, it would be an honor to come to your aid. Even with little magic, give me a weapon and I will draw blood."

What is it with dudes always trying to save you?

"You think you tough, huh?" I give him side-eyes and we crack up laughing. We pass beneath the shade of a particularly bendy jpango tree and for that glimmer of a moment, laughing, the noise of everything fades.

"It is true, I do not have magical relics from the Ancestors, but I can do whoop-ass too."

He's hilarious. I playfully slap his bare shoulder, his rounded muscle flexing beneath my fingers. These folks really need central AC.

"If I ever need help, you'll be the first I call." I don't know if it's true. But it feels good to say.

"I will hold on to that, my Queen." His gaze stays on mine as he presses his soft lips to my knuckles. Heat rushes through me like a waterfall shoved through a clogged drain.

I should pull away, but I don't.

He should let go, but he doesn't.

Somehow we're inches closer than we were a moment ago. My breath is fragile in my chest. His eyes hold me there as if I'm floating.

Say something, stop staring all googly eyed. "I—"

"Ssshhh." He presses a finger to my lips. "We won't say goodbye. Just see you later."

I close my eyes, savoring the moment, when my arm vibrates with a loud buzz. Orange light flashes from my watch, blinding me.

It's Luke.

I put some distance between us and the warmth dissolves as quick as it came. Tiny letters form on the screen.

Luke: RUE, TASHA'S BEEN TAKEN! GET HOME, HURRY!

My pulse spikes. "I'm sorry. I—"

Jhamal stares, confused.

"I—I have to go." I try to run off, but he holds on to my fingers.

"It is quicker on the edge of the island, the Ancestors' burial ground." He glances at my watch. "You are leaving, yes? Something's wrong. I see it in your eyes." He points. "The way you came is long. But on the very edge of the sea, where you saw me training, go there. Your transport signal will work." His fingers still hold on to mine. His words are saying go, but his touch is saying something different altogether.

"Please don't tell Aasim. Don't tell anyone."

He dips his chin in a slight bow, but I can see the disapproval in his stare. I mouth the words "Thank you," savoring the last of his touch. My hand slips from his fingers and I run. Down the path through the trees, the edge of the island looms. I glance at the gold metal peeking from my pocket. "Hope this works."

Choppy waves slap jagged rock as the dining area and surrounding huts grow smaller in the distance. I urge my feet faster, air ragged in my lungs. The sky is stormy, black with cracks of lightening in the distance. The cuffs clank against each other and I zip up my pocket so they're tucked away safe.

Sharp gusts whip my clothes every which way, like hands pulling, tugging me back, begging me not to go. Salty air stings my eyes when I reach the Ancestors' burial ground where Jhamal was training. My fingers hover over my watch.

What do I tell Bri?

Me: Ready my signal to Tasha's NOW! URGENT!!

Bri: ???

Me: No time!! NOW pls.

Bri: Five seconds . . . Rue, don't go alone, please.

Four . . .

Three . . .

Bri: Rue?? Hello??

Two . . .

Aasim's face flashes in my mind.

One . . .

Sorry, Dad. You'd try to stop me.

CHAPTER 31

THE BLOCK IS QUIET.

Too quiet.

A breeze whips by, unsettling a cluster of fallen leaves as I hurry past. Row after row of apartments are on either side, Ms. Leola's door growing larger the closer I get. The moon hangs high in the sky. Somebody should be outside, chopping it up or rolling by.

People 'round the block at night are like eyes and ears. Always watching out. It's like unsaid rules around here. It ain't never quiet. Not like this.

Unless ... folks saw something, gave them a reason to hole up inside.

Hair stands on my neck and I creep closer to Ms. Leola's. This might be the dumbest thing I've ever done, but what choice do I have? I'm counting on these cuffs answering if I need them. Counting on it like my life depends on it. Like all our lives depend on it.

The door handle on Ms. Leola's is chilly and slightly ajar, creaking as I slip it open. I press an ear to it.

Silence.

It pricks my spine like needles. I slip inside and a haze of smokiness and the scent of bacon greet me. Something's burning. Ms. Leola usually sleeps with the hall light on. But it's pitch black.

Closer to the kitchen the burnt grease smell is growing. I peek my head in and cough. Charred strips of bacon are smoking on the stove. Fanning the haze, I flip the burner off and spot a note.

> Going over to Bertha's. Won't be long.
> Make sure you eat yourself something.
> Back soon.
> Ms. Leola

This note is for Tasha. Of course Ms. Leola's at her sister's; Demarcus ain't even in the ground yet.

"T-Tash?"

Panic flutters in me like a moth searching for a place to land. I move down the hall and duck my head into a spare bedroom on the left. Everything's tidy, bed made. The silence is deafening. I strain to hear something, anything, some sound, some hint of life. My breath comes harder and my hands shake.

"T!" My voice is cracked, weak. "Tash, where you at?"

She's not answering.

Something nudges my foot. "Ah!" I scream.

"Meow." Cupcake shoves his head against my leg, purring. I scoop him up and swallow the grimace.

"Cupcake, where is she?" I'm talking to a cat. It's dumb, but desperation is rarely smart. "Wh-where's Tasha?" My eyes sting and I blink faster. "Wh-what happened . . . ?"

He meows again and frees himself from my grasp. He starts to run off, but looks back. *Follow? He wants me to follow him?*

The bell jingling around his neck rings down the hall. I'm on his tail as he slips inside Ms. Leola's room, closing the door behind me. Her embroidered maroon bed cover is straight as a board, without a single crease. A mothy scent reminiscent of old perfume stings my nose. My feet are like bags of wet sand.

I hold the air in because that's easier than breathing. Faint noises float through the air—coming from the bathroom in the back of Ms. Leola's bedroom.

Music.

Old tunes like Moms used to jam play from the cracked bathroom door. Cupcake slips inside. I can't breathe. I can't think. What am I about to see? I grab a wire hanger from the closet. *Just in case.*

"Aaaatttt laasssssst." Etta James's fuzzy voice churns the fear coiled in my gut and I press another foot forward. I wrap my fingers around the cold knob.

One . . .

Two . . .

Three . . .

I whip the door open, yelling.

"Ahhh!" Tasha screams and water goes everywhere.

My heart jumps out of my chest. Cupcake circles my legs. She's taking a fucking bath? *WHAT THE HELL.* I grip my chest and plop on the toilet top, trying to calm my nerves. "Turn off the stove when you're cooking!"

"Oh shoot."

"You gon' burn down the damn house."

"You scared the daylights out of me!" She touches the necklace at her throat before reaching for a towel. "What are you doing here?"

What *am* I doing here . . . ?

Luke.

Luke said . . .

But no one's . . .

My blood stills. *I'm being set up.*

"Get dressed and lock yourself in this bathroom. Lock it. I mean it!"

She hesitates a second, then stumbles up. I dash out the bathroom, across the dimly lit bedroom, and press an ear to the closed bedroom door.

Nothing.

I slip into the hall. Luke set me up? That bastard set me up! Trying to draw me out. The General's dawgs or the General himself are here somewhere, bet. My legs tremble, but I force them still. I check the room with Moms's old stuff. No broken windows, nothing missing. No one's there. I whip open a side closet, hanger clutched in my hand. Still nothing. The kitchen is smoky but otherwise undisturbed. With quiet steps I head to Ms. Leola's back door, peeking through her windows. No one's there.

Weird . . . I exhale.

"T, I'ma check out front. But stay—"

A warm hand smothers me.

I can't breathe.

I claw at his grip, but it tightens. My breath comes out in stutters and I ram an elbow backward at his ribs, but miss. *I-I need air.* I try slamming a heel on his toe. He sidesteps. I pull, yank, writhe every which way, but his arms are like a straitjacket. My scream comes out muffled. *He's too strong.*

"Where's the cuffs?" His voice is low, sharp.

Th-the cuffs?

They know about the cuffs?

But how did they . . . ? *Luke.*

I'm dragged down the hallway toward the room with Moms's stuff. I kick and fight, the wall coarse against my fingers. I claw, scratching, reaching for anything, something. Wood from a picture frame grazes my fingertips, but slips from my clammy grasp.

I strain, fighting him with every bit of strength I have, my lungs screaming for a breath. He doesn't budge and holds my face tighter.

Air, I need air!

"The cuffs! Find them." He shoves us through the doorway and piles of Moms's things lie in boxes. My head feels like a balloon and spots dent the corners of my vision. I reach, grasping for anything, something. Dust coats my fingers as I grab at one of Moms's old bookshelves.

"Hold still, you little—" He hits me in the back and I claw for the spine of a book. It slips, thudding to the ground.

"Which of these boxes has the bracelets?" he says, his grip suffocating me.

Everything's blurry. I reach harder for something on the shelf and my fingers close around cold brass. It's as heavy as lead. I slam it backward toward his head.

Smack.

He grunts, his hand slackening a second. I bite into the fingers clamped to my mouth and taste copper. He howls and I'm able to break free from him. I gulp down air, my lungs parched and jump on him, punching, kicking, screaming.

"Get! Off! Me!" My arms ache and I can hardly see, but I fling blows harder and faster. My fist connects with bone and suddenly my hands are sticky, red.

He reaches for me, one eye open, and I run. If I can get him outside, he's that much farther away from Tasha. He's behind me, so close I can smell him. I whip the front door open.

"Get back here," he yells as he snatches my hoodie, pulling it taut around my neck.

"*Ahhh!*" I strain, forcing myself forward, the threads of my hoodie threatening to rip. I shove my way outside and he spills out Ms. Leola's, losing his grip on my clothes.

Humming streetlights paint the sidewalk orange in the dusky evening light. My body aches and my hand stings, but I keep my eyes on him, fists raised. This ain't over.

He's panting, face bloody, seething mad. A few people rush past, hurrying inside. He swings a jab, but I duck and shimmy sideways— away from Ms. Leola's door. As far away from her door as possible.

A guy with a bat dents my peripheral.

Shit.

And another, this one with a gun in hand.

Shit. Shit. Shit!

My cuffs. I reach for my zipper, but my sticky fingers slip. The guys circle me and Gun Holder points the barrel, gesturing for me to move to the center.

I ball my fists.

"Rue?" Ms. Leola's voice sends a jolt through me. "Baby?" She stands on the sidewalk, holding a bag of groceries. *This can't be happening.*

"No!" I'm surrounded and try to lunge toward her, but my scalp burns like fire when I'm snatched backward by my hair. He holds on tight. The dude with the bloody face and one working eye pulls my hands behind my back, squeezing so hard my bones feel like they might break. I swallow the pain. They won't hear me squeal.

Gun Holder points her way and I can't breathe.

"Back up old lady, get in the house," the voice behind me says. I struggle, but his grip on me is tight. Bat Holder's eyes meets mine and they're heavy with hate. Which is crazy because I don't even know this dude.

But because his racist-ass boss hates me, he hates me too.

A pair of kids on bicycles roll by and my heart stops. They pedal faster, thank goodness. Seconds later a door creaks open and claps shut.

"G-go inside," I plead with Ms. Leola. "P-please, just go inside." She shakes her head no, but I can see the fear in her eyes.

"If you don't want trouble, listen to Rue," the guy holding on to me says.

"You gon' let go of my granddaughter, or so help me!" She balls a bony fist, her wrinkly eyes menacing.

I'm crying.

"P-please, just go inside," I say. This ain't a fight she can win. People start peeping through screen doors, ducking their heads out, then going back in.

"Dave, she got a smart-ass mouth. Snatch her up too." Gun Holder gestures to the one with the bat and he moves toward Ms. Leola. She bred from 'round here, so as he closes in on her she doesn't flinch.

"Leave her alone!" The fingers at my scalp are dug in tight, but I pull and jerk, trying to break free. Dave is inches from her when her groceries hit the ground, one of those giant-ass cans of beans in her hand. She slams it into his forehead and I can hear the *crunch*. He staggers, his bat hitting the ground, rolling away.

"You get away from me!" she shouts, trying to shuffle away as blood drips from Dave's face. He's woozy on his feet, but he goes for her again, rougher this time.

"I swear on my life," I say, thrashing in his grip, "I'll burn you alive if you touch her."

Their laughs taunt me.

"Shut up."

A lump slams into my back and my knees hit the ground. Pain rattles up my spine. Free of his grip, I try to stand but, Gun Holder aims at me. "Sit your ass down."

Dave folds Ms. Leola's arms behind her.

"Let her go!"

"Give us what we came for and we will." The gun is cold on my forehead.

I hold my chin up. "What do you want?"

"You know what we came for. Some pieces of jewelry."

I tuck my elbows tight to my side against the lump in my pocket. "I-I don't know what you're talking about."

"Bullshit. Boss said for sure they'd be here."

The barrel of the gun digs harder into my head as he pulls me to my feet. "I said, where're the bracelets?"

If I give the cuffs to them, my blood will still paint this pavement. Cooperating ain't gon' make me any more alive at the end of this. The bloody-faced dude with strands of my ripped out hair still around his fingers, scoops up the bat and slams it into my legs. Ms. Leola wails.

"No, Rue, baby. J-just give 'em what they want."

"Hey, you—old lady—you know where they are?" Gun Holder's distracted looking her way.

I got one opening.

And I take it.

I slam a fist into his wrist holding the gun. His grip loosens and the metal slips, smacking the ground.

"What the—" he stutters.

Fingers grip my scalp, but I shove an elbow backward and the dude behind me grunts, his hand loosening for a second. I spin around and the heel of my hand slams up into his nose. I've squared up enough to know you aim for the tender parts. And he's got a few.

He barrels over, holding his face, blood trickling between his fingers. Metal glints on my peripheral. *The gun!* Gun Holder dashes for it, but I'm faster, flinging my body forward. My hands close around the metal as I slam the ground. I point it dead at his face.

I lock my elbows in place, hoping he can't tell how bad my arms are shaking. It's so heavy. Heavier than I thought it would be. I keep my eyes fixed ahead.

His hands go up. Coward. For coming for a kid with a gun, beating up on some old lady.

"Drop the bat," I say.

He does.

"And let her go or your friend dies." The guy holding Ms. Leola lets her go.

"Get on outta here," she yells. "Leave us alone." She knees him in the balls before scooting off inside.

"She's right. It's time for you to go. Get out of here."

The guys look at one another, hands up, but their smirks mock me. One even steps toward me. "She doesn't have it in her."

He's right.

He moves closer and my hands shake. I can't hold them still.

"You think I won't shoot?" I shout. He moves closer. "You think I won't take you out? I *said*, leave East Row."

Please don't make me do this.

He takes another step toward me.

I-I gotta show him I-I'm not playing. I aim at the ground and squeeze the trigger.

Crack!

Bat Holder literally jumps and yelps. His hands go up and he leaps back.

My insides scream. *I'm not ever doing that again. . . .*

I'd call the police if I thought it'd help.

But they'd probably arrest *me*.

If I'm lucky.

"Next time, it's your head," I say, hoping I sound tougher than I feel. This is not the way. Not my way. I slip the cuffs out my pocket and their eyes light up like Christmas. I clip them on my wrists one at a time, careful to keep the gun pointed at his head. He's backing away slowly, but practically salivating.

"Get out of here. You're not getting these." *Please, cuffs, whatever you got, I need it now. I do not wanna fire this gun again.*

They turn to go, but keep looking back at me, eyes on my wrist jewelry.

"Keep moving, that's right!" I grip the gun with both hands. They're not walking away fast enough.

Whatever power you want to help me find, Ancestors, please—I need it now.

I reach for the warmth, that familiar tickle inside, willing myself to feel something from the gold on my wrists. Willing myself to hear.

Magic, where are you?

My wrists warm and my heart pounds. *I-is it working?* A tiny burst of energy tickles my chest. *Are they answering?*

Suddenly the guys stop and turn toward me, a sick grin on one of the twisted faces. A shadow moves on the ground and an eerie feeling settles over me.

Everything in me goes cold.

"You have what I want, I see." The General's voice behind me is like ice on my skin. His smug face is somehow even more gross up close. He practically struts toward me, stepping over fallen groceries and past the blood on the ground like he's trying to make sure his polished shoes don't get too dirty.

My magic. I bite down and copper spreads on my tongue.

Even more are behind him, hands full of bottles of liquid with torn rags inside them.

"We can keep this cordial." The General swirls a ball of fire in his hand. "Or I can burn this place to the ground. Hand over the cuffs."

These cuffs are the gateway to reaching whatever magic I'm supposed to have. Without them I don't stand a chance.

I point the gun at him. "No!"

Come on, cuffs . . . Come on. WORK!

He chuckles. "You think you're brave, child. So smart. Like you know so much. And yet you know very little." He steps so close to me I can smell him. There are dozens around us now.

"The cuffs. I'll only ask this once more."

I-I can't. These are my power, my magic, our hope. I study them, glistening on my skin, and they warm a touch.

"A-ancestors, I-I am your Ghizoni daughter and I call on you to help," I mutter. "*P-please* hear me."

The cuffs rattle, warming.

I gasp. *Something's happening.*

"You won't cooperate?" the General asks. "Fine. Just need the proper motivation." His men take off around us.

The cuffs are suddenly piping hot and I reach for a faint tickle in my chest.

It's happening, I can feel it.

Glass shatters in the distance as his dawgs move from house to house, breaking windows, tossing bottles inside. Flames erupt from one of the windows and a woman bursts through the front door, screaming. Mommas hold their babies, fumbling for phones to call someone.

More screams.

More running.

A keyboard and a pair of TVs fall out an upper window, shattering on the ground. Cloudy haze swallows the fire, some man spraying foam from a red can. The fire's out, but another's started as the General's men make their rounds, looting, ransacking.

"*Nooooo!*"

"*Th-they're destroying my home.*"

Rage rips through me.

I tuck the gun in my waist and charge at him.

The General stumbles back and tumbles to the ground. I'm on top of him and my fist kisses his face with a *smack*. I clamp my hands on his head and dig my thumbs into his eye sockets. "GET! OFF! MY BLOCK!"

He thrashes, pushing, punching my side as streams of fiery

magic buzz past my head. Sirens yowl in the distance. People everywhere are bawling, shouting. East Row is a symphony of chaos. My
leg pulses with pain. Someone pulls me backward and I punch and
kick, ripping myself away. I'm up on my feet, hands up, guarding
my face. There are two guys clawing at my wrists, hitting me from
behind. I guard my head and a blow rams into my arms. *The cuffs.*

Focus.

Dig.

My wrists tingle.

Yes, that's it. I can feel it. Something warm moves through me
like a thread of fire, getting hotter, stronger by the second, when a
burst of light slams into me, knocking me to the ground.

My back smacks the pavement, and I gasp for air.

The cuffs slip from my wrists and land with a *tink* and roll away.
NOOOOO!

I peer in every direction, but my head swims and warmth trickles
down my cheek.

Wh-where'd they go?

Another crash of furniture hits the ground. More glass breaks.

Th-the c-cuffs. I n-need the cuffs. Th-they were about to work. I
blink, over and over, the world growing a little clearer.

I have to find the—

Another *crash*.

Piles of things are on fire, burning. People are crying, fleeing.
Muddled voices and the *clack* of the General's footsteps grow louder.
He's coming for me.

The cuffs . . . wh-where are they?

Streetlight glints on something metal and shiny.

I crawl, feverishly, asphalt ripping my jeans, scratching my knees. Everything in me aches, but I lug myself forward across the ground, reaching, clawing, my arms burning. I try to stand up, but his crew pins me down, their feet on my arms. I groan, but I won't scream. I won't.

The General wipes the blood from his lip with a handkerchief. "You people are animals." He scoops up the cuffs, eyes bloodshot.

Nooo!

"You have any idea how hard I've been searching for these? Thought they were a myth." He squats to face me, and his face is blurry. "The Chancellor isn't keen to let me keep playing my little games here, if I don't keep my word to him."

The cuffs glisten in his fingertips. If they burn him, I can't tell. "Let's at least make this fun, shall we? Let her up." His boys let me go and I stagger to my feet. The world is sideways.

"You want them back?" The General turns the cuffs in his hands, his smile curling upward.

I can't take my eyes off the gold. *I do.* It's my magic. Our hope. Our everything.

He tosses the cuffs high in the air. "Fetch."

I bite back the pain and dash for it.

He squeezes an eye shut, pointing. Magic shoots from his fingertip and slams into the cuff and it shatters into a cloud of golden dust.

"Nooooo!" The scream rips from me as my knees slam the asphalt. Golden ash falls like snow and tears burn my face. *No, h-he c-can't!* I pound one bloody fist to the ground after the other. Sirens wail louder, but the sounds of looting and cries of East Row drown them out.

"Cuffs, destroyed." The General dusts off his hands. "Chancellor's orders."

"You can't!" I yell, again and again, louder and louder, until my throat is raw. Gilded ash flickers through the air, my failure taunting me.

He's in my face. So close I can smell the sweat on his pasty skin. "You're a pain in the ass, you know that? If my men would've taken care of you a year ago like they were supposed to, the Chancellor wouldn't be breathing down my neck now. But no, your bitch mother had to get in the way." He smiles, satisfied with himself. "But I guess we took care of her."

M-my mother?

H-he . . . he killed my mother?

I can't think.

I don't feel.

I only see red.

I fling a jab at his disgusting smirk, but streams of magic pummel into me, throwing me back before I can reach his face.

He stands over me, the commotion of chaos pounding in my head.

This is the end. H-he's going to kill me.

He killed my mother and now he's gonna finish me off.

He smirks. "Killing you wouldn't be nearly as satisfying as watching you suffer." He blows me a kiss, turns on the spot, and disappears.

People shriek, crying, begging for the gang to stop.

My home is in pieces.

The gateway to my magic is shattered, gone—a heap of ash.

I feel nothing. I'm as good as dead.

CHAPTER 32

THE SIRENS CRY SO loud my head feels like it might implode. Smoke stings my nostrils, and the sound of gushing water rings in my ears. The fires are all gone, but the people stand around mourning broken treasures, stolen mementos, the terror of being hated and hunted.

Phones are out everywhere, but no news crews or cameras. If we're going to document injustice, we gotta capture that shit ourselves. A cluster of people stand a few feet away on the basketball court, watching.

I sit on the ground, hugging my knees.

If I don't move, maybe the world will stop spinning.

The hope for protecting my sister, my neighborhood, is in a million pieces on the ground. And I'm empty, like a gaping hole has been ripped open inside of me. Boots shuffle around me, tending to the chaos. An ambulance blares in the distance and police sirens howl.

It's over. I'm useless.

People like me never win.

My knotted hair is tight between my fingers. I grip and tug, digging my nails into my scalp. It should hurt, but I'm numb. There's no fix to dull the pain, and nowhere to hide my shame, so I cry out here in front of everyone, looking weak AF.

A man in a paramedic uniform's words are a dull buzz in my ear. I shoo him away like a gnat. The weight on my chest says it's useless to breathe. It rises and sinks, slower. I don't care. I'm so stupid, so reckless. My eyes burn at the corners and I rock back and forth.

Alaya nah, ick e'bah.

My father said *grow stronger in the pain.* Moms said *make a way.* How? Maybe if I could hear it from them. Be reminded one more time. Why is time like that? Only precious when you don't have it?

I need to hear I'm capable.

I need to hear I'm strong.

Maybe then I'd believe it. I rock back and forth, harder. Moms said I'm strong like a diamond. I shine under pressure. My father and his people acted like I'm some Ghizoni queen. They got me mistaken.

I'm nothing—a no one from the gutters of a block that only bleeds.

Another helper stops by, this one in a cop uniform. I see him touch my arm, but I don't feel it. He tugs and I'm standing, somehow. He pulls me over to an ambulance and I'm sitting.

"People are saying you were at the center of what happened. Can you tell—" His mouth is moving, but I don't really hear any of it. When he tucks his notes away in a forgotten file drawer, we're still picking up the pieces of our lives off the street, bracing ourselves for the next tragedy.

It's a few minutes of a job for him.

This is life for me.

I'm supposed to think they trying they hardest and pour out my heart so he can scribble some words on that notepad. I'm supposed to believe what I tell him will actually lead to someone like him coming to the Row's defense. But he won't, because it's always something. . . .

They don't have any leads.

They don't know where his people stay.

They don't have any hard evidence to pin to him.

Excuses.

But let homey stop in a mini mart in a rich white neighborhood with his hands in his pockets just because, and they busting down his family's front door minutes later. Moms raised a diamond and diamonds are sharp. How do I even know this dude ain't working with Litto's crew? I glue my lips shut.

The cop taps his paper. "Okay, well, if you don't have anything to share, I guess I'll—"

His mouth slacks and the words come out slower. His whole face freezes and dust hangs in the air. Nothing around us shifts, like sound itself is muted.

Time stops.

Someone from Ghizon is here.

There in the middle of the chaos is a broad-shouldered figure in the shape of my father.

"Dad!" I barrel into him. He hugs around me, squeezing, and I squeeze back. I'm a child in his arms. And for once, I don't care. He's here to help, to really be there for me. He's never done that . . . or maybe he has, and I was too stubborn to see. I press in to him tighter, his heart thudding against me.

My father is here to help! I—

Wait, does this mean?

No.

No, no, no!

"Your magic—it's . . ." My mind is all fog, a tangled mess of thoughts. "Dad, your magic . . . it's cursed . . . the death toll! Y-you can't . . . the transport spell you took to get here." I shove his chest. "Go, just go, get out of here before it's too late, *please!*"

"It's okay." He strokes my hair. The hug that comforted me seconds ago stings.

"Rue." He grips my arms, eyes hard, firm. *He's strong. So very strong. How did I not see that before? All this time, his tough choices were made from strength, not weakness.*

"You can't be here." Sniffles muffle my words. "I won't lose both of you. I won't!"

He shudders. "The poison . . . I don't know how much time I have. We must move fast."

"This is all my fault. I did this, coming here all alone."

"If this is anyone's fault, it's mine. Come on now, we don't have long. Minutes."

An antidote. Where can I find him an antidote? That would take forever. We don't have forever . . . not anymore.

His eyes droop and his warm skin drains to pallor. A gust of wind sweeps through, blowing the pile of ashes that once were my cuffs.

"H-help me lie down. Hurry, Rue, before the bits of the cuffs are all gone." He speaks as if each word pains him as he settles on the ground. I tuck my head under his chin. I can't believe this is happening. My father's here to save me, but saving me means death.

His chest is firm against my face, thumping with life, his beard, grayer than I remember.

This can't happen. I won't let it.

It's a lie, but I cling to it. Squeezing my eyes shut tight, I imagine I'm little. The hem of his shirt is soft like silk, rising and falling with each breath.

Seconds zip by and I try to hold on to each of them.

"You were raised to be a thinker," he says. "Quick on your feet. No one gets one over on you, Rue. You're stubborn to a fault. That is your determination. Your mother swore to me, raising you here in East Row would make you resourceful, protective, a thinker—a leader."

Sh-she said that?

"And when you were ready, she'd bring you to me. Let you see your other home. Embrace your other half."

Embrace my other half . . .

Embrace that I-I'm Ghizoni . . .

The cuffs. I gasp. The cuffs started to respond when I whispered to the Ancestors that I am their daughter, their chosen.

When I embraced *all* of who I am.

"You are destined for greatness, Jelani. I tell you not to be sentimental, I tell you because it is true. Look at what your Ancestors have come through—that greatness flows in *your* veins."

I am greatness. . . .

He pulls himself up on shaky elbows. His eyes are all fire. "If you remember nothing else, remember this . . ."

Tears swallow my face. I don't want my daddy to die.

"Do not let the past chain you." He grits his teeth, his words pained stutters as the poison sets in. "Make it your strength."

I am strength. . . .

"You're a warrior for your people—*all* of them—every little one without white skin. They look to you to guard them from those who would destroy them. They look to you to heal generations of pain. This is your destiny, child. I am just a mere step along the way."

"No, please stop." I bury my face in his chest. "I can't. I-I can't. . . . Moms gone, you leaving me too? I-I can't do this all alone."

"Rue, look around you. From East Row to Yiyo, you're never alone."

"I can't—"

"You *can*. And you *will*."

I am unstoppable. . . .

He plants a kiss on my forehead. The kiss of a father to his daughter.

I hug his neck. The hug of a daughter to her dad.

His grasp slacks and he trembles. "Our time is about up," he groans, hunching over in pain. "The cuffs . . . before the wind blows all the remnants away. It's a tricky spell, but I think I can do it." He lies back.

"N-not, yet, please. I-I'm sorry I couldn't . . . didn't forgive you sooner." My voice cracks. "I-I'm sorry we didn't have more time." Tears dangle from my lashes and another tremor shakes his finger. "I-I'm scared. Underneath it all . . . I'm terrified. What if I screw this all up?"

He presses a finger to my lips. "Greatness . . . power . . . strength. H-hold my head up and don't let go." I cradle my father's head in my lap. His chest rises and falls, slower each time. He pulls back his sleeves and raises his hands like he's commanding the very sky to answer him. He twists one around the other and golden ash fills the air, flocking to his hands like a swarm of locusts. He twists harder. Another twist and pieces of gold gather in his hands. Veins bulge from his arms as gold sweeps around us like a dust storm.

The curve of metal slowly reform in his grasp and I gape in utter disbelief. Little by little the cuff's pieces forge themselves back together. His chest quivers and he inhales deeply, but he keeps twisting, groaning, as if it hurts him. I look away, wishing I could say stop. But I know this is the only way.

Why does life have to hurt so bad?

Why do we have to learn through pain?

Chimes fill the air as my bracelets crystallize fragment by fragment, piece by piece, back together before my eyes. I blink several more times and I've forgotten how to breathe.

My father's hands tremble. Up and down, his chest still rises and falls, steadily, but slower—much slower. I cry harder, ripped to shreds, a hurricane of relief and agony. The air clears as the last piece of the cuffs snap in place.

His head falls limp.

Everything is foggy. I take the cuffs and holding them again is like fresh oxygen to my lungs. I know what the Ancestors wanted. I know when I put them on this time it'll be different. I slip them on and warm all over.

"D-dad?" I feel his cheek and check his forehead. "T-talk to me . . ."

His head thrashes. *The curse has set in.* I show him the cuffs, shiny and undamaged. He smiles, but his eyelids hang low.

"O-one more thing," he mumbles.

"Anything." I sniffle.

He motions for my head, too weak to lift himself up. Confused, I lean over him. His breath is ragged, slow. He runs his fingers through the roots of my hair and latches on tight to my skull. Calm wraps around me like a fleece blanket on a chilly afternoon.

The world goes dark.

Cool drips pierce my skull like trickles of ice water, swelling behind my eyes as images—memories—flash like a slideshow in my mind.

I see a tree on Christmas morning next to a stocking with my name. A plate with cookies and both my mother and father shoving me toward a floor full of wrapped presents.

The scene dissolves and another appears.

I see my little hands holding tight to covers and my father stepping into my room, book in hand. He kneels beside my bed and I throw my arms around his neck, grinning.

And another.

Moms is dancing in the kitchen in her favorite yellow robe. I see Daddy holding her around the waist, belting a backup tune. There I am playing my guitar mini broom.

I see an auditorium of faces I don't know and two I do. I'm dressed as Cleopatra and a camera flashes from the corner, my dad's face behind it.

Memories of a life I never knew flood my mind and I weep uncontrollably.

He tightens his grip and I see him chase me around the room, waddling with kinky pigtails and a soggy diaper. He snatches me up and tickles me in the air. I see him fast asleep on the sofa with me wrapped up, drooling on his chest. I see him come home with a puppy. My eyes light up and Moms frowns. I see him teach me to drive and shoo boys away from the front step.

Thousands of memories of the life he would have given me crash in a tidal wave of grief.

He squeezes my hand. "I wish they could be real."

"Th-they are to me." I squeeze back. "Please, stay. Please, don't go. There was the one time I lost my tooth and thought it was a seed, so I planted and watered it for weeks." I sob, words gushing from my lips. "A-and this one time I aced a really important math test and got an award." I cry harder. "Another time, Momma took me to ride a horse. A real live horse." I shake his shoulders. "Dad, please!" I shout, beating his chest. It barely rises, almost still. "*Please*—don't go. I have so much I never got to tell you. . . ."

"Alaya nah, ick e'bah," he mumbles.

"Grow stronger in the pain."

He smiles, brushing a hair out my face. "Spoken like a true Ghizoni."

"I *am* Ghizoni," I say, and his smile deepens.

The cuffs rattle on my wrists, gleaming. *It's happening.*

His eyes close and he exhales.

The cuffs cinch tighter.

His chest stills and the skin on my wrists burns, like the cuffs are piercing the marrow of my very bones.

He shudders and his time spell dissolves, the world whirring back into motion. The sound of sirens wailing, people chattering, clamor for my attention. But I only have eyes for my dying father. He stares up at me and his eyes are as deep as the ocean, but still.

He's gone.

The finality of it washes over me, when faint whispers play in my ear.

Ancestors . . . I hear you.

I am listening.

Really listening.

Something wiggles more violently. I'm so close, so close to this power I can feel it. I squeeze my eyes shut, urging my fury to dance with my pain, clutching my dead father's robes.

People stop and stare. I don't care.

"Ahhhh!" I cry out. My skin feels like it's been set on fire and turned inside out. Moms's stilled expression flashes in my mind, the Elders uprooting the trees, commanding the rain, my father's dead stare, Brian's blood everywhere . . . the memories wanna choke me. But instead, my anger erupts in flames.

Both cuffs cinch tight and my arms shudder and shake.

I don't breathe.

I can't see.

I bite back a scream as my cuffs melt, molten gold running down my arms like honey, hardening into a shell over my flesh. My arms glisten and voices chant in my ear, "Alaya nah, ick e'bah."

I am stronger. I am.

Greatness . . . power . . . strength.

I feel my magic there like a weight in the deepest part of myself. I reach for it and heat rushes from my center, snatched along like a string. I hold up my hands and release. What feels like a hundred lifetimes of stored energy rips through my hands, gushing like a blowtorch.

The ground shudders.

Thunder rolls.

Lightning cracks.

My magic is back.

CHAPTER 33

EAST ROW'S PICKING UP the pieces around me.

I sent Aasim's body back to Yiyo with a quick spell. People clear away trash piles and hug one another, crying. A few who were around when my magic blasted give me weird looks. But most ignore me. There's so much chaos in repair, I'm a detail on the periphery.

A fire engine and three ambulances sit sideways on the street. Men in hefty yellow suits wrap up hoses. Paramedics have IV drips out, bandaging people up, carting people off on gurneys. I think there's still one police car. But no reporters, no media trucks or cameramen.

My home was terrorized, but that's not newsworthy, apparently.

Not what the world is trying to see from the people around here.

I run a finger under my sleeve, to the smooth metal seared to my arms. Moms said a second chance ain't nothing to waste. That people who look like us, who come from where we come from, don't get second chances. We gotta be twice as good from the start to get half what other people get. People everywhere waiting for us to fail.

This is my second chance, and when I face the General again, it will be his last.

A phone warms my ear, the gentle *brrriinngg* vibrating against it.

"Rue?" Julius answers, voice laced with panic. "You aight? I freaked!"

I haven't seen him since Brian died in my arms. Never said good-bye or told him what's up. Time wasn't on my side then, and it's still not. "Listen, Litto's people rolled through East Row tonight, looting houses, burning people's things. They tried to kill me."

"Shit, Rue! What you need? I can come through."

"Get a crew together from the block. I have a plan to take Litto down for good. Meet me at Ms. Leola's. I have one stop to make first, then I'll be there."

"Done. And Rue—" The worry is gone. Now it's all anger. "We're going to get these fools. Whatever it takes."

Whatever it takes.

The line goes dead. What if my plan doesn't work? What if I make a mistake, screw something up? I don't have time to doubt. Gotta trust my instincts. I ain't no dummy—far from it. I gotta think quick, but be smart and rely on the things I *know*.

And one thing I learned from growing up 'round here—my misstep with Brian—is always have a crew and roll in deep. So if shit goes left, I got a plan B.

I'ma make a way out of no way, like Moms taught me, but I'ma do it with a team.

I'm back in Ghizon in minutes, on the edge of the sea. The wind whips my clothes and hair every which way. Storm clouds loom far in the distance, but they're moving fast. What time is it? Where would Jhamal be about now?

I dart across the Ancestors' burial ground, the pit where Jhamal trained, and hurry up the crooked path, beneath a cluster of black-bark trees. The pathways are empty. Everyone must be in for the night. Clusters of chakusas sit to my right, their grassy walls rustling in the wind.

Someone shouts. Crying.

Is that Bri?

I really don't have time for this.

But the sentiment of what *used* to be a really close friendship has me nearing the door the sounds are coming from. She's curled up on her bed, smoothing tears from her cheeks. A twig snaps under my step. *Shit!*

Bri emerges from the hut, looking both ways. "Who's there?"

I stick to the shadows. *I do not want to do this.* I should walk away and deal with this later. I step out from the shade and she starts to rush toward me, but stops herself.

"Rue? You're back? What happened? A-are you okay?"

"No, but I will be. The General's dawgs ran through East Row looting homes and terrorizing people. He ripped apart my block."

And killed my mother.

The words are glue on the roof of my mouth. Somehow not saying them out loud makes it easier to function despite the hurt.

"The call from Luke was a hoax. Tasha wasn't taken at all. It was a way to draw me out. So the General's men could get me. He wants the cuffs."

She gasps. "Conniving swera. Rue, I—"

"I'll deal with Luke later. Time's short. I came back because I have a plan to take the General down. But I'm here to grab some help."

"I-I'm so sorry, Rue. Y-you wanna come in?"

I cut a glance over both shoulders. No sight of Jhamal.

"Sure." *Minutes.* I can give this *five* minutes.

"Look...," she jumps right in. "I was wrong for what I said about the watch."

Hell, yes you were. "Okay?" I fold my arms.

"I . . . this is just really hard for me." She plops on the bed.

Hard for her? Four minutes.

"Imagine everything you grew up believing being a complete lie," she says, eyes pleading with me.

"Bri, I get that more than you realize."

She turns to me and there's something there in her eyes—like a twinkle of hope. "I mean, what if we didn't out everything publicly, but, like, worked to vote out the Chancellor?"

Is she serious? Her three minutes just jumped to two.

She studies my face and I guess she gathers what I think of her ridiculous attempt at bargaining about this. "Okay, it's just *so much* to lay on people. Uprooting lives, I mean, that's a lot to ask. What if maybe we *do* out the truth, but, like, maybe Old Ghizon could be here and New Ghizon there and we could, maybe, share the mag—"

Okay, nope. Time's up. "Stop. I don't have a lot of time, so I'm going to tell you this quickly. You can't see that what you're saying is actually digging the dagger deeper?"

She twists her head in confusion.

"You don't get it. I see you trying to work through it, but I can't let you keep hurting me or anyone here in the process. Could you really look at those people out there and say that to their faces? After what they've been through? Think about that for a second. I get you're sad.

I get this is hard. But this isn't about you, Bri. And if helping scares you or makes you uncomfortable, then fine. You are welcome to have dinner and go back home. No one's forcing you to be here."

"Rue, I *wanna* be here. I *wanna* help. I do! I *get* that this is wrong. I *hate* that I never knew. . . . Now, I-I'm just not sure what to do, I guess."

"Well, these ideas ain't it. I was actually just looking for Jhamal. If you really want to help, then fine, I'll give you a shot to help."

"O-okay. I-I'm ready. Tell me what to do."

I leave her there with a minute to spare and spot Jhamal paces from the dining hall.

"Jhamal!" I say, sounding a little too desperate, but he smiles and I don't even care how I sound anymore. He bounds his African god–looking self over, shirtless with gilded armor, and I have to look away to remember what the heck I wanted to say.

"Jelani?" he asks. "I thought you were gone. Is everything okay?

"No, listen." I set a hand on his shoulder and my sleeves raise. He gasps, gawking at my gleaming wrists, the moonlight glinting off their metallic surface.

I smile but think of my dad and it fades. "I finally figured out how to get them to work. Anyway, I came back because I said I'd ask if I ever needed help. And I do."

Plates stacking and voices roar louder from the dining room window slit. "So, will you help?"

"It is not even a question, my Queen." He puffs out his chest, as beautiful and hard as ebony. "Tell me what to do."

I lead him back to Bri's room and they sit, watching me pace.

Another thing I learned back home is thinking ahead. I gotta think four, five, six steps ahead because the consequences for screwing up are higher for people who look like me. No more just reacting because I'm pissed. I gotta be *sure* I've thought this all the way through.

I've run the plan in my head a million times. No second guessing. The key to taking all of them down is bringing his dirty work to light. We need evidence.

"I need a recorder type device," I say to their inquisitive stares. "Something that can record and play it back as a hologram."

"A phototrifiter," Jhamal and Bri say at the same time. They look at each other, equally surprised.

Bri talks first, as usual. "It's basically a thin pin that you activate and it'll record a 360 visual feed of everything happening in a ten-meter radius. Pretty simple to make. I have the stuff in my dorm." She slips her glasses back on, jotting down something on a notepad. "I'd want to attach some sort of cloaking spell so—"

"So you have them?" I interrupt.

Jhamal bristles at her talking about using a spell. *I should have warned him.*

"*Or*"—Jhamal cuts in way more dramatic than he needs to—"you could just take a phototrifiter from here. We make them with auto-invisibility cloaking"—he looks Bri up and down—"ourselves."

"*Automatic* cloaking?" Apparently making these things is a big deal because her mouth is wide open. "Y-you can do that?"

Jhamal nods.

"*Wowww.*" Bri's used to being the know-it-all. Color fills her cheeks. "I-I didn't even know those types of capabilities existed."

"We also have nanosynthesizers"—he says, flipping a silver gadget from his pocket—"that work *by magic*. We've warped the frequencies to emit tiny bits of transmitter spells. . . ."

I'm pretty sure he's just showing off now.

Bri gasps again and her jaw drops. "C-can I touch it?"

Everything in Jhamal's eyes says he wants to say no.

"O-okay," I cut in. "Well, the point is, yes, you do have it here?"

He meets my eyes and I can feel him thanking me. "We do, my Queen."

"That's settled. I'll use yours. Bri, I want you to hack into the New Ghizon mainframe so that whatever I record plays on every single screen in the District. Can you do that?"

"I-I—"

She hacks into stuff all the time. Why she hesitating?

"I can. It's a bit different. Instead of getting in and out, I'd have to stay there, monitoring the entire time to make sure the feed doesn't cut out."

"It's risky," Jhamal says, giving Bri side-eyes. "*Much* easier to get caught."

"Yeah, well so is all of this," I say.

He turns to Bri. "Are you willing to risk getting caught? You could go down for this."

Silence.

I tap my foot, trying to be patient.

Bri sits there chewing her lip, calculating the risk, no doubt down to a science. If this is how she acts over the news of what the Chancellor's done, how's the rest of Ghizon gonna react when I out the truth? I bite my lip and it bleeds.

Jhamal must sense my irritation because he cuts in. "My Queen, I can do this too. You won't find more advanced capabilities any-where else. . . ." He bows his head. "Or a more loyal people."

He's laying it on thick and I don't think Bri's face could get any pinker.

Jhamal's about to speak up, but Bri cuts in. "Y-yeah, I-I'll do it."

"Look, Bri, if you not down, don't worry about—"

"N-no, really. Please, I-I w-wanna help. I'll do it."

She gon' take a risk? A *real* risk? I guess we'll see. I give Jhamal a look and it's like he can read my mind, because he nods. I want him to monitor the feed too, just in case.

Always have a plan B.

"It's settled, then." I check my watch. "Wait for my signal. I'll reach out when I've got the General cornered."

"Wh-what are you planning to record?" she asks. "So I know."

"His confession."

Back in East Row, Ms. Leola moves around her living room shuf-fling between clusters of people. Her front room window is half shattered, but the rest of the chaos seemed to miss her brownstone. Chatter buzzes as homies slap hands, handshake, and catch up. Hazy light seeps through mustard-color drapes and scents of onion and Old Bay seasoning linger in the air.

People are everywhere, spread out on her suede couches. Half the block is here, since the Row's in so much disarray. That's what family does when one of us is hurting: We carry it together, in living rooms and over food.

I need to get everybody's attention, tell them the plan. But where's

Ms. Leola? They know her face, how much she means to me. I need her and Tash *out* of East Row for a little bit.

Ole Jesse dips in and around people, offering to take their empty soda cans. His cart is piled high and parked outside Ms. Leola's stoop. Cupcake works the room picking up snuggles where he can. He nudges my foot and I pull him into my arms. His purr warms me on the inside. The room is so crowded I lose Tasha. Last I saw her she was gnawing down on a piece of boudin.

I squeeze past some girls neck deep in a bowl of gumbo, making sure my sleeves are down tight. Don't need *more* questions right now. Another dude at the coffee table cleans his piece, a ripped-up T-shirt sliding back and forth across the metal. I tiptoe for a better glimpse of Tasha's neon-streaked braid and step on someone's toe. A man with tangled gray locs, who I *thought* was asleep sitting straight up, yelps.

"Oops, sorry," I say.

"That's Bo," Julius says, hurrying toward me. "Hangs outside of the shop I work at. He might look sleep, but trust: He don't miss a thing." Julius really came through. So many from the block are here. Kid even showed up. He's glued to somebody's phone and apparently winning whatever game he's playing.

"You really came through with some crew."

"What, you doubted me?" He says, smirking. "You're fam. You know that."

He offers me a fist, but I nudge him instead, playfully. *Can't touch him skin to skin.* I spot Ms. Leola, exactly who I was looking for.

"Excuse me a sec." I walk off, Julius's lingering stare warms me all over. Ms. Leola peers at the people flooding her living room. Her expression is more wrinkled than usual.

Kid barrels into her, hugging around her waist. "Sup, Ms. Leola?"

"Kid, that you? You looking good, boy! Get yo'self in there and get you a plate."

"Yes, ma'am." He bumps his way through the crowd, eye on his video game.

She turns to me. "I didn't know all these people was coming, baby. It ain't no problem. I just—" She primps her clothes and the edges of her hair. "I was gon' head out to my sister's, but it's fine. I'll stay." She counts on her fingers. "Now, I heated a pot of gumbo. Set out some drinks. But I'ma try to get some ham hocks. Do some turnip bottoms."

There isn't time for all that. "Ms. Leola, listen to me. Litto's men fled. But it's like stirring a wasp's nest. They'll be back. I'm sure of it. And this time we ain't losing. So we don't really have time for you to make sure everybody gets a plate."

She looks like someone's slapped her. Flashes of my shattered cuffs blown through the air like ash, the stillness of my father's chest, his empty stare whip through my mind.

I pull her to me firmly. "I need you gone. Just in case, *please.*"

She considers me for a few moments. "I see that look in your eye, *chile.* So I'ma do as you say, but you be careful now, you hear?"

I hug her as tight as I can and she scoots off to get her keys. I spot Tasha's braids moving through the crowd toward me.

"So, what's the plan, Stan?"

"The plan is you're going with Ms. Leola to her sister's."

"What?" She folds her arms. "Why?"

"Tasha, it's about to go down. It's dangerous and—"

"I don't get why you the only one who gets to make a way. Rue,

Momma taught me that too. I don't wanna miss whatever is 'bout to go down at Ms. Bertha's smelly old house."

"T—"

"No, listen to me!" Her voice is about two octaves too high. "Moms raised a diamond. Those ain't just words to me. These people trying to *kill* me. Trying to kill *all* of us."

Chatter quiets.

People are staring.

She goes on. "I'm always sitting on the sidelines watching you protect me. You looked out for me my whole life. Then Moms died and I didn't see you again for a minute. I ain't know *what* to do. I was so scared. I'm staying, Rue. The Row *my* home too."

Am I this stubborn?

"T, this ain't a game. You could get . . ." I can't even say the word.

"Look around, sis. Everybody here is ready to do what we gotta do. What you always say? *We* protect us because—"

"—nobody else going to."

"Exactly. I'm part of that we."

She doesn't know what she's asking. She asking a lot. All this started to protect her, keep her safe. Now I'm supposed to let her walk into the line of fire?

"Please," she says.

Ms. Leola's white hair cap moves through my silent audience. "Alright, baby you ready?" she asks Tasha. Then glances at literally *everyone* staring at me, confusion written on her face. "Was it the gumbo?"

"No," I say. "I—the food is fine."

Tasha narrows her eyes.

I guess I have to let her be who she wants to be.

"Tasha's staying here." I regret the words as soon as I say them. Ms. Leola doesn't like it either, by the expression on her face, but she kisses us both on the cheek. Her bony hand wraps around my wrist with an iron grip. "You keep yo'self and that baby alive, you hear?"

"Yes ma'am."

Ms. Leola shuffles out the door and silence falls on the place. Ole Jesse's arms are overflowing with cans, but his eyes are fixed on me. Julius is posted up on a wall, arms folded across his chest. He's not talking to anyone or looking at anything in particular. His jaw is tight, mean. He's worried. Something twinges in my chest.

He really does cut for me.

Bo's eyes are wide open, and the sound of a gun clicking into place sends a chill up my arm. Spoons chime and bowls set on tables, a sea of eyes staring back at me.

Everyone's watching, waiting for me to speak.

I tap my pocket of recorders. It's time.

"Thank you all for coming." I shuffle on my feet. Public speaking isn't really my thing. "I-I know there's some folks that don't know everything that's been going on, and I swear I'll explain more when I can." I tug my sleeves down. "But most of y'all have seen what the Litto gang did tonight and has been doing around here."

A few disgruntled voices chime in and I raise my voice above them. "Litto is—"

"A racist," someone says.

"Littering our streets," someone shouts.

"Killing our kids," says someone else.

"Yes, all that," I cut in. "He runs most of his drugs through

Jameson High, using students. It's disgusting. And his men trashed half of East Row tonight. He's done so much foul stuff on our block and I'm done just taking it. The police ain't taking him down. It's like no one cares when *our* people dropping dead or getting locked up left and right." A few "wells" and "amens" rise from the crowd. "I'm gonna draw him out, back here, and—"

A gun cocks. "And I'll handle his ass."

"Wait, listen. If we just knock him off and he disappears, one of his minions could take his place. Us taking down some dude on our own, cops would blame us. I say we go about this smart—with evidence. We know what he's up to; all we have to do is prove it.

"We are the eyes and ears of East Row. All of us. We *see* what he's doing to East Row, our high schools, our streets. The twisted-ass cops he has rolling through here. Reporters don't come here. Maybe the world don't wanna see. But we can make them—with proof.

"The world wanna pretend like we not here being hunted because what we look like, where we live. We'll show them. And with all the evidence we'll have recorded, plus his confession, when I'm through with him he'll have *nowhere* to hide."

In either world.

I pull out the phototrifiters and pass them out.

"I'm gonna get Litto himself to confess and this little device will record it."

I hand a phototrifiter to Bo. He examines it and passes it on. The next does the same and the gadgets move down the line.

"You can use your phone if there's not enough to go around, but these buggers are invisible, so he and his dawgs won't even know we're collecting evidence."

"There's a white boy at my school, a big snake tat on his neck," says Kid. "He's always flashing his bankroll to his boys, talking about all Litto's pushing."

"Yes! Video clips of that would be great, Kid. We can get him on drug trafficking, theft, all the stuff he gets away with. With proof, the world will *have* to listen."

I press a button on the recorder and it glows green a second, then vanishes.

Gasps echo around the place and someone mutters, "Oh shit."

"It's recording everything around me, my voice, my face, the entire scene," I say. "When you're done, just touch it and it'll reappear." I swipe the spot where it vanished and the slender metal chills my fingers, flickering back into view.

I mash the replay button and a sliver of orange light bursts from its center like a laser and contorts into the shape of my face. The hologram glitches a moment and in seconds, an image appears like a 3D movie, saying everything I just said.

"See, easy."

Mouths gape open around the room. Kid's enthralled. The game he was playing sits ignored on his lap as he fiddles with the recording gadget. "This is dope."

"Oh nah," someone says from the back. "I don't want nothing to do with no voodoo shit." He puts on his cap. "If you'll excuse me." The door shuts behind him.

Sigh. My people, I swear. "I-I promise in time I'll explain e-everything." Everything I can. "Ole Jesse?"

The man with the cans looks up. "Yea, ma'am. Still here."

"I want you outside Dezignz recording everything you see."

He nods and slips the phototrifter in his pocket. Something about the way he's chewing his tongue makes me think he's contemplating how much he could make on it at the place he sells his cans. I ain't mad at the hustle. Long as he does the recording first.

"And Kid, you're a good size to sneak under their back gate. Get that recorder inside the warehouse where they keep those stacks of moving crates. It might look like industrial goods, but it ain't. That's all their drugs disguised."

He gives me a thumbs-up.

"Bo, I want you posted up outside against Ms. Leola's. Eyes on everything."

"Got it," he says, wrapping himself tighter in his tattered coat. "They'll think I'm sleep."

"Everyone else, I want you keeping eyes out for Litto's boys. The snake tat is the most obvious mark, but they don't all have that. Keep your eyes peeled for people who just don't belong here." Heads nod and a murmur of voices agree.

I turn to Julius. "I need you to get to Dezignz. Take Ole Jesse and Kid. I'm going to make sure all Litto's roaches show up. Hold them there, play along, whatever you need to do to keep them waiting there."

"But how you gon' get all his boyz—?"

"You trust me?"

"It ain't even question." His gaze is soft, tender.

"It's better if you know less right now," I say. "Just do this, please." I should tell him everything. Show him, at some point. After . . . after this is all done I will explain. Julius nods and his eyes flicker with something that twists a knot inside me.

He's a ride or die if I ever had one.

"I got you, Rue. Always." He winks, and he, Jesse, and Kid head out the door.

"Everyone else, go ahead. Get moving, collecting evidence." The door creaks open and people file out the living room.

"*Uhhh*, Rue." Tasha pulls back the polyester fabric at the window. "I don't think we have time to go look for Litto's dawgs—"

My heart stops at her deadpan tone.

"The looters—they're back."

CHAPTER 34

WITH EVERYONE GONE, RECORDERS in hand, I peep for a better view of a group of men disappearing into a neighbor's house. Bo posts up outside Ms. Leola's house for a view of the block. This time I got backup.

I slip past Bo looking like he's fast asleep out against Ms. Leola's siding, the silver clutched in his fingers.

"Now," I whisper, and his recorder flickers in the air then disappears.

I creep through Ms. Leola's hedges toward the neighbor's, on the heels of the men who snuck inside. Another thing I learned growing up 'round here: *Watch your surroundings.* Someone's always watching.

The Row is in a state of repaired disarray. Some houses have cracked doors. Glass and broken furniture lie in piles outside of homes. I step over a prickly rose bush and peek in Ms. Davis's front room window. Nothing. But I hear shouts, banging, then a crash. I'm up the stoop, peeking for a view through the hole in the door.

There's Ms. Davis tied up, knees to her chest next to her granddaughter, Miesha. Their wide eyes dart my way.

I press a finger to my lips and mouth, "It's gonna be okay."

Miesha points and holds up the number three.

There are three inside.

I listen at the door first. Silence. The knob is cold in my palm. I twist and it opens with a quiet click. Ms. Davis's hands are shaking, forehead sweating, and a tiny cut drips above her eye. She reaches her bound hands for a zipped-up pouch inches from her fingers. *Her insulin.* I tiptoe across the carpet and slide it to her.

"I'm going to get them," I whisper and slip the ties off her hands.

Miesha points toward the hall.

"Go out the back," I say to her. "Get her out of here."

Miesha nods, helping her grandmother up.

Banging and commotion spills from the hall. The sound of things knocked over and breaking. They're going to pay for this. In blood. I peek around the corner for a glimpse of the hall. Wooden picture frames filled with black and white photographs line the olive walls.

Metal clicks.

Shit, they have guns.

One's standing there, on watch, with his back to me, the hint of a snake tattoo on his neck. I press against the wall, my heart an earthquake in my chest. If there's only the one in the hall, the other two must be in one of the bedrooms. Another crash and the walls tremble, louder this time, like an entire chest of drawers shattered against a wall.

I dig inside for that twinge of heat—my magic—and picture it like a snake. A coil of light slithers from my fingertip, while I hide around the corner. It twists, stretching across the maroon carpet silently. The guy looks both ways completely unaware. The thread of energy is a thin rope inches from his feet. It tugs from my center, like a jagged thread ripping through me, snaking its way up his pant leg toward his neck. *So close.* If he moves, he'll see it coming.

My shoe catches on the baseboard. *Shit.* He looks my way.

I jerk the rope and it slips around his neck before he can utter a scream. It coils tighter by the second and he drops the gun to claw at his neck. The metal hits the carpet with a muffled *clang.* So much for stealth. I ease around the corner and I can better see his face. It's the guy from the car wreck, the same one on T's Instagram. Anger burns through me and his face turns pink, his lips sputtering.

As it burns hotter, the rope squeezes.

The way he smiled, luring her to get inside . . .

Tighter.

The flames from the car wreck . . .

Pinker.

Squeeeeze.

He falls with a thud and I step over him.

With a flick of the wrist, the thread of energy fizzles out. I shove his gun in my waistband.

Three left.

"Get that stuff, too, over there. The old radio." A guy who held me at gunpoint after the coffee shop turns a drawer of Ms. Davis's things upside down. A porcelain doll that used to sit in her kitchen window smashes the ground. *She loved that piece.*

"You shouldn't be here," I say.

They flip around, shock on their faces. No weapons in their hands because they're neck deep in robbing sweet ole Ms. Davis.

"Oh yeah, says who?" The bigger one kicks a stack of what looks like leather-bound photo albums. He steps on them, walking toward me, and they rip apart.

"Pretty price on your head, little girl."

"You're not leaving here with legs," I say.

He charges at me, but I'm ready. A rush of energy rips from me, slamming into his chest. He flies backward and thuds against the wall. His head flops—his eyes go woozy. I pin him there. My magic spews against his chest like a hydrant, the room glowing blue from the light.

"Ahhh, this shit burns. This stupid girl is crazy. She crazy! L-let me go!"

I push harder and he squirms, his skin growing redder. My arms ache and his cries quiet. I pull back and the stream of magic evaporates as quickly as it came. He plops on the ground, his shirt in shreds. His chest is sunburn-red as he curls in a ball, wincing in pain.

His friend is pale and he falls to his knees. "P-please don't hurt me. I got a family, kids."

"Oh, kids matter to you all of a sudden . . . when they not brown-skinned?"

Tears pour down his face and the crotch of his pants is wet. "Whatever you want. I-I'll do whatever you want."

Coffee shop dude lifts his face, red and blotchy. "Just wait until Litto gets his hands on her. He'll handle her." He tries to get up, but collapses. I ignore him, turning to the scared dude, his pissy scent wafting to my face.

"What's your name?"

"B-Billy."

"Billy, your friend there isn't very smart. The more he talks, the shorter his life gets." Billy's eyes fall to my cuffs and his mouth opens wider.

"But you're not like him, are you, Billy? You're smarter than he is."

His head's nodding, but he won't look away from my wrists. A coiled snake with bared fangs marks his neck. "I just wanted to get some stuff and get out of here."

"I'm going to tell you to do some things and you're going to do them. You understand that, Billy?"

Dude in the corner tries to speak. "Don't listen to—"

I fire an arrow of light and it flies with a swish, slamming into his mouth, clamping it shut. He squirms, and his screams disappear.

Two left.

I turn back to Billy. "First, call your crew, every single one, to Dezignz."

"A meetup like that only comes down from Litto himself. I-I can't do that."

I conjure fire in my palm and hold it close to Billy's face. "Aren't you the smart one?"

"O-o-okay," he stutters, pulling out his phone. The phone's like a wet bar of soap in his hands, but he manages to start tapping. I keep an eye on the mass message.

Orders from the top. Come in.

"N-now?"

"Yep. Right now."

He adds:

2300.

Military time? Weird.

"N-now what?" he asks.

"Now message Litto. Tell him to come here."

"H-here? Not Dezignz?"

"Here."

He hesitates a moment then the message sends with a swish. "Sent."

"Smart boy, Billy."

He smiles; I slam my fist into his face. His head swims, and he falls over on the floor.

One left.

The General.

CHAPTER 35

'M SITTING ON MOMS'S old stoop when the General shows up.
Bo's still in his spot outside Ms. Leola's and Julius buzzed to
let me know he, Kid, and Ole Jesse are in place at Dezignz, and
that the General's goons are pouring in.

I slip the recorder from my pocket and press the button on top.
It hovers a second and disappears. A few taps on my watch and I fire
off a message to Bri.

Me: Recording started.

At the corners of my vision, Bo looks like some homeless dude
catching a nap. A pair of curtains flutter on a window at the far end
of the block. *Tasha's peeking.* As long as she stays inside, we're good.
I'm out here alone on purpose. I want the General to think I'm his
only competition.

He walks toward me, no more than a few stoops away. His
white shirt is crisp; its tail blows in the wind. I don't get up to meet
him, but I tug down my sleeves. Let him think I'm weak. He gazes
around, looking for his men no doubt.

"Rue," he says. "It's poetic you'd be here at Naomi's door."

The sound of my Moms's name on his tongue makes the magic
in my fingers twitch. I want to shoot a dagger right at his chest,

pierce that thumping organ that gives him the freedom to live. A freedom he's taken away from so many others.

Brian, his name is Brian.

But first I need his confession.

The onyx on his wrists mocks me, my anger rising.

"Those cuff bracelets you're after were from ancient Ghizon. The Ghizon you and the Chancellor tried to erase."

He's close now—so close I can smell his stench. His mug is hateful, lips in a permanent grimace. His pasty grayish skin, like all the Ghizonians have, is dull in the lamplight, but his is extra flaky. Or something.

I hate him.

"A-ah," he says, wagging a finger at me. "Now let's not go pointing fingers. That was the Chancellor's doing before I met him. Here, I'm practically following orders." He smiles.

Every second he draws breath, I hate him more.

Confess.

"That's what you call this? Following orders? Flooding East Row with drugs, hanging out at community centers, stalking schools, all the while holing up in Ghizon?"

A smirk splits his lips as if he's savoring this moment. Satisfied with himself like he has me cornered or some shit. *I'll be wiping that grin off your face.* I swallow the spit I wanna hurl at his mug.

"Well," he says as if he's amused, "when you put it like that . . . I'll certainly take credit where credit is due."

I'm up on my feet, inches from him. "Ain't no other way to put it. You bleeding my block. You got a whole world in Ghizon to stir up shit, but you come here."

His skin is even stranger up close.

I slam a finger at his chest. "WHY!"

He grabs my wrist. Tight.

For a second he's so angry his head looks like a pimple that needs to pop. But as his grip tightens on my metal arms, his eyes grow wide.

Yeah, be scared. I shove him. "WHY?"

Confess.

He stumbles back and his jaw tightens. He points at me and the onyx on his wrists swirl with energy.

"You wanna throw down?" I roll up my sleeves and my cuffs gleam in the evening sun. "Go ahead. But before the light leaves your eyes, you *will* say what you did and tell me why."

"You're a waste of space, just like your mother." He shoots first and I dart sideways, a streak of light flying by with a crack.

I fire back, flames rolling from my fingertips. They barrel through the air and catch his shirt. Flames lick up his sides and he growls before putting them out with a spray of water.

We circle. He spins and stretches light with his hands into the shape of a machete. *Oh shit.* He slashes and I jerk left, dodging. It flies by with a *whoosh.* Energy tears through my palms like barbed wire and I shoot, aiming for his head. He spins sideways a second too late and my magic slashes his cheek. He cups his face, gasping.

"Give it up, old man, you ain't winning here."

His blade slashes left, then right, as he steps toward me. The weapon's heat swishes past me, so close. So very close, like dancing with fire. I step back and my heel catches on a crack in the pavement. I slam the ground, pain shooting up my spine.

I try to get up, but his blade is over me like a guillotine. It comes down fast and I shield my head. *Clang.* His machete slams into my wrist, his full weight bearing down overhead.

Up, I gotta get up.

Screeech. His blade scrapes my arms as I push, straining to force him backward.

"Ahhhh!" *He's so strong.* I push, remembering everything I'm fighting for. I thrust with all my might and he falls back, his blade fizzling out.

I gulp down air while he's on the ground, recovering from the blow.

P-pop, pop-p, pop, pop.

I fire blasts one after another, my magic slamming into him with a *hisssss.* He grimaces, clutching each singed spot. I fire again, harder, faster. His body jerks, convulsing with each hit. He tries to get up, but my magic knocks him back down. I push forward, blasting blow after blow, not letting up.

Something behind me that sounds like a door claps closed.

The General hunches over in pain on the ground, his skin blotchy and bloody. His lips are swollen and his trembling fingers conjure a flame that keeps shorting out. I cut a glance at the place where the recorder disappeared. It's getting all of this. But what I need, what I want is him admitting what he's done. I let him get up.

"TELL ME WHY!"

Confess.

He scowls as if he has no plans to say a word.

I pull at the threads of energy sizzling through me and shove with both hands. The air ripples like waves, slamming into him.

He flies backward, lands hard, and howls in pain.

I'm over him now and rage flows through me instead of blood. A flame dances from my fingertips and I hold it to his throat. "Say it. Say what you've done. I wanna hear it."

He flares his nostrils, glancing both ways.

"No one's coming to save you." I hold the flame closer to his throat. "Confess!"

"Confess?" A deranged look, then a smirk flit across his face. "What do you want to hear, huh? How I came to your mother's doorstep looking for you? How I have more drugs running through that one high school than in half the city? That's what you want to know, huh?"

"I want the truth. All of it."

"You want to hear how it's cheaper to buy a cop in this town than a pair of courtside seats? How many faces I've buried for not doing what I say? Where I'm going to hide your body too." His jaw clenches.

He's trying to scare me.

"*I* run your neighborhood. Me! That's what you want to hear, Rue—Rue from East Row? I do things to people like you that make nightmares seem like sweet dreams." He laughs to himself. "Your mother thought she was tough too. But she bled to death like a piece of meat. And so will you. The Chancellor ordered you to be killed as soon he found out what your father did. But we couldn't find you. He was gonna give up searching, thinking you'd never seek out Ghizon." He glances at my cuffs. "But he showed me the books. . . ."

What books?

"And I knew what kind of threat you'd be. I saw it all my life;

I told him, give Coloreds a little power and they'll want to start changing shit."

Wait. "What do you mean you saw it *all your life?*"

He flinches, but I catch it and I let the flame lick his face. The spot it touches turns from gray to pink. *What the?* I slide a finger down his pasty skin and it's gritty on my fingers, like makeup. *The fire's peeling away his gray complexion?*

How . . . unless he's . . . no way . . .

I gasp, the realization sending shockwaves through me. "Y-you're human?"

"Not completely stupid, I see," he says. "But I guess even dogs have brains."

I glance at where the recorder disappeared, and I let out the tiniest sigh of relief. I'm getting all this, all this proof. The Ghizoni won't be pleased.

Looking away was a mistake.

Something slams into me and I fly backward, skidding on the ground. Prickles of pain shoot up my spine and I can't feel anything. My head pounds, throbbing, when a familiar girl's voice swirls in my ear.

"No!" the voice screams.

Tasha?

No! I told her to stay back. The girl yells again, louder. Thoughts tangle in my head as I try to pull myself up on my feet.

"Get off my sister," she yells, slamming into the General's back, her nails digging into his face. She catches him off guard for a split second.

And it's the second I need.

I'm up, still woozy, but I channel every fragment of humming inside me to my wrists and shove. A roar of energy rolls through me, bursting from my hands and slamming into him. He stumbles, but latches onto Tasha by the hair. She howls in pain.

Shit! NO!

I rush toward her. Everything's woozy, but I fling myself forward toward the blurry image of them. I throw a dart of fire in his direction, groaning in pain, still dizzy from slamming the concrete. My shot blows right past him. Before I can fire another, his magic wraps around her like a lasso.

"Let her gooooo!" The words come out like nails clawing a chalkboard. He's marching toward me, dragging her. "Now you'll cooperate, won't you?" he says, tugging at Tasha's scalp.

He's gonna take me back—back to Ghizon.

The recorder. I need the recorder.

Up. I have to get up.

Before it's too late.

Before he zaps us out of here and the only bit of evidence I have stays here.

I stumble up to my feet, but the world is spinning.

"It's too late, Rue," he cackles. "Just quit."

Quitting isn't in my vocabulary.

He shoots and my skin burns like fire's split it open. I force myself to ignore the throbbing and run back toward Moms's stoop where I activated the recorder. My feet are clumsy over each other, but I reach Moms's stair rail and grip it to steady myself.

Panting, I reach for the spot where the recorder vanished, hands swatting the air. *It was here. Somewhere.* I reach higher, grabbing, grasping at nothing. *Shit! WHERE IS IT?*

Fire slams into my reaching fingers. "*Ah!*" Another strike pounds my back and I fall to my knees. Everything hurts.

The recorder, get the recorder.

I strain, reaching around in the air. It was just here. I activated it sitting *right* here. I touch the tip of something cold and stretch my fingers, reaching. *So close. I-I'm so cl—*

Metal handcuffs close around my wrists, subduing my magic.

"No!" *I'm going to Ghizon with no proof of who he is, what he's done.*

He gestures at Tasha. "I'll be keeping her alive *for now*, so you behave." He snatches me up by the wrists and the metal cuffs bite into my skin.

"But, you . . . oh, you will die slowly for being a pain in my ass." He smooths a speck of blood from a gash in his cheek. "But first, the Chancellor intends to have those cuffs, even if he has to cut them off."

He mumbles the transport spell and everything goes black.

CHAPTER 36

BLINK AND GHIZON SURROUNDS me.

Angry stares cling to my skin like sweat on a humid day. It's like déjà vu except this time how do I get away? And now Tasha is a hostage, too.

The sun scorches my head and thoughts rattle in my brain. I'm screaming inside. The Justice Compound—where they keep prisoners—is up ahead, a short walk through Central District. The General touched up his makeup, then called for backup as soon as we arrived, so Patrol surrounds me on either side.

For two "little girls," they sure act scared.

If we make it to that detainment room, we won't make it out alive. Guaranteed.

The General tugs at my wrists to make me walk. It's probably a hundred steps. A hundred steps before they tuck me away and I never see the sun's light again. I pull harder, but I can't get my hands free.

"I'm going to get us out of this," I whisper to Tasha.

"I-I'm sorry," she says, sniffling. "I just saw him trying to hurt you—" Her face is stained and tears mixed with blood slip down her face.

"No talking." Patrol butts the back of her head with a gun and she whimpers. I'm going to hurt him for that. For a second he meets my glare and doesn't look away. I hope he feels my hate, my anger.

If he doesn't yet, he will.

I yank my wrists, but the metal clamped around them won't give. The dorm quad and courtyard on my left is teeming with students.

Ninety steps.

Ninety before they tuck me away and the truth dies with me. With us.

I force down the anxiety swelling in my gut. The crowd glances from the General's bashed face and singed, shredded clothes to me, covered in rips and cuts. They whisper, pointing at the golden cuffs seared into my wrists.

One watcher, a taller fellow with golden hair, almost like a mane, stops tinkering over a cart of baubles and meets my eyes. I don't know him, but something in his stare makes my insides slosh.

Eighty steps.

Time's running out.

The General jerks me harder and Tasha bumps into me. She's still a bit woozy and her lip's busted.

"Can you reach my hands?" I whisper.

"I'll try," she says. Our fingers clumsily try to unlatch each other's restraints. I feel the latch for one and try to open it. *That's it, come on, T. Pry it open.* A Patrolman catches us and snatches us apart, putting himself between us. And just like that our two seconds of progress is gone.

Sixty steps.

We keep moving down Main Street and Golden Mane works

his way through the onlookers, his eyes dead set on me. *Maybe I do know him?* I squint. Nope, I don't. The grease stains on his shirt say he must be Zruki. But the baubles he's peddling look fine, like gold.

Gold.

The detainment area looms ahead and more Patrol, armed with shields, wait. Fear bubbles up my throat.

The crowd packed in around us parts. Golden Mane keeps pace with us, walking along the outside, around and between people, when a commotion breaks out. He pushes one person into another and they start arguing, shoving. *What's he doing?* Golden Mane instigates and their disagreement grows louder. The crowd's fighting spills into our path and Patrol pushes them off, yelling and swatting.

I shove my hands back to Tasha's. "Again, try to get it off. Twist the latch."

Her clammy hands work feverishly, and I feel my cuffs loosening. "That's it, T. Almost."

I pull. Hard. And metal digs into my skin. My entire hand's gonna rip off with the handcuffs. A Patrolman catches me from the corner of his eye. "What the—" He swats at me with the brunt of his gun. I duck and his gun slams into another Patrolman, throwing him off balance. I hook my bound hands around his neck and squeeze. He sputters and I hold him there, his back to me, like a personal shield.

"Behind me, Tasha, now."

She scoots, pressing against my back.

The General whips around pointing a weapon at us and the crowd screams. "Rue, be smart. You're outnumbered, powerless. Let him go."

I stand firm, putting Patrolman in front of me and Tasha. He's not taking us in that prison building, magic or not. Golden Mane catches my eye again, pointing up. Up high. His physique is familiar, tall with lean muscle. Golden rings hug his knuckles and he's done up in some sort of robed costume—*costume.*

OMG, it's Jhamal.

In disguise!

If Jhamal's here in something from a costume merchant, Bri must be close by too. But the recorder, I don't have it. He doesn't know. I try to mouth the words and Jhamal-in-disguise gets closer, squinting. *Ugh. He'll never be able to read my lips from this far.*

"I'll ask one more time, Ms. Akintola," the General's weapon is aimed at my personal shield. "*Let* him go."

I pull the Patrol shielding us tighter to me. He's clawing at his throat, gasping for air. I hold on with every ounce of strength I have.

Jhamal waves at me, pointing to his wrist. He wants me to press play on the recorder. I shake my head, tears stinging my eyes. I don't have it. He and Bri have everything set up to play the damn transmission and I don't have the recorder, the proof.

This is falling apart. My entire plan is falling apart.

"IT'S POETIC YOU'D BE HERE." The General's voice bellows over the crowd, rattling every building on Main Street. There, up high, hanging like white sheets on the front of the District's buildings, is the General's angry face.

I-it worked. Somehow it worked.

There, in the flesh, is Bri standing in front of the General looking up at the recording. Her eyes puffy, hair ragged, and her wrists bandaged like she's a damn mummy. She looks somehow even more pale and is smashing a button on the wristwatch clutched in her hand.

"We backed up the feed," she says smiling nervously. She looks like she's 'bout to pass out. "We got everything. I-it's all here."

The General looks between us and his expression turns from confusion to shock as the video replay shouts overhead.

The people on the street watched, a mix of confusion, shock, and anger written on their faces.

"YOU'RE A WASTE OF SPACE, JUST LIKE YOUR MOTHER." The video plays, East Row's brown brick homes in the backdrop, nestled side by side, so close it looks like they're hugging.

Bri's still standing there finger pressed to the watch, looking like she might faint.

"Turn it off!" the General shouts, and darts of light whistle through the air, knocking Bri off her feet. "Arrest her!"

Bri groans, writhing on the ground. The watch tumbles from her hands and the video glitches. Jhamal intercepts it, scoops Bri up, and disappears in the crowd.

In seconds, the playback starts again.

"This is treason! Arrest them both!" the General shouts, but the video of his gloating drowns out his shouting.

"I RUN YOUR NEIGHBORHOOD! ME!" On the video, a flame from my finger grazes his throat.

People spill out of buildings, streams of students rush from the dorm halls, swallowing the courtyard—everyone's eyes on the replay. The street's a blanket of whispers, and it's doubled in occupancy. All eyes are on the General's gray face turning pink.

"Y-YOU'RE HUMAN?" It's odd hearing my own voice so loud. Gasps erupt like an explosion and a few people glance at me, confusion, surprise, or something written on their faces.

"NOT COMPLETELY STUPID, I SEE."

Patrol's fixated on the video playback, but the General tries to get them to listen. "I said get her, now!"

A pair take off after Bri and Jhamal. The others ignore him completely, gaping at the General's giant head on the screen. His skin's turning red and chatter sweeps through the streets like a swarm of locusts.

"Hurry, Tasha," I say. "While they're distracted."

The metal's confusing between my fingers. I feel for the divot in the restraints and dig my nail in. I strain to pry it open.

"Almost got it," Tasha whispers.

One more hard tug and the cuff on Tasha's wrist snaps open. She's much faster with free hands and my cuffs are off in seconds.

"BUT I GUESS EVEN DOGS HAVE BRAINS," he bellows from a face ten stories tall. Tasha's in the backdrop, and watching his magic pummel into her on screen rips me apart all over again. A few more seconds and the video flickers a moment then fades.

For a second, everything is silent.

Still.

Nothing moves.

No one breathes.

Eyes dart around and the General's sweating bricks, completely unaware Tasha and I have freed ourselves. Patrol even stares.

He's human.

Now they see him as an other.

Chaos erupts in motion. The General runs, shooting at me. He jets off through the crowd, half cursing him and the other half moving out of his way. Screams ricochet off the glass walls around the

District's buildings. Everyone flees in every direction, people pushing and stumbling over one another. Bodies bump into me, shoving. I shove back, fighting to keep Tasha close to me. Patrol tries to keep order, but one gets knocked over and stampeded.

Shouts buzz in my ear. The General's getting away. But Tasha, I can't just leave her right here. I pull her toward me, shielding her under my arm.

Something sounds like glass shattering and I spot giant masses flinging through the air. Shop windows and the Binding Ward's glass walls burst into a million pieces.

Oh my god, this place is falling apart.

Fire erupts from inside the building and in minutes smoke's scratching my throat.

The General—I'm losing sight of the General.

I step up on someone or something for a view above the crowd. As far as I can see, people are destroying buildings, ripping one another apart with magic. Amid the chaos, I spot a spark of light up ahead and a scraggly, almost bald head behind it. *There he is.*

A warm hand wraps around mine and my heart skips a beat. Jhamal. His costume has worn off and his side's sticky with blood.

"Are you okay?"

"I will be fine." He winces when he speaks. "What can I do?"

I place Tasha's hand in his. "Get her out of here. Protect her with whatever you have."

I kiss her forehead. "He'll keep you safe until I get back, I promise." She nods, her everything trembling.

Jhamal darts off as something booms and the tallest residence hall tips over, creaking its way to the ground with a *crash*. The skies rain steel and glass and dust clouds make it hard to see. I hunch down, darting through the crowd in the General's direction.

He's *not* getting away. I refuse to let him.

I push faster, coughing my way through the smoky air. Something stings my side, then feels wet, but I keep pushing. People scream profanities at me or one another, I don't know. I only have eyes on the General.

He turns toward the fallen debris of the residence halls and I pound the ground harder. He glances back at me and darts of magic fly like bullets my way. I dodge left, and the shots whip by. He hops over another chunk of fallen rubble and I follow him inside the crumbled structure that was our old dorm.

Metal groans, then clanks, and the ground shifts. *Bang*. A pile of rubble slams to the ground, blocking his path. He has nowhere to turn but back—to face me.

He's trapped.

We're trapped.

But only one of us is making it out of here.

"So, this is it then, huh?" His eyes are wild, bulging out of his head.

"For you, yeah." I shoot first and our streams of energy meet, crackling like electricity. He groans and presses.

The Ancestors' magic buzzes with my own in some deep crevice inside me. *This. This is what they called me for.*

"Let it go, Rue," he says, groaning to keep his defense up. "You're a forgotten detail of a story that's never been written. This isn't a fight you can win."

"Watch me." I dig, every inch of me aching. Fire pulses through my every limb. Deep inside my magic churns, searing my insides like a violent force trying to rip its way out of me.

I let it.

And I aim for his wrists.

"Ahhh!" Air buckles and cracks, rippling like waves. The General flies backward and slams into a piece of steel. His onyx pops from his wrists and hits the ground, rolling to my feet. I scoop them up and put them in my pocket.

"You lose." I heave a wad of spit at his face. "*We* win."

CHAPTER 37

NEW GHIZON BURNS.

Smoke billows toward the sky, kissing the sun. The General's bound by his feet and hands, attached to a rope I hold over my shoulder. His head drags the pavement, his eyes batting in and out of consciousness. I make my way up the street, around piles of rubble, dragging the General. A simple spell helps him come along weightlessly. His groans are muffled and restraints are on *his* hands.

He's done.

Almost.

I *do* have one more thing for him.

But first, I have unfinished business here.

He didn't act alone.

I'll have the Chancellor's head, too.

The city's in ruins. People stare as I pass. A few mutter things under their breath. Others bow, saying thanks. The city is falling whether they like it or not. I sift through faces, looking for someone I know.

That's when I see him and my blood runs hot again. I yank the dead weight behind me faster and approach Luke, who's chewing out some frail woman. His nails are dug into her arm.

I'm at his back before he knows I'm there.

"O-ooh, R-Rue! So ni—"

I slam my fist into his teeth and he staggers before stumbling to the ground. I straddle him and punch him again. *Lying asshole. Two-faced.*

"I'm sorry! The General s-said if I cooperated and got in good with Bri to spy on you, he'd promote me to Patrol. He even said he'd give my family new designations, Dwegini. . . ."

"You'd let my people die to up your status?" He'd fit right in where I'm from. I kick him.

"Mind if I?" The familiar voice of a girl I used to call my best friend tickles a special place inside me. Bri's definitely looked better. Her knees aren't shaking anymore, but she's covered in scrapes and dried blood. The bandages on her wrists are blotchy with red stains.

"Your wrists?" I ask.

"I-I asked Bati to have my onyx removed, Unbound." She holds her hands up. "No more magic, officially."

"Bri, I—I don't know what to say."

"Rue, I've always envied your ability to just be you. You've never fit in here, so to speak, and you never tried to. You're comfortable in your own skin. I want that. I want . . ." She gazes off in the distance. "I guess I want to stop caring about being the best at what *they* say I need to be and figure out what being the best means to *me*. Starting with getting rid of that stolen onyx on my wrists. And I know it doesn't fix anything, but I want *no* part in what the Chancellor did. It was wrong. It *is* wrong. And I'm still working through it all, to be honest." She shifts her weight and winces. "But I want to do what I can to help. I'm sorry, Rue. I'm so sorry."

I hug her and it feels good. Luke groans in pain, trying to get back up. I kick him and he barrels back over.

"If I screw up . . . ," she starts.

"*When* you screw up," I say.

"*When* I screw up, call me out on it, please."

"Oh, I will. Trust. Let's just hope your know-it-all ass listens."

We laugh.

"Being you unapologetically, Bri, is the best goal you've ever set for yourself, I gotta say."

She blushes. "I'm gonna do my best. Trying to be like you."

We laugh again. "But hey, have you seen the Chancellor?" I ask.

"I haven't. He's probably trying to get as far away from here as possible. This place is coming apart. Some are shouting for the Chancellor's head and others are fighting them for saying it. It's scary seeing people like this. What's gonna happen?"

Smoke stings my eyes. "I don't know, but you're right, it's a war zone. I'm going to reinforce the barrier over Yiyo to keep any Grays from going that way." I nudge her. "Except you, of course. So, you better head that way and soon."

She nods, but won't meet my eyes. "Luke had been acting really weird, controlling almost, with questions about stuff he didn't need to know," she says. "I should have seen it sooner. I'm really sorry, Rue."

"I didn't see it either, to be honest. He always seemed cool."

She mouths "sorry" again and squeezes my hand. I squeeze back. Feels good to have my friend again. Luke groans and Bri slams the toe of her shoe into him. "You bastard!" Another blow. "How could you?" And another. She's going in.

As I turn to leave her to it, I spot slick skin like polished mahogany and I melt.

Jhamal.

He's bandaging his shoulder and side. Cuts and scrapes line his arms and a nasty slash mars his cheek. The world fades to a whisper. Jhamal is all I see.

"Rue? What you . . . *oooooh*," Bri says when she sees who I'm staring at. "Go ahead, girl."

My feet stick to the ground like cement.

Time is fleeting.

We gotta say the things we think and feel while we can.

My dad taught me that.

I rush over. Jhamal spots me and limps toward me. Steps from him, his cuts are easier to see. A small gash runs down his temple, and thin red slashes color his cheeks. His pants are torn, his armor battered and caked in blood. And there's Tasha behind him.

I squeeze her. "Sis, you okay?"

She nods. "I'm okay. Some old dude running through here tried to grab me, but your friend here hemmed him up." Tasha grimaces, glancing at Jhamal's wound.

Everything that comes to mind to say sounds stupid. How do I thank him? What words are enough?

"Thank you." I throw my arms around his neck and he hugs back. "I'm so glad you came through. The costume was genius."

His chiseled arms are tight around me. I can't breathe in his grip and I don't want to.

"I told you I can do whoop-ass too." He chuckles. I laugh, his heart thumping fast against me. He's so corny and cute.

Tasha looks between us. "I can take a hint." She slides off and my cheeks burn. His lips part in a sideways smile and it's sexy as shit.

"Your sister is very fierce, like you. She bit the man who tried to hit her." He laughs.

"That's T. By the way, have you seen the Chancellor?" I ask.

He points. "Heading that way, yes. I didn't approach because I had Tasha with me. Then he just vanished on the spot."

I'll find him. "Jhamal, really though . . ." I meet his eyes and I could stay there, swim there, forever. "Thank you. Coming through with the photofri—whatever they're called. The recorders. And looking out for T." My insides shudder as lines dance up his biceps. I'm warm all over, trying to play it off.

"It is an honor, My Q—"

"Jelani," I say.

"Jelani," he says, holding my gaze. "Once things calm down and you finish knocking off whoever else is on your list . . ." He chuckles and his chiseled cheeks send a wave of heat up the back of my neck.

"Maybe we can do something other than fight the next time we see each other?" He flashes his pearly whites again.

"Yeah. I'd like that. Maybe we can catch the latest action flick back home."

"Flick?"

"A show, like a movie. We can watch a movie in a theater."

"In Ghizon, we have warriors fight wildebeests as part of training. Now *that* is a good show."

I snort. "It's a little different there."

His touch is warm when he takes my hands. "I would like that very much." He brings my knuckles to his lips and his breath grazes my hand.

Time is fleeting.

No regrets.

Before he can kiss my knuckles, I pull his face to mine.

Everything spins around us and his breath licks my lips. Never have I wanted something so badly. My insides flutter and I grip his arms, pulling him even closer. Our noses touch. Sweat and earth, brawn and strength, dance in my nostrils, curling my toes.

"Are you sure?" he whispers.

I press my lips to his and for a moment there's no world around us. I'm not in my hood or Ghizon. I'm not a warrior or a Ghizoni queen. I'm a flicker, a feeling, a flame that can't be quenched.

His arms fold around my neck and he pulls me deeper in to him.

His mouth is fire.

My tongue dances with his flame.

Seconds move like days and my insides scream more alive than they've ever been. We pull apart, foreheads pressed together, out of breath.

Whatever this is, I don't want it to end.

He holds my face in his hands. "I hope we can see this movie together soon."

I sigh. I want to tell him back at home Edwards Theater off Highway 59 stays open until two a.m. I want to say I'm a normal girl and having a boyfriend is totally something I can do. I want to promise him we can walk away from this place and be regular people.

But it's not true. I *still* have people to look out for, battles to fight. The Chancellor's still out there.

"I hope so too." I tuck a hair behind my ear and tighten the grip on the rope over my shoulder.

The General grunts in pain.

"But first, there's one more thing I need to do."

CHAPTER 38

AM A RACIST.

The letters on the sign at the General's feet are painted in red, for blood. I'd have used his actual blood, but it was sticky as hell. Marker was easier. But the message is the same. He's tied to a chair, his mouth bound, cuffs on his hands.

He tried to destroy my home and hide in another world.

Now he's going to sit on my block and own what he did.

East Row surrounds us. Not just the buildings, the homes, the cars blasting jams, but the people. The grandmas hollering at kids to get out the street, the plates going from one door to the next, the shuffle of shoes on the basketball court.

Kids on bikes roll past with a glance. Some stop and stare, phones out at the busted-up white dude in his crisp collared shirt. Some keep moving.

I clamp a hand on his shoulder and squeeze. "You gon' look at this place, these people, and face what you did."

No closed courtroom doors.

No expensive lawyers.

No whispered conversations.

No under-the-table deals.

No power.

No privilege.

This is justice the block is gon' see.

If he hears me he doesn't respond. He keeps his eyes shut. It's so funny how hard people work to not see their wrongs. This dude won't even look.

But that's alright.

Soon.

I check my watch. TV and news crews thought I was joking when I called and said I'd caught the leader of Litto's crew. Somebody must have believed me, because in minutes it was all over blogs and calls started coming in. I had told them all the same—meet me in East Row.

Justice is going down here.

I told the reporters to expect a big bust going down at Dezignz, too, where Julius is holed up. He was freaking out by the time I called. He had said the guys in the warehouse were starting to get suspicious, but he was able to keep them there under the threat that Litto himself would be there any moment.

It probably helped that I put the General on speakerphone, and with some fiery prodding—literally—he said just what I told him to. Nobody budged after that. I had told Julius on the low to just sit tight and wait for the Feds. And that thanks to recorders from Kid, Bo, Ole Jesse, and the others, plus what the General 'bout to admit to the world here, there'll be enough evidence to lock him up for life.

His head hangs and the crowd around us grows. A woman walks up holding a poster with a picture of a boy about Tasha's age.

"I saw all that stuff online." She wears a neon yellow shirt that matches the poster. Two years are scrawled on the shirt, with a hyphen in between. "So it's true?" she asks. "That's him?"

I nod, my chest aching at all the blood shed here from this dude's hate. I embrace her and she smudges away a tear from under her sun shades.

"Thanks for being here," I say.

"Thank you for bringing him down. He been terrorizing East Row for years." Her voice cracks. "Enough is enough." She rocks back and forth on her feet, humming, clutching her sign, holding in her pain.

The General's eyelids are still closed. "You never told me, why . . . why you hate us so much."

It's not a real question. There's not an answer that'll make sense or lessen the blow. But I can't shake wanting to hear what he'd say. A group of reporters, cameras on their shoulders, move our way and he parts his chapped lips.

"I don't have anything to say to you people."

You people. "You will do as you're told willingly," I whisper the words he'd told me back in Ghizon, "or you'll be *forced* to do as you're told." Now the ball's in my court. I slip the vial of clear bubbly liquid from my pocket that I stole from Luke forever ago and shake it in his face. His eyes grow as I drip the tiniest bit of the truth serum on his lip.

He tries to spit it out, but it's too late. His pupils dilate and he's somewhere between lackadaisical and pissed. I force another drizzle down his throat. People stare, gasp, chatter, but no one stops me.

"I asked you a question."

He speaks between gritted teeth. "It's funny, you know, when I stumbled on that island with my buddies decades ago, they were stupid. They wanted to try talking to the natives. Not me. I stayed hidden in the foliage. That's how I got out of there alive. I came back here and tried living a normal life. Joined the service, worked my way up to a one-star. But some Black, affirmative action-type two-star did me in. He took my place. I never liked Coloreds, not one bit. That two-star had heard some things he shouldn't have about my business and told people that didn't need to know. He got me discharged, the bastard. When they cut me loose from the military, I told myself to move on. But I couldn't forget that cold winter and those dirty people with abilities that shouldn't be possible. I wanted it when I'd first seen it, but I didn't have means then. But oh, it's amazing the connections you make working for the government in Intelligence. The friends. People who owe you favors. The things you can get away with."

He laughs to himself and a reporter tips closer, holding a microphone under his mouth.

"It's not hard watering a seed in a mind that's already planted it. So I went back to the island when I got out of the service and sold myself better than any resume ever could to that greedy Chancellor. I told him I'd make sure the Americans never came for his island again. And if even a whisper of those brown-skinned people he killed off surfaced, I'd take care of it. It'd be a pleasure." He smiles. "And the Chancellor couldn't say yes fast enough. He was hungry before I met him, but he was even hungrier then. All I wanted in return was to be Bound to magic to do my business here. No Colored would ever out-rank me again, in stars or power. I pulled my gang together, fashioned myself a new surname—Litto—and built more wealth and power on these streets than you'll ever see in your lifetime, girl."

"But back in Ghizon, how did you"—the words are bile in my mouth—"rise in the ranks there?"

"The Chancellor fashioned that paste for my skin to take on that grayish color, strapped me up with plenty of Yoheem Elixir to metabolize my genetics, replenish my fitness levels. Same stuff Patrol takes to keep them in youthful shape. Same stuff the Chancellor takes to keep his cells regenerating at the rate of a twenty-year-old. The man's, like, a hundred and twenty-five years old, you do realize?"

The reporters look at one another, brows furrowed, completely bewildered.

"Once I looked the part, he told the people I was an old buddy from Moyechi, his tribe. He announced I'd be heading up the territory's security measures. Tightening things up to keep us safer from outsiders. Given their history, they bought it, of course."

The lies. So many lies.

Still, that doesn't explain everything.

"What does my mother have to do with any of this?"

"When the Chancellor found out about you, it rattled him," he says, reluctantly. "You see, I'm a sea of calm under pressure. Not him. He was hasty, and ordered me to find you and your sister. He demanded I snuff out your entire bloodline to be sure Aasim's seed was cut, root and stem. We weren't sure about Aasim's relation to that Tasha girl, but didn't want to take any chances. I sent a few guys from my crew here to keep Patrol's nose out of it. I couldn't have them knowing about my dealings here, because that would blow the Chancellor's and my story. The Ghizoni believed I was from there, see. An old friend of his. But they made mistakes. They killed your mother, but couldn't find you or the other one."

My mother and sister might have been an order from the Chancellor, but the General's smug grin makes it clear he was happy to carry it out.

"The Chancellor keeping Aasim alive, believing he could make a 'son' out of him in case he needed his raw magic later, was a costly, arrogant misstep." He turns from the camera to me. "Had he made absolutely sure he killed all those brown fuckers when he united the tribes, you wouldn't exist. And I wouldn't be sitting here now."

I slap him so hard my hand stings. Reporters and bystanders with phones out swallow us on this tiny patch of concrete in the center of my home. I slap him again.

"Are you admitting to colluding to commit genocide against . . . ?" The reporter looks to me for clarification.

"All kinds of brown-skinned people, Black people," I say.

". . . Black people?" She finishes the question and holds the microphone to him. More microphones pile in next to hers.

"I did it and I'd do it again," he says. "Only smarter next time."

I clench my fists. I want to clock him, just one more time. But the lady with the yellow poster holds me back. "You're a racist and you chose to take out your hate on my community! You will rot for this."

The reporter prods him again. "Are you the notorious boss of the Litto gang? The gang allegedly responsible for strings of unsolved murders, armed robberies, and drug trafficking across the city?"

He struggles with the words, fighting the serum, but they force their way out anyway. "I am. You say it like it's a big deal. These people don't matter. Never did. Never will."

I bite my knuckle to keep from punching him again. Our crowd has swelled, more parents showing up. Between families and the media, there are a hundred around us, maybe more. I recognize Demarcus's mom, Aunt Bertha. She's holding a poster with Demarcus's face grinning at me in his starter jersey from the Jameson basketball team. And like a trigger, more memories play on repeat in my head.

Brian, his name was Brian.

Reporters crowd me and video lights turn on.

The world is watching, Rue, what you gotta say?

"Brian, his name was Brian," I say. "He was in the National Honor Society and he was Homecoming King. I didn't know him personally, but he was Black, like me. He refused to sling drugs. I saw it. And they killed him for it." I face the General. "Brian, his name was Brian, and *he* mattered. SAY IT, or so help me I'll burn your eyes off your face!"

Anger rises off him like steam. "B-Brian. H-his name w-was Brian...."

"And?"

If looks could kill. "A-and h-he m-mattered."

Aunt Bertha's crying hard, shoulders shaking. I pull her to me. She points to her poster. "H-his name was Demarcus a-and he mattered." Her voice cracks, but another mother holding a different poster loops her arm in Aunt Bertha's.

The General scowls, glancing at me, then speaks. "D-Demarcus. H-he m-mattered." The words leave his tongue as if they taste like rotten meat, but I'll take them.

Another mother speaks up. The one looped in Aunt Bertha's

arm. "And my daughter's name was Ebony. She was so bright. Only fourteen, and she mattered."

He repeats Ebony's name, seething. More lines of onlookers face the General and tell him their children's names. He repeats each one, saying they mattered, begrudgingly.

It doesn't bring them back.

It doesn't change that they're gone.

But in a small way, it means something.

Tires screech and the brown brick apartments around us glow from blue to red. A siren *woops* and my heart jumps. A caravan of blacked-out SUVs line the perimeter of the block.

Feds.

Black-suited men and women step out, guns raised, and swarm around us. My breath catches. But for the first time in as long as I can remember, their barrels are pointed at the *right* person—the puppetmaster, this racist-ass white dude.

More guns than I can count are aimed at him, and a lady in a really fancy pants suit with tan skin and dark hair offers me a card. "We should talk. You've done good work here."

I lean back on my elbows at Moms's old stoop and Julius leans back too. A lady named Keisha lives here now. I explained to her that it used to be my home and how Moms died here. She told me to come back as often as I wanted, that it was as much my home as hers.

By the time the Feds cleared out the warehouse, Julius was sweating bullets. I had told him I called in to the tip line and left clear evidence and instructions that he was working with me, but still, cops. Guns. That shit's scary.

Julius throws an arm around my shoulder. "Yo, what the fuck just happened? You gotta catch me up on the *whole* story, fam."

I do. I really do owe him an explanation, after all this. I laugh. "You don't realize what you're asking."

He pushes his lips sideways. "Am I fam or am I fam? Do I come through or do I come through?"

I nudge him with my shoulder in that way I used to do and set my head on his shoulder. "You right, you fam. You already know."

"But foreal though, some folks 'round here wary of all this talk about magic and shit. You know I always have your back. That's a given. But I ain't know what to say because you ain't really told me what's what. So, what's up? I'm listening."

If I can trust no one else on this entire planet, I know I can trust Julius. He knows me like no one else and he's as good as family. I pull the pieces of onyx from my pocket and turn them in my hands. "Okay . . . you asked. And it's easier if I *show* you instead of *tell* you."

He looks confused.

"Here goes." I lace my fingers between his and he sucks in a breath, holding it in for a long minute, shock stamped on his face. I hold my hands tight to his as he absorbs all my memories of Ghizon and everything that just happened. His eyes dart around every which way behind his eyelids. Several moments pass. Then he gasps and I break our grip.

"WHAT THE FUCK?!"

"*Yeahhhh*," I say.

"You . . . I mean . . . and that General dude . . . your pops too . . . damn, I'm so sorry." He brings my forehead to his. "How could you not tell me this, yo?"

"I didn't want you at risk, that's all. Keeping fam safe is what I do. You're fam."

"I'm more than fam." He winks and rubs a thumb across my lips. It sends tingles through every part of me. But I pull away gently and put my head back on his shoulder.

"So what now?" he asks, taking the onyx from my hand. He examines it closely. "All that power can be put in this little tiny stone."

"Wild, right?"

"*Ow.*"

"What?"

"Is it supposed to be warm?"

"Yeah, when it's Bound to your skin and filled with magic, it warms when your mag—" *Wait, what?* "It's warm?!"

"Yeah, it—"

My wrist buzzes and I'm up on my feet, Julius peeking over my shoulder.

Bri: They broke through the barrier.

Me: What barrier? Who?

Bri: Rue, the Chancellor! He's marching on Yiyo Peak.

Julius grabs my arm. "Take me with you, I wanna help."

"You don't know what you're asking. It's different there."

"Don't sound like it." He doesn't get how dangerous this could be. "Rue, come on. It's me."

His words jar me. I hadn't realized until that moment how protecting the people I care about is my knee-jerk reaction. So much so that I shove them away, which probably hurts them, too. It's a mistake I'm not about to make with him. The world isn't on my shoulders alone.

"I'm stubborn."

"Say what?"

"And I don't listen." What I want to say is that I wish I'd stopped and thought more. Pondered choices. Set aside my emotions for a moment. Reckless love might still be love, but it can destroy so much in the process. But those words get stuck in my throat.

"I-I just needed to say it out loud. I'm going to do better. I can't fix everything. But together, maybe *we* in Ghizon and in East Row can fix a lot."

"I ride for you, Rue. Always. You know that." He laces his fingers between mine and it does something to my insides that I try—and fail—to ignore.

"I know you do. I really do. So, okay. You wanna come to Ghizon and help? I'm not going to say no."

"*Whaaaa?* Rue gon' accept some help?" He teases, laughing into his fist.

"Shut up." I shove him. "But let me go there first. See what's what, because I don't know what we'd be walking into."

"Aight. That's a plan."

"We'll figure this out together. I'll take all the help I can get." I give his hand one more squeeze and try to let go, but he holds on. "I really have to go. But I'll be in touch as soon as I can. Promise." My fingers slip from his. "Oh, here, take this, too." I hand him my watch. "Be my eyes and ears here on the block, for now. Anything happens, I'm here in a heartbeat."

"You don't need this to get back undetected?"

"Nope, using a good ole-fashioned spell. Let them trace me, I'm not hiding anymore." I walk away, letting the East Row sun warm me all over.

For so long, I've felt like I lived in two worlds.

But that's because I was forced to choose one over the other.

I'm not choosing anymore.

I'm both Rue from East Row *and* a Ghizoni queen.

I slip my hoodie off and toss it. Sunlight glints off the golden metal pattern written into my arms. I don't care who sees. This block is family and they're gonna know all this power stands with them.

A few straggling reporters rush my way; their cameras swivel in my direction. Microphones are shoved at me. Video lights shine in my face.

I ignore it.

Let the world see.

Let them know we're not broken here. We are *strong*—nobody's prey.

And we are taking our magic back.

I mumble the transport spell with the world watching, twist on the spot, and I'm gone.

AFTERTHOUGHTS

People see my life. The eroded buildings and cracked sidewalks.
To them I am the building, my life the concrete.

I'm not broken.
Don't pity me.

They see the drugs, but not the dreams. The pain but not the joy.
The headlines paint a picture. A picture, incomplete.
Their eyes are half open. So much do they miss.
Bonds forged, beyond our blood, through struggle is the core of our richness.

See me as I am, not as you would have me be.

My hood is my home. Not my prison.
The springboard to my future. You see poverty. I see promise.
My story makes me strong. Resilient. Unshakable.
I'm a force to be reckoned with. A mountain that won't be moved.

For I am the blood of the old gods, a Ghizoni queen.
I wear richness on my shoulders money can't esteem.
My skin is the color of earth, and greatness pulses through my veins.
And yes, I come from poverty. But no, I'm not ashamed.

I am not who you say I am or who you say I will be.
My wounds are outshined by the radiance of my true identity.
One as bright or brighter than yours.
Not high or mighty, you say?

I say, watch.
And you'll see.

ACKNOWLEDGMENTS

First, I'd like thank God, without whom none of this would've been possible, for blessing me with so much more than I even dreamed.

And thank you to my husband for encouraging and supporting me to chase even my wildest dreams. For patience as I learn to juggle my many hats. For late-night taco runs, for celebratory chocolate, for supporting my deadline-induced ice cream obsession. For being utterly convinced—in this writing career thing—I've finally found my calling. Thank you, babe.

And thank you to my three little mini mes for loving me through the hard writing days. Letting me take time away from you that I can never get back to chase this dream. Thank you for such grace. You are my daily reminder I've so much to be grateful for. Momma-ing you taught me a new level of patience and I couldn't have navigated this industry without it. Mariah, you remind me that love and kindness is the greatest gift we can give anyone. Daniel, you remind me to see sunshine in each day no matter how cloudy. Sarah, you remind me never to take time for granted. If this book was never a thing, my life was already full enough just with you three to love on. This author dream is just a cherry on top of an already gargantuan ice-cream sundae.

Huge thanks to my editor, Denene Millner, for seeing me. For believing in what this book could be. For giving this love letter to my community a platform, a place, a chance. I'm in awe of your editorial brilliance and the inspirational Black woman you are. And thank you to Justin, Alyza, Chloë, Taj Francis, who designed this dope cover, Shivana, Milena, and the entire S&S team for your support and the expert brilliance you put behind this project.

Thank you to my agent and birthday twin, Natalie Lakosil, for always believing even when I don't, for letting me be a bundle of nerves and never complaining at my need to verbally process pretty much everything, lol. For patience and optimism that know no end. Thank you for the hours of phone calls and hundreds of e-mails. For Stone brussels sprouts and pancetta, for laughs, tears, for making this dream real.

To Paige and Naomi, who I wrote this book for. You always tell me you look up to me because I'm your big sis. But hear me, Boos. This is for you. It's always been for you. Rise. Do. Achieve. You are magic and the world is at your fingertips. Take it.

And thank you to my number one STAN, my momma, who filled my childhood with imagination and nurtured my love of reading. For pushing me to believe I can do anything. That failure is a critical part of success. For insisting I will rise from any obstacle because it's just who I am. I hope to even come close to all you see in me, Mommy. I love you.

To my grandma, who raised me to be a thinker, resourceful, and ambitious. For always reminding me to keep my priorities in line and never let fear be an excuse to not try. For insisting the only place my chin belongs—is up. You've always been an example of the woman I hoped to become. To my grandpa, my Ace, my Main Squeeze. For staying on your knees for me with fierce determination my entire life. For showing me grace lived out and being the coolest Gramps on the block. For always letting me sit on your lap no matter how old I get. To both my grandparents for being proud of me. That alone is worth more than anything any of this has given me.

To Rocqell, Roslyn, Aunty Regina, Uncle Chuck, Micah, Syd, my entire family that's always believed I could do whatever I set my mind to.

Thank you to my OG BFF Jennifer for always riding with me, letting me drag you into my millions of wild ideas. For loving me despite my flaws and pushing me to be the woman, mother, writer, and friend I was created to be. You keep me grounded. I could not do any of this without you.

Thank you to Marquet for fiercely believing in each of my endeavors (no matter how random) through the torrent that is often life. For being unwaveringly sure I would soar as a writer before I'd even written a word of this book. You're the carrots to my peas. The one riding in the lifeboat with me whenever there's a storm. Love you to the ends of eternity.

And to Diarra, my ride or die, my Brooklyn Queen, the syrup on my sammich, the glue to my wig, thank you for inspiring me to be Piano-in-the-Desert-Extra unapologetically. You remind me to hold fast to joy and love and live like there's no tomorrow. And to my sweet Alyssa, thank you for being a pillar of wisdom, a role model for my babies to look up to. For your heart that gives more than you take and touches every life you meet. I wrote this for you, boo. You are a queen.

Thank you to every CP and beta who took the time to read my very imperfect words and helped me make them shine. Thanks, Jessica F, for reading every word I've ever written. For the hours upon hours of Marco Polos and Facetime calls. For letting me cry to you, squeal to you, thank you. And thanks Brittany, my Birdie, for being a fiercely loyal CP and friend. For laboring with me, draft after draft. For knowing this story would make it when I didn't. And Emily, thank you for loving Rue from the very start and seeing how powerful this story could be. For endless willingness to read again and again and again. For helping me learn and grow as a writer. And to Sarah, thank you for being there from the query trenches. For golden feedback and always believing I'd have an actual writing career when I'd only hoped to get this one book out. I'll always cherish you and the window of time we shared. And to Del, thank you for always being #TeamJess but more importantly #TeamRue. You are a gift.

Thank you Jeff for seeing Rue in her earliest drafts and saying (and believing without a doubt), "This is the book that's gonna make it, Jess." Thank you Graci, my publishing twin and favorite Rick Riordian princess. It's been a dream to have your talent in my corner. And an even bigger dream to call you friend. To Alechia, you taught me so much in those trepidatious querying and sub months. I will forever be grateful. Thank you Mary for seeing Rue and valuing her anger. For getting the necessity of this book. For fighting for girls like Rue. Thanks to Jessica L for always being there to gush and let me pick your genius editorial mind. I cherish our friendship. And thank you to Taj, who always knew Rue would make waves.

Thanks to Naz, Olivia, Tasha B, and Ryan for always being there to share advice, read, or let me vent. I'm so thankful for each of you. Thank you Beth Phelan for creating DVPIT. And thanks to the Female AOCs group for the constant hilarity and just being a safe space for a Black woman to exist on Twitter. Love y'all to the moon and back. Thank you to Mrs. Monock and her students at America's School of Heroes and Mrs. Brown's students at Vista Alternative HS for loving this book concept before it was a thing and working hard every day to fight for *your* dreams. Your tenacity and resilience reminds me why I write.

You inspire me!

Thank you to Nic Stone, my Slytherin twin, for pouring out wisdom on me time and time again. For helping me better understand how to survive in this industry and constantly reminding me what I'm worth. Your friendship is a priceless gift. Thank you for being the queen you are and helping pave the way so that books like mine even have a chance. And special thanks to Angie Thomas for helping create a space for stories like mine to exist. Thank you for pioneering, inspiring, leading with such joy and humility. You are a beacon.

Thank you to Clem, Michael, Bethany, Johan, Tiffany, and the entire I Hope U Die crew for being there from the very beginning. Thanks to my SubWarriors peeps and the best encouragers anyone could ask for: Tashie, Molly, Ana, Ayana, Alaysia, Heather, Kelis, Kris, Jasmyne, Sue Ellen, Jess S, Alexa D, Llama Mama—Cat, Sonora. Jessica O, Deborah, and Ciannon, it's been an honor to debut with you queens. Thanks, DViants and YAY Squad for being my sounding board, a safe place to vent, shout, cry. I love all of you and can't wait to hold your books too. Thanks to my Bradford Agency family. And thanks to my entire Twitter family for keeping me going every time I wanted to quit. For flooding my feed with hilarious gifs, for making my ice cream stress eating feel validated (looking at you, Sabaa), for laughs, for productivity, for constant encouragement. To Rue's Crew and my Queen Squad, thank you for riding with me! Kris, Kel, Lisa, Steph, get ready, you're next!

And extra special thanks to all the Diamonds I've met (and have yet to meet) along the way: my Cullen Bobcats, the young, Black Kings and Queens on their grind, the teachers putting in work every day like the ones who refused to give up on me, the endless number of hood Aunties, the community that loved, reared, and raised me . . . thank you for pouring into me, so I could pour out.

This is for *us*.

And George Floyd:
Rest easy, fam.
This is for you.

Turn the page for a sneak peek at
Ashes of Gold

THE ENEMY LIES IN wait to bleed my people.

To litter the homeland with our bones.

To bury its secrets.

But first he has to go through me.

I crouch in the brush surrounding Yiyo Peak for a better view of the Chancellor and his men. The sun washes Ghizon in shades of evening. Bleak wasteland stretches before me, scorched and burning. Blackened jpango trees are claws raised in sacrifice to the Ancestors. An armament of uniformed Patrol stand where there was once a field of lush vegetation and wispy grass, onyx glowing on their wrists.

Pangs churn in me—for justice, for the death of my parents, for the terror the Chancellor has caused my Ghizoni people, for the magic on his wrists that isn't his own. He'd made sure the treachery was scrubbed from the island's textbooks. But bones whisper from their graves if you listen hard enough.

My gilded arms warm instinctively with power, but I blow out a breath. *Easy, Rue.* With my Ghizoni people nearly magicless, it's basically me against thousands of Grays, the Chancellor's men. I have one shot at this and timing is everything.

Yiyo, the home my people have hidden in for years, sits behind us, perched in the middle of the forest. The Ghizoni and I hide in the foliage around it, clad in armor. I duck down lower behind thick waxy leaves to get a better glimpse of the enemy's movement. Everything he and his men have touched in the past three days of this siege has been destroyed. The Chancellor paces so rigidly, I expect to see steam rise off him. As if he'd burn every piece of beauty in the world if it would secure his power.

The destruction out here in the wilderness ends abruptly at a barrier as transparent as glass, which forms a dome over us and the mountain. Bri, in her haste to get me here quickly, said he'd broken through the barrier. Thankfully she was wrong. But he's about to. And it's the only thing keeping them from us.

It glistens, hanging above us. Thin cracks spiderweb on its surface and my heart ticks faster, my fingers twitching. The Chancellor scans the area and I hide myself behind a smooth-barked tree that's as wide as I am. Thousands of Patrol surround him. There's so many of them. So few of us. I swallow and gaze at the trees at my back, but my people are well cloaked, tucked into nooks of branches and wide leaves, in pockets of shadow, waiting, watching. The lines written into their faces are more determination than fear.

The Chancellor's nostrils flare and he shouts. Because of the barrier, I can't hear it. But his men raise their arms in unison. I clench, my muscles tightening in angst as I watch them aim magic at the barrier. The cracks on its glossy surface spread. Their arms lower. He yells and they fire again. It's been going on like this for days. But each "aim and fire" twists the corkscrew in my chest. That dome breaks, then what? I clench my fist.

I fight.

Outnumbered and all. I picture Moms's face. There's no other way. The General's demise must have reached the Chancellor's ears while I was in East Row. He is always poised, pensive, stoic. Three days ago, when they started this siege, they were collected, organized. But now, his reddened complexion, his corded throat, say the orders he's shouting are rooted in exhaustion and frustration, not control. Which I intend to exploit.

I wish I could have seen his face when he learned that hundreds of my people still exist. That some actually got away when he showed up to unify the tribes under him. And that they've been hiding inside *Yiyo* for generations, their magic fractured, a wisp of what it used to be. But even still, resiliently hopeful, strong, and ready.

A twig snaps behind me and I turn to find Jhamal pressing in beside me. He's no more than a breath away, a wall at my back. The siege glows orange in his ebony eyes.

"They won't break through," he says.

They will. I'm sure of it. But I swallow the words. I don't want his hope to falter. Hope is its own kind of magic. But Jhamal studies my eyes and finds the truth. The lines deepen on his face and I squeeze his hand in reassurance.

He gestures for everyone to come together and hundreds in shining gold armor emerge from the shadows. They surround us, eyes flicking between the two of us.

"It appears the barrier will break today," Jhamal says, broadening his shoulders, forlorn shadowing his expression.

"It will," I say. "But we can exploit the Chancellor at his most vulnerable point."

"The island is our home," says a Ghizoni clad in armor with bear-claw insignia perched on his shoulders. "We know these paths better than anyone. We should take cover in the thickest leaves and let them come to us. Ambush them." He tightens his grip on his curved blade.

"So we line up here," a girl with a braided topknot says, digging the tip of her shield into the ground, drawing a picture of the plan.

I glance for another view of the Chancellor. The barrier's thinning with every attack, magic sizzling its dulled surface. Rage is burned onto the Chancellor's skin. *I'm the true threat. The opposition to his power. What if . . .*

"I'm the carrot. Dangle me."

Their expressions twist in confusion.

I stand. "Listen, we don't have time to strategize. For three days we've been hunkered down in this forest with no clear consensus of a plan, watching his movements, studying him. I've got to get out there. Before it's too late."

"We've learned a lot about his movements these past two days," the Ghizoni says.

Crack. I suck in a breath, glancing at the barrier. The spiderweb of cracks I'd just seen has doubled in size. "I'm not trying to minimize that and I'm sorry if it came out that way. I'm just saying, the Chancellor wants *me*." I hold out my golden arms. "These. And they outnumber us greatly. I'ma fight him one-on-one. That's our chance. Our only chance."

Heads turn in silent conversation with one another.

"Jelani," Jhamal starts. "Don't do this. What is the full plan? Lay it out."

All eyes on me.

I step back. "To get out there. To fight." They're wasting time. I leave the huddle and creep closer to the task at hand.

My Ghizoni people are like collateral damage to the Chancellor. He's razing the land where our Ancestors grew their food, the chakusas where my father's father raised his family and buried our dead, where aunties and their daughters picked kaeli berries for their turning out ceremonies. Anger moves through me in a rush of heat. I don't want to sit and talk about a plan for another minute. That barrier is going to fall. And I need to be in position to end him.

"And what would you have us do while you're out there?" someone shouts at my back. I don't know. I just know they can't die for this. They've suffered enough at the hand of the Chancellor. The Ancestors gave me this magic. My parents died so I'd have it. So I could do this. So I could fight.

Crack.

I summon heat to my fingertips, keeping to the edge of the tree line so I can see him, but he can't see me. A flicker of hope thuds in my chest mangled with fear. *I can do this. I have to do this.*

My people call for me, but I jet off. The Chancellor's narrowed eyes search for me at the edge of the trees. Patrol snaps to attention. Magic flies through the air, slamming into the glass dome overhead. It shutters.

I can't stop them from shattering the barrier, but I can be ready when they do. The second before the barriers opens up wide enough for him to step through, I'm going to reveal my position and fire at him before he can fire at me. I'm counting on catching him off guard. I blow out a breath. It's gon' work.

A crack cuts through the air and the protective dome above us cracks like an egg. I summon that familiar heat; magic swirls in my hands.

"Jelani," Jhamal says, his clammy hands curling around my wrist. As if the sweat on his palms is just as much about me as what we're all up against. The last time we were together, my lips were pressed to his. Aching churns in me for the simplicity of that moment again. The moment of peace and comfort it gave me. Especially amidst so much loss.

I rub his hand on mine and his eyes soften. But the moment is interrupted when a glassy chunk of the barrier falls from the sky like a jagged piece of hail. A rip slides down the side of the barrier, its glass splitting in two.

"It's going to fall in any moment."

The Chancellor practically salivates, a crack widening right in front of him. It's time.

"I have to," I say, tugging my hand from Jhamal.

"I'll come with you," he says.

He doesn't have magic. He can play defense only.

"No," I say. "Not if you don't have to."

He tucks his lip and nods. I hold on to his fingers as long as I can before letting go and leaving him there.

I step from the clustered jpango, and the Chancellor's eyes snap to me like a magnet, the cracking glass splintering the image of his face. The gap in the barrier widens, its edges being chiseled away by Patrol's magic. Delight curls his lips and my fingers twinge with heat.

Minutes. I have minutes.

I picture my magic slicing through him, ripping his stolen power from his bare hands. I close an eye to gauge my vantage point, the split second I'll have.

Crack.

I straighten. I just need one clean shot. One. I swallow. Magic pools in my wrists as the Chancellor holds a hand at the ready, waiting to signal his men. Bits of glass fall to the ground like snow.

The crack widens.

My heart beats in my throat.

Magic jitters through me and I tremble for fear I might burst. Everything my father died for, my mother was sacrificed for, amounts to this moment. This man.

Crack.

The final pieces of the barrier fall, shattering like glass. A cloud of dust surrounds us from the impact. I cough, lifting my hands. Weapon and shield in hand, Jhamal suddenly frees himself from the brush, armored in a gold breastplate lined with bits of fur, and sticks to my heels.

No! Dammit, Jhamal.

With no time to yell at him I turn back to the task at hand.

"Aim," I say, squeezing an eye shut, the Chancellor's head in my sights.

His men's arms raise in unison, all pointed at me.

I root my feet, hold in a breath. "And *fire*." My magic flies straight for his face. His eyes widen in anticipation and he shifts aside at the last second. My magic darts past, grazing his face, leaving his cheek red-streaked.

Close, so close. *We could win this.* I raise my shaky hands, suck in a breath for fear if I breathe too deeply, the pressure will shatter me in a million pieces. Patrol fires back and a cloud of crackling energy streams at me overhead. I retreat back into the cover of the trees. Their magic slams into the blackened wood, lighting up the edge of the forest like a firework display.

I zip through the branches, over a stump, and book it to the farther end of the forest so I can attack them on their flank. I find the perfect spot and aim at the sides of their faces. Glass rains around us, my sliver of an advantage buckling like a dam as magic barrels from my fingertips toward the Chancellor. Hope swells in me like a balloon. I clench my fists as streaks of light zip past the trees, through the air, and slams into them like dominoes.

A few falter, their heads turning my way, now aware of my new position. The Chancellor fumes, reforming his men up. I aim for him again and heat tugs through me like live wire. I bite my lip until I taste copper, watching my magic fly through the air straight toward him. Yes, yes, that's it. I bite into my knuckle.

"Raise," he shouts, and Patrol raises their arms. "And fi—"

His expression widens with fear when he spots my magic barreling toward him. He jerks the man beside him in front of him as a shield. My magic slams into the man squarely in the face. The Chancellor tosses him out of the way, his jaw mean. He points in my direction, shouting at his men. The small advantage I'd had is disappearing like fresh rain on dry soil.

"Ahhh!" Desperation rips through me as I urge my magic to burn through me, firing in succession as fast as I can. I manage to hit a few Patrol who fall over and don't move.

"Charge!" The Chancellor orders his men and their ranks break, running toward me. The cloud of dust thickens under their stampede. I blink but the haze of dust stings my eyes. The glass has stopped raining, but panic has hold of me.

I look for a target, something to fire at, but it's harder to see. Something sharp grazes my back and I turn to find flames flying through the air at me. *Run!* I take off toward the tree line, skimming for anything to use as a shield. The sound of glass crunching underfoot crushes my confidence. A fireball pummels through the air and I jump sideways, its heat warming my face. I spot Jhamal dodging fuzzy strands of magic behind his shield.

"Jhamal!" But he doesn't turn in my direction. Can he even hear me over all the screaming? More Ghizoni emerge from the forest, vengeance rooted in heartbreak behind their battle cry. *No, they have to go back!* Another blow flies at me and I dodge, covering my head. Jhamal runs toward me and a swirl of magic chases him.

"Get down!" I charge his way, push him down, and kick off the ground. Up. Up. Air whips beneath me and my wrists connect with the magic midair. It sizzles then fizzles out. I land hard.

"Jhamal, you okay?" I ask, panting.

He nods, gripping my hand and I tug him up to his feet. He falls in behind me, back-to-back.

"You need a shield!"

A burst of magic flies toward us. He pulls us aside, this time, dodging the blow. The Patrolman stumbles in shock at his miss. Jhamal takes advantage of the moment, slamming his knuckles into the Patrolman's face. Violence erupts in explosions in every direction. I aim and fire toward them, heat pulling through me like a rope tethered to my chest. Magic flies from my hands slamming into someone with a Ghizoni in a headlock. Jhamal and I rotate. I aim and fire. Aim and fire again, until my wrists ache from the recoil.

Something slams into me and the world goes sideways. I stagger. Pain pinches my knees as they slam the ground. The world goes black.

Silence.

I'm a fragment, a feeling, a thought. I am air.

Smoke stings my nose.

Boom.

"Ahhh!" Shouts blare in my head.

For several moments the world is silent. Death is all I hear.

I blink and the sky is a blur. I blink again and sounds swell around me. Magic sizzling armor, groans, screams. The battle rages.

"Up, Jelani," someone says, pulling me up by my arms. "Can you hear me?"

I cup the Ghizoni's face expecting to see Jhamal, but it's not him. My hand is warm and sticky. "Th-thank you . . ." I gesture for his name, blinking his blurry face into focus.

"It's Rahk."

"Thank you, Rahk."

"You were out for some time."

"I-I was?"

"They ambushed us," he say. I take in the scene around me when an explosion pops overhead. We tuck our heads and run, skirting around fallen bodies, crumpled armor tangled around bleeding Patrolmen.

The battle has turned.

And not in our favor.

What have I done? Why didn't I tell them to stay in the forest? Or take cover somewhere or . . . something. My eyes sting. I try to blink the shame away and look for Jhamal.

I-I did not think this through. There are too many of them.

Panic grips my throat. Magic zips past in a streak of light and I halt, stumbling backward. I turn but there's magic coming from that direction, too. Cornered, bodies barrel into me. I hold my wound with one hand and fire darts of magic at the shooters.

Jhamal sprints toward us. His arm is streaked with red and he holds his elbow.

"Rahk." Jhamal greets him with some special handshake.

"All the others I was with have fallen," Rahk says to no one in particular, but his stare is fixed on me. "What should we do?"

Jhamal throws his blade; it swivels and whistles over my shoulder. Somewhere behind me someone groans before hitting the ground. Rahk covers himself with his shield, the ferocity in his eyes dimming. The ground is a sea of carnage and ash on both sides.

"What should we do?" Rahk asks again, his gaze darting between us. Jhamal looks at me too.

"I—" I break out into cold sweat.

"Jelani?"

"I, uh—" My heart races. "Go back through the forest. We need cover. You all do. Get inside Yiyo Peak. Bar the door shut. I'll finish them off out here."

"What?" Jhamal cuts in, but Rahk doesn't wait to hear. He runs off to grab the others.

"Jhamal, go with them. Defense isn't enough. Without you all armed with magic, it's— I missed the moment I needed. Having you out here now is too big of a risk."

"No." His jaw flinches and he deepens his stance, his mug mean.

"You have to listen to me!" I grip his arms. "You will die out here, you hear me? GO!" I shove his chest. "Listen to me, dammit!"

His nostrils flare.

"Please."

He doesn't move for several moments. We cut down three others, back-to-back, before he pulls me to him, presses his lips to mine, and retreats into the forest.

I sense the Chancellor before I see him.

"It's finally just you and me then, Jelani." His eyes flick to my gleaming wrists and I swear he licks his lips. I raise my arms, summoning my magic. A ball of light glows brighter between my shaky hands.

Magic flickers on his fingers, but I react first.

"Ah!" I fire at him.

But the world goes lopsided.

My head is wet and sticky, my fingers red. I blink. Someone pulls me. No, I try to say, but the words only play in my head. I spot Jhamal, running faster than the wind toward me, fury in his eyes. His javelin flies from his fingers and someone holding me lets go. But others grab hold of me. I can't move. I can't breathe.

"No!" Jhamal roars, fighting through the army of them growing around me. Their prize. The prey they've hunted for so long. Captured. I look for someone, anyone, to help. But all I smell is the mountain where I sent my people—burning.

RIVETED

BY *simon* teen ♥

BELIEVE IN YOUR SHELF

Visit RivetedLit.com &
connect with us on social to:

DISCOVER NEW YA READS

READ BOOKS FOR FREE

DISCUSS YOUR FAVORITES

SHARE YOUR IDEAS

ENTER SWEEPSTAKES FOR THE CHANCE TO WIN BOOKS

Follow @SimonTeen on

to stay up to date with all things Riveted!